The

RESISTANCE
BAKERY

BOOKS BY SIOBHAN CURHAM

An American in Paris

Beyond This Broken Sky

The Paris Network

The Secret Keeper

The Storyteller of Auschwitz

The Secret Photograph

The Stars Are Our Witness

The Scene Stealers

Frankie Says Relapse

Sweet FA

NON-FICTION

Something More: A Spiritual Misfit's Search for Meaning

Dare to Write a Novel

Dare to Dream

Antenatal & Postnatal Depression

SIOBHAN CURHAM

The

RESISTANCE
BAKERY

bookouture

Published by Bookouture in 2024

An imprint of Storyfire Ltd.
Carmelite House
50 Victoria Embankment
London EC4Y 0DZ

Storyfire Ltd's authorised representative in the EEA is Hachette Ireland
8 Castlecourt Centre
Castleknock Road
Castleknock
Dublin 15 D15 YF6A
Ireland

www.bookouture.com

ISBN: 978-1-83525-183-6
eBook ISBN: 978-1-83525-182-9

The fine arts are five in number, namely: painting, sculpture, poetry, music, and architecture, the principal branch of the latter being pastry.

— MARIE-ANTOINE CARÊME

PROLOGUE
OCTOBER 1943, PARIS

People sometimes like to ponder the question: if you knew you were going to die, what would you choose for your last meal on earth? But as a pastry chef, I've always wondered, if I knew I was going to die, what would I choose to bake? Now I'm confronted with that question for real, there's only one answer—the most spectacular of all the French pastries, the most extravagant of all the confections—the croquembouche.

Meaning "crunch in the mouth," the croquembouche is one of the hardest cakes for a chef to master, a towering pyramid of cream-filled pastry puffs, all bound together with golden spun sugar and delicate shards of caramel. I look down at my recipe book and scan the handwritten list of ingredients. I've decided to fill my pastry puffs with a variety of flavored creams—coffee, chocolate, praline, vanilla—to make them as irresistible as possible. My stomach twists into a knot at the sight of *poudre de succession* written between flour and butter in the ingredients for the choux pastry.

It's not too late, I tell myself. *I don't have to do this.* But then I think of all that's happened—all the death and violence and deception—and my resolve hardens. This is the only way I'm able to fight back and I'm going to take it. I *have* to take it, even though it will undoubtedly lead to my death. I have nothing left to lose.

All around me, the men in the kitchen banter and joke in German, while upstairs my Resistance comrades are being interrogated and tortured. Their laughter grates like a poorly played violin. They won't be laughing for much longer, though. Soon, they'll all be reeling from shock.

I tip some flour onto the weighing scales and glance around to make sure no one's watching, then I take the pouch of powder from my purse. *Poudre de succession*—the powder of inheritance, as it was known among the French elite in the seventeenth century. I suppose I should have renamed it the powder of revenge for my recipe, but maybe that would be too obvious. I open the pouch and sprinkle the powder into the flour. "May all who eat this pastry die a miserable death," I whisper as I stir it in and I'm filled with the hysterical urge to laugh.

In a few hours, the highest-ranking officers of the German Intelligence Service will be gathering in the restaurant next door for dinner and I'm going to create a dessert so astonishingly beautiful that they won't be able to resist. I picture their greedy hands grasping at the pastry puffs. I imagine their murmurs of delight as they bite through the crunchy caramel to the airy pastry and rich, velvety cream beneath. And then, as the powder of inheritance—or arsenic as it's more commonly known —begins to do its work, I picture their eyes widening in horror as they're greeted with a sight they've inflicted upon so many here —the grim and merciless specter of death.

1

JUNE 1940, PARIS

Madame Monteux used to say that if you only wait long enough, you will see that there is a rhyme and reason to everything. Heartbreak, illness, loss, they all have their purpose, according to my eternally optimistic benefactor and friend. She was once even able to find a silver lining in the onset of hemorrhoids—admittedly, after consuming half a bottle of Veuve Clicquot. "If it hadn't been for my obvious discomfort, I wouldn't have been offered the spare box seat at the opera," she told me, gaily waving her flute glass in the air. But it was easy for Madame Monteux to have such a rosy view on life. She hadn't just been born with a silver spoon in her mouth—the only child of a diamond merchant and sole heir to his fortune, she'd been born with an entire silver service.

I, on the other hand, came from far humbler beginnings. The humblest, in fact. As a baby, I was found abandoned on the doorstep of a bakery in Malakoff on the outskirts of Paris, swaddled in a bright orange towel. I was taken in, named Coralie after the color of the towel, and eventually adopted by the elderly baker, Arnaud, and his wife, Olive, who had never been able to have children and saw me as a somewhat belated gift from God. They taught me how to bake, and in doing so introduced me to my life's passion. Meeting Madame Monteux when I moved to the Left Bank at eighteen helped me see that someone with a passion for pastry being abandoned as a baby at a bakery had a certain air of fate to it. But as I walked to work that terrible night in June 1940, I found it impossible to find any kind of meaning in the Paris streets stripped of life and hope.

"Now I know how the people of Pompeii felt when they fled Vesuvius," a man muttered grimly as we watched a procession of people scurry past with their belongings piled high in prams and barrows.

I nodded, but privately I disagreed. The people of Pompeii knew exactly what they were trying to escape from as the volcano belched red-hot lava into the air. These Parisians were fleeing an unseen and impossible-to-predict threat, and something about that made it infinitely more menacing. We knew that the German army was approaching from the north and the east, like a noose tightening around the city's neck, but no one knew when and how they'd arrive and what they'd do once they got here.

I hurried along rue de Sèvres, past the shut and hastily barricaded cafes and stores. The night air smelled of smoke from the endless bonfires of documents being burned outside the Ministry buildings, and a stray dog scampered past, whimpering for the owners who'd no doubt deserted him in their haste to leave. I passed the boarded entrance of Le Bon Marché store and into Square Boucicaut. The garden in the center was eerily quiet and I suddenly felt as if I'd been left to roam an empty movie set.

Don't be afraid, I told myself. *Maybe one day, you'll find a rhyme and reason to this.* But for once Madame Monteux's cheery words brought no comfort.

As I reached boulevard Raspail, the Hotel Lutetia loomed

into view. But today the majestic Art Deco facade, with its ornate grapes and cherubs carved into the milk-white stone, failed to take my breath away. The windows at street level had been covered with makeshift shutters made from pine branches, and wire fencing had been erected around the revolving door. More reminders of the German troops building like storm clouds on the horizon.

Thankfully, Baptiste, my favorite concierge, was standing on duty just inside the door. As always, he was wearing his pristine black uniform with its peaked cap and gold brocade, but his chestnut eyes had lost their sparkle and there was no sign at all of his customary grin.

"Coralie!" he exclaimed, clearly surprised to see me. "You've come to work."

I nodded. Half the hotel staff and most of the guests, many of whom had come to Paris after fleeing the Nazis in Germany, had left, but I needed the distraction. I needed to keep my mind and hands busy.

"They're saying that the Germans will be in Paris by tomorrow," Baptiste said, causing me to shiver.

Just like the streets outside, the normally bustling lobby was eerily quiet. I glanced over to the grand piano, gleaming in the low lamplight. The piano was part of the folklore woven into the fabric of the Lutetia. The author James Joyce, who would come to the hotel to escape the cold of his apartment, used to tinkle the ivories while singing Irish ballads to an adoring crowd. But now the leather tub-shaped chairs clustered around the piano were empty, and the only faces to be seen were staring mournfully from the gilt-framed portraits lining the walls. I looked down at the mosaic of a storm-tossed ship embedded in the floor. It was the symbol for Lutetia—the Roman name for the site that became Paris—set above the Parisian motto: *Fluctuat Nec Mergitur*, meaning, "Beaten by waves but never sinks." Oh, how I hoped those words were true, for it felt as if the worst of all storms was about to hit us.

I heard footsteps echo across the lobby and turned to see Raphael, the hotel's head sommelier, hurrying toward us. He was a heavy-set, square-jawed man of about forty with slicked-back hair and eyebrows so thick and dark they looked as if they'd been painted on with shoe polish.

"Is it done?" Baptiste said and Raphael nodded.

"Is what done?" I asked.

"I've walled off the finest wines in the cellar," Raphael muttered, glancing around furtively as if an advance party of Germans might be hiding behind the reception desk. "There's no way those animals are getting their hands on our Chateau Cru Godard."

I laughed but once again shivered. It seemed impossible to imagine Nazis here in the hotel that had until recently been a refuge for the artists, writers, musicians and politicians who'd opposed them in Germany.

"I thought Marianne had left?" Raphael said to me.

"She has." Marianne, my boss, had left Paris the day before to go and stay with family in Royan on the southwest coast. Apparently, her elderly aunt had taken sick and needed help. It was incredible how many Parisians suddenly had sick relatives to attend to—and all so far away from the advancing Germans. Not that I could blame them. Maybe I would have had a sick relative too, if I had any family members to invent ailments for.

"Our Coralie is made of sterner stuff," Baptiste said with a wink.

"I certainly am," I replied with a lot more bravado than I felt.

"Good for you," Raphael said rather patronizingly, and I scowled in response. He might have been an expert in wine and excellent with the guests, but there was an arrogance about him that really got under my skin.

"I'll get to work then," I said, and padded off along the thick burgundy carpet lining the hallway housing the hotel stores.

The owners of Le Bon Marché had built the Lutetia back in 1910 to give their customers and suppliers somewhere to stay in Paris where they would want for nothing. Consequently, the hotel was like a small town, with an array of bars, restaurants, a hairdresser's, newsagent's, tobacconist and grocery store. The patisserie, where I worked, was midway along the corridor.

I took my key from my bag and unlocked the door. Some might have said that I was in denial, adopting a business-as-usual approach when so many had left, but my role as a patissier didn't feel like a job, it felt like my very identity and I couldn't bear the thought of losing it. I was going to keep baking for as long as I could.

I made my way through the darkened store, past the gleaming glass cabinets at the counter and into the kitchen at the back. I was the one who did all the work anyway, I tried reassuring myself. My glamorous boss, Marianne, preferred being front of house, chatting and flirting with the customers rather than getting her perfectly manicured nails greasy with cream or butter. Her departure would make very little difference.

I fetched my mixing bowl from the shelf and some yeast from the larder. Desperate times called for the most comforting of cakes, so I was going to start by making a kouign-amann. As soon as I put on my apron and rolled up my sleeves, the tension began fading from my body. I turned on the wireless and moved the dial until I found some rousing music. Then I went over to the barrel of sugar and took out a scoop.

Instantly, I heard the voice of my adoptive father, Arnaud, in my ear: "Leave some for me, sugar-snatcher!" and I smiled at the memory of my childhood self snatching tiny handfuls of sugar from the barrel in his bakery.

What would he make of what was happening to France, I

wondered, and for the first time since his death from consumption five years ago and Olive's just months later of a broken heart, I felt a sense of relief. At least they weren't there to witness what was happening to our country.

I combined some water, sugar and yeast in the bowl and while I left it to rest, I thought of how Arnaud always told me the stories behind the cakes he taught me to bake. Kouign-amann began life in 1800s Brittany purely by accident when a chef named Yves-René Scordia ran out of desserts, so he decided to experiment with some leftover bread dough. The result was one of the richest, most delicious confections ever created and I loved the notion that a last-ditch experiment could become one of the most popular cakes in France. It was a lesson that had folded itself into my own baking over the years, as I came to rely more on trial and error than rules and recipes.

Humming along softly to "*J'ai deux amours*" playing on the radio, I melted some butter, which I added, along with some flour and salt, to the yeast mixture. Then it was time for my favorite part—kneading the dough. I dusted the surface with flour and threw down the sticky lump. I had to be careful, I cautioned myself. There was so much fear sloshing around inside of me, I had to make sure I didn't pummel it into the cake. I closed my eyes and thought happy thoughts of Arnaud and Olive.

"Let this cake bring comfort to all who eat it," I whispered as I kneaded. I wasn't a religious person, but I always whispered these kinds of prayers into my pastries. Madame Monteux was convinced that this was the secret to my success. I wasn't sure. All I knew was that on the rare occasion I forgot to bless one of my creations and infuse it with positive messages, the pastry would be too heavy, the sponge too dry or the bread soggy. "Please, let it melt their cares away," I added, and I pictured hope shimmering like starlight out of my fingertips and into the mixture.

Once the dough had softened and become more elastic, I placed it back in the bowl, covered it with a towel and left it to rest by the warmth of the pre-heating oven. While I waited for it to rise, I would make some tarte tatin. The song *"Parlez-moi d'amour"* came on the radio and as I started peeling a bowl of apples, I allowed myself to pretend that nothing had changed. I imagined that the hotel bar still tinkled with the laughter of the last of the night's revelers, and the long corridors of darkened bedrooms above sighed with the soft whispers of sleep.

The next few hours passed by in a haze as the kitchen filled with the aroma of apples, cinnamon and caramelized sugar. But then, just as the clock outside struck six in the morning and I was about to take the tray of tarts from the oven, Baptiste burst in, his shirt collar undone and his face ashen.

"They're here!" he gasped, leaning on the door frame. "The Germans are inside the city gates."

2

JULY 1984, SAN FRANCISCO

It sounds like such a cliche for a teenager to say this, and I normally avoid cliches like the plague, but I hate my parents. Firstly, I hate them for not taking the threat of nuclear war seriously. Secondly, I hate them for arguing almost every day of my childhood. And not in the passionate way of fiery lovers, but in a low-level peck-peck-pecking at each other, which is totally exhausting to be around. But most of all, I hate them for shipping me off to my grandma's for the summer. Apparently, they need "time and space on their own to see if they can save their marriage," but why should I be punished for their relationship issues? When I said this to Suzette last night—I'm now refusing to call her Mom—she said I wasn't being punished for their relationship issues, I was being punished for skipping school to go on protest marches and for displaying "other problematic behaviors." The fact that she sees my trying to save the planet over learning algebra as problematic only confirms my suspicions that she's deeply selfish or incredibly stupid, or both.

I follow the passengers from my plane out into the arrivals hall, dragging my backpack on the floor behind me. A line of eager-faced people are there to greet us, many of them holding signs with names on. It's been so long since I've seen my grandma I hope she's thought to do this and I scan the crowd for someone with white hair holding a card with the name Cindy. I doubt my self-obsessed parents have told her I prefer going by the name Raven now.

I study the faces, trying to look calm and cool. *We could all be about to be incinerated to a crisp*, I remind myself. *You've got way bigger things than airport arrivals to be afraid of.* I picture a nuclear mushroom cloud blooming on the horizon, my go-to thought when I need to get things into perspective. But still, you'd think she'd be here for her one and only grand-daughter who she hasn't seen in five years, and who has just taken her first solo flight at the tender age of thirteen.

My throat begins to tighten the way it always does when I hear the low whine of Suzette and Frank pecking at each other. *What if she's forgotten I'm coming? Do people start losing their memories at sixty-six? What if she's out playing bowls with her other elderly friends or at a sewing circle?* Not that I can remember my grandmother playing bowls or sewing. The only thing I remember about her is her baking. The last time she visited us in Brooklyn, she brought the most incredible cake that was soft as a cloud in the middle but crisp and sugary on top. I can still remember how warm and happy it made me feel. Clearly it didn't have the same effect on Suzette, who ended up accusing Grandma of being a terrible mother and wishing that it had been her and not Grandpa who'd died the year before. My grandma left the following day, never to be seen again.

My panic grows. *What if she's a terrible grandmother as well as mother and she's decided to not come get me? What will I do if I'm all alone in San Francisco? What would the heroine in a Judy Blume novel do?* I ask myself. But, for once, my beloved favorite author fails to inspire me.

The other passengers all melt off outside or into the arms of the people waiting and I stand there feeling my cheeks burn. I scan the hall for white hair and those grody nylon pant suits older women love to wear and practically jump out of my skin when I feel a tap on my shoulder. I turn to see a sprightly woman with short dyed black hair wearing a Grateful Dead T-shirt, pinstripe pants and a pair of green sneakers.

"Yes?" I say, looking over her shoulder for any sign of my grandmother.

"Cindy, is that you?" She gazes at me, open-mouthed, a stunned expression I realize I must be mirroring.

"Grandma, is that you?"

She throws back her head and laughs. It's a nice laugh, light, like the pealing of a bell, rather than the tight, sarcastic sniggers of my parents.

"*Mon dieu!*" she says in her strange, half-American, half-French accent. "You look so much older than I was expecting."

"And you look so much younger," I can't help blurting out.

She laughs even louder. "Why, thank you!" She touches my arm. "Isn't it funny how we women long to look older up until a certain point, and then we'd give anything to be told we look young again."

I want to smile at this. I like the fact that she's implied that I'm a woman. I'm sick of my parents treating me like a kid. But I've been angry for so long, it feels as if my face has seized up into a scowl.

"I'm so sorry I'm late," she continues, giving me a hug, and I catch a waft of her perfume. It's rich and floral and makes me think of those glamorous Hollywood actresses from black and white movies, who smoke cigarettes in fancy holders and huskily drawl things like, "Come up and see me some time." "I had a nightmare getting parked." She grabs my backpack. "Come on, let's get out of here."

As I follow her through the arrivals hall, my brain races to process what's just happened. My grandma doesn't seem nearly as bad as I'd been expecting, but I mustn't lower my guard. We take the elevator to the parking lot and she leads me through the rows of cars to a ramshackle pick-up truck. A faded bumper sticker on the back reads: *Lead me not into temptation for I'll find it myself*, which is kind of gross coming from someone her age.

"What ees up?" she says in that weird accent of hers.

"Nothing," I answer automatically—my stock answer when my parents ask me this question, having learned that, in the drama of their marital breakdown, I don't get to play a speaking role.

"I guess this isn't as fancy as you're used to," she says, following my gaze to a patch of rust on the wheel arch. "But I need something that drives well in the forest."

I want to ask, *What forest?* but reply, "Fair enough," instead. Then I try to open the passenger door, but, of course, it's locked. My cheeks burn. I don't want to be here. She unlocks my door with her key but doesn't open it for me. I wonder if I've upset her. I don't like being obnoxious, but if I am, maybe she'll send me home early. A plan begins hatching in my mind. "So where do you live exactly?" I ask as I clamber into my seat.

"Sonoma County, it's about an hour's drive from here, so buckle up."

"I don't do seat belts."

She turns to look at me. "Well I do."

"Go for it." I stare at her. I can't believe I'm being so rude, but I'm tired and it's baking hot, and she probably doesn't want me here either. If I can speed up my being sent home, I'll be doing us both a favor.

She turns the engine off and reaches in front of me to the glove compartment, taking out a pack of cigarettes. Just before she shuts it, I see something that makes me gasp.

"Do you have a revolver in there?"

"Uh-huh." She winds down her window, lights a cigarette

and leans back in her chair, closing her eyes as if she's relaxing on the back porch.

"What are you doing?" I ask, bewildered.

"Having a smoke, seeing as we won't be going anywhere."

"What do you mean, we won't be going anywhere?"

"You refuse to put on the seat belt, I refuse to drive." She takes a drag on her cigarette and blows out a thin plume of smoke. As it mingles with the humid air, I feel it clinging to the insides of my nostrils.

I make a big drama of winding down my window, then yank on the seat belt. If it was my mother, I'd refuse to cave, but this is my grandmother, and she has a gun in her glove compartment. "OK, you can go," I say as I clunk the seat belt into the clasp.

"*Merci beaucoup!*" she exclaims and turns the key in the ignition. Some old sixties band comes blaring out of the tape deck and I feel another flush of embarrassment. Especially when I notice a really cute boy in a CND tee walking toward us. I wind up my window and sink down in the seat, as low as the stupid belt will let me, anyways. To make matters even worse, my grandma starts singing along at the top of her voice. It's like she's deliberately trying to embarrass me.

We drive out of the airport and onto the highway and I feel a tightening in my throat. I don't want to be here with this grandmother I barely know on the opposite coast to my best friend, Melissa, and my home. Not that it feels like home. Nowhere feels like home. My throat gets even tighter as the harsh reality of my lousy life hits me. My parents don't want each other and they don't want me. A sob escapes just as the song comes to an end. I try to disguise it with a cough and wipe away my tears, staring out of the side window so my grandma won't see.

She turns the tape off. "I guess life's been a little tough for you lately. Suzette doesn't tell me much, but I know she and Frank have been having some issues."

"Uh-huh," is all I can trust myself to say without crying again.

"Do you want to talk about it?"

"No."

"OK." She turns the radio on. The news is all about the Olympic games, which Russia has boycotted due to them taking place in America. When the Kremlin first announced the boycott, I got it into my head that it was because they were going to nuke America during the games and didn't want their athletes to be here. "Do you think there's going to be a nuclear war?" I blurt out. I didn't mean to say it, but sometimes my fear of the mushroom cloud gets the better of me.

"I hope not." She turns the radio off. "It seems impossible to believe that there was once a time when Russia and America were allies."

"During the Second World War?" I reply, recalling my history class.

"Yes. Back then, Germany was the big bad monster everyone hated and feared." She laughs, but it isn't light-hearted like her laugh in the airport. It feels tinged with something else —sadness maybe.

"Weren't you in France during the war?"

"Yes. In Paris."

"You must have hated the Germans back then."

To my surprise, she shakes her head. "Not all of them." She looks at me, her expression deadly serious. "The whole point of war is to get us to hate each other, but for what?"

I'm not sure what to say to this. "But if another country, like Russia, is threatening to nuke us, isn't it natural to hate them?"

"In my experience, it's a lot more complicated than that."

We drive on in silence. My grandma isn't at all how I

remembered her or expected her to be, and I really can't decide
if this is a good or bad thing.

3

JUNE 1940, PARIS

Once Baptiste had returned to the lobby, I paced around the patisserie kitchen, unsure what to do. The counters were lined with trays of pastries—croissants, madeleines and gleaming tartes tatin, and presiding over them all, the golden dome of the kouign-amann. I felt a little like a drunk must do when surveying a sea of empty bottles after a binge. *What had I been thinking, baking so many cakes? What had I been thinking, baking at all?* I knew the Germans were coming, and now they were here. Surely none of our remaining guests would be venturing out of their rooms, and if they did, they would have no doubt lost their appetites.

The door burst open, and Baptiste reappeared, eyes wide. "One of the bellboys just arrived," he whispered. "He said the Germans are here on the Left Bank and they're coming down boulevard Saint-Michel!"

I instantly thought of Madame Monteux. Despite being Jewish, she had refused to leave Paris, scared that if she left her beloved apartment, she might never get it back. I had to go to her and make sure she was all right. I would take her some cakes. I fetched a box from one of the cupboards and put the kouign-amann inside, along with a couple of tartes tatin and some croissants. "Please, help yourself," I said to Baptiste.

He glanced at the crowded counter-tops and shook his head. "I feel too sick to eat. Shall we go and see what's happening?"

"See the Germans?" I stared at him in horror.

He nodded. "I think I need to witness it for myself to believe it's really happening."

I nodded grimly. Perhaps he had a point. "But then I need to go to Madame Monteux."

"Of course. Tell her I'm here if there's anything she needs." Baptiste adored Madame Monteux and loved to flirt with her whenever she came to see me at the hotel, calling her the Duchess, and kissing her hand. She would always feign embarrassment, but I could tell from her stifled smile and rosy blush that she loved it really.

When we got outside, I was surprised to see that the street was busier than it had been in a while, with a steady stream of people making their way toward boulevard Saint-Michel, as grim-faced and silent as a funeral procession. Clearly we weren't the only ones who wanted to see if our worst nightmare had come true.

I heard them before I saw them—a man speaking French with a strong German accent through some kind of loudhailer.

"You are now under German occupation," the voice boomed from a car that was rounding the corner. "You must surrender any private weapons immediately and anyone who commits a hostile act against the occupation authorities will be met with the death penalty."

Baptiste and I exchanged anxious glances.

"A curfew is now in place, from nine o'clock at night until six in the morning," the voice continued as the car crawled past us. "And from now on, you will be observing German time, so please reset your clocks and timepieces accordingly."

"There's no way I'm moving my watch forward an hour for them," Baptiste muttered with a glare.

I nodded in agreement. But, oh, how I wished we could move time forward until the moment the Germans were defeated and leaving our beloved city with their tails between their legs.

As we drew closer to the boulevard, I heard the low hum of engines and a patrol of German soldiers on motorcycles appeared. My stomach clenched. Hundreds and hundreds of them glided past in their gray-green uniforms on their gleaming machines. Baptiste and I came to a halt and watched in stunned silence. More and more people joined us on the sidewalk, all gazing, dumbfounded, at what was unfolding. I felt a stab of anger as I noticed the smug smirks on some of the soldiers' faces. What must they think of us, all standing there so passively accepting our defeat? Then I heard another sound over the motorcycle engines, the clip-clip of what sounded like hundreds of feet. Rows of soldiers appeared, all marching in formation, holding rifles across their chests.

As the first of the foot patrols reached us, they greeted us with beaming smiles and I was momentarily taken aback by how normal they looked. I was not sure what I'd been expecting —fangs bared and dripping with blood, perhaps. One of them threw a chocolate to a little girl beside me. The girl gazed at him, eyes saucer-wide, then she began to grin.

Don't fall for it! I wanted to yell. *They're our enemy, not our friends!* I bit my lip and looked down at the ground.

"I need to go and see Madame Monteux," I said to Baptiste, having seen more than enough.

He nodded grimly. "Chin up, Coralie, and give my love to the Duchess."

I hurriedly wove my way through the growing crowds on the sidewalk. A couple of soldiers were lowering the French flag displayed over one of the buildings and my stomach churned as they replaced it with the red, white and black of their dreaded swastika.

By the time I arrived at Madame Monteux's apartment building by the Seine, I was full to the brim with dread and fear. I glanced across the river and saw more German troops marching along the other side. There were so many of them; it felt as if Paris had been flooded by a murky gray-green wave.

Fluctuat nec mergitur, the motto of Paris came back to me. We might be rocked by this wave, but we would not sink.

I slipped through the ornate glass doors and into the marble-floored foyer of the apartment building. The concierge, a small, birdlike woman named Brigit, waved at me from her office over to the right. I waved back but didn't stop. Brigit took the sport of gossiping to an Olympic standard and this was definitely not the time for tittle-tattle.

Madame Monteux lived on the top floor, so while the tiny elevator made its way up, I took the opportunity to compose myself. The last thing she needed was my anxiety. She had much more to fear from the Nazis than me.

I walked along the wood paneled hallway and gave my customary three sharp knocks on the door. She opened it swiftly, as if she'd been standing there waiting for me. She was wearing a plum satin dress and her long silver hair hung, sheet-like, down her back.

"Oh, Coralie, what a dark, dark day for our city of lights!" she declared, beckoning me inside with her pearl-embossed cigarette holder. "I've been watching them across the river from the window."

"They're here on the Left Bank too." I followed her through to her living room. Light and airy, with huge floor-to-ceiling windows and an intricately carved cornice, it was my favorite room in the apartment—although it hadn't been when I first came here in my old role as her housekeeper and I had to do the dusting. A pile of old copies of *Paris Vogue* were strewn across the table and a recording of her favorite opera, *La Traviata*, was crackling away on the gramophone. Madame Monteux had been an opera singer when she was younger and now taught trainee singers.

"I've been trying to comfort myself with some rousing Verdi," she said, perching down on the red velvet chaise longue. "But it isn't working."

"Perhaps some cake will do the trick?" I said, putting the box down on the table. "I made your favorite."

"Kouign-amann?" she asked, her dark eyes widening. Although she was almost seventy, her long hair and doe eyes gave her a beautiful girl-like quality.

"Yes, and I kneaded plenty of comfort and courage into the mix."

She clasped her hands together, the oval moonstone in her favorite ring glimmering. "Oh, Coralie, you are such a comfort to me."

"It might not be too late to escape." I'd been trying to convince her to flee to a safer part of France for months but as she had no family left and all of her friends were in Paris she'd stayed put. Perhaps now she'd seen the Germans arrive, she'd feel differently. But she shook her head.

"Never! I love this city. The only way I'm leaving is in a coffin."

My skin prickled with goosebumps. "Don't say that!"

"Why not? It's true."

"Let's eat," I said, deciding to steer the conversation away from coffins and onto the far more comforting subject of cake. I fetched some plates from the kitchen, but as soon as she saw them, she shook her head.

"What are you doing with those old things? An occasion like this requires my finest porcelain."

I frowned, confused. "There's nothing to celebrate. You just said this is one of the darkest days our city has ever seen."

"Exactly, so we need to create our own light. Let's use the Chinese tea set."

As we sat down at the gleaming mahogany table to feast on jade porcelain, I was reminded again why I loved her so. She had the most irrepressible spirit I'd ever encountered.

"In a world ruled by hatred and fear, happiness is an act of rebellion," she said, raising her delicate teacup. "To being happiness rebels."

"Happiness rebels," I echoed, chinking my cup against hers, and the aria on the gramophone reached its stirring crescendo.

I returned to the Lutetia that evening to find Alexandre, the hotel manager, pacing up and down the deserted lobby. The armpits of his shirt were dark with patches of sweat and his chin was gray with stubble.

"I thought Marianne had left," he said to me, looking confused.

"She has, but I wanted to stay until the end. Not that I want there to be an end," I hastily added. "I'm here until you no longer need me."

He gazed at me vacantly, his mind clearly elsewhere. "Thank you," he muttered before hurrying off.

I was about to go to the patisserie when I spied a figure sitting hunched over in one of the armchairs.

"Greta?" I called, hurrying over.

Greta Fischer was a German artist and outspoken critic of Hitler, who had fled to Paris from Berlin to escape the Nazis. She'd been a daily visitor to the hotel patisserie ever since she'd arrived and was one of my favorite customers.

"Oh, Coralie, it's so nice to see you." She smiled up at me, but the whites of her eyes were stained pink as if she'd been crying.

"Are you all right?" I asked.

"I don't know." She sighed. "I don't know what to do, or where to go." Her eyes darted around the lobby, reminding me of a frightened little sparrow. "Do you think the soldiers will come here, to the hotel? Do you think they'll check who's staying here?"

"I don't know. I hope not. Surely they'll have more important things to do."

She nodded and gave me a weak smile. "That's what I've been hoping, but it's so scary knowing that they're now here in Paris."

I crouched in front of her and took her hand in mine. It was icy cold despite the summer heat. "I'm sure you'll be OK. They have no idea that you're here."

She nodded and her smile grew.

"And first thing in the morning, I'm going to make some of your favorite cakes."

"Religieuses?" she said hopefully.

"Absolutely."

She leapt out of the chair and hugged me tightly. "Thank you! And thank you for not leaving like so many others have. It's such a comfort knowing you're still here too—and I'm not just saying that because of your cakes!"

"Of course!" I replied with a grin. "I'm not going anywhere. And the good thing about the others leaving is that there's all the more pastries for you."

She laughed. "I can't wait." She picked up her bag from beside the chair. "I'm going to try to get some sleep. I'll see you in the morning."

"Yes, goodnight."

I watched her head over to the elevators with a heavy ball of dread forming in the pit of my stomach. I really hoped my optimism was warranted and she'd be OK.

· · ·

I went through to the patisserie pantry, where I had a small daybed I'd sleep on when I wanted to get an early start on the next day's baking. I snuggled under the blanket, my body feeling like a lead weight from the stress of the day. *The Germans are here, in Paris*, echoed through my mind, but I batted the thought away and focused instead on the religieuses I would make for Greta, deciding to fill them with chestnut crème pâtissière instead of ordinary cream or custard. I drifted off to sleep picturing fat juicy pears and a creamy hazelnut paste.

I woke at four and, after freshening up in the ladies' bathroom by the lobby, I set to work making the choux pastry. Religieuses were made of two choux buns, one on top of the other, and meant to resemble chubby nuns, hence the name. I began by heating a pan of butter, salt and water. As I brought it to the boil, I thought back to my childhood and how religieuses had been my favorite of all the cakes Arnaud made. They were delicious and always made me giggle when I thought of what they were named after. But my thoughts kept straying back to the Germans and I burnt my finger. The pain snapped me back to my senses and I took the pan from the heat and tipped in the flour and began to stir.

"Please fill this pastry with courage," I whispered. "Make Greta feel as brave as a lioness as soon as she eats it."

I kept stirring until the dough was smooth and had formed a ball, then I transferred it to a bowl and began adding the eggs. Once the dough was ready, I piped neat lines of choux balls onto baking trays—some large for the nuns' bodies and some smaller, for their heads. Being forced to concentrate on the piping helped loosen the tension in my shoulders, and just like the day before, I began losing myself in my baking.

A few hours later, once the religieuses were made and iced, and trays of golden croissants and brioche had been baked, I put my wares on display in the glass-fronted cabinets in the store.

There were a lot less pastries than normal, but at least I'd made something and hopefully they'd bring some cheer to Greta and the remaining guests.

I heard a sound from the hallway outside and hurried over to the door, hoping it was Greta coming for her breakfast. I flung the door open and froze on the spot. The hallway was full of German soldiers, all marching towards me.

4

JULY 1984, SAN FRANCISCO

We arrive at my grandma's house late in the afternoon. I knew from my mom that my grandma had moved to a new place after my grandpa died so I'd been expecting a condo in a retirement complex but it couldn't be more different. A wooden one-story, situated at the end of a long dirt track and surrounded by towering pine trees, it's more like something out of a fairytale. The sun is lowering in the sky and causing golden shafts of light to filter between the branches, which only adds to the magical feel.

"*Bienvenue*," she says as we step inside the house. It's dimly lit and smells of sugar and cinnamon. I inhale deeply. It's so different from the artificial pine air fresheners and bowls of "Floral Fantasia" pot pourri my mom insists on dotting throughout our apartment. And that's not the only difference.

As she leads me through the living room, I see that my grandma's furniture is much older and none of it matches, yet it all seems to go together somehow. She shows me down a narrow passageway to a guest room at the back of the house, over-looking a lake. Unlike my bedroom in New York with its constant soundtrack of honking taxis and siren wails, all I can hear are the birds chirping in the trees outside, and the whir of cicadas.

"Take a moment to freshen up and get settled in," she says, showing me the en suite bathroom. "I'm going to make you a cake. It's one I haven't made for a very long time, but I have the feeling it's exactly what you need."

I'm not sure what she means by this, but I nod, grateful for some time on my own to get my bearings and, more importantly, to figure out the fastest way to get banished back to New York so I can be reunited with Melissa.

After lying on the bed for an hour, I'm no closer to coming up with a plan for getting sent home—other than being generally obnoxious—and the smell of baking drifting in under the old wooden door is making my mouth water and my stomach gurgle. It's a rich, chocolatey aroma with the hint of something familiar that I just can't place—vanilla maybe. I can't resist going to investigate.

I haul myself up off the bed and glance out the window. The sky is streaked tangerine and pink and the sun is setting over the water, turning it a deep shade of red. A heron drifts into view and splashes down. It's breathtaking.

I read somewhere that in the event of a nuclear attack, the sky will fill with radioactive particles of debris and soil and it will go as dark as night. I shiver and fetch a sweater from my backpack. I can't understand why humans waste their intelligence and imaginations on increasingly horrific ways to destroy the world when it's full of views like this. Whenever I think of this, it makes my heart break, so I think of Melissa instead. We've made a pact that if and when the bomb drops, we'll meet our deaths together. But now she's all the way on the East Coast alone. If the Russians nuke us while I'm stuck in California, I will never, ever forgive my lousy parents.

I venture out of the bedroom and into the darkened hall-way. The aroma of baking is so intense, I can practically taste the chocolate in the air. Instantly, I feel a pang of guilt. I wish my parents hadn't dragged my grandma into their battle. She seems nice, and kind of interesting, and I don't want to hurt her feelings. But I have to get back to Melissa.

I follow my nose like a hound down the hallway and into the living room. Some movement through the window catches my eye and I see my grandma in the garden watering her plants. This is more how I'd imagined someone of her age to be. I hadn't imagined her wearing a Grateful Dead T-shirt and swig-ging from a glass of wine while she gardened though.

I sigh and go through to the kitchen. Unlike the kitchen back home in New York, which is the size of a postage stamp and so white and pristine it looks more like an operating room, my grandma's kitchen is huge and a riot of color. I do a full turn and drink it all in. Copper and iron pots and pans hang like bats from the ceiling and the long windowsill is lined with plants. A huge wooden dresser stands against one of the walls, its shelves full of brightly painted crockery, and a jug of wild daisies sits in the middle of the table.

I go over to the window and peer out onto the porch. The empty swing seat is gently swaying as if it's being pushed by a ghost. Feeling almost drunk on the intense smell of chocolate, I go over to the table and sit down. There's an ancient-looking leatherbound notebook next to the fruit bowl, its cover splat-tered with grease stains. I glance at the door. If you look inside something that's lying out in plain sight, can it really be deemed snooping? My mother certainly didn't seem to think so the day she revealed that she'd read my journal.

My cheeks burn at the memory. Her reading an angry rant in which I wished I could divorce my parents was what sealed my fate and led to my banishment here. That and the gushing account of my love for Jet—a guy who works in a record store on

Bleecker, and the many and detailed ways in which I'd show my love for him if I ever got the chance. My embarrassment turns to anger and I flick the old notebook open and start thumbing through the yellowing pages. Why should I care about anyone else's privacy?

The book is full of what look like handwritten recipes. I know from my school language class that the first couple are in French, the handwriting looping and slanted. But then I turn the page and the writing changes, with the letters becoming smaller and more square. I frown. The first recipe looks as if it's written in German; I recognize the word bratwurst. I keep flicking and find more recipes in the same writing, interspersed with the ones in French.

I turn to the inside page and see some kind of handwritten dedication. It's in the square handwriting and in German. *Die Rezepte des besten französischen Konditors der Welt und eines bescheidenen deutschen Kochs!* Below the inscription, there's a date: *Mai 1941*.

I think back to what my grandma said in the car about the Germans having been the monsters back then, but not having hated all of them and the book suddenly feels like a grenade in my hands.

I flick to the back and find an old postcard tucked inside. There's a picture of the Eiffel Tower on the front and on the back the person with the square handwriting has written, *Ma chère Coralie, merci pour cette belle journée*. I know enough French to be able to figure out that it means, *my dear Coralie, thank you for this lovely day*.

I frown at the postcard like the TV detective Columbo, piecing together the clues. My grandmother and this mysterious German person used the book to record recipes in Paris during the war. But the postcard would indicate that they socialized together too.

I stare at the words *Ma chère Coralie* and a chill goes right through me. Is this why Suzette has hardly anything to do with my grandma? Is this why she called her a terrible mother? Was Coralie some kind of Nazi sympathizer?

"What are you doing?"

The sound of my grandma's voice from behind me makes me jump and I drop the postcard onto the table.

5

JUNE 1940, PARIS

I locked the patisserie door and raced into the kitchen, my heart pounding, fit to burst. The Germans were in the hotel.

Their voices grew louder and I risked peeping around the kitchen door. They were all streaming along the corridor outside. I prayed that none of them glanced to the left and saw the cakes on display.

I heard the rattle of the door handle being tried and I lurched back out of sight. Thank goodness I'd locked it. I slid onto the floor, leaning against the wall, my head in my hands. What were so many of them doing in the hotel? And, more importantly, what should I do?

I jumped as I heard yelling and the pounding of feet marching across the floor above. Instantly, I thought of Greta. Her room was directly above the patisserie. We used to joke about cutting a hatch in the floor so she could lower a basket on a rope for me to fill with pastries. I looked up at the ceiling, terrified. Were the soldiers there to arrest her?

I heard a scream and a thud and then what sounded like something, or someone, being dragged across the room. *This can't be happening. This can't be happening*, my mind repeated incessantly. But it was. *Why oh why had I reassured Greta that she'd be OK?* I should have urged her to leave. I needed to help her, but how?

I stood up and glanced frantically around the kitchen for some kind of inspiration. My heart sank. A five foot two woman with a rolling pin would hardly be a match for the might of the Nazis.

Things quietened down upstairs and I decided to risk checking if the coast was clear. I couldn't stay cowering in the kitchen forever. I'd have to take my chances and see if Greta was OK. Grabbing my jacket and bag, I slipped into the shop and stopped dead. One of the soldiers was peering in through the patisserie window. He'd taken his hat off and was holding it to his chest, revealing a head of curly hair the color of caramel. As I stood frozen in the kitchen doorway, I realized that he hadn't noticed me at all, he was too busy staring at the cakes. I was about to step back out of sight when he looked up and for a second our eyes met. To my relief, he looked as startled as I was and hurried off.

I crept over to the door, and, after checking the hallway was clear, I slipped out, making sure to lock the door behind me. As I drew closer to the lobby, I heard the hum of men's voices all speaking in German. *Damn!* I turned to head back to the patisserie but saw to my horror that more soldiers were making their way toward me along the corridor. My stomach flipped as I caught a glimpse of Greta's red hair in the middle of them. I stood stock-still, back to the wall as they frogmarched her toward the lobby. As she drew level, I opened my mouth to say something, but she looked at me and shook her head. Panic swirled inside of me. Where were they taking her? What were they going to do to her?

Once they'd left I made my way to the lobby, which was bustling with Germans—mainly officers, judging by the hats they were wearing and the stripes on their coats. To my surprise, I saw Raphael weaving among them, holding a tray full of glasses of champagne. He had a smile fixed to his face, but his eyes were steely. Alexandre, the hotel manager, was deep in conversation with two German officers by the reception desk. It all felt like a surreal dream.

I spotted Baptiste hovering by his office and made a beeline for him.

"They've taken Greta," I whispered, and saying the words out loud jolted me from my numbness. This wasn't a surreal dream. This was our harsh new reality.

"I know. They've taken the other guests too," he replied, grim-faced. "They must have heard that the Lutetia had been a safe haven for those fleeing them." He shook his head; all the color had drained from his face. "And now it's going to be their home."

"What do you mean?" I hissed.

"They're moving in," Baptiste replied glumly.

I stared at him in shock. "How many of them?"

"All of them. They're taking over the whole hotel."

We watched as some soldiers marched in through the main entrance laden down with boxes and crates.

Baptiste gestured at me to follow him into his tiny office.

"That's not the worst of it," he whispered, closing the door behind me. He took off his peaked cap, revealing his thick thatch of silvery hair.

I steeled myself for whatever could possibly be worse than this.

"They're the *Abwehr*."

"The German Intelligence Service?" I replied, horrified. Greta had told me about the *Abwehr* and their notorious interrogation and torture techniques.

Baptiste nodded. "They're making the Lutetia their headquarters."

I placed my hand against the wall to steady myself. "So

that's it then. It's all over." I felt crushed. The Lutetia had been the scene of some of my happiest memories. It was where I'd become an adult and found my place in the world. Or so I'd thought.

"It certainly is," he muttered grimly. I watched as he took a box from the shelf and began filling it with his personal possessions—his pipe and beloved harmonica and the framed photograph of his grandchildren that always had pride of place on his desk.

"What will you do?" I asked. What would we both do?

"I don't know." It was horrible seeing the normally jovial Baptiste look so utterly defeated.

Once he'd packed up his belongings, I followed him numbly back to the lobby. But just as we were about to leave, I remembered my treasured baking utensils. I couldn't leave without them; they were my only remaining connection to Arnaud and Olive. Baptiste had already slipped out through the revolving door and I saw two armed German guards standing where he used to greet the guests.

I turned back into the lobby and saw Alexandre heading toward me.

"I need to speak with you, Coralie," he said, ashen-faced.

"It's all right, I'm leaving. I just need to collect a couple of my things from the patisserie kitchen."

He shook his head. "They've asked if you will stay."

"Who?" I murmured, praying I'd misunderstood.

"The Germans. They need some food and all our restaurant staff left yesterday. I said you might be able to provide them with some pastries, until they have their own kitchen staff in place." I must have looked horrified because he touched my arm sympathetically. "It's only for today, until their own chefs have got set up in the restaurant kitchen."

A German officer with a thin, perfectly manicured mustache approached. "Well?" he said to Alexandre.

Alexandre looked at me hopefully. I thought of the beautiful copper canelé molds and shell-shaped madeleine baking pans Arnaud had gifted me. If I refused, I'd probably have to leave immediately and never see them again. Even worse, they might end up in the thieving hands of a German chef.

I nodded. "I'll do it." It was only one day after all.

Alexandre gave a relieved smile. "Excellent. They need any pastries you've already got up in the conference room now." He looked at the officer, who nodded curtly in response, then turned on his heel and marched off.

I made my way through the thronging lobby, unable to believe I was surrounded by the enemy I'd dreaded and loathed for so long. Every time I saw the swastika on their armbands, I shuddered. The nightmare was going from bad to worse.

When I reached the relative safety of the patisserie, I drew a breath. All I had to do was deliver the pastries up to the conference room, then I could leave and never come back. But rather than bringing relief, the thought almost floored me with a feeling of loss. This place had been such a haven to me.

I took a tray of religieuses from the refrigerated cabinet and winced as I thought of the love and courage I'd infused into the chestnut cream. I'd made these for Greta, but now she was gone. If only I'd known who'd be eating them, I'd have infused them with pain!

Just as I was about to leave with the pastries, a German soldier appeared at the door, the one with the caramel-colored hair who'd been drooling at the cakes before.

"I... uh... I've been sent to help you," he said in French, looking slightly embarrassed. As well he should, the lousy invader.

"With what?" I replied curtly.

"Bringing the pastries upstairs." He looked at the tray of religieuses, his bright green eyes widening. "Is that real cream?"

he asked in the kind of hushed tones you might use to refer to a miraculous religious sighting.

I nodded. What a strange question. "You can bring those if you like," I said, nodding to the trays of croissants and brioche.

"Of course."

We took the trays of food along the corridor to the elevator.

"I'm Reinhardt," he said as we stepped inside.

"I'm Mademoiselle Donnadieu," I replied, hoping to make it clear that I did not wish to be on first-name terms with him.

"What are they called?" he said as the elevator began its ascent.

"Pardon?"

He nodded at the tray I was holding. "The pastries, what are they called?"

"Oh... religieuses," I muttered. "They're supposed to look like nuns."

He laughed. "Very round nuns."

"Yes," I replied curtly. It was bad enough that I had to supply them with my pastries, I was not about to make small talk with this invader.

But my bravado waned as soon as we arrived at the conference room and I saw about ten German officials sitting around the table. They all fell silent as we walked in. A shaft of sunlight fell upon my tray, causing the chestnut brown fondant to gleam. One of the officers looked at the cakes and licked his lips. Another said something in a suggestive tone while looking at me. The others sniggered and I felt a tightening in my chest.

We placed the trays on the table and Reinhardt said something in German. It was clear from his uniform and the deferential way in which he spoke that he was their subordinate. The officer at the head of the table nodded and barked what sounded like an order.

"Come," Reinhardt said, ushering me from the room. "They

want us to make a dinner," he said as soon as we were back in the corridor.

"Us?" I stared at him.

"Yes."

I thought maybe his French wasn't as good as it seemed and he'd misspoken or I'd misunderstood. "You and me?" I pointed at us both to make sure he knew what I meant.

"Yes." He pressed the call button for the elevator and when he turned back, I saw that his cheeks had flushed pink.

"I don't understand."

"There are some very important people arriving here this evening. They want us to prepare a menu for them. I'm to make the main course and you're to make the dessert."

"But..."

He opened the elevator door and stepped back to allow me inside first. "I'm a chef," he said.

I looked pointedly at his uniform. "So, you're not a soldier?"

He shook his head. "I was a chef in Berlin before the war broke out. Then I was recruited to cook for the *Abwehr*. Some of the officers used to eat in my restaurant."

"Oh." If he'd been trying to impress me with this, his words fell upon distinctly unimpressed ears.

"I know this must be very difficult," he said quietly as the elevator began going down.

Very difficult? I wanted to spit back but said nothing. All I could think was, *How can I get out of this?* I could feign illness. Or tell him that I needed to go to the bathroom and slip out of a fire exit. But then I'd lose my precious utensils.

The elevator arrived back on the ground floor and he followed me like a puppy dog to the patisserie.

"There's a kitchen in the restaurant, you know," I said as he followed me inside. "For you to make your dinner. I'll make the dessert here."

"Oh, yes, of course." He smiled at me, and in any other

circumstances, I would have found the warmth of his gaze comforting, but instead I found it unnerving. "I was just wondering what you were planning to do, or if you needed any help," he continued.

"Help?" My voice came out a lot shriller than I'd intended.

"Yes."

And then it happened—all of the anger I'd been suppressing surged into my head and I was blinded by a red mist. "I'm a French pastry chef," I spat. "French pastry chefs are the best in the world, and I've been baking since I was five years old. I don't need any help, least of all from..." I managed to stop myself, but it made little difference. It was obvious what I was about to say.

His smile faded and he gave me a brisk nod. "Very well. I'll be back in a couple of hours. We need enough desserts for fifty people." He stalked out and off down the corridor.

As soon as he disappeared from view, I wanted to kick myself. What had I been thinking, speaking like that to a German? Even if he was a chef, he worked for the *Abwehr*, who were known for their brutality. Arnaud and Olive used to laughingly refer to my flashes of temper as my "saucepan boiling over moments," but I hated how they'd so often land me in trouble.

I took three long deep breaths, the way Olive had taught me, and I pictured my anger leaving my body as I exhaled.

More soldiers began filing past outside and my heart broke for the Hotel Lutetia. One thing was for certain, there was no way I was making dessert for those monsters and their victory dinner. I was going to collect my baking pans and sneak away and they could go to hell.

I hurried into the kitchen and gathered my precious tins into a basket. Then I came back into the shop and looked around forlornly. The two years I'd worked there had been the happiest of my life. It was torturous thinking of the Nazi pigs setting foot in there. I trudged over to the door, but just as I opened it, Reinhardt reappeared. He was holding a crate full of vegetables and a large iron pot.

"I have to cook here, with you," he said, looking slightly sheepish.

"What? Why?"

"I think someone sabotaged the restaurant oven. It's broken."

I thought of Xavier, the head chef in the hotel restaurant. He'd made no secret of his hatred for the Germans before he'd left to stay with his family in Provence. I pictured him setting about the oven with a meat mallet and fought the urge to smirk.

"Would it be OK if I used your stove to make a stew?" Reinhardt asked.

"Do I have any choice?"

"Not really, no." Again, he gave a sheepish smile.

Before I could respond, I heard voices and Reinhardt's smile disappeared and he stood to attention.

I peered up the corridor to see an older man with neatly parted white hair and bushy eyebrows approaching. He was wearing an officer's uniform with an iron cross pinned to his chest. A much younger woman in a rose-pink dress walked beside him, talking ten to the dozen. Her brown hair was elegantly rolled and her full lips were painted pink to perfectly match her dress. Combined with her flawless white skin, she looked like a china doll.

I instinctively stood straighter, trying to make all five foot two inches of me count. *What you lack in stature you certainly make up for in spirit*, Olive used to tell me when I'd come home from school indignant because the other girls had teased me, calling me petit four. She said it to me so often, I truly came to believe it.

You might have won the battle, but we will still win the war, I thought to myself as the pair came to a halt beside us.

"A patisserie!" the woman exclaimed, looking up at the gold lettering on the shopfront.

Reinhardt said something to her in German and they all looked at me.

"What is your name?" the woman asked.

"Coralie," I muttered.

"And this place is yours?"

I nodded, although my proprietorship of the patisserie was going to be tragically short-lived.

"Well then, you and I are going to be very good friends," she said and the man she was with laughed and nodded.

They continued on their way and Reinhardt took off his hat and gave what sounded like a sigh of relief.

"Who was that?" I asked.

"That was Admiral Wilhelm Canaris," he replied. "The head of the German Intelligence Service."

6

JULY 1984, SAN FRANCISCO

Feeling sticky and hot with embarrassment, I turn to see my grandma standing in the doorway brandishing a trowel. "I was just..."

"Looking at my personal things." She marches over and scoops up the postcard and recipe book. "Didn't your mother ever teach you that it's wrong to go through another person's things?"

"No, actually, she didn't," I reply sullenly, thinking of the Daughtergate Diary Scandal, as Melissa and I had named the whole sorry affair.

"Well, it is—very wrong," she mumbles, clutching the book and postcard to her chest, as if they are her precious babies.

There's something about the way she says this—the obvious disapproval in her tone—that causes my vision to go blurry with anger. "Well, clearly you didn't teach your own daughter that, because she thinks it's perfectly acceptable to read my private journal." I stare at her defiantly.

"Suzette read your journal?" I'm slightly comforted by the fact that she looks horrified at this.

"Yes, trying to find reasons to get rid of me." Much to my annoyance, I feel dangerously close to tears.

"Oh, I'm sure she wasn't trying to—"

"Of course she was!" I interrupt. "The only person my mom and dad hate more than each other is me!" And now the tears start spilling onto my face. I wipe them away angrily.

"Oh, Cindy."

"I'm not called Cindy anymore. I'm called Raven!" I mutter. "And I don't want to be here any more than you want me here."

"But I do want you here!" she exclaims, and her tone is so warm and genuine, it catches me off guard and more tears fill my eyes. "Wait a second," she says, touching me gently on the shoulder, then she goes through to the living room and I hear a drawer sliding open and closed. She returns without the postcard and book. "I've been so looking forward to your visit," she remarks, instantly causing me to feel a pang of guilt at my outburst.

But she might have been a Nazi sympathizer, I remind myself. I desperately want to ask her about what I saw in the book, but that would mean drawing attention back to the fact that I snooped.

"Have you really?" I ask suspiciously. "It's OK, I can take the truth. I've become very used to dealing with disappointment."

"Oh dear," she says, sitting down beside me and biting her bottom lip as if she's trying not to grin.

"It's not funny!"

"I know, it's just that you..." She breaks off.

"What?"

"You remind me a lot of myself."

I'm not sure what to make of this, but before I can say anything, she leaps back up. "Ooh la la! The gateau!" She races to the oven and takes out the cake.

The smell is so intoxicating, I can feel my mouth start to drool. I mustn't weaken though. I can't spend an entire summer without Melissa. And I can't spend an entire summer with someone who once had a "lovely day" with a Nazi.

My grandma puts the cake on a wire rack on the side and returns to the table.

"I want to go home," I mutter, unable to look her in the eye, but more out of embarrassment than anger now. "Please can you call Suzette and get her to book me on a flight to New York?"

To my horror, she shakes her head. "I can't."

"Why not?"

"I'm under strict instructions not to bother them."

I hunch in my chair like a deflating balloon. The fact that my mother would beg my grandma not to bother them—and that she sees me as a bother—sums up my sorry life perfectly. A montage of scenes featuring Suzette and me starts playing on fast-forward in my mind. All the times I tried to win her approval through my perfect grades and track scores. All the times I tried to grab her attention through being funny or smart, and then when that didn't work, through yelling and slamming doors. And all the while, my father drifting by in the background, always on his way someplace else—the office, the Giants game, the bar—anywhere so as not to have to face the unhappiness of his wife and kid.

I sigh. Even Judy Blume wouldn't create a family this dysfunctional. Her characters' parents might be annoying at times, but they all have good hearts, and none of the grandmothers are potential Nazis. I slump forwards, my head in my hands, and I hear my grandma get up and move around.

"I'm sorry, Raven," she says softly. "Why don't you try some of this? I guarantee it will make you feel better."

I peer through my fingers and see that she's placed a giant slab of chocolate cake in front of me. It looks so moist and smells so delicious, I can't resist sitting up just enough to break off a piece and shove it in my mouth.

"Would you like some of my orange iced tea? It goes really well with the cake," she says and I nod as my mouth is parched.

I hear the clink of ice cubes and, next thing, a tall thin glass is placed in front of me. I pull myself upright and take a sip. It's citrusy and fresh with a hint of cinnamon.

"I have a proposal for you," my grandma says, sitting down beside me.

I take another bite of cake. She's right, it goes really well with the tea.

"We can either see you being sent here as bad news..."

"Yes." I nod emphatically.

"Or we can choose to turn it into good news."

"But how?" I ask, genuinely bewildered.

She laughs. "Clearly it's going to take some effort on your part, but I could suggest some ways."

"Go on then." I take another mouthful of cake and have to fight not to gasp in pleasure. It seems to be getting richer and gooier with every bite. I've never tasted anything like it.

"Well, the reason that I'm seeing your visit as good news is that it means I can finally get to know you—the real, grown-up you."

"You see me as a grown-up?" I can't help asking, aware that my behavior since I arrived here hasn't been the most mature.

"Well, sure. The last time I saw you, you were only eight. And, sadly, my visit got cut short." She clears her throat, looking a little awkward at the memory. "But now you're a young woman and I'm intrigued to learn all about you."

I stare at her suspiciously.

"Especially as you seem so interesting," she continues.

"You don't need to patronize me."

"I'm not. I really like the way you dress and how you have your hair."

"You do?" I scrutinize her face for any sign that she's lying. Suzette freaked out when I dyed my hair black and had the sides shaved off. She said I looked like the newest member of the Addams Family.

"Yes," she replies, nodding emphatically. "I love people who create their own style and who aren't afraid to stand out, especially at your age when there's so much pressure to fit in."

"Thank you," I say, and I mean it. The day I debuted my new hairstyle at school, my skin had to thicken like a cow's hide to deflect the sniggers from the jocks and their cheerleader sidekicks.

"I've always marched to the beat of my own drum when it comes to personal style too, as you can probably tell." She gestures at her Grateful Dead tee and pinstriped pants ensemble and grins. "And I can tell from the CND badges on your backpack that you're a deep thinker and you care about life, and that makes you very interesting to me."

I'm not sure if it's the deliciousness of the cake, or the warmth of her praise, but I can feel my defenses starting to weaken. It feels so good to be noticed by an adult for once—like, noticed in a good way, instead of being wrongly judged.

"I don't want to perish in a nuclear war either," she continues, "so we have that in common too." She laughs, but in a gentle rather than mocking way.

I take another mouthful of cake. And another.

"Good, it's working." She nods approvingly. "I wasn't sure it would after so many years."

"What's working?"

"The cake."

I'm not sure what she means by this, but I suddenly feel really bad about what happened before. "I'm sorry I snooped in your book," I say softly.

"It could have been worse." She shrugs.

"How?"

"It could have been my journal." She gives me a sympathetic smile. "I'm sorry that happened to you."

"Thank you."

She tops up my glass from the jug of iced tea.

"Can I ask you a question?" I ask cautiously.

"Of course."

"The book?"

"Yes?"

"Were the recipes in it yours?"

She nods. "Well, some of them were."

"And whose were the others?" I ask, praying she won't get defensive and clam up.

"Oh... uh, just a work colleague," she replies, looking away.

"Was the colleague... were they German?" I hold my breath, hoping she'll answer. "It's just that I noticed some of the words were in German," I add.

"Yes, they were," she says quietly. "More cake?" She gets up and hands me the knife. "Just help yourself."

"Are you sure?" This is so different to home, where everything I eat is strictly portion-controlled and nowhere near as delicious. I can't quite believe my luck.

"Of course. I made it to be eaten." She sits back down and looks at me. "I worked in a hotel in Paris before the war, as a pastry chef."

"Oh, I see. But the date in the front of the book..." I break off, aware that I'm revealing the extent of my snooping.

"What about it?" she asks.

"It was during the war."

"Yes. The Germans who took over the hotel asked if I would make pastries for them."

"Oh." I breathe a sigh of relief. My grandma working for a German hotelier is definitely preferable to what I'd been imagining. I cut myself another slice of cake. "Were they just normal Germans then? The ones who took over the hotel?"

"What do you mean, normal?"

"Well, not soldiers."

She nods. "No, they weren't soldiers."

I take another bite of cake, my relief growing.

"They were spies."

"Spies?" I almost spit out my cake.

She nods. "They were called the *Abwehr*—the German Intelligence Service. The hotel became their headquarters."

I put my fork down, suddenly feeling sick. "So, you worked for them?"

"Yes, until..." She stands up again, looking uneasy suddenly. "I should wash the cake tin."

I stare at her back as she goes over to the sink. "Until what?" I ask softly.

"Until I started working against them," she replies, before turning the faucet on.

7

JUNE 1940, PARIS

Reinhardt stared wide-eyed into the patisserie fridge as if he were gazing upon a set of crown jewels.

"I've never seen so much cream," he whispered.

"What do you mean? You're a chef." I'd fully intended to ignore him completely, but his strange reaction to the cream piqued my curiosity.

"We haven't been allowed to use cream since 1938," he said.

"Who hasn't?" I asked, bemused.

"Us Germans." He sighed. "I've had to make an ersatz version using egg white."

I stared at him, horrified by the mere thought. "But why?"

He shifted his gaze from the cream to me and his expression saddened. "Food shortages."

"Because of the war?" If it was, he surely wasn't expecting me to feel sorry for him.

"Yes, but not this one," he replied.

"What do you mean?"

"Do you really not know?"

I shook my head.

He frowned at the crowded fridge. "We've suffered chronic food shortages ever since the Great War and the blockades ordered by the Treaty of Versailles."

"Oh."

He looked at me, as if expecting me to personally apologize. I bit down on my lip. There was no way I was apologizing to a Nazi for anything. For all I knew, he could have been lying.

"So, how many people am I making dessert for?" I asked, eager to get on with my work and get out of there as soon as I could.

"I'll need you to make fifty desserts, plus something special for the Admiral and his staff."

I gave him a curt nod. I really didn't like the way he was talking like he was my boss.

It's only for one night, I told myself. *Then you'll never have to see him again.*

I pondered what to make for our uninvited occupiers. I'd never felt less enthused to bake and it was an unnerving feeling. Baking had always been such a source of joy to me. In the end, I decided to make a selection of different flavored éclairs and a hazelnut dacquoise.

"Where would you like me to set up my station?" he asked.

Well, that was something, at least. I pointed to the smaller counter in the darkened far corner, certain he wouldn't accept, but, to my surprise, he went straight over and started arranging his vegetables.

"Won't you need more utensils?" I said, looking at his solitary pot. If he thought he was going to borrow any of mine, he had another thing coming.

He shook his head. "I grew up with *Eintopfsonntag*. I'll be fine."

"What's that?"

"It means one-pot Sunday."

I looked at him and shrugged.

"It was a government initiative in Germany to encourage us to make a stew using just one pot on the first Sunday of every month."

"Why?"

"To help the poor."

I tried not to splutter at the notion of the Third Reich wanting to help anyone.

"On the first Sunday of the month, they would ask all families to eat a one-pot stew instead of their normal roast lunch," he continued, "and wealthier families would donate the money they saved to charity."

I turned away, feeling uncomfortable. On the face of it, this one-pot stew initiative sounded like a lovely idea, but I'd read all about what the Germans had done to the Jews in Austria and in Poland. If he thought he was going to warm my heart with his tales of Nazi compassion and one-pot stews for charity, he could think again.

"So, how about you?" he asked. "How long have you been working here?"

I inwardly groaned. How could he possibly think I'd be in the mood for small talk on a day like today?

"Three years," I replied. "Best three years of my life," I couldn't help adding sullenly.

"And why do you love being a pastry chef?"

"Because it feels like being a magician," I answered instantly, turning to look at him. He was leaning back against the counter, hands in his pockets and smiling that warm, relaxed smile of his. "Or, at least, how I imagine being a magician feels."

"What do you mean?" His green eyes shone with a genuine interest that was hard to resist.

"Well, French pastries aren't just about the taste, they're all about the appearance too. Ever since I was a little girl, I would feel wonderstruck at how a cake could taste so delicious *and* look like a work of art. It felt like magic to me."

His smile grew. "Wonderstruck. I like that word. It's how I felt earlier when I saw your cakes—the fat nuns. It was as if I'd been struck by a bolt of wonder." He clapped his hands to his chest as if mimicking being struck by lightning and I couldn't help laughing.

"Oh—uh—thank you."

"You're welcome."

We smiled at each other, and for a moment I forgot all about what was going on and felt touched by his interest and enthusiasm. But then I heard a man barking something in German in the corridor outside and all the warmth I'd been feeling instantly drained from my body.

"I'd better get started," I muttered, turning on the oven.

"Yes, of course."

Thankfully, I had some hazelnuts already ground and roasted so I was able to get straight to making the meringue for the dacquoise. I separated some egg whites and added a pinch of salt. Then I took my whisk from a peg on the wall and set to work. Normally, I found whisking extremely therapeutic, especially if I was feeling angry or down. But the more I whisked the eggs, the more I seemed to whisk myself into a bitter froth. I thought of the hotel guests and staff who'd had to flee and the smug arrogance of the men who now occupied the Lutetia in their place. The fact that I had to make these men a celebratory cake really was, well, the icing on the cake.

"Aren't you forgetting something," Reinhardt said, snapping me back to my senses.

"I'm sorry, what?"

"The sugar," he said with a smile. "I take it you're making meringue."

"Thank you very much, but I know what I'm doing," I snapped, feeling flustered. Why was he watching me?

Shouldn't he be getting on with his own meal? "The later you leave the sugar the lighter it tastes," I lied.

"Is that right?" I could tell he was stifling a smile and it made me want to hit him round the head with my whisk.

I grabbed a handful of sugar from the barrel and flung it into the bowl.

"Don't you need to weigh it?" he asked.

"No. *I* don't."

My natural instinct when it came to measurements was another thing that had convinced Arnaud I was some kind of child genius. I personally didn't see myself as any kind of genius, it was just something that came naturally to me. The same way an artist just knows how to create entire landscapes with random brushstrokes, or a sculptor is able to find a perfectly formed statue in a chunk of stone.

I looked back into the bowl and could tell that it needed more sugar. For a moment, I thought of sabotaging the meringue and throwing in a handful of salt instead, but my pride and passion for baking wouldn't allow me. I'd show those German monsters with their dull one-pot stews that they didn't have the imagination or the flair to beat us. They might have rocked Paris, but we'd have the last laugh, of that I was certain.

I threw in some more sugar and whispered a prayer into the mixture. "*May all who eat this cake soon taste bitter defeat.*"

8

JUNE 1940, PARIS

After what felt like the longest, most arduous baking shift I'd ever experienced, the desserts were ready. Four trays of éclairs, flavored chocolate, coffee, rose and almond, and one hazelnut dacquoise. As I arranged them on platters, I realized that Reinhardt was watching.

"They look incredible," he said. "The way you work it reminds me of..." He broke off.

"Of what?" I asked.

"The way my mother used to cook."

"She was a pastry chef?"

"No, but she had the same flair and imagination, even though she had hardly any money for food. She used to dance as she cooked, the way you do too."

"I don't dance!" I said indignantly.

"Oh but you do." He picked up the ladle he'd been using for his one-pot stew and began twirling it the way I liked to twirl my mixing spoon, adding in a comical pirouette for good measure. "And she'd talk to her ingredients as she was mixing them just like you do."

Damn! I'd been trying so hard not to move my lips as I

stirred my silent prayers into the food. Clearly he hadn't heard what I'd been saying though. I doubted he'd have been smiling at me if he had, and it seemed like a genuine smile, and not at all mocking. I frowned. He wasn't going to trick me with his gentle smile and his twinkling eyes and his heartfelt tales of his mother. "Maybe if you cooked more interesting food you wouldn't have the time to spy on me!" I retorted.

"I wasn't spying on you, I was admiring you." As soon as he said it, his face flushed. "In a professional way, obviously."

I looked at his pot bubbling away on my stove, making the patisserie kitchen smell of carrots and turnips, and I felt the sudden urge to tip it onto the floor. The whole experience was so infuriating and humiliating. "I don't want your admiration," I muttered. "I just want to go home."

"Oh." He instantly looked disappointed.

I took my apron off. "I've done what was asked of me. I've made your desserts, now I want to leave."

"Of course." His look of dejection grew, and I felt a pang of guilt for hurting his feelings, which only annoyed me even more. Why should I care about the feelings of a German after what they were doing there in the hotel and in Paris? What the hell was wrong with me?

I knew that the sensible thing would be to slip out without saying another word, but my pride wouldn't allow it. I wanted him to know what he and his precious Führer had cost us, the pain they'd caused.

"Coming to work here was the best thing that ever happened to me," I said, putting on my jacket and picking up my bag. "And having it stolen from me is the very worst. I want you to remember that when you're cooking here. That you are responsible for the worst day of my life."

"But—"

"And I'm taking these," I continued, picking up the basket

of baking tins. "They were a gift to me from the people who took me in when I had nothing and no one."

"I'm so sorry," he said, and once again I was struck by how genuine he seemed.

Don't waver, I told myself sternly. But before I was able to make my grand exit, I heard the patisserie door open, causing us both to jump.

"Wait there," Reinhardt said before going into the shop.

I listened as he spoke in German to another man and my anger turned to frustration at myself. What had I been thinking, talking to him like that again? He might seem genuine and caring, but he worked for the German Intelligence Service and the place was now crawling with German spies who were known for their fondness for torture.

I went to pick up the basket and, in my agitated state, knocked it onto the floor, sending the tins flying. I dropped to my knees, trying to retrieve them as quietly as possible.

After a couple of seconds, Reinhardt's feet appeared in front of me. "If you want to leave, you have to come with me now as it's almost curfew," he said quietly. "They've asked for you to wait on them at the dinner, but I can say that you had to go as you weren't feeling well."

I scrambled to my feet and scooped up the basket, desperate to get out of there.

"Quick," he said, ushering me out of the kitchen.

We hurried along the corridor and into the lobby. German officers were now sitting in the armchairs around the piano where James Joyce had once sung his ballads and the air was thick with cigar smoke and laughter.

Reinhardt said something to the armed guards on duty and to my relief they opened the door.

"Thank you for your help," he called after me, but I didn't reply. And I didn't look back. I couldn't. The fact that on this terrible day, a German had shown me some kindness only made me feel sadder and more confused.

I hurried along the street fighting the urge to cry from despair. In the craziness of the day, I'd forgotten all about the stupid curfew. The notion that we were now banned from the streets of our own city after nine o'clock at night felt so offensive I could barely breathe. Too upset and angry to return to my lonely studio apartment, I decided to visit Madame Monteux and ask if I could stay the night there instead. I needed her warmth and eternal optimism to re-center me.

Madame Monteux opened the door to me with a relieved smile lighting up her face. "Oh, Coralie, I've been so worried about you. I heard what happened at the hotel."

I stepped into her arms and burst into tears. "I'm so sorry," I sobbed. "I'm so sorry."

"Oh my goodness, child, what for?"

"They... they asked me to make some desserts for them. I should have refused. I should have walked out like Baptiste did, but I'd left my baking tins in the kitchen, the ones Arnaud and Olive gifted me. And I couldn't bear the thought of the Germans getting their hands on them."

"It's all right. Slow down." She stroked my hair and my sobbing subsided.

I looked up at her through teary eyes. "You don't think that I betrayed you?"

"Of course not." She led me into the living room. "Although I really hope you didn't fold any love into the pastry!"

"No!" I exclaimed. "I stirred in the bitter taste of defeat."

She laughed, but I noticed that it wasn't her usual hearty chuckle. "What a terrible day."

"The worst."

"But I do have some good news though."

I laughed through my tears. "Only you could have good news on a day as bad as this."

"That's because I choose to make my own good news," she replied, going over to her drinks cabinet and taking out two champagne flutes.

I grinned at her. "Sometimes I think you only like to make good news so you have a reason to drink champagne."

"Well, it's certainly a delightful perk." She took a bottle of Veuve Clicquot from the small champagne refrigerator she kept in the living room and deftly popped the cork.

"So, go on, tell me? What on earth could we smile about today?" I asked as she filled the glasses and handed one to me.

"I have a gift for you," she said, her smile growing. She reached into the pocket of her gown and pulled out an old iron key.

"A key?" I frowned in confusion. "To what?"

"Your future."

"I don't understand."

"To hell with the Germans taking over the Lutetia," she said defiantly. "I've bought you your own patisserie."

9

JULY 1984, SAN FRANCISCO

I lie in the bed gazing up at the ceiling fan as it goes round and round and round. My body feels exhausted, but my mind won't stop racing. After dropping her bombshell that she ended up working against the German Intelligence Service, my grandma hastily changed the subject and we spent the rest of the evening talking about me. I have to admit that it felt nice to be the focus of someone's attention for once, and she seemed genuinely interested, asking me all about my day-to-day life and my hopes and dreams, and really cool random questions like, "If you could take a year to travel the world, where would you go?" but since coming to bed all I can think about is the recipe book and the postcard tucked inside. Who was it from and what could it mean? And why did my grandma clutch them to her chest the way she did, and hide them away in the living room? What was she scared of me seeing?

I sit up and peer out of the window. A thin crescent moon hangs in the sky, surrounded by more stars than I've ever seen. We never get to see stars like this in New York due to the light pollution. It's breathtaking. I crouch beside the window and drink it all in. I wonder if the people who invented the nuclear bomb ever saw a sky like this. Surely they couldn't have or they'd never have wanted to create something capable of destroying it. Hot tears start blurring my vision. There's no way I'm going to sleep now. I don't want to start torturing myself with thoughts of nuclear destruction, so I decide to go get a glass of milk.

I tiptoe over to the door and open it slowly. My grandma's bedroom is on the other side of the house, but it's the kind of old place full of creaky wooden floorboards and heavy old doors on squeaking hinges that makes sneaking around really difficult. I creep along the narrow hallway and through the living room into the kitchen. The cool air still smells of chocolate cake and I instinctively lick my lips.

I take a carton of milk from the refrigerator and pour myself a glass. Hopefully it will help me sleep. But as I drink it, my head fills with questions again. Why was my grandma so quick to hide the recipe book away? What was she scared of me seeing? I gaze into the darkened living room. I know that the book is in a drawer in there somewhere, but dare I try to find it?

I take another sip of milk and weigh up the alternatives— return to bed and torture myself with thoughts of nuclear Armageddon and missing Melissa, or try to get to the bottom of the mystery of my grandma and the Nazis. I ask myself my go-to question in times of doubt: *What would a Judy Blume heroine do?* and I instantly stand up and listen for any sound of my grandma.

It's so silent, even the cicadas outside have stopped their whirring. I can't remember ever experiencing such an absence of noise and I'm not sure if I find it soothing or terrifying. *This is probably how the world will sound after the nuclear apocalypse,* my inner voice of fear whispers.

Desperate for a distraction, I march into the living room and look around. Straight away I see a set of drawers in one of her old cabinets. I go over and very slowly pull the top one open. It's full of napkins. The second one contains place mats and the third is full of sets of coasters. I sigh and look at the other side of the room. There's one drawer in the unit housing the record player, but it turns out to be full of cassette tapes. So where did she put the book?

I tiptoe over to the old desk in the window and my pulse quickens. There are two drawers either side of the chair. This has to be it. This has to be where she's put the book. I open the first drawer and feel around inside, but it's just a mess of paper clips and elastic bands. I grope around in the second drawer and feel a burst of excitement as my fingers brush against the edge of a book—no, two books. I take them out and tiptoe back to the kitchen so I can see them in the light.

I look at the recipe book first, carefully turning the pages for any more hidden postcards. But all I find are recipes. There's a faded brown fingerprint by a recipe for Gateau Chocolat. I put my finger on top of it, imagining my grandma all those years ago, touching the page, her fingertip sticky with cake mixture. Someone has jotted something in the margin beside the ingredients, some numbers in blue ink. I guess it must be an adjustment to the recipe.

I turn my attention to the other book. It has a red leather cover and I can see that it's some kind of photo album. Turning it over, I gasp. The words *Meine Dienstzeit* are inscribed on the front. But it's what's below the writing that fills me with dread—a thick, black swastika.

10

JUNE 1940, PARIS

"*Et voilà!*" Madame Monteux cried as she removed her hands from my eyes. "So, what do you think?" She looked at me eagerly.

The first thing I thought as I looked at the building in front of me was, *How is it still standing?* Everything seemed to be hanging by a thread. From the faded, peeling sign on the front, to the wooden shutters and even the door.

It was the day after I'd left the Lutetia for good and as soon as the cursed curfew had ended, she'd brought me to a little side street off boulevard Raspail. It was only a couple of blocks away from the Lutetia but a world away in terms of appearance. It all felt so surreal and I still couldn't believe that she'd bought this for me.

"I know it needs a bit of love and attention," she continued. "But it has so much potential. Wait till you see inside." She stared at me pointedly. "Well, go on then, unlock the door."

I took the old key from my purse and cautiously turned it in the lock.

"Go on!" Madame Monteux urged, looking as excited as a child who's just been visited by Père Noël.

The door opened with a loud creak and as soon as I was inside, I saw what she meant. Everything was faded and shabby and covered in a thick layer of dust, but as I gazed around, I was able to see beneath that, to what it used to be, and what it could be again. I pictured the empty shelves at the back stacked with bags of macarons and cookies, tied with ribbon, and the curved glass cabinet beneath the counter filled with pastries every color of the rainbow. A huge, old-fashioned cash register squatted at the end of the counter and I could hear the ding of the bell and the clatter of the drawer opening as I served eager customers.

I turned to look at the front of the shop. There were large windows either side of the door. A wooden counter ran along one of them, and in my mind's eye, I saw people sitting on the stools that had been tucked beneath, eating éclairs and watching the world go by. A deep display cabinet sat in the other window, and I imagined arranging a beautiful display of pastries there to entice people inside.

I turned back to Madame Monteux, who was standing by the counter looking at me expectantly.

"Can I look at the kitchen?" I asked.

"Of course you can," she exclaimed. "It's yours!"

I let myself behind the counter and went through a pair of swinging, saloon-style doors into the back. A huge oven took center stage on the back wall. To the left, there was an ancient-looking refrigerator and, to the right, a huge square stone sink. I went over to a door at the back and pushed it open to reveal a set of stone steps leading down to a cellar. The perfect place to keep pastry cool during the summer.

I looked at Madame Monteux, overwhelmed with gratitude and disbelief. "Is it really mine?" I murmured.

"Absolutely." She took my hands and squeezed them tightly.

"But, why?" was all I was able to say in response.

"Because you deserve it." She looked me dead in the eyes.

"You're way too talented to be working for someone else—especially that frivolous fool Marianne. I couldn't bear the way she took all the glory for your pastries, while you slaved away like Cinderella in the kitchen. I want to see you shine, Coralie. I want other people to see and acknowledge your talents."

"I didn't mind working behind the scenes, you know. I was just so happy to be baking."

"I know, but talent like yours should be rewarded. And I realize that it's not the best of times, but the war won't last forever. And you now own this place outright, so you don't have to worry about paying rent. And I'll pay for whatever you need to get it shipshape again and up and running."

"Oh no, that's too much!"

"Nonsense." She reached in her bag for her cigarettes. "And by accepting this gift, you'll also be doing me a huge favor."

"How?"

She lit a cigarette, her expression grave. "It won't be long before our occupiers try to steal Jewish assets and property. We've seen what they've done in Austria and Poland. Obviously, I'm hoping that the government will protect me as a French citizen, but I can't be certain and I'd much rather invest some of my money in you than let those pigs get their hands on it. And it is such a wonderful investment." Her eyes became shiny with tears and she looked away.

"Thank you." I swallowed hard, so moved by her generosity and faith in me, I felt close to tears myself. Ever since I was a child I'd dreamed of owning my own patisserie but just like trying to catch a bubble without it bursting, it always felt like a dream too delicate to be able to grasp hold of and make a reality.

"So?" She looked at me hopefully. "Do you agree? Is it good news?"

"Of course it is. It's the best!" I flung my arms around her and hugged her tightly. "Oh, Madame Monteux, I love you!"

"I love you too, Coralie. And please, I wish you would stop with this Madame Monteux nonsense and call me Suzette."

"I'll try."

"And as a return on my investment, I would like a box of your finest cakes every week."

I laughed. "That, I definitely can do."

And so, the miracle worker Madame Monteux even managed to turn the arrival of the Germans into something positive. For the next couple of weeks, we worked tirelessly to get the patisserie shipshape, as she called it. I enlisted the help of Baptiste, who was equally delighted to have something to do at a time when we thought we'd lost all sense of purpose. He set about restoring the floorboards to their former glory and painting the shelves at the back primrose yellow. I so badly wanted to bring some color back to Paris, I decided to have the storefront painted yellow too, and the sign fern green with cornflower blue lettering—as soon as I'd decided on a name for the place.

A week into the renovations, I bumped into Raphael walking along boulevard Raspail, in his sommelier's uniform.

"Are you still working at the Lutetia?" I asked, shocked. Before the occupation, he'd made his hatred for the Germans clear in many a late-night rant at the hotel.

He nodded, grim-faced.

"But why would you want to work for *them*?" I whispered, checking there were no patrolling soldiers nearby. Ever since their arrival they seemed to have infiltrated every nook and cranny of the city.

"I have my reasons," he said in that smug way of his.

"Fair enough. Good luck." I started walking on and he grabbed my arm.

"How about you?" he asked. "What are you doing now?"

I told him about the patisserie and how Baptiste was

helping me renovate it. "If you know anyone who has a spare refrigerator, let me know," I said.

"I will," he replied, and I really didn't expect to see or hear from him again. But the following day he turned up at the patisserie with what looked like a brand new refrigerator in the back of his brother's van.

Baptiste was overjoyed to see his old colleague and once we'd got the new fridge in place and the old one in the back of the truck to be dumped, I made us all coffee and we sat at the stools in front of the now clean and sparkling window.

"I don't understand why you're still working at the Lutetia," Baptiste said to Raphael, echoing my thoughts from the day before.

Raphael looked up from the cigarette he was rolling, his expression deadly serious. "I thought it might be useful," he replied.

"Useful to who—the Germans?" I exclaimed.

"Of course not!" He glared at me. "Think about it. While I'm there blending into the background and serving them drinks, I'm also able to hear what they're talking about."

"But surely they'll be speaking in German," Baptiste said.

"Yes. And little do they know that I can understand every word," Raphael replied triumphantly. "I learned German when I was a boy, but, of course, I haven't told them that. I just pretend that I know the basics."

I stared at him, slightly taken aback that there was more to him than an arrogant attitude and a pair of overly intense eyebrows. "But for what purpose?" I asked.

"Did you hear Charles de Gaulle's speech the other night on the BBC?"

Baptiste and I shook our heads.

"I'd heard he was in London," I said. The French army officer had been a regular visitor to the Lutetia before the war and had even spent his wedding night there. It felt surreal thinking that he was now exiled to London while the *Abwehr* had taken over the hotel.

"He's going to be broadcasting again tonight," Raphael said. "On Radio Londres. Take a listen and then you'll understand why I'm still working at the Lutetia." And on that enigmatic note, he lit his cigarette and left.

Later that evening, when I was alone in the patisserie painting the walls of the kitchen, I tuned the radio to BBC Radio Londres and my skin erupted in goosebumps as I heard de Gaulle's voice crackling over the airwaves. At first, he spoke about the French defeat in the Battle of France and how we had been outnumbered by the Germans in terms of men and of equipment.

"But has the last word been said?" he continued. "Must hope disappear? Is defeat final? No!" he exclaimed, causing me to shiver with excitement. He went on to talk about the might of our Allies, the British and Americans, and then he appealed to any French soldiers who were able to join him in Britain. He was clearly building a new army. "Whatever happens, the flame of the French Resistance must not be extinguished and will not be extinguished," he concluded.

I turned the radio off and sat there for a moment on the floor of the patisserie kitchen. I thought back to what Raphael had said about his reason for still working at the Lutetia and now it all made sense. He was responding to de Gaulle's call to fan the flame of the French Resistance. My excitement grew. Raphael was staying at the Lutetia to gather information. He was going to spy on the German spies for the French Resistance. And then an idea occurred to me—an idea so simultaneously thrilling and terrifying, my skin erupted in goosebumps. What if I did something similar? What if I tried to get some work at the Lutetia so that I too could spy on the Germans? Perhaps I could go and see

Reinhardt, the chef, and ask him if he'd like me to make them some more desserts. He'd certainly seemed very enthusiastic about my work. Maybe he could put in a good word for me with his bosses in the *Abwehr*. I decided to talk to Raphael about my idea and my heart swelled. The Germans might have thought that victory over the French was easy, but what they hadn't counted on was our spirit of hope, resistance and resilience.

I scrambled to my feet. Finally, I knew what to have painted on the sign out front. I went through to the darkened store and smiled as I took in the freshly painted shelves and gleaming glass cabinets all ready and waiting to be filled with my pastries, at the Patisserie Resilience.

11

JUNE 1940, PARIS

Thanks to the hard work and generosity of my friends, the Patisserie Resilience was ready to receive customers within a couple of weeks. I decided to have the grand opening on the last Monday in June and woke the day before at the crack of dawn, a bundle of nerves. I'd given up my studio apartment by that point and moved into the rooms above the store, but Madame Monteux had invited me to stay at hers for the weekend.

I went over to the window of her guest room and peered outside. The rising sun was causing the Seine to shimmer gold and it looked so peaceful that for a moment it was possible to imagine that the occupation had just been a bad dream and it was a normal Sunday morning. But, of course, it was anything but a normal Sunday. Paris had become like a ghost town, with its remaining inhabitants hiding away like mice in the floorboards, only coming out when absolutely necessary. What if no one found the patisserie tucked away on its narrow side street? What if I had no customers at all?

Hearing some movement from the living room next door, I went through to find Madame Monteux pacing up and down, fully dressed in a pale blue skirt and matching blouse and shoes.

"Oh good, you're up!" she exclaimed. "I couldn't sleep. I'm too excited about your grand opening tomorrow."

"Me too!" I replied. "Although I'm more nervous than excited. What if no one comes? What if the oven breaks? What if—"

"What if, what if, what if!" she chirped like a bird. "You know the best thing for an attack of the what ifs?"

"No," I laughed.

"A long walk." She looked at the clock on the mantel. "The curfew is over; why don't we go for a wander?"

"Really?" Ever since the Germans had arrived, the notion of wandering anywhere had seemed distinctly unappealing for fear of running into them.

"Yes," she replied. "Why the hesitation? They haven't made walking illegal yet. Let's wander while we still can. Let's wander to our hearts' content!" She waved her hands in the air as she spoke as if she were conducting an orchestra.

I laughed and nodded, infected with her enthusiasm as always. "Let's do it."

We set off across the river and into the Marais. It was a beautiful morning, but the streets were deserted.

"It's so empty now so many have fled," I said with a sigh.

"We have to look on the bright side," Madame Monteux replied. "We have the city all to ourselves." And for a moment it really felt like that—until I saw that the street sign at the junction had been replaced with one in gothic German lettering.

We carried on walking until we reached the 9th arrondissement.

"Feeling better?" Madame Monteux asked, linking her arm through mine.

"Absolutely. Thank you. You really are my fairy godmother." I felt her squeeze my arm tighter.

"And you, my dear, are a ray of sunshine." She grinned at

me. "Let's go to the Opera House. It always conjures such lovely memories for me."

As we made our way to place de l'Opera, Madame Monteux regaled me with wonderful tales of operas past, but just as we reached the square, we heard the rumble of engines. A cavalcade of open-topped cars swept past, coming to a halt outside the opera house, where some French police in black capes stood on duty. The policemen sprung into salutes as German soldiers got out from the cars. I prickled with indignation at their traitorous display. They all hovered around one of the cars and we watched in silence as a man in a peaked cap and long leather coat got out. He stood and gazed up at the opera house, as if in awe of the majestic building.

"Who do you think it is?" I whispered to Madame Monteux with a growing feeling of unease.

"I don't know but he must be some kind of bigwig. The French police are practically curtseying to him." She tutted and shook her head.

We watched as the man strode up the stone steps, pausing to once again drink in the grandeur of the building. When he reached the top, he stopped and turned, and for the briefest of moments, his gaze fell upon us, and as it did, it felt as if my blood had turned to ice.

"Oh *mon dieu!*" I gasped as I saw that infamous stubby black mustache.

"It's him," Madame Monteux hissed, clasping my arm. "Hitler is in Paris."

A second later, he'd turned and disappeared inside the building, his flock of soldiers right behind him.

Madame Monteux had turned as white as a sheet and it struck me how horrifying this must be for her. The opera house was her favorite place in the capital. Now it would never be the same again. "I can't believe it!" she said, her voice trembling. "I can't believe he's here."

I nodded, too horrified to speak. It had been bad enough seeing all of the soldiers invading our streets, but to see their Führer—the man who was causing so much devastation to the world—right there in front of us was beyond comprehension.

"Let's go home," Madame Monteux murmured and I readily agreed.

We walked back to the Left Bank in stunned silence.

"Are you all right?" I asked Madame Monteux as we entered her building.

She nodded, but for once she didn't have anything upbeat to say. For once, she seemed incapable of creating her own good news. The bad news we'd just witnessed was too overwhelming. The only vaguely positive thing I was able to cling to was my idea for helping the French Resistance and I resolved to speak to Raphael as soon as I could. Perhaps there were other ways I could help as well as trying to get some work at the Lutetia. After what I'd just witnessed, I was willing to do anything.

Thankfully, my beloved friend recovered her *joie de vivre* in time for the store opening the following day, arriving on the doorstep with her arms full of pink and yellow roses.

"Congratulations, my dear!" she cried as she stepped inside, thrusting the flowers at me.

"Thank you." I held my breath as she gazed around the store. I hadn't allowed her to set foot inside while Baptiste and I had been doing our renovations as I'd wanted it to be a surprise. I really hoped she was happy with her investment.

She went over to the cabinet in the window and examined the trays of macarons I'd placed there, hoping the pretty shades of lilac, primrose, orange and green would lure people inside. Still not saying a word, she moved across to the glass-fronted counter, which housed éclairs in three flavors—coffee, chocolate and raspberry, rows of plump religieuses oozing with hazelnut cream, custard-filled canelés with a thick caramelized crust, choux buns fat with chestnut crème pâtissière and gleaming with chocolate fondant, and a tray of Paris-Brests filled with praline cream and covered in flaked almonds. Two large wicker baskets full of freshly baked croissants and brioche stood at the end of the counter by the old cash register. Everything on display had hope, resistance and resilience sifted, folded and baked into them.

"Well?" I exclaimed, unable to bear the suspense any longer.

Madame Monteux gazed at me, eyes wide. "Oh, my dear, it looks divine and smells delicious!"

"I'm so glad you like it." I exhaled. "It's unlike you to be so quiet!"

"I don't just like it—I *love* it! I was quiet because you'd rendered me speechless." She grinned. "Thankfully, it was only a temporary affliction."

"Thank goodness!" I laughed with relief.

I divided the roses into two vases and placed one by the cash register and one in the window.

"Do you think anyone will come?" I asked anxiously as I peered outside. "There are so few people left in Paris and this is such a quiet street. What if we have to eat all the cakes ourselves?"

"I can think of far worse fates," Madame Monteux quipped, gazing longingly at the choux buns. "Don't worry, my dear, once people know you're here, you're going to have queues out the door."

As if on cue, the door opened and Baptiste walked in, dressed in his Sunday best suit, all crisply pressed.

"Coralie! Congratulations!" he cried. "It looks incredible."

"Thanks to you," I said, giving him a hug.

On seeing Madame Monteux, Baptiste took off his hat. His silver hair was shiny with pomade. "Good morning, Duchess, so lovely to see you," he said, kissing her hand and bowing deeply. "You are looking more magnificent than ever."

"Enough of that nonsense!" she exclaimed, but with a giggle.

I looked at them both and my heart filled to the brim with love and gratitude. Who cared if no one turned up. It was so wonderful to see my old friends laughing and joking again. If only Arnaud and Olive could have been there too—they would have been so excited to see me open my very own patisserie.

When no one had come in after half an hour, I sent Baptiste and Madame Monteux outside with plates of macaron and canelé tasters, and it wasn't long before a queue was forming. It wasn't quite out of the door, but I had my first customers!

The rest of the morning passed in a blur and by mid-afternoon I'd sold out of éclairs and choux buns and almost all the croissants. Thankfully, the street we were on was so narrow you'd miss it if you didn't know it was there, so all the customers were locals and I didn't have to serve a single German.

"I would like to invite you both for dinner at mine," Madame Monteux said at the end of the afternoon as I took the empty trays from the cabinets to be washed. "To celebrate the success of the Patisserie Resilience."

Baptiste grinned from ear to ear. "It would be a privilege and a delight, Duchess."

"All right, all right, no need to over-egg the pudding." She raised her thin eyebrows and shook her head before turning to me. "What do you say, Coralie?"

"I would love that. Why don't you two get going and I'll meet you there once I've cleaned up." I put some religieuses in a box and handed them to her. "Dessert."

"*Merci beaucoup!*" She turned to Baptiste and offered him her arm to link. "Come on then, don't just stand there dawdling."

He clicked his heels together and gave her a salute and as he escorted her out of the store, he grinned and winked at me over his shoulder.

I took the trays into the kitchen and filled the sink with soapy water. It was only then, once I was on my own and washing the dishes, that the reality hit me. My patisserie was open and my first day had been a success. Even in these dark days of war and occupation, my fairy godmother Madame Monteux had given me a reason to feel hopeful and smile again. I wasn't sure how I'd ever be able to repay her.

I heard the bell above the door jangle and smiled, ready to greet my last customer of the day.

"*Bonjour!*" I cried as I came through the swing doors, only to stop dead at the sight in front of me. A German soldier in that dreaded green-gray uniform was standing in the middle of the store, like a cloud blocking the sun.

"I found you!" he exclaimed, taking off his hat, revealing a crop of golden curly hair, and I realized that it was Reinhardt, the German chef.

"You were looking for me?" I replied, my mind whirring into action as my shock wore off. This could be the perfect opportunity to try to get some work at the Lutetia.

"Yes. I've been to just about every patisserie in Paris. I knew that a chef as talented as you wouldn't be out of work for long." Coming from another person this might have seemed too slick, but I could tell by his warm smile that he wasn't feeding me a line and that he really meant it. "I have something for you." He put his hand in his pocket and pulled out a copper canelé case. "You left this in the hotel kitchen." He placed it on top of the counter. "You said they meant a lot to you. I didn't want you to be without the full set."

I grabbed the case and stuffed it in my apron pocket. I wasn't sure what to make of him traipsing around Paris with my canelé case like some kind of Prince Charming trying to find the owner of the glass slipper. I didn't know whether to be flattered or concerned that he cared enough to bother, but then I realized that I could use it to my advantage.

"So, this is where you work now?" he said, looking around.

"I own it actually," I couldn't resist saying.

"It's yours?" He stared at me, clearly shocked.

"Yes," I replied. "A friend bought it for me after I lost my job at the Lutetia."

He shifted uncomfortably. "I'm really sorry about that."

"It's OK. I'm actually really glad to see you again."

"You are?" He looked at me hopefully.

"Yes. I was wondering..." I broke off, my heart beginning to thud. I hadn't been able to run my idea past Raphael yet, to check if my working at the Lutetia would be useful for any kind of Resistance movement, but this was too good an opportunity to miss. "Do you have any need for a pastry chef, on a part-time basis? It would be so helpful to have the extra work while I get this place up and running." I swallowed hard before uttering my next line. "And maybe your officers would appreciate some authentic French desserts."

"Oh, I'm certain they would," he said enthusiastically. "They loved what you made before."

I fought the urge to retch at the thought of the *Abwehr* officers enjoying my pastries. "That's wonderful!" I exclaimed, forcing a smile onto my face. "So would you put a word in for me?"

"Of course. Although..." He looked at the cabinet under the counter, where a solitary Paris-Brest still lingered. "I might have to buy that cake for research."

"Research?"

"Yes, to see if you're up to the job." He grinned. "Think of it as an edible job interview."

I couldn't help but laugh and put the pastry on a plate and passed it to him. "*Et voilà!* My interview on a plate."

"Thank you." He placed some francs on the counter. "Is that enough? I'm still not used to the different currency."

"I'm not sure you've got the hang of this job interview business," I joked. "You're not supposed to pay the candidate."

"No, no, I insist," he said, pushing the money toward me.

"Thank you." I put the money into the cash register and when I looked back at Reinhardt, he was taking a huge bite of the cake.

"Oh!" he gasped, his green eyes wide as saucers. "This cream is incredible. How did you get this flavor?"

"It's from praline—ground caramelized almonds and hazelnuts," I said. Once again, I found his enthusiasm both disarming and infectious and I couldn't help grinning as he took bite after bite.

"It is delicious," he mumbled through a mouthful and a dollop of the beige cream dropped onto the front of his uniform. But like a man possessed, he kept on eating. It reminded me of how I would eat Arnaud's pastries as a child. Olive would scold me for getting cream all over my clothes and face and sometimes even in my hair, but Arnaud would shush her, telling her that pastries were made to be devoured, not daintily nibbled.

"Pastries are made to be devoured," I said softly, instantly blushing as I realized I'd spoken his words out loud.

Reinhardt looked at me and smiled. "Yes!" he exclaimed, and took another bite, sending yet more cream oozing onto his uniform. "Devoured. Yes, yes!" Flakes of almonds fell from the cake onto the floor as he finished the last piece. It was only then that he noticed the cream on his uniform. "Uh-oh." He took a handkerchief from his pocket and tried to wipe it away, but it only made the stain worse. "I don't suppose I could have some soap and water?" he asked. "To try to clean this off."

"Can't you clean it at the hotel? They have a laundry room there."

He shook his head. "My gluttony will have brought shame

upon the Reich," he muttered, sarcastically. Or at least that's how it sounded.

"What do you mean?"

"Well, they're so obsessed with appearances."

Our eyes met and for a moment I got the strangest feeling that maybe, just maybe, he wasn't that much of a fan of the Reich either. The moment passed and he looked away, his cheeks flushing as if embarrassed that he might have said too much.

"All right, come through." I beckoned him behind the counter and into the kitchen, where I soaked a cloth in warm water and added some soap. Then I went over to him and began rubbing at the stain.

"Thank you," he said with such obvious relief, I realized that he must have been genuinely afraid of going back with cream all over him. "I don't know what came over me." He gave an embarrassed laugh.

I looked up from the stain and smiled. "You were possessed by a pastry demon. That's what my adoptive father used to say when I was a kid and he caught me stealing a bite of his cakes. He was a baker too."

"Was he the one who gave you the cake tins?"

"Yes." I carried on scrubbing away at the stain.

"If his pastries were anything like yours, I'd completely understand."

I couldn't help smiling as I thought back to Arnaud. "He used to tell me that pastries aren't like any other kind of food, where you just throw the ingredients together. He said that making a pastry is like conducting a chemistry experiment."

"I think I understand," Reinhardt replied. "For pastry you need the right conditions as well as the ingredients. The temperature of the room, the way you knead the dough..."

"Yes, exactly! And you have to be prepared to mess up, to keep trying new methods."

I felt a spark of recognition, a connection to a kindred spirit. But that was impossible, I told myself quickly. This man in front of me might have been a chef, but he was still working for the German Intelligence Service. He was still one of our occupiers. I felt a hot wave of shame at feeling any kind of connection with him, and our close proximity felt suddenly and awkwardly intimate.

"There, all done," I said, taking a step back.

He clearly felt some awkwardness too as his cheeks flushed and he backed away toward the door. "Thank you for the cake," he murmured, "and for cleaning up my mess."

Before I could reply, the bell jangled over the shop door. "Ooh, looks like I have another customer," I said gaily, but my voice sounded shrill in my ears.

We walked out of the kitchen and my heart sank. Raphael was standing by the door. When he saw Reinhardt behind me, he instantly frowned.

"Thank you so much," Reinhardt said, holding his hand out for me to shake. It felt oddly formal and I couldn't help wondering if he was doing it to put things back on a more professional footing. "And I'll be in touch about you coming back to the Lutetia."

"That's great!" I exclaimed, relieved to be reminded of our earlier conversation. "Thank you."

Reinhardt nodded to Raphael as he walked past him and out the door.

"What was that about?" Raphael asked, scowling after him.

"He's the new chef at the Lutetia."

"I know who he is," Raphael said, turning his scowl on me. "I see him every day at work. What was he doing here?"

I took a breath, trying not to let his patronizing tone rankle me. "I had an idea, inspired by you," I said, deciding to appeal to Raphael's vanity. It appeared to work and his scowl faded.

"Go on," he said, locking the shop door and coming over to the counter.

"I heard Charles de Gaulle's radio broadcast," I whispered, "and I want to do my part, fanning the flames of the French Resistance."

Raphael raised his thick black eyebrows.

"I've asked the chef if I can go back to the Lutetia on a part-time basis to make their desserts."

"But what about this place?" he asked.

"I'll fit it around this place." I leaned over the counter closer to him. "I want to spy on the *Abwehr* too."

I held my breath and waited, praying he didn't dismiss my idea out of hand. But, to my delight, he began to nod.

"That's actually an excellent idea," he said, his voice full of surprise, like he never would have imagined me capable of such a thing. Even when he praised me, he somehow managed to make it sound like an insult. It was a rare talent indeed. "No one would suspect a woman of being a spy," he continued, nodding thoughtfully. "They'd probably be a lot more indiscreet around you. Can you speak any German?"

I shook my head. "But I can learn."

"Good. I'll get you some books."

A shiver ran up my spine. The notion that I might be in a position to spy on the German Intelligence Service filled me with nervous excitement.

I smiled at him, emboldened. "And if there's any other way I can be of help, just let me know. This place is really hidden away—which isn't so great for getting customers, but it's out of the sight of the soldiers."

He nodded thoughtfully. "You might be on to something there. Maybe we could use this place to pass messages."

My feeling of nervous excitement grew. "To who?"

"Other Resistance members." He leaned closer and lowered

his voice. "There are a lot of us out there and the fightback is already beginning. I'll be in touch."

He turned on his heel and let himself back out onto the street.

I stared after him, my mind racing and heart thudding. My prayers had been answered, I'd found a way to fight back against the Germans, but in doing so I'd also volunteered to walk straight back into the lions' den.

12

JULY 1984, SAN FRANCISCO

I stare at the album with its swastika glaring up at me like a neon sign, trying to think of an innocent reason why my grandma would have it in her possession, but I can't. Part of me wants to put the books back in the drawer and go back to bed, but I know that if I do, I'll only be plagued with more questions. I have to look inside the album.

I take a breath and open the cover. The first pictures are of famous Paris sights—so famous I recognize them without ever having been to France before. There's the Eiffel Tower and the Arc de Triomphe and one taken from a bridge over a river that I guess must be the Seine. I turn the page and see the picture of a store. I squint to read the sign above the door. It says Patisserie Resilience. The photo next to it is of some cakes. Did my grandma make them? I wonder. But why would they be in a photo album with a swastika on the cover?

I hear a door squeaking open on the other side of the house and my heart pounds as I race into the living room and shove the books back in the desk drawer. I just make it back to my seat at the kitchen table when my grandma appears in the doorway.

Her face is shiny with moisturizer and she's wearing an over-sized Jim Morrison T-shirt as a night dress.

"Oh, you startled me!" she exclaims. "What are you doing up?"

"I couldn't sleep," I mumble, barely able to look at her.

"Me too. I get terrible insomnia, it drives me crazy. Are you hungry? I could fix us some French toast."

The choice between staring at the ceiling fan thinking about nuclear Armageddon or feasting on eggy bread is a total no-brainer, especially if her French toast is anything like her chocolate cake. "That would be great, thank you."

She looks so happy at my reply, it makes me feel warm inside. It feels so good to be invited to stay instead of being constantly told to go to my room.

As she takes some eggs from the refrigerator, I decide to see if I can get her to open up some more about the war. Obviously, I can't let her know that I've been snooping again, but maybe if I get her talking, I can find out why she's in possession of a Nazi photo album. Just thinking about it sends a shiver through me.

"So, have you worked anywhere else as a pastry chef?" I ask, thinking of the photo of the patisserie in the album.

"Yes, actually, I had my own patisserie. A very good friend of mine bought it for me during the war."

My mouth goes dry. "That's so cool. What was it called?"

She turns to me with a strange expression on her face, and I hope she can't see my cheeks flushing. "It was called Patisserie Resilience. Why do you ask?"

"Just curious. I—uh—like knowing the names of things." As soon as I say this, I realize how lame it sounds and my cheeks burn even hotter. "Cool name," I say, trying to add credence to my supposed love for titles.

She gives a sad smile. "Yes. It's a shame..." She breaks off and fetches a loaf of bread from a cupboard.

"What is?" I press my chilled milk glass to my cheeks while she isn't watching to try to cool them down.

"That it ended the way it did. Would you like syrup with your toast?"

"Yes please." I watch her glide around the kitchen with the grace of a ballerina as she assembles a pan, a whisk and a mixing bowl. "How did it end?"

She turns to me and sighs. "In the very worst way imaginable."

13

SEPTEMBER 1940, PARIS

It was a beautiful sunny day in late September, that kind of fall day where the colors have never seemed more vibrant, and I was preparing for another day in the store. In the three months since I'd opened the patisserie word of mouth had spread and I'd grown a loyal and friendly band of customers. Due to some shortages of sugar and dairy produce, I'd had to change my menu, featuring more icing and less cream, but I'd still managed to make a tray of éclairs, which took center stage in the cabinet beneath the counter. I'd made a pistachio fondant for the top in a striking shade of green so they made the perfect centerpiece. Either side were trays of chocolate brioche, oat and raisin cookies and croissants and pains au chocolat, glowing with a gold, buttery sheen. The display case in the window was filled with raspberry and walnut meringues, light and fluffy as clouds. I was standing back surveying my wares when the door burst open and Madame Monteux came in, on a cloud of her favorite perfume.

"Oh, my dear, have you heard the news?" It was immediately obvious from her worried expression that she wasn't bringing glad tidings.

"What is it? What's happened?" I asked, instantly feeling panicked.

"The government are going to start rationing our food."

My panic grew. "What kind of food?"

"All of it. Even the basics. Cheese, sugar, milk, bread, chocolate."

I looked at the cabinet as she spoke. She was listing all my key ingredients.

"And the amounts are so paltry," she continued. "We're only going to be allowed eight grams of butter a day. And one egg. Can you believe it?"

"How are we supposed to survive?" I sat on one of the stools by the window, feeling utterly devastated as I thought of my beloved customers and the millions of other people all over France struggling to cope on such meagre offerings.

"Maybe we're not supposed to." Madame Monteux came and sat beside me. "Maybe the Germans are planning on starving us into submission."

"So much for their posters claiming to be our saviors." Anger started burning through my shock. I wanted to march outside and tear down their stupid propaganda. It was a good thing I hadn't heard from Reinhardt about working at the Lutetia. If I'd been working there when this happened I might not have been able to control my response. "And what will become of this place?" I looked at her, helplessly. "There's no way I'll be able to make my pastries if all of my ingredients are to be rationed."

Madame Monteux pursed her lips and frowned, the way she always did when she was deep in thought.

"I've got it!" she finally exclaimed. "You need to apply the same creative magic to this shop that you use when you're baking."

"I don't understand."

"Think about how you bake. You never follow the rules. You always use your imagination."

"Yes, but I can hardly imagine away the government rations."

"No, but you can *reimagine* what you make in this store."

I gave a sigh of despair. "And make cakes out of thin air?"

She laughed. "No, but you could start making bread."

"Bread, but why?"

"Oh, Coralie, I credited you with more imagination than this," she gently scolded. "Bread is being rationed, which means it's one of the things we will still be allowed to eat. Which means there will still be a need for it. Which means—"

"Bakers will be allowed the ingredients they need to supply the bread rations," I cut in.

"Exactly. And I know that your passion is for pastry and not the humble baguette, but if it means you can keep this place going, and keep baking..."

I gave her a weak smile. It wasn't ideal, but at least it was something.

"So, what do you say?" she asked eagerly.

"I say that once again you have waved your fairy godmother's wand!" I leaned forwards and kissed her cheek. "Thank you."

"Excellent!" She stood up and marched behind the counter.

"What are you doing?"

"I'm going to serve your customers while you get baking. You need to establish this place as a boulangerie as well as a patisserie so you'll be able to stay open." She went into the kitchen and returned holding my apron out to me. "So go on, get baking!"

As soon as the smell of freshly baking bread filled the store, Madame Monteux opened the door so the aroma wafted onto the street and drew passersby inside. And in between serving customers, she designed some beautiful posters saying Boulangerie Resilience, which we stuck in the windows. The transformation into a patisserie-boulangerie was complete, but would it be enough to help me survive the new rationing system?

Late in the afternoon, Madame Monteux left to teach one of her singing students and I sat behind the counter with a notepad and pencil, dreaming up ways I could make baguettes more interesting. I could add finely chopped nuts, perhaps, or a sprinkling of cheese on top, but then I remembered the news about the rations and my spirits fell. Were nuts and cheese about to become luxuries from the past, consigned to our distant memories?

I was distracted by a movement in the window and felt the sick feeling that had become a reflex action every time I saw the green-gray German uniform, or the "haricots verts" we Parisians now mockingly called our occupiers. I prayed that the soldier who was looking at the cakes in the window didn't come in. I was in no mood to serve food to the very people who now wanted to starve us.

I peered over the counter and saw that the soldier's face was obscured by a camera. A lot of the German soldiers in Paris could now be seen with cameras on leather straps around their necks, taking photographs of famous sights such as the Eiffel Tower and the Arc de Triomphe, as if they were harmless holidaymakers rather than occupiers. I'd never seen one of them take a photograph of my pastries though and it was too much to bear. I jumped up from my seat and marched over to the door.

"Why are you taking a picture?" I asked as I flung it open, my voice shaking with anger. It was only then that I realized it was Reinhardt. I hadn't seen him since he'd returned my canelé tin so I'd given up hope on going back to the Lutetia. What if he'd come to offer me a job after all? And what if I'd blown it by being so surly?

"Oh, I'm sorry, they just looked so..." He broke off, looking embarrassed.

I took a breath, to try to regain my composure. "That's OK. I'm sorry I shouted, you just took me by surprise."

"No, it's my fault, I should have asked your permission before taking the photographs." He gave me an apologetic smile and, once again, I found myself confused by the mixed feelings he created in me. I really didn't want to like him, but he made it very difficult. "We've been given these cameras to take pictures of the beautiful sights in Paris," he continued. "And I couldn't think of anything more beautiful than your pastries." He put the camera in his jacket pocket.

"So you wanted to capture them before you take away my right to make them," I muttered sarcastically. I knew I shouldn't get cross with him. I knew I needed to keep him on side if I was ever to return to the Lutetia, but it was all so unfair. I turned and went back into the store, feeling sick with disappointment.

"What do you mean, I'm going to take away your right to make them?" he asked, coming in behind me.

"With your new rationing system." I went back behind the counter. "How can I make my pastries when I'm no longer allowed sugar or butter or cream?"

"And you think that's my doing?" he asked, sounding wounded.

"Well, maybe not you personally, but it's coming from your leaders."

We stared at each other for a moment.

"And whose leaders were responsible for the blockades against Germany after the Great War?" Reinhardt asked with a frown. "Whose government caused thousands of German children to starve to death and thousands of others to die of malnutrition."

"I don't know what you're talking about," I muttered.

"My mother lost two of her siblings to starvation after the

First World War. And she spent years desperately trying not to lose her own children to the same fate." He sighed. "We have been living on rations for years and years. You worry about getting your precious cream, but we had entire winters where practically all we had to live off were turnips." His face flushed.

"I'm sorry," I said, suddenly feeling very tired. If what he was saying was true, the world was an even bleaker place than I'd imagined, and what I'd said about my pastries must have seemed crass and insensitive. "I didn't know that had happened in Germany. I'm so sorry your mother experienced that."

To my relief, his expression softened. "I'm sorry too," he said quietly. "I'd actually come here because I have some good news. At least, I hope it's good news." He gave me a sheepish smile. "I'd been hoping to come sooner but it's all been a bit chaotic for me at the hotel trying to get my kitchen staff organized. But now they're finally all in place and I'd love to offer you some work as a pastry chef. I had a word with my bosses and your desserts were very popular before, especially with Admiral Canaris and his secretary Inga. You might remember meeting them?"

I thought of the older man and the woman who looked like a porcelain doll and nodded, trying to disguise my relief and excitement. I hadn't blown it after all. He was offering me an opportunity to spy on the *Abwehr* at the very highest level, although, of course, he didn't know that. "What would the work involve exactly?" I asked.

"We'd like you to come to the hotel every Sunday to make pastries for the evening meal," Reinhardt replied. "You'd be working in the restaurant kitchen alongside me. We'd provide all the ingredients you need."

I forced myself to smile, but inside I could feel my anger bubbling up again. So, while we had to try to survive on their paltry rations our German occupiers would be gorging themselves on our finest ingredients.

I took another calming breath before responding. "That sounds wonderful. And Sundays are perfect as this place is closed."

He grinned. "Excellent. I look forward to working with you again."

"You too."

There was a beat of silence. Reinhardt opened his mouth as if he was about to say something, then closed it again.

"So, I'll see you on Sunday then," I said, trying to break the awkwardness.

"Yes, if you could get there at three o'clock, that would be great. Tell the guards on the door that you're there to see me. They'll be expecting you."

My stomach churned as I thought of the soldiers I'd seen there before. *You're doing this to help get rid of them*, I reminded myself and forced myself to smile and nod.

About ten minutes after Reinhardt had left, the bell above the door jangled again.

I came out from the back to see Raphael shutting and locking the door. He'd been a regular visitor over the past three months, giving me updates about the fledgling Resistance movement and asking if I'd got the job at the Lutetia. I smiled. Finally I'd be able to get him to stop with the questions.

"I have something for you," he said, marching behind the counter as if he owned the place. "Come." He gestured at me to follow him into the kitchen.

"What is it?"

"A Resistance newspaper," he whispered.

He opened his satchel and took out some papers. The heading RESISTANCE had been stenciled in large letters across the top.

"Where's it from?" I whispered, staring at it in awe.

"Some comrades at a museum here in Paris produced it. It's best I don't tell you which one. The less we know about who's involved, the safer it is for everyone."

I shivered at the implication of his words: that it was safer in case we were ever arrested and interrogated by the Germans. "What do you want me to do with them?"

"You're to give them to people who are going to distribute them." He split the papers into four piles. "You'll know who they are because they'll ask for a box of macarons for their cousin Claude's thirteenth birthday. You're to put one of these piles of papers in the bottom of the box."

I nodded, filling with excitement that, after months of waiting, I was finally going to be able to help—and hopefully in more than one way. "I have some news for you too."

"Oh yes?"

"The German chef came back. They've agreed to my offer to return to the Lutetia. I'll be making pastries in the restaurant kitchen every Sunday." I searched his face for some sign of approval. He raised his furry caterpillar eyebrows, which was about as enthusiastic as Raphael's facial expressions got.

"Excellent. It will be good to finally have you there. I'll come by before Sunday to brief you on what we'll need from you, and what to expect. I hope you have a strong stomach."

"What do you mean?"

He grimaced. "It feels as if they've been having one long party since they got there, the gloating bastards."

But rather than make me feel sick, hearing this only strengthened my desire to get back to the Lutetia—so that I could help to kick the gloating bastards out.

14

JULY 1984, SAN FRANCISCO

Needless to say, it took me forever to fall off to sleep, and when I finally did, I had a really stressful nightmare in which I discovered that my grandma was working in secret for the Russian president, Konstantin Chernenko.

I wake to the sound of birds chirping right outside the window and the smell of something buttery and delicious creeping in beneath the door. My stomach instantly gives a hungry gurgle and I get out of bed and pull a sweatshirt on over my pajamas and what happened last night comes flooding back to me. After telling me that her patisserie came to some kind of terrible end, my grandma swiftly changed the subject, which was incredibly frustrating. If only I could talk to Melissa, she might be able to help me make sense of it. But what if she came to the conclusion that my grandma had been a Nazi? I'm not sure I could handle the embarrassment. It's been bad enough that she's had to witness my parents' mortifying behavior over the past few years.

I make my way into the kitchen to find my grandma standing by the stove with her back to me, humming away as she mixes something in a bowl.

"May all who eat this brioche feel peace and love," she murmurs as she mixes, causing me to frown. She sounds more like a hippy than a Nazi—and she looks like one too, in her long floaty dress and sandals.

I take a breath and clear my throat.

"Ah, Raven!" she cries, turning to face me. "Good morning, *ma chère*! How did you sleep in the end?"

I shiver as I remember the words *ma chère* on the postcard. "OK, I guess. How about you?" I sit down at the table, which has been laid with a plate of golden crescent-shaped pastries and jugs of coffee and orange juice.

"So-so," she replies with a shrug. "Please help yourself to the croissants. They're still warm from the oven. I hope they taste all right. They're another thing I haven't made since leaving France."

I take a bite and can't help letting out a little moan of pleasure. The pastry is so light and buttery, with a hint of salt.

"Is it OK?" she asks, looking concerned.

"Oh yes!" I exclaim, taking another bite. "This is honestly one of the best things I've ever eaten."

"Oh good!" She gives me a beaming smile. "It's been so long since I made them, I was worried I might have lost my touch."

"No, not at all." I pour myself a glass of juice. "Do you not do much baking anymore then?"

She shakes her head. "I gave it up after I married your grandpa and moved to the States."

"Why?" I take a sip of juice.

"My heart wasn't really in it anymore." She gives a sad smile. "I'd make the occasional cake for a special occasion, but that was it."

I think of the cake she brought the last time I saw her, when she visited us in New York, and feel a pang of sorrow that she'd seen it as a special occasion, only for Suzette to yell at her that she wished she'd died.

But that might be because Suzette knows what she did during the war, I remind myself and I take another bite of croissant. It seems to grow more delicious with every bite and I have to fight the urge to cram it into my mouth in one go.

"Well, I'm really glad you baked these," I mumble through a mouthful. "And the cake last night. And the French toast. They're all delicious."

Her face lights up. "Thank you!" She puts whatever she's been making in the oven and wipes her hands on her apron. "In that case, I'm going to make you something extra special for dessert this evening." She unties her apron and takes it off. "But I'm going to need to go to the grocery store. Will you be all right on your own for about half an hour?"

"Of course," I reply, feeling a burst of excitement. I could use the time alone to have a better look at the photo album and try to figure out why it's in her possession.

"Excellent, thank you!" She comes over and kisses the top of my head and I instantly feel guilty for planning to snoop again. But what choice do I have if she won't tell me what happened?

I stay at the table eating croissants until I hear her truck bumping its way down the track and into the distance. Then I stand up and take a deep breath. *I'm not being a snoop*, I tell myself. *I'm just trying to get to know my grandma better*. I know I'm kidding myself, but my curiosity is too strong and propels me into the living room and over to the desk. I listen for a second to make sure the truck isn't coming back, then I open the drawer.

15

SEPTEMBER 1940, PARIS

A couple of days later, I was woken in the middle of the night by a thudding sound coming from the passageway beside the store. Thanks to the curfew, the streets of Paris were deader than the grave during the night, with the only sound that of the dreaded clip-clip of the patrolling soldiers' jackboots. I was so tired, I put it down to being a stray cat or dog and rolled over and went back to sleep. But when I got up at four to start baking, I looked outside and found two sacks. My first thought was that Raphael had left me something else to hide for the Resistance. But surely he wouldn't be so careless as to leave it out in plain sight.

I crouched down and undid the cord binding one of the sacks and felt inside. I could tell instantly that it was sugar. I quickly pulled the sacks inside and opened the other one, which contained flour and a large slab of butter wrapped in brown paper. I smiled. Had Madame Monteux worked her magic again and got them for me on the black market?

I noticed an envelope stuck to the top of the butter. Inside was a piece of paper and a photograph. On the paper was written, *I'm sorry. See you on Sunday.* I turned the photograph over and saw that it was of my meringues in the shop window. It had been taken at such an angle that the sunlight was shimmering off the top, giving them a slightly ethereal glow. On the back was written, *The most beautiful sight in all of Paris.*

But rather than make me angry, I felt relieved. Now I had enough ingredients to make croissants as well as bread so I could give my customers a surprise gift along with their paltry bread ration.

When people came to exchange their bread coupon that morning, I slipped an extra croissant in the bag with their baguette. To those who noticed, I'd simply wink and whisper, "Shh." It felt wonderful being able to play fairy godmother.

Midway through the afternoon, when the shop had quietened down, a thin-faced woman in shabby clothes came in, her dark eyes darting this way and that.

"I need a box of macarons for my cousin Claude's birthday," she muttered.

"I'm so sorry, madame, but I haven't been able to make any macarons due to the rations," I replied, completely forgetting the secret code.

"I need them for my cousin Claude's *thirteenth* birthday!" she said again, more urgently, thankfully prompting me to remember.

"Oh, yes of course! Wait there."

I hurried into the kitchen, my heart thudding, and took a cake box into the pantry where I'd hidden the Resistance papers. I quickly put one of the piles into the box, covered them with a lining of greaseproof paper, and filled the box with some old macarons I'd been keeping for just this purpose.

"Your macarons, madame!" I called before heading back into the store.

The woman stood staring at me open-mouthed and ashen-faced, and I had to stop myself from gasping when I saw the reason for her fear. Reinhardt was standing right behind her.

"You have some macarons?" he said, and I thought my heart might pound right out of my chest.

"Unfortunately, this woman bought the last ones I had in stock," I said quickly.

He sighed. "What a shame."

I held the box out to the woman and she took it, her hands trembling violently. My blood ran cold. If she dropped the box and revealed the papers, she could get us both arrested.

"Let me get the door for you," I said, eager to get her out of the store.

"Allow me," Reinhardt said, and I watched, heart in mouth, as he accompanied the woman and her box of Resistance newspapers to the door.

Thankfully, she made it out of the shop and off down the street without incident.

Reinhardt returned to the counter with a shy smile on his face. "I came to see if you got my peace offering."

"I did. Thank you." I leaned on the counter; my legs felt like blancmange.

"I'm sorry I got angry the other day," he said, looking down at the floor. "It was just so hard seeing what my mother went through."

"I'm sorry too," I replied. "I know I probably seemed really spoiled to you, moaning about not having cream, but baking is so much more than a job to me. Being a pastry chef gave my life meaning. It gave me an identity when I had none. It scares me to think of a life without it."

I immediately felt annoyed at myself for revealing so much, but, to my relief, he was nodding as if he completely understood.

"Becoming a chef saved my life too..." He paused. "After my mother died."

"She died?" I stared at him, shocked.

"Yes. When I was sixteen. I had to get a job in a kitchen to make ends meet, but it ended up being so much more than that. It gave my life structure again; it made me feel part of a family. And realizing that I'd inherited her love for cooking made me feel as if..." He gave a sad smile. "As if she was still there, somehow, beside me."

"I understand," I murmured, baffled that I should feel this kind of connection with a German.

"It seems that you and I have some things in common," he said softly.

"Yes." And despite who he was—and my better judgment—I felt a charge pass between us.

"I should get back," he said with a smile.

"Of course." I began rearranging the remaining baguettes on display as he headed over to the door.

"Oh, by the way, Admiral Canaris will be at the Lutetia on Sunday night, hosting a party, so you're going to be baking for the high command of the *Abwehr*."

"That's wonderful," I replied, my stomach churning from a mixture of nerves and excitement.

"Glad to see you're not intimidated." He grinned.

"Not at all," I replied. Oh, if only he knew!

16

SEPTEMBER 1940, PARIS

I decided against telling Madame Monteux I would be catering for the *Abwehr*. Remembering what Raphael had said about the importance of knowing as little as possible when it came to Resistance activities, I wanted to protect her. But, more than that, I really didn't want to upset her.

Madame Monteux had invited Baptiste and me to dinner on the Friday before I returned to the Lutetia and as I made my way past Brigit, the concierge, and up in the elevator, I silently chanted in my head, *Don't mention the hotel, don't mention the hotel.*

"Oh, Coralie, have you heard the news?" Madame Monteux exclaimed as she opened the door to me.

I stepped inside, feeling a stab of concern at her appearance. Her long hair had been piled into a misshapen bun that had slid halfway down the side of her head and her eyes were rimmed red as if she'd been crying.

"What's happened? Are you OK?"

"Come through, come through." She ushered me into the living room, where Baptiste was standing, scowling, by the window. When he saw me, he simply nodded rather than give his normal cheery greeting.

"What's happened?" I asked again, panic rising inside of me.

"The government have brought in a statute against the Jewish people," Madame Monteux said quietly.

"The *French* government?" I stared at her in horror. I knew that our new prime minister Pétain was weak-willed, but I never would have imagined he'd do something like this.

Madame Monteux nodded.

"That spineless Pétain is nothing more than Hitler's puppet," Baptiste muttered.

"What does the statute say?" I asked, dreading the answer.

"We've been banned from working in certain professions," Madame Monteux said, putting a fresh cigarette in her pearl holder. Quick as a flash, Baptiste was there with a book of matches to light it for her. "I'm no longer allowed to teach my singing students."

"No!" I clamped my hand to my mouth. "That's terrible."

"I can't believe I fought in the Great War to see this happen to France," Baptiste said, shaking his head.

"This is only the beginning, you mark my words," Madame Monteux replied, her eyes wide with fear. "They'll be coming for our property next." She looked around the room frantically. "What if they take my home?"

Baptiste stood up tall and puffed up his chest. "They'll do that over my dead body, Duchess."

His words brought a tear to my eye. While his loyalty and defiance were admirable, a sixty-two-year-old man would be no match for the might of the Nazis.

"I'm so sorry," I said, my voice catching, and I gave her a hug. "I wish there was something I could do."

"Oh, my dear, just by being in my life you give me so much," she replied, holding me tight.

"But it isn't enough." Anger boiled inside of me. I pulled back and looked her straight in the eyes. "I promise you I'm going to do everything I can to help defeat those monsters and get them out of our country."

"That's the spirit!" Baptiste said, patting me on the back before looking back at Madame Monteux. "The French government might have let you down, Duchess, but the French people won't. We won't let them get away with this."

"No, we won't," I said firmly. I thought of my job at the Lutetia and my resolve stiffened. The stakes had been raised and I had to find a way to turn it to the Resistance's advantage. I wasn't going to sit by while they persecuted my dearest friend.

I set off for the hotel on Sunday, filled with a steely determination. Reinhardt might have melted my defenses with his tales of his mother and the hardships they'd faced, but I could no longer afford to be sentimental. Nothing was more important to me than Madame Monteux, nothing and no one.

The sight of armed German soldiers standing guard by the revolving hotel door caused my confidence to waver slightly, but I gritted my teeth and marched up to them.

"My name's Coralie Donnadieu," I announced. "I'm here to make some desserts. Reinhardt, the chef, is expecting me."

The soldier gave me a cursory nod and disappeared inside. My pulse began to race. What if Reinhardt hadn't given them my name? Or, even worse, what if they somehow knew I'd been helping distribute the new Resistance paper? My mouth went as dry as sawdust as my panic rose—a state made even worse by the fact that the other soldier was standing there staring at me.

You're doing this for Madame Monteux, I reminded myself and I calmed down a little.

After what felt like forever, the guard returned and, thankfully, beckoned me inside.

It felt so strange returning after so long, and after so much had changed. As I walked into the lobby I instantly bristled at the sight of German women in their dreary uniforms behind the reception desk. *This place doesn't belong to you!* I wanted to yell. *And you don't belong here!* It felt as if they were a dense gray fog obscuring all the colorful memories I had from my time at the Lutetia before. But the sight of them only strengthened my spirit of resistance and I vowed there and then to do all in my power to drive them from France.

I followed the soldier across the lobby, my utensils clanging in my bag with every step. If I'd wanted to make a subtle entrance, I'd failed miserably and everyone I passed greeted me with a cold stare as if I was the intruder and not them. What a difference three months had made. It was hard to imagine that this had once been a safe haven for those fleeing the Nazis. Again, I thought of Madame Monteux. Would she end up having to flee too? But where would she go? And how would she make it past the German checkpoints?

The soldier escorted me all the way to the restaurant kitchen, even though I knew exactly where it was. *I know this hotel way better than you,* I wanted to yell at him. He opened the kitchen door onto a hive of activity. The warm, steamy air smelled of vegetables and roasting meat. An army of line cooks worked away at their stations, chopping and peeling and frying and stirring, and there at the heart of the kitchen waving his arms and shouting orders, like a conductor in an orchestra pit, was Reinhardt. Dressed in chef's whites, he looked completely different to how I was accustomed to seeing him. More confident and masterful, and completely at ease.

"Wait," the soldier barked at me, and I watched as he marched over to Reinhardt and said something in his ear. Instantly, his face lit up and he came hurrying over. The sleeves on his chef's jacket were rolled up, revealing a pair of muscular, tanned arms.

"Mademoiselle Donnadieu," he said with a smile. "Welcome! Come. I'll show you to your station." He led me over to a counter in the corner, next to a colossal refrigerator. I'd only been in the restaurant kitchen a handful of times before, usually to borrow an ingredient for the hotel patisserie. For a moment, it didn't feel all that different with the staff all at their stations, hard at work. The only obvious difference was the fact that they were speaking in German. But as Reinhardt led me to my station, the voices faded, and an awkward silence fell.

"This is Mademoiselle Donnadieu," Reinhardt called, addressing the elephant, or rather the small French woman, in the room. "She's an extremely talented pastry chef and she will be making the desserts here every Sunday."

A chunky, ruddy-faced man peeling a huge pile of potatoes muttered something in German and the others began to snigger. Quick as a flash, Reinhardt was over to him and, despite being half his size, he began talking to him sharply. To my surprise, the man turned away like a scolded puppy with his tail between his legs. Reinhardt looked around at the rest of the kitchen staff and said something in a firm tone. They all nodded and glanced at me. One of them, a young boy who looked to be no more than eighteen, gave me a warm smile. I couldn't help feeling slightly impressed. Clearly, Reinhardt commanded their loyalty and respect.

"I'm sorry about that," he said in French as he returned to me. "No one will bother you now. And if they do, you must tell me immediately."

I nodded and set my bag of utensils down on the counter.

Reinhardt showed me my oven and opened the fridge to reveal a plethora of butter and cream. The shelves above my station were laden with sugar, flour, chocolate and jars of nuts. It was a sight that simultaneously made me excited and sick. Tonight, I would be baking for the *Abwehr* using food stolen from the French, and while the French tried to survive on their meagre rations. The injustice of it all made me furious. *Remember why you're here*, I reminded myself before my hot head got the better of me.

"Do you have everything you need?" Reinhardt asked.

"Yes. Thank you." I took a mixing bowl from the shelf, my heart pounding. This was without a doubt the strangest setting I'd ever had to bake in. I decided to make a gateau Saint Honoré first as the cake was dedicated to the French patron saint of pastry chefs and, Lord knows, I needed to enlist his help to get me through this ordeal. As I kneaded the puff pastry dough, I imagined my fists pummeling the stupid fat head of the potato peeling man who'd mocked me and I felt my tension begin to ease.

Once the dough had formed a ball, I scored the top with a knife and placed it in the refrigerator to chill, then I began making the pâte à choux for the balls that would go on top. As I heated some butter, sugar and salt on the stove, I was aware of frequent glances in my direction, but thankfully no one said anything. Reinhardt was in the opposite corner of the kitchen, garnishing a large joint of meat with sprigs of rosemary. I thought about what he'd told me about the food shortages he'd experienced growing up. It must surely feel like heaven to have so many ingredients at his fingertips now—food stolen from us, though, I reminded myself with a frown. I was here to find a way to help Madame Monteux and the people of France.

Once both lots of dough were chilling, I started making some vanilla crème pâtissière, to fill the choux pastry puffs. My mind raced as I tried to come up with ways I could possibly spy on the Germans. My plan had seemed good in theory, but now I was at the hotel, I could see some obvious flaws. To find out anything about the *Abwehr*, I'd have to get out of the kitchen. But how, and when? I could tell Reinhardt that I needed to use the bathroom, but that would hardly buy me enough time to do anything without arousing suspicion. Perhaps I could pretend to be taken ill, but that would probably only see me getting escorted off the premises. If only they'd asked for my services as a waitress rather than a chef, at least then I'd be able to mingle with the guests, but, of course, I couldn't understand German yet. Reinhardt was my only hope. I'd have to try to engage him in conversation later, once the food was made and we were less busy, to see if I could glean anything of any use from him.

I glanced in his direction and saw that he was looking over. He smiled as I met his gaze and I smiled back. I'd have to make more of an effort to be friendly if I wanted him to open up to me.

The next few hours passed in a haze as I baked up a storm in my corner of the kitchen. It felt so good to have access to such a wide range of ingredients again, and I let my imagination run riot, creating éclairs with pistachio and raspberry flavored icing, an almond fraisier and a custard-filled puits d'amour. I was slicing some strawberries for the fraisier when the young boy who'd smiled at me before came over.

"Hello, I am Hans. It is very nice to meet you," he said in stilted French, repeatedly wiping his hands on his apron as if he was nervous. There was a sweetness about him that was quite disarming.

"Hello, I am Coralie. It is very nice to meet you too," I replied.

"Reinhardt, he is trying to teach me French," he said, his face flushing bright red. "I hope how I speak it is OK."

"It's very good," I replied and finally he made eye contact with me and gave me a shy smile.

"Thank you."

The ruddy-faced man, who was now washing pots in a nearby sink, saw us talking and called something out in German and some of the other men looked over and laughed and jeered.

Hans's face flushed even redder. "That is Gunter. He is, how do you say? *Merde!*"

I burst out laughing. "Yes. Yes he is!"

"It is very nice to meet you," Hans said, backing away, his face now so red, I half expected it to burst into flame.

After that, the rest of the staff seemed to forget I was there and the kitchen hummed with friendly banter and chefs barking orders. Whenever I glanced over at Reinhardt, I'd find him engrossed in something, whether it was the dishes he was preparing or helping one of his colleagues. He seemed to rule his kitchen with a mixture of passion and good humor—although I couldn't understand what he was saying to his staff, it elicited frequent guffaws of laughter, and this in turn helped me relax. It was nice seeing him so lit up too. It reminded me of Arnaud, and how, when he was at work in the kitchen, joy shone from him like the sun.

I was just adding some more caramel sauce to the top of the gateau Saint Honoré when I heard the soft clip of women's heels behind me. I turned to see the beautiful doll-like woman I'd met that awful day the Germans had arrived, the secretary to Admiral Canaris.

"Well, hello again," she said with a smile. "Reinhardt told me you'd be making desserts for the party tonight, but I had to come and check with my own eyes." She gazed at the cakes on the counter. "These look incredible."

"Thank you." I put down my piping bag and wiped my hands on my apron.

"What is this called?" she asked, pointing to one of them.

"It's a puits d'amour," I replied. "It means well of love."

She looked at the pastry, with its custard filling and golden puff pastry handle. "I see! It is like the bucket in a well, no?"

"Exactly. It was a favorite with the court of Louis XV." I omitted to tell her that King Louis' court had had great fun giving another, smuttier meaning to the "well of love," relating it to part of a woman's anatomy.

"How interesting." She cocked her head to one side, as if thinking of something. "I have an idea. Why don't you come and serve the cakes to us yourself? You have no idea what a treat French pastries are for us, and I'm sure the other guests would be fascinated to hear the history behind them."

A shiver ran up my spine at the thought. "I'd love to," I replied.

"Excellent! I'll send someone down to collect you when we're ready for dessert."

I watched her walk away and my stomach churned. I'd just been invited to serve the Admiral in charge of the German Intelligence Service and his cronies. This could be the opportunity I'd been hoping for to spy on the *Abwehr*.

17

JULY 1984, SAN FRANCISCO

I gaze into the desk drawer, my heart pounding. Now it's daylight, I'm able to see an old envelope sticking out from beneath the recipe book and photo album. I take it out and see that there's no name and address on the front. I feel inside and remove a folded piece of paper that's soft and yellowing with age. I recognize the handwriting immediately, from the German recipes in the book. But this writing isn't recipes, it's a list of sentences, under the heading: *Deutschunterricht für Coralie.*

Danke für dich
Ich liebe dich
Darf ich dich bitte küssen?

I sigh with frustration. Other than *"danke,"* which I think means thank you, I have no idea what it says. But I do know from the heading that it's to do with my grandma, Coralie. If only I had access to a German dictionary. I look at the phone on the desk and have a light-bulb moment. Melissa!

I pick up the receiver and dial her number, remembering to add the New York area code. It's only when I'm listening to the long purr of the ringtone for the seventh time that I realize she's now three hours ahead of me, making it late morning there. She's probably gone to the record store. My heart twinges as I think of her standing by the counter in her Frankie Say Relax T-shirt and pedal-pushers, asking Jet about the latest twelve-inch singles in stock. I'm about to hang up and wail in despair when the call is answered.

"Hello," I say nervously, praying that it's her and not her mom. As much as I love Melissa's mom, she can chat for hours, and I don't have time to spare.

"Raven, is that you?"

I feel an instant mixture of relief and sorrow at hearing Melissa's voice. "Yes! Oh, Lissa! It's so good to hear your voice!"

"Yours too. I'm missing you so much! How's it going at your grandma's? What's she like?" She puts on the fake British accent we use when we want to be melodramatic. "Are you positively dying of boredom, my precious darling?"

"Um, I wouldn't say that I'm bored exactly," I reply, looking at the swastika on the photo album. "I need you to do me a favor."

"Of course."

"I have some words in German I need to translate. Is there any way you could go to the library or the bookstore and use a German dictionary for me?"

"Wow!" She laughs. "I was not expecting that!"

"I'll explain more later." I lean over the desk and peer out the window to make sure my grandma isn't coming back early. "Can I dictate the words to you?"

"Sure, hold on."

Once Melissa is ready with a pad and pen, I spell out the words.

"This is all super intriguing," she says when I've finished. "Please tell me your grandma isn't making you study while you're staying there. You're meant to be on vacation!"

"No, not exactly." I clear my throat and put on my own British accent, but in the style of James Bond. "This is more like a secret mission, Miss Moneypenny."

"Holy moly! What do you mean?"

"I can't explain right now," I reply in my normal voice, "and I probably won't be able to when you call back, but I promise I'll spill as soon as I'm on my own and I know the full story."

"You'd better!"

"I will." I read her my grandma's number from the center of the dial and we say goodbye.

I put the receiver down and look back at the piece of paper. What do the words mean? I wonder and I feel a rush of fear. What if it's something I'd rather not know?

18

SEPTEMBER 1940, PARIS

By the time I was summoned to present my desserts to the *Abwehr* officers, I was practically giddy with nerves. I'd had plenty of time to think of all the things that could go wrong, all the ways in which I could be uncovered, which was ludicrous given that I didn't even really know what I was doing myself. Thankfully, Reinhardt had offered to accompany me and act as my translator.

As soon as we arrived in the restaurant and I saw the German officers sitting where the guests used to dine, my resolve hardened. They didn't belong here and anything I could do to hasten their demise had to be worth the risk. Reinhardt had appointed some of his staff to carry the desserts in and we followed in a weird, slightly awkward procession. I saw Inga sitting beside Canaris at the head table. When she saw me, she smiled and waved and said something in his ear. He tapped his knife on his glass and silence fell upon the room. He announced something in German and the other men laughed.

"He said that they are all in for a treat tonight," Reinhardt whispered in my ear. "As well as the finest French champagne, they will be experiencing the finest French desserts."

I felt my hackles rise but managed to paste a meek smile to my face.

Inga beckoned us over and we went and stood beside their table. Three other men were sitting there and another, stern-faced, woman.

"Perhaps you could tell us what each of these desserts is called, and the history behind them, especially this one." She grinned and pointed to the puits d'amour.

"Of course." Just as I was about to speak, I saw a man step forward to refill Canaris's champagne glass and realized that it was Raphael. "Er, this dessert is, er called the puits d'amour," I stammered.

Thankfully, Inga interjected at that point to translate in German, which gave me a few seconds to regain my composure.

"It is so-called because it resembles the bucket from a well," I pointed to the puff pastry handle. "And it was very popular in the court of Louis XV."

As Inga translated, I was met with blank stares.

"This one is called tarte tatin," I said, pointing to the caramelized apple tarts. "And they came into being purely by accident."

"How?" Inga asked.

"Two sisters were baking some ordinary apple tarts one day, and one of the tarts accidentally flipped upside down as she was putting it into the oven. She didn't realize what had happened and when they took the tart out, they discovered that the top had caramelized and it tasted so delicious they baked them like that ever since."

"That's a fun story," Reinhardt whispered to me as Inga translated what I'd said into German. This time, she was met with a slightly more enthusiastic response.

One of the men at her table looked up at me and smiled. "Your desserts are like works of art," he said in broken French. "They are almost too good to eat." He laughed. "Almost, but not quite." He said something to Inga in German and the others laughed.

"He says, enough talking, more eating," Inga said to me with a grin. "Thank you so much for your time. I look forward to you baking for us again."

"I look forward to that too," I said, my heart thudding, and with that I followed Reinhardt back out and into the kitchen.

"I hope that wasn't too difficult," he said as we went back over to my station. The other men had all gone on their break and, apart from the drip-drip of a tap, the kitchen was totally silent.

"Of course not, why should it have been," I said breezily.

He stared at me curiously.

"I'm always happy to talk about desserts," I said, trying to make light of it. I was realizing quickly that if I wanted to use him as a source of information for the Resistance, I would have to walk a thin tightrope between being friendly and enthusiastic, but not suspiciously so.

To my relief, he laughed. "I'm the same with food. Get me talking about a recipe and I won't shut up."

I nodded and smiled, although I couldn't quite see how it was possible to be enthused about a stew cooked in one pot.

"Would you like a drink?" he said, taking off his chef's hat and running his hand through his hair, causing his golden curls to spring back into life.

I nodded. "That would be nice." It could potentially be helpful too, I thought to myself as he fetched a bottle of red wine from a cupboard and poured a couple of glasses.

"So, who exactly was I making dessert for tonight?" I asked, once we'd sat down at a counter at the back of the kitchen. "I always like to know who I'm baking for," I added with a smile.

He laughed. "Well, you'll now be able to say that you've catered for all the top brass in the *Abwehr*. The man who spoke to you was Friedrich Rudolph, he's Canaris's second in command and in charge here in Paris. The two other men at the head table were Rudolph's officers, Oskar Reile and Arnold Garthe."

I quickly repeated the names a couple of times in my head to try to commit them to memory. "Isn't life full of surprises?" I said with a sigh. "I never in my wildest dreams imagined that I'd one day end up baking for the German Secret Service." I tried to ignore the bitter taste these words left in my mouth and smiled.

He gave a little laugh. "I know what you mean." There was something about the way he said this, a slight air of something to his tone, that I couldn't quite identify, but it sounded a little like regret. "Still, sometimes life's surprises can be wonderful."

"What do you mean?" My pulse quickened. Was he saying that his working for the *Abwehr* wasn't wonderful?

"Getting to come to Paris," he murmured. "I always wanted to come here. My mother filled my head with stories about it as a kid." His cheeks pinkened and he looked away.

"Your mother had been to Paris?"

"Yes. Her mother was French. That's why she taught me the language. She always wanted me to come to France." He gave a wry laugh. "I'm not sure what she would have made of me coming under these circumstances though."

I stared at him. "What do you mean?" I whispered.

But before he could answer, some of the kitchen staff came barging back in and Reinhardt leapt to his feet.

"You should get going," he said. "Would you like me to walk you home?"

I frowned. The thought of walking back to the patisserie in the pitch dark with the city now crawling with Nazis was hardly appealing. But, on the other hand, I didn't want anyone I knew to see me with a German.

Before I could answer, Raphael came striding into the

kitchen. He stared pointedly at the glasses of wine in front of us.

"Hello, Coralie, I didn't expect to see you here," he said and I felt a moment of confusion before realizing that he obviously didn't want Reinhardt to know that we'd been in touch.

"Yes, I've been asked to come back and work here every Sunday," I replied.

"I'll walk you home," Raphael said, and I thought I saw a flicker of disappointment on Reinhardt's face as he stood up and cleared away our glasses.

"Thank you so much for your work tonight," he said, his tone now businesslike. "I look forward to seeing you again next Sunday."

"Yes, you too," I replied.

I packed up my things and put on my coat and followed Raphael into the lobby, past the guards and out of the revolving doors. I took a deep lungful of the cool night air and tried to breathe the tension of the evening from my body.

"Well, you two seemed to be getting very friendly," Raphael muttered as we made our way along boulevard Raspail. As was the norm by now, the street lamps were all out and the darkness was so thick, it seemed to catch in the back of my throat. On the plus side, the stars had never seemed brighter. I gazed up at them and took a deep breath of the cold night air.

"I'm doing what you asked me," I whispered. "I thought he might have told me something useful for Charles de Gaulle and the Resistance."

"What would a chef know?" Raphael said dismissively, instantly making me want to give him a kick.

"I found out who the men at the head table were," I whispered, eager to prove him wrong.

"Canaris, Rudolph, Garthe and Reile," he rattled off. "Tell me something I don't know."

"Well, I might have got further if you hadn't barged in and demanded to walk me home."

We continued walking in silence until we reached my little side street.

"I don't want you getting too friendly with him," Raphael said quietly as I came to a halt. "It could backfire on you."

"What's that supposed to mean?" I asked indignantly.

"There are already enough French women fraternizing with the enemy. I ought to know, I have to serve them at the hotel parties." His voice was laden with disgust.

I pulled myself up as tall as I could, although this only brought me level with his barrel-like chest. "But I wouldn't be fraternizing with the enemy," I hissed. "I'd be working for the Resistance."

He stared down at me. "So, you're really serious about this?"

"Of course! I want them out of France just as much as you do."

He remained silent for a moment, looking at me intently, then nodded. "OK. Good."

"I'm glad you approve," I said sarcastically, but, privately, I fizzed with excitement as I turned and headed down the street. Raphael could be as sour as he liked; after my night at the Lutetia I no longer felt helpless. I was finally in a position to be able to help, and it felt fantastic.

19

NOVEMBER 1940, PARIS

I gazed down at the bowl of watery soup in front of me and fought the urge to weep.

I will not be broken by a bowl of soup, I vowed silently. *I am made of far sterner stuff.*

I glanced across the table at Madame Monteux, who was staring at her own bowl as if it were a hideous toad.

She looked up and caught my gaze. "Those monsters have taken away my two main passions—food and teaching," she said glumly.

I looked back at the insipid vegetable soup in front of me and I couldn't help thinking of what Reinhardt had told me about food in Germany when he'd been growing up. "Perhaps we need to develop a new passion for carrots and turnips," I said, "then we'll never be disappointed."

Thankfully, she took the joke and ran with it. "What an excellent idea!" she exclaimed. "I hereby declare my undying love for the turnip! Oh, how I adore its wrinkly beige skin."

"It really is a most characterful vegetable," I quipped, before taking a spoonful. "And as for its bitter taste—simply divine!"

Madame Monteux giggled. "Not to mention exquisite."

A sharp rap on the door interrupted our laughter and we looked at each other anxiously. Ever since the government statute against the Jews in September, rumors had been rife about German troops requisitioning Jewish apartments and property.

"I'll get it," I said, standing up, my pulse quickening as I made my way to the door. "Who is it?" I called. Hopefully it was just Brigit with some mail.

"It's Père Noël, with an early gift," Baptiste called back and I felt a surge of relief.

I flung the door open to see him holding a long package wrapped in brown paper.

"What is it?" I asked.

"A trout."

I gave a gasp of joy. "It's OK, Madame Monteux," I called as we hurried into the living room. "It's Père..." I broke off, looking around the room. Madame Monteux appeared to have vanished into thin air. "Madame Monteux, where are you?"

There was a rustling sound and she crawled out from under the table.

"What were you doing under there?" I asked, shocked.

"I thought it was the Germans. I didn't want them to find me."

Seeing her so vulnerable caused my heart to break.

"Oh, Duchess!" Baptiste exclaimed. "You shouldn't have to crawl around and hide in your own home like this. I'd give you a hug if my hands weren't so full of fish."

"He's brought us a trout!" I exclaimed, desperate to raise her spirits.

Madame Monteux gave us both a weak smile. "That's wonderful," she said, but she still looked really shaken. She'd always seemed so indestructible. It was horrible to see her like this. My hatred for the Germans grew. They'd sucked all the light and life out of Paris and now they were doing the same to my beloved friend.

The following morning, I woke to find that Père Noël had paid an early visit to the store too and left the gift of a sack of something on the doorstep. I hoisted it inside and saw a note pinned to the top and recognized Reinhardt's handwriting: *Something different for you to experiment with.*

I opened the sack and put my hand inside. It felt like flour but coarser than usual. I took out a handful and saw that it was wholegrain. I frowned. Surely it would be too heavy for baguettes or croissants. I looked back at the note. I liked the fact that he'd remembered me talking about my love of experimenting, and it was always a challenge I rose to.

I fetched what I had left of my plain flour and poured a mixture of both into a bowl. Perhaps if I used half and half, I'd be able to come up with something interesting. I started with one tray of croissants, not wanting to waste valuable ingredients in case it didn't work. The result was surprisingly satisfying. The wholegrains gave the croissants a rich, nutty flavor. It was different, but in a good way. And now I'd be able to make some extra to bump up people's rations.

Reinhardt's flour had the same effect on the baguettes and soon the whole place was filled with the aroma of baking bread. By the time I was ready to open the doors at six in the morning as curfew ended, I had baskets of baguettes ready, plus a hidden basket of croissants under the counter to slip as a bonus to anyone who looked in need.

The morning flew by, and I was so busy, I hadn't noticed Raphael had entered the store until he was standing right in front of me.

"Good day, Coralie," he said curtly.

"Good day," I replied.

"I have the butter you were asking for," he said, which I knew was code for him having another delivery of Resistance newspapers. He could have picked a less busy time to deliver them though. "It's a different kind," he whispered.

"Please, bring it through to the kitchen," I said, raising the hatch in the counter to let him through. Apologizing to the woman behind him and telling her I wouldn't be long, I followed him into the back. "What is it?" I whispered.

"Flyers," he replied, his eyes gleaming with excitement. "The students are having a demonstration against the Germans."

I felt a mixture of excitement and fear at his words.

"They're protesting about their Jewish professors no longer being allowed to teach. On Armistice Day at the Champs-Élysées." He put the package in the pantry. "Someone will be along to collect them later. They'll say they're here to get some bread for their grandmother Audrey."

"OK." I followed him back into the store, my heart pounding. Could the fightback be about to begin in earnest? First the students, then maybe the rest of the Paris population would take to the streets. I began humming *"La Marseillaise"* under my breath. Never had the call to fight tyranny felt more rousing.

I was still humming the anthem at the end of the afternoon as I prepared to close. All the bread had been sold, or exchanged for ration coupons anyway, and I'd given away most of my strange new croissants as bonus gifts. I couldn't wait to go straight to Madame Monteux's to tell her the good news about the protest. But Madame Monteux, it turned out, had decided to pay me a visit. I was just taking the trays out of the window when she strode through the door on a cloud of Chanel.

"Madame Monteux, you will never guess what's happened!" I blurted.

"Have the Germans left?" she asked hopefully. "Was it all a bad dream?"

"Sadly, no, but I do have some good news." I grabbed her arm. "Come with me to the kitchen."

"Have you made me a cake?" she asked, eyes wide.

"No, although I do have a croissant with an unexpected twist."

She looked at me and laughed. "Oh, Coralie, I do so love your endless imagination."

"Well, you're going to love this even more," I said, producing one of the leaflets from the pantry with a flourish. "The students are having a protest about their Jewish professors no longer being allowed to teach."

I watched as she studied the handwritten leaflet and then, to my surprise, her eyes filled with tears.

"Don't cry," I said. "It's happy news. The fightback against the Germans is beginning."

"These are happy tears," she said. "But do you really think it will achieve anything?"

"Of course!" I exclaimed. "It will wake the rest of the French from their stupor. I'm sure it won't be long before we're all taking to the streets to protest. The fire of the French Resistance won't be extinguished. Now come through to the store and try one of my new croissants."

The bell above the door jangled. I walked back into the store and came to an abrupt halt. Reinhardt was standing there in his cursed green-gray uniform.

"*Bonjour*, Coralie," he proclaimed cheerily just as Madame Monteux joined me behind the counter and I heard her give a tiny gasp.

"*Bon-bonjour*," I stammered, glancing at Madame Monteux. She was staring at Reinhardt as if frozen to the spot. And then I saw something that made my heart almost stop. She was holding the leaflet about the protest in her quivering hand.

There must be some way I can explain this, I thought to myself as time seemed to stand still. But Madame Monteux still didn't know I'd been working at the Lutetia, so how on earth could I explain why I was on first-name terms with a German?

"Did you get my gift?" Reinhardt asked with one of his twinkly-eyed smiles.

"Oh, er, yes, thank you."

"I have to go," Madame Monteux said, in a tight little voice I'd never heard her use before. "Thank you, Coralie, for the *surprise*." She strode out from behind the counter and Reinhardt sprang to open the door for her.

"Please, allow me," he said, turning his smile on her.

She stopped and stared at him, still holding the leaflet, and not saying a word. I wondered if he'd noticed the gold Star of David pendant around her neck. My heart began pounding, fit to burst. Finally, she marched out.

"Did you use it?" Reinhardt asked, approaching the counter, blissfully unaware of the pandemonium he'd unleashed.

"Use what?" I replied, distracted. All I could focus on was Madame Monteux and what she must be thinking.

"The flour."

"Oh, yes."

"It's a lot healthier, you know."

I stared at him blankly.

"Wholegrain flour. In Germany, our bakeries are encouraged to come up with their own *Vollkornbrot* recipes."

"*Vollkornbrot?*" I echoed.

"It means brown bread." He smiled hopefully. "Maybe one day I could show you how to make traditional *Vollkornbrot*. It's really delicious."

The notion of talking recipes with him while Madame Monteux was so clearly distraught felt horrendous, and it took everything I'd got not to ask him to leave. *You're being friends with him in order to help Madame Monteux,* I reminded myself. As soon as he'd gone, I'd go after her and reassure her that everything was OK.

"That would be great," I said numbly, and I took one of my wholegrain croissants from the basket beneath the counter. "Perhaps you would like to try a *Vollkornbrot* croissant?"

"Of course!" He took it from me and bit into it. "Oh, this is delicious," he said through a mouthful, causing flakes of golden pastry to flutter like petals to the ground. "It gives it a really nutty flavor."

"That's exactly what I thought!" I exclaimed, immediately kicking myself for being so effusive. But when it came to the subject of pastries, it was almost impossible for me to remain restrained.

"Was your friend all right?" he asked after taking another bite.

"My friend?"

"The woman who was here before. She looked upset."

Instantly, I was on my guard. *Why would he ask this? And how should I respond?* "She... she has a lot to worry about at the moment."

His smile faded. "I'm very sorry about that."

He looked so concerned, I wasn't sure what to make of it. Had he seen her Star of David pendant? If so, he would probably understand what I meant. But part of me wanted him to see what his leaders were doing, the pain they were causing.

"I should get back to the hotel," he said, now looking awkward and embarrassed.

"OK."

He cleared his throat. "I—uh..."

"Yes?"

He frowned, as if deciding against whatever he'd planned to say and looked at the half-eaten croissant in his hand. "I—er, I'm glad you were able to make use of my gift."

"Oh—yes, thank you."

He went over to the door, then stopped. "Goodbye, Coralie. See you on Sunday—I hope?" He looked at me questioningly over his shoulder.

"Yes, of course. See you on Sunday."

His face broke into a smile of relief. "Thank you!"

I stared after him as he left. What on earth had made him act so strangely? Could it be that he felt badly about what the Germans were doing to the Jewish? I shook my head. I couldn't allow myself to think such things. I couldn't risk lowering my guard.

I closed the shop and hotfooted it to Madame Monteux's apartment building.

"What's the weather like out there?" a disembodied voice echoed across the foyer as I came racing in. I turned to see Brigit peering out at me from her hatch.

"What? Oh, it's—uh—cold but not too bad," I replied.

"I heard that the Jews aren't allowed to teach anymore," she said, leaning through the hatch. "So I suppose your friend won't be having any of her music students visiting again."

"That's right," I replied noncommittally as I hurried over to the elevator. I really didn't have time for her small talk this evening, especially if it was about Madame Monteux.

"Oh well, she was probably thinking of retiring soon anyway," Brigit continued.

I felt a rush of indignation at her blasé attitude but thought better than to say anything and pulled the elevator door open and stepped inside.

"Have a nice evening," I called sharply before pressing the button.

When I gave my customary three knocks on Madame Monteux's door, there was no answer. I tried again and again. Perhaps she hadn't gone home after what had happened in the shop. Maybe she'd gone to see Baptiste. I was just turning to leave when the door inched open.

"What do you want?" Madame Monteux muttered from inside.

"Thank goodness you're home, I want to explain." I waited for her to open the door wider but she didn't. "Please," I said. "It wasn't how it looked."

"It looked pretty self-explanatory to me," she said haughtily. "You've been fraternizing with a German. Is that how you've managed to keep the shop open? Is a Nazi funding my investment?" Her voice cracked.

"No, of course not!"

"So you're just accepting gifts from him then? I was right there, Coralie, I heard what you both said."

"It was only some flour."

"So he *is* helping to support the store."

"No—yes, but it's not how it looks."

She gave a dramatic sigh. "I can't believe you would do this, after everything I've done for you."

"And I can't believe you'd think I'd betray you!" I pushed the door open and stepped inside. I had to take control of the spiraling situation.

Madame Monteux trudged down the hallway into the living room and I followed hot on her heels.

"I'm working for the French..." I broke off in shock. The normally elegant living room looked as if it had been ransacked and the floor was covered in crumpled sheets of paper. "What on earth has happened?" I bent down to pick up a piece of the paper and saw that it was sheet music—or what was left of it. "Who did this?" I looked around for any other signs that the Germans had ransacked the place, but her valuables all still seemed to be in place.

"I did it," she said defiantly. In the light from the lamps, I saw that her cheeks were streaked black from what was left of her eye makeup.

"But why would you do such a thing?"

"I no longer need it anymore, thanks to your friends, the Germans."

"Oh for goodness' sake!" I took hold of her arms. "Will you listen to me, please? They aren't my friends. I didn't want to tell you this because I didn't want to endanger you by association, but I'm working for the French Resistance—or hoping to at least! I want to help you, the way you've helped me. I've been using the patisserie as a place to distribute a Resistance newspaper and..." I paused for breath. "I've gone back to work at the Lutetia every Sunday as a way of possibly gathering information. That's how I know the German who came to the store. He isn't a soldier, he's a chef."

Madame Monteux stared at me and for an awful moment I thought she didn't believe me, but then she threw back her head and she began to laugh. "Oh, Coralie, I can't believe I doubted you. I fear the stress of this all is driving me crazy."

I looked around at the carnage on the floor. "I fear you

might be right," I said in an exaggeratedly grave tone. We both laughed and I pulled her into a hug. "But now you know, you mustn't breathe a word to anyone, not even Baptiste. It's too dangerous."

"Of course. And thank you," she said. "For bringing me good news. With the students protesting and people like you being brave enough to fight back, I no longer feel so helpless."

"Unlike your poor sheet music," I joked, looking back at the jumble of papers.

The day before the student protest on Armistice Day was a Sunday and as I walked to the Lutetia, I couldn't help feeling anxious for the students. The Germans had strictly forbidden any kind of commemoration for the Great War, so I dreaded to think of how they might respond to an open protest against them. Perhaps they wouldn't realize until after it was all over, I tried reassuring myself, although I knew this was naïve and overly optimistic.

As I approached the main entrance of the hotel, I saw the distinct cape and hat of a French policeman coming down the road toward me and going up to the German soldiers standing guard at the entrance.

"I'm Sergeant Francois Blaise. I'm here to see Oskar Reile," I heard him say.

Instantly, he had my attention, as I was certain Reile had been one of the men present the night I served my pastries to the *Abwehr* officers. Why would a French policeman be paying an officer in the German Secret Service a visit? I stared at his back indignantly. Was he here to betray his fellow countrymen? *Sergeant Francois Blaise*, I repeated his name over and over in my head so I'd be able to remember it and tell Raphael. The guard let him in then turned to me. Thankfully, this time he recognized me and let me in without any fuss, and without insisting on accompanying me.

I looked at the policeman making his way across the lobby. Could I risk following him to see why he was here to see Reile? He was going in the opposite direction to the restaurant kitchen, but if stopped, I could always say I was going to use the ladies' bathroom. Before I could talk myself out of it, I followed him across the lobby and into the bar. I stopped just inside of the entrance and pretended to look for something in my bag. A German woman in a gray uniform walked past and gave me an enquiring stare, making me want to grab my egg whisk from my bag and beat her round the head with it.

Don't be ridiculous, stay focused, I told myself as I watched the policeman approach a man sitting in an armchair. My stomach clenched as I recognized him from the head table the night I'd served my desserts—Oskar Reile. Thankfully, he was sitting in an alcove right next to the bathrooms. I just had to walk past really slowly and see if I could overhear anything.

I took a breath and stood up straight. I could do this. I *had* to do this, for Madame Monteux.

As I drew level with the men, I heard Reile ask, "What is his name?"

"Dubois," the police officer replied. "Bernard Dubois."

I walked past and stopped a couple of feet behind them, hoping to overhear something else, but then a stern-faced woman appeared in front of me. She looked vaguely familiar, but I wasn't sure where I knew her from. She said something to me in German and I shrugged helplessly.

"I'm sorry, I'm French," I murmured, still trying to keep an ear on the conversation.

The policeman appeared to be giving Reile an address, but I only heard the word boulevard.

"What are you doing here?" the woman said in broken French.

"I'm a pastry chef. I'm here to make some desserts."

"In the bar?" She scowled.

"I need to use the bathroom. I worked here before. I know there's one just over there." As I pointed to the bathroom, Oskar Reile stood up and my heart began to pound. What if she told him she'd caught me acting suspiciously?

"Thank you very much," he said to the policeman, shaking his hand. "We will send someone round to see Mr Dubois and put a stop to his activities." There was an ominous tone to his voice that sent a shiver up my spine.

Thinking on my feet, I gave the woman an embarrassed smile. "It's my time of the month and I really didn't want to use the staff toilet in the kitchen. It's so full of men."

She pursed her lips tightly and gave a curt nod. "All right, but then you're to go straight back there."

"Of course." I glanced at Oskar Reile and my heart skipped a beat as he met my gaze. "Thank you," I said to the woman and started hurrying to the bathroom.

"Wait," Reile called out and I almost dropped my bag in shock.

I stopped and slowly turned.

"Don't I know you from somewhere?" he said.

I was aware of the woman's eyes boring into me.

"I don't think so," I replied, thinking it was better to not show that I recognized him. "I'm a pastry chef. I work in the kitchen."

"That's it!" he exclaimed, his face breaking into a smile. "That cake you made was the most delicious thing I've ever tasted." He patted me on the arm. "I'm very happy you're back."

"Thank you."

I hurried into the bathroom, locked myself in one of the stalls and pressed my burning cheek to the cool wall. That had been way too close for comfort. But at least I'd overheard Reile's conversation with the policeman, or part of it. Maybe Raphael would know who this Bernard Dubois was. I'd have to try to find him as soon as possible, though, if Dubois was to be warned he was due a visit from the *Abwehr*.

I took a moment to compose myself, then walked out of the bathroom. Thankfully, the woman had disappeared. I hurried out of the bar and across the lobby, banking on the fact that, as dinner hadn't been served yet, Raphael would be down in the wine cellar. The cellar had two entrances: one in the restaurant kitchen, and one behind the bar. As soon as the coast was clear, I slipped down the corridor behind the bar and through the door, making up my excuse for being there as I went. I wanted to make a gateau with cherry brandy in it; I was going to see Raphael to get some.

"Hello," I whispered as I reached the bottom of the stairs. The cellar was lit by flickering lamplight, only adding to my nerves. "Is anyone here?"

Raphael appeared from between the shelves and I had to clamp my hand to my mouth to stop myself from yelping in shock.

"What are you doing here?" he hissed.

"Don't worry, no one saw me—and if they did, we can say I've come to get some brandy for a dessert." I took a step closer and lowered my voice to a whisper. "I have some information for you."

"OK." He nodded tersely and I explained what I'd overheard. "I haven't heard of him, but I'll ask my contacts," Raphael replied. "I don't suppose you got the name of the policeman?"

"I did!" I exclaimed, eager to prove that I had what it took to be a spy for the Resistance. "It's Sergeant Francois Blaise."

"OK, that's really helpful because now we can be sure that he's working for the *Abwehr* as an informant." For the first time since I'd known him, he gave me a look of respect, and even though he irritated the hell out of me, I couldn't help feeling a burst of pride at having won his admiration.

"I'd better get to the kitchen," I said.

"Yes. Good luck. And good work."

I made my way up the stairs, grinning, his oh so rare words of praise ringing in my ears. I could do this. I had what it took to spy on the Germans.

21

NOVEMBER 1940, PARIS

I woke the next morning with a jolt and that strange feeling you get when you know that something big is happening but your brain is too foggy from sleep to remember what. It was only as I got out of bed and made my way across the cold floor that it hit me. It was Armistice Day—the day of the student protest. I'd arranged to go with Madame Monteux and Baptiste and they arrived in the store early afternoon, both grinning excitedly. Bizarrely, Baptiste was holding two fishing rods.

"Are you planning on doing a spot of fishing while we're there?" I said, staring at him baffled.

He chortled. "No, it's for the protest."

"It really is genius." Madame Monteux beamed.

I stared at them blankly. "I don't understand."

"*Deux gaules,*" Baptiste said.

"Two rods," I repeated, still not understanding.

"*Deux gaules,*" he said again. "As in Charles de Gaulle."

I burst out laughing.

"I told you it was clever." Madame Monteux looked at Baptiste and raised her perfectly plucked eyebrows. "I had no idea you were such a wit."

"Duchess, I'm offended!" he exclaimed, clapping his hand to his heart. "I thought my humor was what most attracted you to me."

"The cheek of it!" she exclaimed, the color rising in her face.

"I'll bring some sables in case we get hungry," I said, putting some of the buttery vanilla biscuits into a paper bag.

"Oh, isn't this fun!" Madame Monteux remarked. "It feels as if we're going on an adventure."

"Or a fishing trip," I said drily.

As we made our way to the Champs-Élysées, my spirits lifted higher and higher. V for victory signs had been chalked all over the walls.

"Do you think many people will turn up?" I asked.

"Maybe a hundred?" Baptiste said.

But as we drew closer, we heard what sounded like hundreds of voices.

"Goodness!" Madame Monteux exclaimed as the Champs-Élysées came into view. It was full with what looked like thousands of people. And they weren't just students. There were people of all ages and from all walks of life. Some of them, like Baptiste, were holding two fishing rods.

"This is incredible!" I exclaimed.

Baptiste nodded, clearly speechless.

"My faith in the French people has been restored!" Madame Monteux declared. "Look, they're laying flowers at Clemenceau's statue."

We watched as a woman and her child laid a bouquet of white roses at the foot of the statue to the former prime minister. The ground all around the statue was covered in bunches of flowers, all tied with tricolor ribbons. Georges Clemenceau had led France to victory in the Great War and as such was an arch-enemy of the Germans. What would they make of this?

I glanced around nervously for any sign of soldiers, but,

thankfully, there were none. A small group of French policemen stood at the side of the street, looking on. I thought of the police officer I'd seen at the hotel the previous day and shivered. It was a horrible feeling knowing you could no longer trust the people who were supposed to protect you.

We continued walking deeper into the throng, leading up to the Arc de Triomphe.

"*Vive* de Gaulle!" the students kept crying in between singing rousing choruses of "*La Marseillaise.*" "*Vive les Français!*" They exuded a jubilant kind of defiance and it was infectious. I could feel it traveling like osmosis into every cell of my body.

"It's like we've reclaimed Paris," I said, turning in a full circle to drink it all in. Ever since the Germans had begun their occupation, their troops had daily parades along the Champs-Élysées to the Arc de Triomphe, as if to rub our noses in their victory. It felt so sweet to see so many people reclaim the wide road from them.

I took the bag of sables from my pocket and offered them to Madame Monteux and Baptiste.

"This is the happiest day I've had in ages," Madame Monteux said before taking a bite of her cookie. "Oh, and now it's even better. This is delicious, Coralie. The vanilla is divine!"

"Thank you, I—" I broke off, catching sight of a man in a suit with a thin mustache talking to some of the policemen nearby. My jubilation was instantly replaced with a feeling of dread. It was Oskar Reile, the *Abwehr* officer. He began turning in our direction and I quickly spun round so my back was to him. "I have to go," I said.

"What? Why?" Madame Monteux looked at me, concerned.

"I can't stay here, it isn't safe. And I don't think it is for you either." I grabbed the sleeve of her fur coat. "Come on, let's go."

"What's happened, Coralie?" Baptiste asked, looking confused.

"Please, just trust me."

Linking arms with them both, I steered us over to the sidewalk and through a line of policemen.

"What's happened? What did you see?" Madame Monteux asked anxiously.

There were so many people now, it was starting to feel a little claustrophobic, especially as more police had arrived, all holding rifles. I heard a rumbling sound and looked round to see a stream of German trucks approaching.

"Oh no!" Madame Monteux exclaimed.

"Quick." We hurried down a side street. I glanced over my shoulder to see scores of German soldiers spilling out of the back of a truck and onto the sidewalk, rifles drawn with bayonets fixed.

"What's going to happen to the students?" Madame Monteux cried.

"I'm going back," Baptiste said, brandishing his fishing poles.

"No!" I cried. "It isn't safe."

"I fought in the Great War."

"Yes, but not armed with two fishing rods," I exclaimed, grabbing his arm. "Please!"

"The students need me," he said.

Madame Monteux stepped in front of him, blocking his way. "I need you," she said, her voice breaking.

I stared at her, shocked. This was the first time I'd seen her open up to him like this in all his years of unabashed adoration. It was simultaneously heartwarming and heartbreaking.

Judging from his stunned expression, Baptiste was as shocked as I was. "You do?" he said.

"Yes. So don't you dare leave us here all alone to get home."

To my huge relief, he nodded and lowered his fishing rods. "I'm sorry."

"Quick, let's go," I said, terrified that Oskar Reile would come round the corner at any moment and see me with Baptiste and his *deux gaules*. If an *Abwehr* agent knew I'd been at the protest march, my position as a Resistance agent in the Lutetia kitchen would be over before it had even begun and I'd probably be arrested.

We hurried up the street and then a cracking sound pierced the air.

"What was that?" Madame Monteux asked.

"A gunshot," Baptiste replied grimly.

22

JULY 1984, SAN FRANCISCO

After my call with Melissa, I get dressed in my favorite CHOOSE LIFE T-shirt and black pants covered in silver zips. My grandma might have been involved with a Nazi, but the nice things she said about my style have filled me with a newfound confidence. For once when I look in the mirror to style my hair, I'm not struck by the usual pang of self-doubt that I might look stupid. I add a final blob of gel and sigh. If only my grandma didn't appear to have such a dubious past, I could have really started to like her.

I hear a vehicle approaching and make my way into the kitchen. My grandma comes in through the porch door holding two brown paper bags full of groceries.

"Hey!" she says with a smile. "I love the T-shirt."

"Thank you." I smile back, but all I can think about is the note I found in her drawer and what it might mean. "It's by a British designer named Katharine Hamnett. It's her way of protesting against war."

"It's very cool." She takes some apples from one of the bags. "I hope you like apples, I forgot to ask."

"I love them," I reply. I wonder if Melissa has gone in search of a German dictionary yet. I really hope she doesn't ring back while my grandma and I are in the same room.

"Excellent. Perhaps you could help me to peel them?"

"Peel what?" I say distractedly.

"The apples of course," she says with a laugh.

She puts the radio on and the kitchen fills with the sound of Fleetwood Mac. As we start peeling the apples, she tells me this really fun story about how the apple tart she's going to make began life as an accident when a French woman was baking a traditional apple tart but it flipped it upside down as she put it in the oven, making the apples go all golden and crispy.

"And now tarte tatin is one of the most popular desserts in France," she concludes with a grin. "And people love the caramelized top."

"It sounds delicious," I say, as I dump my apple peelings into the trash.

"It is and it just goes to show that sometimes the best things in life can be a mistake," she remarks.

I nod. As someone who is always being nagged at by my parents to behave impeccably at all times and achieve perfect grades, I love the notion that an upside-down, partially burned pie could end up taking the French dessert world by storm. It feels like a parable of hope for misfits everywhere. I make a mental note to share the story with Melissa.

Next, we core and quarter the apples and my grandma shows me how to arrange them in tight circles inside a pie dish. Then she heats some sugar on the stove until it starts to smoke and caramelize, adds some butter and brushes the fruit with the golden syrup. She places the pie dish in the oven and takes a disc of pastry from the freezer. "One of the bonuses of having insomnia is that I'm able to prep in the middle of the night," she says with a laugh. "I made this after you went back to bed."

After about thirty minutes, she takes the dish of apples from the oven. "Now we have recreated the accidental caramelizing of the apples, it's time to add the pastry," she explains before placing the pastry lid on top, tucking the edges inside and pricking the top with a fork. She pops it back in the oven. "Let the baking of an upside-down tart begin," she says with a grin.

I giggle and sit back down at the table. But now we've made the tart, my anxious thoughts from earlier make an unwelcome return. What if the German note reveals something sinister? How can I get to the bottom of it without letting her know I snooped on her again?

"Shall I make us some iced tea while we wait?" she asks, taking off her apron.

"Yes please."

She's just made the tea when the phone on the wall starts to ring, causing me to jump.

"Hello!" my grandma answers in a singsong voice.

I look down into my lap, praying it isn't Melissa as it will be super awkward having to take the call in front of her.

"Oh, hello," she says. "Yes, of course. Raven, it's a friend for you." She stretches the phone cord across to the table and hands me the receiver.

"Oh, uh, thank you." I feel my face flushing. "Hello," I say nervously into the receiver.

"Hey," Melissa's voice crackles down the line. "Your grandma sounds nice. It's so cool that she calls you Raven."

"Yes—uh—she is—it is," I stammer.

"Well, Agent Double Oh Seven, I am happy to report that I've done my homework for your secret assignment," Melissa continues in her fake British voice.

I watch as my grandma sits down at the table and pours us both a tea.

"Oh yes?" I say nonchalantly.

"It was actually really fun," she says. "And so romantic!"

"Romantic?" I can't help repeating, and I notice my grandma raise her eyebrows.

"Yes. Are you ready for the translation?"

"Sure." I sit back in my chair and try to look as if I don't have a care in the world.

"So, the heading means, German lessons for Coralie. Who's Coralie?" Melissa asks.

"OK," I say pointedly.

"You can't say?" she guesses, lowering her voice.

"Uh-huh."

"Ooh the plot thickens." Melissa giggles. "Well, whoever she is, she's a lucky lady because the other sentences say, thank you for you, I love you, and, get this..." She pauses dramatically, and my heart begins to thud. "Please can I kiss you? Isn't that adorable?"

"Yes," I say, but my voice comes out like a squeak. I take a breath to try to regain my composure. "OK, well, thanks so much for letting me know." As soon as I say it, I know it sounds weird, too fake and officious.

"Promise me you'll call me as soon as you're able to tell me what's going on," Melissa pleads.

"I will."

"Swear to me on all you hold precious. Swear on the life of Jet at the record store."

"I swear," I mutter. "Thank you. Bye." I get up and hurriedly put the receiver back on its cradle on the wall.

"Everything OK?" my grandma asks, looking across the table at me.

"Sure," I reply, sitting back down. But I feel the very opposite of OK. Not only do I know that my grandma worked for the German Secret Service and socialized with at least one of them, but I now know that she and that German were in love!

I glance at her across the table, innocently sipping on her tea. She seems so nice, but I know from my history class that the Nazis were anything but nice. How could she have fallen in love with one of them? And why has she kept the recipe book and photo album all these years, even after marrying my grandpa and coming to America? Surely you'd only keep mementoes like that if you still had feelings for the person concerned.

I feel a tightening in my chest. Is my grandma still in love with a Nazi?

23

FEBRUARY 1941, PARIS

Over the next couple of months, Paris was gripped by a bitterly cold winter, the relentlessly gray skies forming the perfect backdrop for a city that had been stripped of its *joie de vivre*. The hunger from the rationing was really starting to bite and some people had even begun breeding rabbits in their apartments as a way of getting meat. Thanks to Baptiste and his contacts on the black market, Madame Monteux and I would sometimes be lucky enough to dine on chewy lamb chops or a dry fillet of fish, and, naturally, we never went short of bread.

Working every weekend at the Hotel Lutetia hadn't been as rewarding as I would have hoped as my movements were strictly limited to the kitchen. Nevertheless, I spotted an opportunity to develop my skills as a spy, suggesting to Hans that he teach me some basic German in exchange for some French lessons, to which he readily agreed. The books Raphael had given me had been helpful to a point but I'd realized that the best way to really learn a language was to speak it. I also worked on deepening my friendship with Reinhardt—not that it felt like work. As much as I hated to admit it, I admired the calm and light-hearted way in which he ran the kitchen and commanded the respect of his men, and I'd really come to enjoy his company. It had become clear though that he didn't know much about the Secret Service agents he was cooking for, or, if he did, he wasn't at all forthcoming.

The one thing that kept fanning the flames of my hope was the Resistance newspaper that I was helping to distribute. Raphael still hadn't told me which museum was producing it, but twice every month, he'd arrive at the patisserie with a bundle of the papers, and every month, different people would turn up at the store to collect them, uttering that month's secret code. Through reading the paper, I learned of the budding Resistance movement growing underground in Paris like bulbs before spring and that thought kept me going.

Then, one weekend in mid-February, I finally had a breakthrough when Inga appeared in front of me in the restaurant kitchen.

"I was wondering if I could ask a special favor?" she said with a smile so pleasant and warm it was hard to reconcile with the fact that she worked for the head of the *Abwehr*.

"Of course," I replied.

"Would you be able to bring some of your delicious cakes up to my room? I have a lot of work to do tonight and I need something sweet to keep me going."

"I have just the thing." I nodded to a bowl of canelé mix resting on the side. "They'll be ready in about an hour."

"Excellent. I'm in room 317."

"I'll bring them up to you as soon as they're baked." My skin prickled with goosebumps. Finally, I had a reason to venture upstairs, and hopefully to have a look around while I was up there.

I quickly put the mixture into the tins and placed them in the oven. When the top of the cakes were perfectly crisp and caramelized, I took them out and arranged them on a plate to let them cool.

Hans, who'd been fetching some milk from the fridge, came over and gazed at them longingly. "They look so delicious," he whispered in French.

"I think you should have one for doing so well in your French lessons," I whispered back. I'd grown really fond of him over the past few months. He was so young and so open-hearted it was easy to separate him from the atrocities committed by his nation.

He grinned and grabbed a canelé from the plate, stuffing the entire thing in his mouth, causing his rosy cheeks to puff out like a hamster's. "Oh," he gasped, "they have custard in the center!"

"They certainly do."

"*Merci beaucoup! Merci beaucoup!*" he kept saying over and over as he munched away.

"You are very welcome," I replied in German, before taking off my apron and heading over to Reinhardt with the cakes. "Inga asked me to bring these up to her," I said, holding my breath and hoping that he wouldn't tell one of his staff to take them instead. Thankfully, he was busy adding the final garnish to piece of fried fish, so he just nodded.

Look straight ahead and with purpose, I told myself as I walked across the lobby. Fortunately, it was quiet as most of the staff were in the restaurant having dinner. Deciding to avoid waiting for the elevator in case I got apprehended, I slipped through the doors into the stairwell. As I reached the first floor, I peered through the small panes of glass in the doors leading to the rooms. Could I risk taking a quick look? I could always say I'd got lost if I was caught, and feign ignorance, and Inga would be able to vouch for the fact that she'd asked me to bring her the cakes.

I pushed through the doors into the corridor before my fear stopped me. Signs in German had been put on the bedroom doors, above the room numbers, and midway along the corridor they'd hung a large portrait of Hitler. Spying a door near the end that was slightly ajar, I kept walking toward it, my pulse quickening. *I'm trying to find Inga*, I mentally rehearsed my cover story in my head. *She asked me to bring these cakes.*

I slowed right down as I drew level with the door and glanced inside. The former guest bedroom now contained a row of desks housing typewriters. There didn't appear to be anyone inside. Could I risk taking a proper look? If I got caught, I'd be in trouble for sure as there was no way I could say I was there for Inga. Seeing a desk just a couple of feet inside, I decided to take the risk. An open box of index cards sat in the middle, with a card out beside it. The name Albert Gaveau was written at the top, along with an address. Something else was written underneath and the name Boris Vildé. I stared at the card trying to memorize both names. Albert Gaveau was clearly French, but why did the *Abwehr* have his details?

Before I could think anymore, I heard footsteps coming toward me along the corridor. Damn! I quickly slipped behind the door, so that if whoever was coming glanced inside, they wouldn't see me. If they came in, however, it would be a completely different story. As the footsteps drew louder and closer, I was hit by a waft of caramel from the canelés. What if they smelled the cakes too and came in to investigate? *Please, please, please, whoever you are please be suffering from a blocked nose,* I silently prayed.

The footsteps stopped as if whoever it was was looking in. Then, to my horror, the door closed and I heard a key turn in the lock. I almost dropped the tray of canelés in shock. How was I going to get out of there? How was I going to explain being locked in there? I looked around frantically and saw a door on the other side of the room, which I assumed led to the bathroom. I hurried over, my heart pounding and my face burning. This was a complete disaster. Why did I think that I had what it took to spy on the Germans? I should never have left the kitchen.

As I'd predicted, the door opened onto a sumptuous bath-room, complete with claw-footed tub. There was another door on the opposite wall, by the sink, but did it lead to an adjoining room, or was it merely a closet? Being careful not to make a sound, I placed the plate of cakes on the side by the sink and tiptoed over to peer through the keyhole. To my relief, I saw that it opened onto another bedroom, although it too had been turned into some kind of office. As far as I could make out, there was no one in the room, so I took my chances and slowly turned the handle. The door opened with a theatrical creak. I picked up the cakes and tiptoed inside. Every desk in this room housed a transmitter radio. What were they for? I wondered. Transmit-ting messages, or intercepting them? I took a quick look around, but I was too concerned with trying to escape to have a proper look.

I went over to the main door and said a quick prayer before trying the handle. When it opened, I almost passed out from the relief. I stood with the door ajar for a moment, checking there was no sound of anyone coming, then I slipped back into the corridor and raced toward the stairs. In my haste, one of the canelés dropped to the floor, but before I could pick it up, I heard a door opening behind me so I had no choice but to leave it there.

Back in the stairwell, I took a moment to try to compose myself. My hands were trembling and my skin was covered in a clammy sweat. That had been way too close for comfort. I hurried up to the third floor, my relief soon replaced by a feeling of panic. Someone was bound to find the dropped cake. Wouldn't they wonder how it got there? I couldn't afford to worry about that now, though, I'd already been gone long enough. I had to get the remaining cakes to Inga and get back to the kitchen.

I made my way along the corridor and knocked on her door, my hand still trembling.

"Come in!" she called.

I opened the door and stepped inside. This room still had a bed, but a large desk had been placed by the window, where Inga sat, bathed in the golden glow of a lamp. Some papers were spread out in front of her. She quickly opened the top drawer of the desk and swept them inside.

"Oh, thank goodness!" she exclaimed with a smile. "Please, come in."

I took the cakes over to her and placed them on the desk.

"Oh my," she said. "They look delicious."

"They're called canelés. They originated in Bordeaux." I glanced down at the desk, wondering what it was she hadn't wanted me to see. I decided to keep talking to try to buy myself some more snooping time. "The winemakers there used to use egg whites to clarify their wine, so they'd give the surplus yolks to the local convents and the nuns invented canelés as a way of using them up. The word canelé means fluted, and they're made in special fluted copper tins." I noticed an open wooden box on the desk. There were three compartments inside; one of them was open and contained a rubber stamp, the kind you'd use for official documents. "They have to be copper as copper is a great conductor of heat and makes the outsides of the cakes nice and crispy."

She laughed as she closed the lid on the wooden box. "You really are a mine of information."

"Sorry, I'm just passionate about pastries."

"Please don't apologize, it's so nice to talk about something lovely like cakes for a change. It's so nice to talk to a woman." She smiled at me again, but this time it was tinged with something else, a wistfulness perhaps.

"Yes, I suppose you must spend a lot of your time here with men," I offered, spotting an opportunity. "A bit like me, down in the kitchen."

"Yes!" she exclaimed. Her gaze flitted to a small corner table housing some glasses and a couple of crystal bottles of liquor. "I don't suppose..." She looked back at me. "Would you care to join me for a drink?"

"Oh—uh—that would be lovely, thank you," I replied, surprised, but eager to make the most of this unexpected opportunity.

"Whisky or brandy?" she asked. "I'm afraid I don't have anything lighter. As I said, I spend most of my time these days in the company of men."

"They certainly can drive you to drink," I quipped and she giggled.

"Oh, I didn't mean it that way, but yes, yes they can!"

"Brandy please," I said, and she gestured at me to sit down on one of the armchairs by the fireplace. My mind started racing as I watched her open an ice bucket and clink some cubes into the glasses using a pair of silver tongs. I needed to be careful not to stay too long as I couldn't afford to upset Reinhardt, but, on the other hand, I'd waited so long for an opportunity to get closer to a member of the *Abwehr*. And getting closer to Admiral Canaris's secretary felt like hitting the jackpot.

"So, tell me, what's it like down there in the kitchen?" she asked, bringing our drinks over and sitting down beside me. "Some of the men down there seem a little..." She paused, a smile playing on her rosebud lips.

"Neanderthal?" I suggested, thinking of Gunter.

Inga burst out laughing. "Yes! I was trying to find a more subtle word to describe it, but yes, neanderthal."

"It's actually not too bad. Some of them are quite sweet and Reinhardt, the head chef, is really great to work for." To my annoyance, I felt my face begin to blush as I said this. I think Inga noticed too, as she gave me a knowing smile.

"Yes, he really is a lovely man and such a talented chef. I'm always glad when I'm sent down to talk to him about a menu. It makes a very pleasant change."

I wondered if she meant compared to the *Abwehr* agents. "I'm guessing the men you normally have to deal with can be quite intimidating," I said, in what I hoped was a casual tone.

"Huh. I don't tend to get intimidated by men all that easily," she said with a shrug. "Sadly, I find a lot of them distinctly unimpressive." She leaned closer and lowered her voice. "Even the Führer."

"You've met Hitler?" I fought to not look too shocked.

"Of course." She gave me a conspiratorial grin. "Very little charm, and terrible skin," she whispered. "He has these huge pores on his neck, like the skin of a chicken."

I leaned back on the sofa and laughed. Then it occurred to me that this might be some kind of test to see how I felt about Hitler, so I quickly wiped the smile from my face. "Your French is very good," I said, deciding to change the subject. "I'm trying to learn some German at the moment, to make my work easier in the kitchen, and I'm in awe of anyone who's fluent in another language."

"I can actually speak three," she said, taking a sip of her drink. "German, French and English. My father sent me to school in England and I stayed on at college there, and the London School of Economics."

"Oh." Again, I fought to contain my surprise, but she clearly noticed it as she started to frown.

"Please don't tell me you're one of those people who are shocked at a woman getting a further education. I thought you French women were feistier than that."

"We are. And I'm not!" I exclaimed. "I was more shocked that your father had sent you to England—rather than have you educated in Germany," I added.

She nodded. "Let's just say that my father thought it would be better for me to be out of the country, but then the war started, so I had to go back to Berlin."

"And that's when you started working for the *Abwehr*?" I risked asking.

"Yes."

I wasn't sure if I'd asked a question too far, as she downed the rest of her drink and stood up.

"Well, I'd better get back to my work," she said.

"Yes of course. Me too." I put my glass down on the side table and stood up. "It was lovely talking to you."

"And you." She walked me to the door. I felt a growing sense of dread that I might have ruined my opportunity, but, to my relief, she gave me a warm smile. "Thank you so much for the lovely cakes. They will make my night's work a lot more bearable, I'm sure."

"You're very welcome. I hope your work goes well."

What could she be doing, I wondered, that would keep her working late into the night?

I made my way downstairs, planning to find Raphael at the first opportunity. Finally, I had some tangible information to share with him, and hopefully he'd be pleased at my attempts to befriend Canaris's personal secretary, and someone who had met Hitler. But as I reached the bottom of the stairs, I heard a commotion coming from the lobby. A crowd of *Abwehr* agents were coming in through the revolving doors, and as they got closer, I saw that they were frogmarching two men in civilian clothes. I stood, still as a statue with my back pressed to the wall, as the group approached and marched right past me to the elevators. As they passed, I saw that the officers had a woman captive too. She looked terrified.

One of the Germans started to laugh as they waited for the elevator to arrive.

"Did you really think that the *Abwehr* wouldn't find you?" he said in French in a mocking tone. "Now you will see what we do to the people who resist us."

For a fleeting second, the woman's terrified gaze met mine and it was as if her fear coursed right through me.

24

FEBRUARY 1941, PARIS

The next day, I was so distracted I committed the mortal sin of forgetting to add the yeast to my bread and I had to frantically try to salvage things and make a new batch of baguettes. I'd barely slept at all when I got back from the hotel. All I could think about were the people I'd seen being dragged into the Lutetia and the look of terror in the woman's eyes. What had the *Abwehr* agent meant when he'd said "now you will see what we do to people who resist us?" Was he talking about torture? It was a chilling reminder of what could happen to me if I got caught. Any time I thought of the canelé I'd dropped, I felt a fresh surge of fear.

The morning passed in a numb haze of baking and serving people their bread rations. When Raphael appeared at the end of the afternoon, I almost collapsed to my knees in relief to see someone I could confide in. My relief was short-lived, however.

"Something terrible has happened," he said by way of greeting, locking the door and closing the shutters.

"What is it?" I asked, instantly feeling panicked.

He took off his hat and came over to the counter. His normally immaculate hair was unkempt, and his chin dark with stubble. "The people who produce the Resistance paper have been caught."

"No!" I exclaimed.

He nodded, grim-faced. "Somebody informed on them to the *Abwehr*."

"When did this happen?"

"Yesterday."

I shuddered. "Did the *Abwehr* bring them to the Lutetia?"

"I don't know, I wasn't working yesterday."

"I was, and I saw some people being brought in by the *Abwehr*. Two men and a woman. I heard one of the agents say that they were going to learn what they did to people who resist them."

Raphael slammed his hand on the counter. "*Merde!*"

"Do you—do you think they're going to torture them?"

"I'm certain of it. Where are the papers I gave you to distribute?"

"Down in the cellar."

"You need to burn them. Right now." I'd never seen him look so rattled and it was really unnerving.

"Of course." Then I remembered what I'd found on the first floor of the hotel on my way to seeing Inga. Perhaps it would be of some use to Raphael. "I saw something in the hotel last night, before I saw the people who'd been arrested."

"Oh yes?"

"Yes, I snuck into one of the rooms and I saw some index cards on a desk. One of them had two names on it. Boris Vildé—"

"Boris Vildé?" He visibly paled.

"Yes, do you know who he is?"

He nodded. "He's one of the producers of the paper. He was arrested yesterday. What was the other name?"

"Albert Gaveau."

"Right. I wonder..." He frowned.

"What?"

"If he was the informant. Good work, Coralie."

"Thank you." I breathed a sigh of relief.

Raphael gave me a grim smile and put on his cap. "I need to go. Don't forget to destroy the papers, and if anyone comes here with the code to collect them, you're to pretend you don't know what they're talking about, because it could be a trap."

"Understood."

I locked the door behind him, then hurried through to the kitchen and retrieved the pile of Resistance papers. As I scanned the stenciled header with its little hand-drawn flame as the dot above the i, my heart ached for the brave men and women who'd risked everything to produce it. What would become of them now? How would the *Abwehr* punish them?

I lit a fire in the small grate in the store and threw the papers on top, watching as they started glowing red at the edges before bursting into flame.

"I'm so sorry this happened to you," I whispered as I watched their words go up in smoke.

A loud rap on the door tore me from my sorrow and sent me into an instant panic. What if it was the *Abwehr*? What if one of the people they'd captured had broken under torture and exposed the distribution network? Or what if someone had discovered the canelé I'd dropped on the floor? My fear rose as there was another knock on the door. I could pretend to be out, but they'd no doubt see the smoke coming from the chimney. I prodded the burning pages with the poker to encourage the fire to burn faster, then unlocked the door. As I opened it a couple of inches I saw the green-gray of the German uniform and my stomach dropped.

25

FEBRUARY 1941, PARIS

Time seemed to stand still as I stood frozen to the spot but then I heard Reinhardt's voice. The blood was pumping so fast in my ears I couldn't make out his words.

"Pardon?" I squeaked in response, opening the door a few inches more.

"I've brought you a present, to say thank you for your great work last night," he said, holding out a container.

"Oh." I thought of the Resistance papers still burning in the grate and felt paralyzed by fear.

"It's Strasbourg sausage."

"Oh," I said again, still numb with shock.

"I thought you might be hungry."

My shock finally wore off. *Everyone in France is hungry*, I wanted to yell, *apart from you Germans.*

"You don't have to have it if you don't want to. I just..." He broke off. "It was my favorite meal as a child and I wanted to share it with you."

I heard footsteps approaching along the street. "OK, come in," I said, quickly ushering him inside. The last thing I needed was one of my loyal customers seeing me fraternizing with a German.

"Ah, it's so nice and warm in here," he said, making a beeline for the fire.

I watched, horrified, as he put the food down on the counter and warmed his hands in front of the flames. What if the papers hadn't all burned properly? What if he saw the Resistance header?

"Come with me, let me get you a drink," I said, grabbing Reinhardt by the arm and steering him behind the counter.

"Thank you, that would be lovely." He gave me a grateful smile.

I glanced over his shoulder and my heart almost stopped beating as I saw a piece of paper curl and spiral up the chimney, the letters RESIS still clearly visible. I grabbed Reinhardt's arm and practically dragged him upstairs.

"I'm afraid I don't have much room," I said as his eyes scanned the studio, taking in the armchairs, the small kitchenette and the unmade bed in the corner. "Please, take a seat." I steered him over to the kitchen table and lit the candles in the middle. *Why oh why hadn't I made my bed?* And what if he thought I'd brought him up here for a reason other than to eat and drink? One of Olive's lectures from my childhood came back to haunt me. "Never let a man see your petticoat, never let him touch your knee, and never, under any circumstances, invite him into your bedroom—unless you're married to him." What would she think if she could see me now?

"Are you sure this is all right?" Reinhardt said, as if detecting my unease. "My being here, I mean."

"Of course!" I replied gaily, pulling out a chair for him. "But I want to make it clear that I have only invited you into my kitchen. The fact that it is also my bedroom is just an unfortunate twist of fate and due to a chronic lack of space."

"Oh, yes, yes, of course." He glanced at the bed and his face flushed and I realized to my relief that he was just as embarrassed about it as me.

I took two plates from the cabinet above the sink and put them on the table. "Would you like to do the honors and serve?" I asked.

"Of course." Clearly relieved to have the focus move away from my boudoir, he opened the container and dished the food onto the plates. As well as the sausages, he'd made golden roast potatoes and creamy mounds of pale orange mashed vegetables that I guessed were a mixture of carrots and turnips. The smell instantly caused me to drool and I felt a stab of annoyance at myself for being so weak-willed. I shouldn't feel grateful to him for feeding me—his leaders were the ones starving me after all.

But then I took a mouthful of the sausage, and another, and I was flooded with gratitude. It was so good, so flavorful. The seasoning was exquisite and the gravy was like nothing I'd ever tasted before—rich and oniony with a hint of red wine. And the contrast between the crispy exterior of the roast potatoes and the soft fluffy interior was divine.

"This is incredible—delicious," I said in my novice German through mouthfuls.

"Thank you." He smiled. "That makes me very happy to hear. And to hear it in German too. Hans is teaching you well."

"Never mind me learning German," I replied. "I want to learn how to make this gravy. Did you make the sausage too?"

"I did."

"I've never tasted anything like it!"

He grinned from ear to ear and it made me feel warm inside to think that my opinion clearly meant so much to him. It also made me like him more, to see him so humble despite his obvious talents. It was a very attractive trait. "I'm so glad you like it. I was experimenting with the seasoning."

"Well, it worked. You'll have to tell me the recipe."

"A good chef never discloses his secrets." He grinned. "Although..."

"What?" I was aware that there was gravy trickling down my chin, but I didn't care. It had been so long since I'd had a hearty meal like this, I felt slightly out of control.

"If you were prepared to teach me how you make pastry, then perhaps I could find it in my heart to let you know the secret to my sausage and gravy. I think it would be a fair exchange—even though you, as you've previously pointed out, are one of the best chefs in the world and I, a mere novice." His eyes twinkled at me in the candlelight and I couldn't help grinning back. He had such a knack for putting me at ease.

"Hmm, perhaps I could teach you one form of pastry in exchange for both the gravy and the sausage recipe—given that I am one of the world's best."

"It's a deal." He held his hand out to me across the table and we shook. His hand was warm and his grip surprisingly strong.

"So, you're not cooking at the hotel tonight?" I said after shoveling down some more of the food.

"No, it's my night off."

We continued eating in silence for a while, then he looked at the radio.

"Do you like listening to music?"

"I love it."

"Shall we put the radio on?"

"Of course." It was only when I stood up that I realized I had it tuned to BBC Radio Londres.

I glanced over my shoulder and saw that he was watching me. *Damn.* I moved to try to block his view and quickly turned the volume right down before turning the radio on and moving the tuning dial. I turned the volume back up and the room filled with the crackling sound of static. While I tried to find some music, I reminded myself that my main priority should be helping the Resistance and Reinhardt was my best potential source of information about the *Abwehr*, especially now he was in my kitchen away from the prying ears of the other Germans.

"Can I ask you a question?" I said as I sat back down.

"Of course." He wiped his mouth on his napkin.

"I saw something yesterday, at the hotel, and it confused me."

"It wasn't Gunter's attempts at a soufflé, was it?" he joked. "That confused me too. He took them out of the oven way too soon."

I forced myself to laugh, but inside my nerves were building. I needed to be really careful about how I phrased my next question as I didn't want to arouse any suspicion. "I saw some people being brought into the hotel last night—one of them was a woman and she looked really upset. I think they might have been arrested."

"Oh." His whole demeanor changed and he looked down at the table, his shoulders hunched. "I don't know anything about that," he muttered.

Worried that I might have blown it, I decided to try a new tactic. "I hope you don't mind me asking, I just get so scared sometimes."

He instantly looked concerned. "Of what?"

"Of doing or saying something wrong. It's a very strange feeling, having another country occupy yours and bringing in so many new rules."

"I don't think you have anything to worry about," he said warmly. "Especially if you keep making those delicious pastries. Most of us have never tasted cakes like that before." He smiled. "I've never seen *Abwehr* agents moan with pleasure the way they do over your desserts. It's as if you've cast a spell over them."

"That's good to hear." I smiled back at him, relieved that I seemed to have repaired any damage my previous question might have caused. I was fast learning that life as a Resistance agent meant becoming adept at finding the conversational sweet spot between asking too much and not enough.

"Please don't be scared," he said softly and he looked so concerned, I actually felt a little guilty for lying to him.

"I won't be now you've put my mind at rest," I said, deciding not to push it any further. "Thank you."

He smiled and leaned back in his chair. "So, when do I get my lesson in pastry making?"

"How do I know I can trust you?" I joked. "What if I disclose my top secret and you never tell me how to make the sausage and gravy."

He looked thoughtful for a moment, then his eyes lit up. "I have a proposition."

"Go on."

"How about every week we meet for a cooking lesson and we each share a secret recipe? Or I share two for every one of yours," he added, raising his eyebrows.

I nodded. I liked this idea for two reasons—firstly, it would mean more time with Reinhardt to build his trust and try to find out more about the *Abwehr*, and secondly, I was always open to the idea of learning new recipes. "I think that's a very good idea," I said. "It sounds like fun."

"Oh, there'll be no fun in my lessons," he said mock seriously. "I demand utter silence and a somber mood at all times in my kitchen."

"Well, I know that isn't true," I replied. "I work in your kitchen, remember? I've seen the way you are with your staff. I like the way you joke with them but still command their respect. You create a really nice atmosphere."

He gave me a grateful smile. "Thank you. That really means a lot to me." He looked down at his plate and fiddled with his knife and fork. "Do you remember me telling you how going to work in a kitchen saved me?"

"After your mother died?"

"Yes."

I nodded.

"Most of the other men in my kitchen come from difficult backgrounds too, especially Hans—he was orphaned as a young kid."

I felt a pang of sympathy as I thought of the sweet-natured Hans.

"I'm willing to guess that most kitchens are the same," Reinhardt continued. "And because I understand that, I try to make it feel like a family, where everyone's accepted and respected, as long as they work hard."

"I really like that." As I contemplated his words, I forgot about the wider situation and the occupation and the war. All I could think about was how I, too, had found my sense of purpose and self-worth in a kitchen, through baking. "I was found abandoned as a baby," I said quietly.

He stared at me. "What do you mean, abandoned?"

"My real parents, whoever they were, left me on the doorstep of a bakery, wrapped in a towel."

He gave a whistle of surprise.

"Thankfully, the owners of the bakery took me in and named me after the towel and—"

"They named you Towel?" he interrupted, eyes wide.

"No!" I laughed. "Coralie, after the color. The towel was a bright orangey-pink."

"Oh, I see."

"And the bakery owners eventually adopted me," I continued, "but I always felt a strange sense of not really belonging, and a feeling of..." I paused.

"Yes?" he said softly, leaning closer.

"Not being good enough," I muttered.

"What do you mean?" He looked at me intently. "Did your adoptive parents make you feel like that?"

"No. They were lovely. It was my real parents. The fact that they were able to just leave me there on my own in the cold, that feeling of not being wanted. I was never able to shake it. I hated not knowing where I came from."

He nodded. "That must be hard."

"I loved what you said about your mother, about the way you see her passion for cooking in you, and how it connects you to her even though she isn't here anymore."

He gave a sad smile.

"I don't have that, and I never will. I'll never know who I come from, who I truly am." My voice began to waver, so I stopped talking and took a sip of my drink. What was I doing, confiding in him like this? I'd never even told Madame Monteux these things. "But once I discovered my love of baking, I finally had something—something I was good at, a sense of worth and identity."

He nodded. "I understand completely."

I gulped hard, feeling close to tears.

"Can I say something?" he asked, leaning even closer across the table.

I nodded and a tear spilled onto my cheek.

"You don't need to know who your birth parents are to know who you are. Can I tell you who I see when I look at you?"

I nodded again.

"Yes, I see a talented pastry chef, but I also see someone who is brave and strong and who won't be pushed around."

"What do you mean?" I felt a flurry of panic. Had he worked out that I was working for the Resistance?

"Well, for example, that time you told me in no uncertain terms that you didn't need any help from me as you were a French pastry chef and they were the best in the world."

I cringed. "I hope you didn't think I was conceited."

"Not in the circumstances, no."

"What do you mean?"

He paused for a moment as if unsure whether to continue. "I feel pretty certain I would have reacted the same way if the situation had been reversed."

I gave him a relieved smile.

"I think you're a great person, Coralie, and I only wish..."

"What?" I whispered.

"That we'd met in different circumstances."

"Thank you. I wish that too." And I realized in that moment that I really meant it.

He smiled and got to his feet. "I should get back, but I'd really like it if we could give each other cooking lessons."

"I'd really like that too." I stood up and accompanied him downstairs. The fire in the grate had gone out and it was pitch-dark.

"Goodnight, Towel," Reinhardt said as we reached the door.

I burst out laughing and jokily hit him on the chest.

"Sorry, *Coralie*," he said and for a moment we were so close, I could feel his breath on my cheek and it made me shiver.

"Goodnight, Reinhardt," I said, returning to my senses and unlocking the door.

As I watched him walk away into the night, I tried to process what had just happened. What I'd just felt. I knew he was a German, and as such, I couldn't afford to trust him, but our conversation had changed something deep inside of me. It was as if by opening up to him, he'd knocked a chink off the armor guarding my heart.

26

JULY 1984, SAN FRANCISCO

"How was your friend?" my grandma asks, as we wait for the tart to bake and I continue to ponder how and why she could have fallen in love with a Nazi.

"Oh, OK I guess," I answer distractedly.

"Was she calling about an affair of the heart?" she asks, and now she has my full attention.

"I'm sorry?" I say, staring at her.

"Did she have news of a romantic nature?"

"How did you..." I break off, remembering how I'd blurted out the word "romantic." "Oh, uh, yes, kind of."

"I'm sorry, I couldn't help eavesdropping." She gives me a guilty grin.

"No problem. I was right in front of you. You had no choice but to overhear."

"Yes, but there was a time when I was a professional eavesdropper." She laughs. "So I'm afraid my ears have been trained to overhear things."

"What do you mean?" I ask, instantly curious and wondering if she's talking about her life during the war.

"Oh, it's a long story." She waves her hand as if batting my question away. "I'd far rather hear about your friend. What's she like? How long have you known her? What does she want to do with her life?"

Once again, I feel conflicted about my grandma. She might have a dark past, but it sure is refreshing to have an adult genuinely interested in me and my friends.

So I tell her all about Melissa and how, like me, she dreams of the day when the countries of the world will live together in peace and how she wants to be a music journo and she writes mock reviews of the latest records in her exercise book during math class. And how she hates math and thinks that if God had wanted us to know algebra, he would have given us at least one situation in life when we would actually need it.

My grandma snorts with laughter at this. "She sounds a little like my friend Madame Monteux," she says. "She had a great sense of humor too."

"Had?" I say softly and her smile fades.

"Yes. She's no longer with us sadly."

"When were you friends with her?"

"Oh, years and years ago—in Paris."

"During the war?" I quickly ask.

"Yes, and before."

I note that she doesn't say after.

"You know the cake I made for you yesterday?" she says.

"How could I forget it?"

She gives a shy smile. "Thank you. Well, I first created it for her, over forty years ago, when she was going through a tough time."

"Wow, that's a long time ago."

"I know! And I hadn't made it ever since. That's why I was so relieved you liked it."

I feel a tingle of excitement. This could be my opportunity to get her to open up some more. "What made you make it for me, after so long?"

"I could tell you'd been going through a hard time too and..." She breaks off with a smile.

"Yes?" I say gently.

"Madame Monteux liked to believe that my baking had special powers because I'd always stir an intention into the mixture."

"What do you mean?"

"It seems silly now," she says, clearly a little embarrassed, "but I'd picture myself stirring things like love or strength or happiness or hope in with the other ingredients."

I have a flashback to earlier that morning when I'd found her whispering into the mixing bowl about love and peace.

"I bet you think I'm crazy." She laughs. "Please don't tell Suzette. She'll probably have me shipped off to a home for the old and senile."

"I won't." I grin.

"I named your mother after Madame Monteux, you know. Her first name was Suzette."

"Oh wow, I always wondered how Mom got to have such a cool name. Is it French?"

She nods.

"How come you call her Madame Monteux instead of Suzette? It sounds kind of formal for a friend."

"She was my boss when I moved to the center of Paris when I was eighteen. I was her housekeeper. And she was such a formidable character, it kind of stuck, even when she asked me to call her Suzette." She gives a wistful smile. "She was always Madame Monteux to me, even when I no longer worked for her."

"Oh, I see."

"As soon as she tasted my baking, she insisted I get a job as a pastry chef, and that's how I ended up at the hotel I told you about."

"Working for the Germans?" I ask, jumping at the opportunity to steer the conversation in that direction.

She hesitates before replying. "Yes. And she was the friend who bought me the patisserie when the German occupation began."

I think of the photo of the Patisserie Resilience in the album with the swastika and a shiver runs up my spine. Could I finally be about to find out how it got there? And how the album got in her drawer? I need to go gently though, not make her clam up again. "What was she like?" I ask.

My grandma gives me a sad smile. "She was one of the most positive and hopeful people I ever met, and she lived her life to the absolute fullest until..."

"Until what?" I ask softly, crossing my fingers beneath the table. *Please, please, please, let her answer.*

She gets up from the table suddenly. "I need to check on the tart."

"No!" I can't help exclaiming and she stares at me, shocked.

"Why not. We don't want it to burn."

"I wasn't talking about the tart," I mumble, looking down at my lap, my face flushing. *Damn my stupid mouth!* Suzette is always telling me I need to think before I speak, but sometimes the words shoot straight past the thinking part of my brain and burst right out—and often in the worst of circumstances. Like right now.

"What *were* you talking about then?" my grandma asks, and a terrible silence falls upon the kitchen.

27

MAY 1941, PARIS

For the next couple of months my life fell into a new routine. Working in the patisserie from Monday to Saturday, at the Lutetia on Sundays, and having cooking lessons with Reinhardt every Monday on his night off. On the night of our first class he arrived at the store with a brown covered notebook.

"I thought we could keep a record of the things we make," he said. "Somewhere for us to write down the recipes."

"So, you're planning on making this a regular thing?" I said, trying to ignore the feeling of excitement I was experiencing at this prospect.

"Oh, yes, uh, if that's all right with you?"

I smiled and nodded. It felt surprisingly, almost worryingly all right with me. I opened the book and saw that he'd written an inscription in German on the first page.

Die Rezepte des besten französischen Konditors der Welt und eines bescheidenen deutschen Kochs!

Thanks to my German lessons with Hans in the kitchen I was able to translate some of the words. "The best recipes ... French ... world ... German ... cook," I said falteringly.

"The recipes of the best French pastry chef in the world," he said with a grin, "and a lowly German cook."

I burst out laughing and shook my head. "I never said that I was the best in the world."

"Hmm, I think you did." He stepped closer and just like that evening by the store door, the air between us seemed to crackle and spark. "If I remember correctly, upon meeting for the first time you informed me that, as a French pastry chef, you were the best in the world, and had been since you were five years old."

I picked up a tea towel and flicked it at him. "I didn't say I'd been the best since I was five!" I paused. "I didn't become the best until I was seven at least!"

"Ah, such modesty." He chuckled. "I feel so honored to be in your presence." He pulled the towel from my hand and clutched it to his chest.

"What are you doing?" I asked.

"Trying to absorb some of your greatness. Perhaps you have left a trace on this cloth." He made a show of clutching it even tighter.

I grabbed the end and tried to tug it back, but he wouldn't let go and pulled me closer to him instead, so close our faces were only inches apart. For a brief, charged moment, I felt the strongest impulse to kiss him.

Quickly coming to my senses, I dropped the towel and took a step back. "Enough of this nonsense," I said in a stern tone, hoping he hadn't noticed my blushes. "Let our first class commence." I picked up a pen and wrote *The World's Greatest Puff Pastry* on the first page.

Our cooking classes soon became the highlight of my week. For a few hours, I was able to escape my thoughts and fears of the war as we cooked and chatted and laughed and listened to music. Reinhardt always brought a bottle of wine and at the end of the evening, we'd have a drink and feast on whatever we'd made. I'd have moments when I'd wonder if it was wise to become so close to a German, but the truth was, I'd come to treasure our friendship and I always was able to console myself with the thought that I was getting close to Reinhardt in order to help the Resistance.

It was impossible to forget about the war at any other time, though. In April 1941, all Jewish bank accounts were frozen and although Madame Monteux tried her hardest to remain cheery, the cracks were beginning to show. Baptiste and I took it in turns to visit her to make sure she never had to spend a day alone.

Then, one day in the middle of May, she arrived at the store, ashen-faced.

"It has begun!" she cried as she hurried over to the counter.

"What has?"

"They're deporting the Jews."

I stared at her, horrified. "Who are? Where to?"

"The government. The police tricked foreign Jews living in Paris to report to the authorities. They made it sound as if it was just a routine status check, but when they got there, they were arrested on the spot. Thousands of them have been deported on trains from Gare d'Austerlitz. Oh, Coralie, what am I going to do?"

It was the first time I'd seen the normally formidable Madame Monteux so openly at a loss, and it was a terrifying sight.

"Did you say it was foreign Jews?"

"Yes, Poles mainly and I think some Czech."

As much as this sickened me, I had to try to find some hope for her to cling to. "Well, I'm sure that as a French Jew, you'll be safe. I know our government is lousy, but there's no way they'd deport their own people."

"But don't you understand?" she cried, her dark eyes wide with alarm. "They no longer see me as one of their own. They see me as a Jew. They've taken away my right to work. They've taken away my money. Of course they'd be willing to deport me too."

Just at that moment, Baptiste arrived in the store, looking dapper as ever in his suit and fedora. "Duchess!" he exclaimed. "I'm so glad I've run into you. I was wondering if you'd do me the honor of escorting me on a walk." But when she turned to him and he saw her tear-stained face, he let out a gasp. "What's wrong?" As she told him the news, his expression changed from one of concern to horror and then anger. "How can this be happening?" he said furiously. "After everything we went through in the Great War. Georges Clemenceau must be spinning in his grave." He took hold of her hands. "I know you're as grand as a duchess and not accustomed to expressions of physical affection from the hoi polloi, but would it be all right if I gave you a hug?"

She nodded and he wrapped his arms around her and, while I found their show of affection heartwarming, I still felt sick. What if Madame Monteux was right? What if the French Jews were the next to be deported? Where would they be deported to? I thought better of asking Madame Monteux this question for fear of upsetting her further, deciding to ask Raphael if he knew the next time I saw him.

Once Madame Monteux and Baptiste had gone for their walk, I locked the store and went upstairs. I had a cooking class with Reinhardt that night and I'd been planning on teaching him how to make éclairs, but now my heart wasn't in it. All I wanted to do was bake something for Madame Monteux, something to make her feel better, but how on earth could a cake possibly help at a time like this? I sat at the table feeling utterly despondent and I still hadn't been able to shake the feeling when Reinhardt arrived.

"What's wrong?" he asked as soon as we were upstairs in the kitchen.

"Nothing, what makes you ask that?" I said hastily.

"You're not your usual color."

"My color?" I looked down at my green dress. It was one I'd definitely worn before. Thanks to the clothes rations, my wardrobe hadn't been updated in a long time.

"Yes." He looked embarrassed. "This may sound stupid..."

"That's never stopped you before," I couldn't resist quipping.

"I always associate people with colors. It's something I've done since I was a kid. I thought it was normal, until I told my mother about it and she told me no one else does this." He laughed.

"Go on?" I asked, intrigued.

"I'm not sure what it is—something about the way a person acts or how they look, but I've always translated that into a color. For example, Gunter in the kitchen is beet purple."

I thought of Gunter's ruddy cheeks and laughed. "Yes. I can see that. And what about Hans?" I asked.

"White," he answered. "He's so pure."

Again, it made sense.

"So what color am I normally?"

"Yellow," he replied without missing a beat. "Like sunshine."

"Really?" I stared at him, incredulous. Ever since the occupation had started, I'd felt more like a dull rain cloud than bright sunshine. I pulled a mock frown. "I hope this isn't some elaborate line you're feeding me, Chef. Just because I happen to have a bed in my kitchen, it doesn't make me a loose woman."

"No, of course not!" he exclaimed, falling for my joke, and his face flushed bright red. "You just always seem sunny to me."

"I think you must bring that out in me then because most days I feel exceptionally cloudy, especially today."

"Why today?" He looked at me curiously.

Damn, yet again I'd said too much. "I'm just worried about a friend. She came by earlier and she was very upset."

"Is it the same friend I saw here once before? The woman with the long silver hair?"

I thought back to the day he'd seen Madame Monteux when she'd been holding the flyer—an occasion so fraught with fear, it had been seared into my memory. "Yes, and I wanted to make her a cake to cheer her up, but I couldn't think of anything. It's the first time that's ever happened to me. Normally, I always know what to bake."

"Hmm." He frowned.

I wondered if he was remembering the gold Star of David pendant Madame Monteux had been wearing the day he saw her and if the reason for his frown was because I had a Jewish friend. I felt my hackles rise. If he dared say anything to that effect, he'd see my color change to an angry shade of red.

"It sounds as if you're thinking too much," he said finally. "I have an idea." He paused. "It involves me blindfolding you; would that be OK?"

"What?" I stared at him. "I repeat, just because I have a bed in my kitchen, it doesn't mean—"

"I promise I'm not trying to seduce you," he interrupted with a laugh. "You have to trust me."

It was a very ironic statement given the circumstances, but the truth was, by that point and in that moment, I did trust him, implicitly, so I nodded.

"Excellent." He looked around and spotted one of my scarves hanging on the back of a chair. "May I?" he asked.

"I suppose so." I sat there while he gently tied the scarf around my eyes, trying to ignore how I shivered when his hands touched my hair.

"It's not too tight?" he asked.

"No."

"But you can't see anything?"

"No."

"OK, good."

I sat and listened as I heard a rustle of the bag he'd brought and things being placed on the kitchen counter. Finally, he came back over and placed his hand on my arm.

"Do you remember our class from a couple of weeks ago, when you told me how your lavender choux buns came to be?"

"Yes. When I had the strangest hunch that lavender might work well with lemon," I replied, smiling at the memory.

"Exactly. And you told me that so much of what you create in the kitchen is based on instinct and intuition."

"Yes."

"The day you told me that changed everything for me."

I fought the urge to tear off my blindfold so I could look at him. "What do you mean?"

"I do the same thing now, when I cook, and it's become the most incredible experience." He laughed softly. "I never know what's going to happen! So now I want to return the favor and remind you of what you taught me."

I gave a bemused smile. "By blindfolding me?"

"I've arranged a variety of ingredients in dishes on the counter. I want you to think of your friend and how you want your cake to make her feel and then reach for the ingredients that feel right."

"But I won't know what they are."

"Exactly." He laughed again. "You'll need to use your intuition more than ever before."

I thought he was crazy for suggesting such a thing, but I did as I was told and closed my eyes behind the blindfold and thought of Madame Monteux. As Reinhardt led me over to the counter I pictured her biting into something I'd made her and all the sadness melting from her face and her mouth curving up into one of her beautiful beaming smiles. Then I put my hands out in front of me and instinctively reached to the right and my hands felt a dish.

"This one," I said.

"OK, good." He took the dish and I heard him place it on the table. "And what else?"

I allowed my hands to hover over the counter as if I was divining for water. "This one," I said, as I felt my hand being drawn to the left. And so it continued until I'd chosen five of the dishes.

"And now for the big reveal," Reinhardt said, before untying the blindfold.

I blinked and looked down at the table. I'd chosen a dish containing chunks of dark chocolate. Another containing vanilla pods. So far so good. Then I spied a bowl of courgettes and let out a hoot of laughter. The other two dishes contained cinnamon and cardamom.

"What do you think?" Reinhardt asked eagerly.

"I think I could create something from all of them—apart from the courgettes."

"I'm very disappointed in your lack of imagination, Chef," he retorted. "It could have been a lot worse, you could have picked the turnip."

"There was a turnip?" I looked at the counter and, sure enough, a slightly misshapen turnip was squatting there in the middle. "What is it with you Germans and your root vegetables?"

He laughed. "So, are you up for the challenge or not? Do you have what it takes to make the cake from these ingredients?"

"Of course I do." I shoved past him and put on my apron.

He patted me on the back. "That's the spirit. And now you've got your color back."

I smiled. There was no denying that his crazy experiment had lifted my spirits.

It turned out that making a chocolate cake using finely grated courgettes didn't taste nearly as strange as I'd imagined, in fact, they made the texture melt-in-the-mouth moist and incredibly moreish.

When I brought it to Madame Monteux the following morning and she took that first bite, her face was exactly as I'd imagined it, and she treated me to a beaming smile.

"Oh, Coralie, you are a magician!" she exclaimed. "I don't know what you put in this cake, or what intention you folded into the mixture, but it's working."

I took hold of her hands and squeezed them tight. "I pictured your sadness melting away, and turning to hope, and I stirred in strength and happiness."

She hugged me and I felt her body quivering with silent sobs.

"You're not alone," I whispered in her ear. "I'll never let them take you, I promise you."

28

AUGUST 1941, PARIS

"Hey, Springerle," one of the line cooks shouted to me. "Have you got any sugar?"

"Why?" I called back in German. "Need to sweeten that sour personality of yours?"

As the other men started laughing, I marveled at far I'd come since I'd begun working in the Lutetia kitchen. Not only could I now speak enough German to join in with the men's banter, thanks to my lessons with Hans, but they'd bestowed a nickname upon me—Springerle—the name of an intricately designed German cookie, which I took as compliment and a sure sign I'd been accepted into the fold. Of course, I constantly had to override my feelings of guilt that the fold in question was German and remind myself that it was all for the sake of the French Resistance.

It was a swelteringly hot day in August, and as we were all busy prepping for the night ahead, a man I'd never seen before strode into the kitchen. He was wearing a sharply cut suit and a pair of patent leather spats like a 1920s gangster. His face was jowly and his slicked-back hair glistened with pomade. I pretended to be fully focused on icing the buns laid out in front of me, all the while shooting him curious glances.

"*Guten Tag!*" he boomed but in what sounded like a distinctly French accent. "I need something to eat."

"Dinner isn't being served until six," Reinhardt said in French, and there was a curtness to his tone that took me by surprise.

"Yes, well, I won't be here at six," the man replied. "I have urgent business to attend to." His closely set eyes scanned the room and I quickly looked back at the piping bag in my hand. Who was this French man so full of swagger in the headquarters of the *Abwehr*? The hairs on the back of my neck stood on end as I realized that he had to be working for them, and for him to strut into the place like a prize cockerel meant that they must hold him in high regard. Which in turn meant that he was probably an informer and a traitor to his own country. Out of the corner of my eye, I saw him make his way up the central kitchen aisle. I kept on icing my pastries. Hopefully if I stayed in my own little bubble, he wouldn't notice me.

"A couple of these sausages will do," the man said, stopping by Gunter's station.

"Of course," Gunter replied, his tone far warmer than Reinhardt's.

"Mmm," I heard the man say and my throat tightened as I realized he was strutting my way. "Now, what do we have here?" I caught a waft of expensive cologne—another sign of his treachery, for most people in Paris couldn't even afford soap anymore. The most common aroma on the Metro or in stores those days was stale sweat. "Luc Laporte," he said, extending a chunky hand to me. There was thick gold signet ring on his little finger engraved with some kind of crest. "And you are?"

"Coralie Donnadieu," I mumbled, putting down the piping bag and reluctantly shaking his hand. His sausage-like fingers were hot and clammy.

"You're French?" he asked.

"Yes." I felt sick at the notion that he might see me as a fellow collaborator.

"I should have guessed, with pastries as good as that. These Germans might have been able to conquer the world, but there are certain areas where we French are the best, no?" He gave a snort of laughter.

Spotting an opportunity, I smiled and nodded. "What is it that you do for them?"

He gave me a smug grin. "Now that would be telling. Let's just say I'm in the business of persuasion."

I heard Gunter snigger behind us.

Laporte cracked his knuckles and looked back at my pastries. "I think I'll take one of those for my dessert."

"They aren't finished yet, but I could bring one to you when they're ready," I said, seeing a chance to find out where in the hotel he worked.

He gave me a hard stare. "I hope you're not trying to get me alone in my room."

I heard more sniggers from Gunter and a loud pounding sound from Reinhardt, who was hammering the hell out of some cutlets with a wooden meat mallet.

"We all know what these French women are like, eh?" Laporte said, raising his voice to address the room.

I gritted my teeth, aware that I was dangerously close to having one of my saucepan bubbling over moments. The nerve of him, a French man criticizing French women so he could suck up to the Germans. He made my skin crawl, strutting around in his spats like some poor imitation of Al Capone.

"OK, bring some up to me when they're done. I'm on the fourth floor. Room 414."

He marched back over to Gunter, who'd plated him up some sausages, potatoes and sauerkraut.

"Thank you," he said before turning back to me. "And I'll see *you* later," he added suggestively.

"Ha, Springerle, looks like you've got a date," one of the fish chefs quipped.

On the other side of the kitchen, Reinhardt continued hammering at his cutlets, louder and louder.

"Not interested," I retorted. "You know what they say about French men—and their bravery—or lack of." It was a low blow, but it got the desired laugh from my colleagues and even Gunter managed a smirk.

"Laporte's one French man I wouldn't want to cross," Hans muttered as I returned to icing my pastries.

"Why?" I asked, but he shrugged and looked away as if he'd said too much.

As I finished my icing, I thought about what Laporte had said about working in persuasion. Did that mean interrogation? Surely the Germans weren't getting French men to do their dirty work. But the more I thought about it, the more it made sense. As he was fluent in French, he'd be better able to tell if someone was lying. What a traitor.

As soon as the pastries were ready, I put a couple on a plate.

"*Bonne chance!*" one of the men called as I walked past, prompting knowing laughter from the others. When I reached Reinhardt's station, he looked at me, concerned.

"I can send someone else up with them if you like?" he said, meeting my eyes.

I cringed as I shook my head, aware that it must look as if I wanted to spend more time in that idiot Laporte's company. But I couldn't afford to worry about what Reinhardt thought of me. I had an opportunity to find out something for Raphael and the Resistance and that was all that mattered.

"It's fine. I won't be long, and I could do with a walk."

"OK then." He turned away, looking distinctly unimpressed, and I felt an annoying pang of dismay at having upset him.

Stop worrying about what he thinks, I silently scolded myself and I thought of Madame Monteux and everyone else I was trying to help.

I took the stairs to the fourth floor to buy myself some thinking time and all the way my apprehension grew. *Reinhardt knows where you've gone*, I reminded myself. If anything bad happened and I didn't return soon, surely he'd send someone to come and find me.

I emerged onto the fourth floor and was once again hit by a wave of sorrow at what had become of the Lutetia as I saw the German signs on the doors and another portrait of Hitler on the wall. I fought the nervous urge to giggle as I remembered the drink I'd had with Inga and how she'd said Hitler's skin was like a chicken's. Sadly, she hadn't invited me to her room again and I'd barely seen her in the past few months.

I was halfway along the corridor when I heard something strange coming from one of the rooms. It was a mewling sound, the kind an animal makes when they're in distress. I stopped by the room and pressed my ear to the door.

"Oh," a voice cried feebly. "Oh."

I stood frozen to the spot, unsure what to do. Perhaps someone was having a medical emergency and needed assistance. *Whoever it is was they're the enemy, so just leave them to it*, I told myself. But when they cried out again, it was impossible to ignore.

I knocked on the door softly. "Are you all right in there?"

"Help, please," they cried out in French and I instantly felt sick.

I tried the door handle, but it was locked, and then I heard another door opening further along the corridor.

"Please!" the person cried out again.

"Shhhh," I hissed before hurrying on my way, and just in time, as I saw Laporte emerge into the corridor.

"Aha! My dessert has arrived!" he said with a smirk, looking me up and down and ignoring the cakes.

All I could think of was the poor soul trapped in the room. If they cried out to me again we'd probably both be for it.

"I hope you like your dessert," I said loudly, for the benefit of whoever was in there. Thankfully, it seemed to work and they remained silent.

"Oh, I'm sure I will. Come." He beckoned me to follow him to his room.

Feeling a sharp pang of anxiety I stepped inside and the smell of his cologne became overpowering. He'd obviously reapplied it, but why? I really hoped it wasn't on my account. I quickly scanned the room. The bed was unmade and some shirts were hanging on the back of the closet door. The desk in the window was covered with cardboard files. A large pair of gold pliers sat on top of one of the piles. My anxiety grew as I wondered what they might be for.

"You can put them down over there," he said, gesturing to his nightstand.

I approached the bed, feeling increasingly cornered.

"Thank you." I looked over my shoulder to see him move to the door. Was he about to close it? But then another cry rang out from down the corridor and instantly his smile turned to a scowl. "You need to go," he said sharply.

"Yes, of course. I hope you like your dessert," I squeaked as I hurried past him and into the corridor. This time, I made my way to the elevator so I wouldn't have to go back past the person trapped in the room. As much as it pained me to ignore them, there was nothing I could do to help and if I tried it would only make things worse.

My fear rising, I pressed the button again and again. After what felt like forever, the elevator arrived and the door slid open. I was so het up, I didn't notice Inga was in there until I'd stepped inside. She was tucked in the corner, fiddling with something in an envelope.

"Oh, hello," she said, clearly ruffled. "What are you doing up here?"

"Somebody requested some of my pastries," I replied, trying to compose myself.

"I'm not surprised." She gave a half smile, clearly distracted by whatever was in the envelope.

There was an awkward silence as we waited for the elevator door to shut.

"Come on, hurry up!" she muttered, clearly as eager to get out of there as I was. She leaned forward and stabbed the button for the ground floor again and again, and as she did so, the contents of the envelope spilled onto the floor.

I started bending down to pick it up.

"No!" she yelled just as the elevator door shut and we finally started going down.

I stared up at her, shocked.

"I'll get them," she said, her eyes wide with what looked like panic.

I looked back at the floor to try to see what she'd dropped, but she'd crouched over it now and was obscuring my view.

The elevator juddered to a halt on the first floor.

"Shit!" she exclaimed, shoving whatever she'd dropped into her bag.

The door slid open and a man in a black SS uniform stepped in.

"*Guten Tag,*" he said curtly.

Inga clutched her bag to her, looking as if she might be about to pass out. Clearly she didn't want him seeing whatever was in the envelope, either, but why? They were on the same side, and she worked for the man at the very top of the *Abwehr*.

Surely I was the one who ought to be pale and sweating, trapped in an elevator with both of them.

After what felt like forever, the elevator reached the ground floor and we all stepped out. The SS man strode over to the lounge and Inga breathed a palpable sigh of relief.

"Is everything OK?" I asked.

"Of course it is!" she muttered crossly.

"Right, well, enjoy your day," I said curtly and stalked off toward the kitchen. *What the hell was her problem?* I berated myself for ever having fallen for her winning smile and warm words. She was just as bad as the rest of them—maybe even worse as she looked so deceptively sweet.

I arrived back in the kitchen to find Reinhardt pacing up and down by the door.

"Oh, you're back," he said, sounding hugely relieved.

"Of course. I was only going to drop the pastries off."

He nodded, then stepped closer. "If he asks you to his room again, you should say no," he whispered in my ear.

"I'm perfectly capable of taking care of myself," I said, prickling with indignation again. I'd had a bellyful of these people telling me what to do.

"Trust me," Reinhardt replied gravely. "He is not someone you want to get to know."

I nodded and reminded myself that I was supposed to be gathering information for the Resistance, not letting my pride get the better of me. "I was surprised to see a French man with a suite here at the hotel," I said quietly.

Reinhardt gave a dry little laugh. "Don't be."

"What's that supposed to mean?"

He cupped my elbow with his hand and steered me over to my station, away from the others. "Nothing makes sense in this place," he muttered. "That's why I focus on my cooking and try not to think about anything else. If I thought too much about what's happening here, I'd..." He broke off as Gunter came striding over, his white kitchen jacket straining to contain his ever expanding belly.

"What veg do you want me to prep, Chef?" he asked in German.

"I'll come and show you," Reinhardt replied.

As I watched them walk away, my skin prickled with goosebumps. What had Reinhardt meant about nothing making sense here? And what had he been about to say before Gunter came over? Whatever it was, it certainly didn't seem positive. My feeling of nervous excitement grew. Could it be that Reinhardt really didn't like the Nazis? This wasn't the first time he'd alluded to being unhappy. I took some dough from the refrigerator and began rolling it out as I pondered the implications of this latest development. If Reinhardt really didn't like his bosses, he could potentially be an excellent source of intelligence, and make up for the lack of headway I'd made with Inga. I just had to get closer to him to make him open up more.

I placed a pie tin on top of the flattened dough and cut around it to make a pastry lid and another thought occurred to me—one that made me feel even more excited. If Reinhardt really didn't like his Nazi bosses, it meant that ultimately we were on the same side, and I would no longer have to feel guilty about how much I'd grown to like him.

29

JULY 1984, SAN FRANCISCO

"Why did you shout no?" my grandma asks, breaking the terrible silence, and I can't tell if her expression is curious or annoyed.

"I didn't shout," I say, trying to avoid answering the question. "I exclaimed."

"Is that so?" I feel slight relief as I notice she's trying not to grin.

"Yes. According to Suzette, I have an overexuberant personality. I tend to exclaim a lot."

"Can a person be too exuberant?" my grandma asks, and my relief grows. I appear to have steered her right off the subject.

"What do you mean?"

"Well, I think exuberance is a very good thing." She smiles wistfully. "I wish I could have more of it."

"Stick around and some of mine might rub off on you," I joke.

"I hope so. Ooh, the tart!" She hurries over to the oven and takes the tart out and the aroma of caramelized apples grows so strong and so delicious, I can barely think straight.

"So, what shall we do today?" I say gaily, praying that she's completely forgotten about no-gate, as I shall name it when I recount the terrible tale to Melissa.

"They said on the radio that there's going to be a peace protest in the Mission District," my grandma says, putting the tart on a wire cooling rack and coming back to the table.

"Cool."

"I thought you might like to go to it."

"Are you being serious?" My mouth falls open in shock.

"Absolutely. That's if you don't mind going with your old grandma."

"Of course I don't mind." I leap from my seat and give her a hug.

"Oh!" she laughs. "I wasn't expecting such an enthusiastic response."

"Are you kidding?" I'm about to tell her that my parents have forbidden me from going on protests in New York, then think better of it in case it might make her change her mind. "I'm an overexuberant person, remember?"

"Oh yes." She laughs. "How could I forget?"

This time, when I get in the truck, I put on my seat belt straight away.

"Thank you," she says before turning the key in the ignition and jiggling the stick shift.

When her old sixties rock music comes blaring out of the stereo, I wind the window down and sing along. It feels so good to be able to be my true self in the company of an adult, I no longer care what she did during the war, I'm too full of gratitude.

We get back home just as the sun is dipping behind the trees and the edges of the clouds are glowing gold. Both of us are starving, so we head straight to the kitchen, where Grandma cuts me a generous slice of tarte tatin with cream.

"Something to tide you over until dinner's ready," she says. "And speaking of dinner..." She disappears off into the living room and returns with the old recipe book.

Instantly, I feel a buzz of excitement. We've had such a nice day together, perhaps I can use the book to finally get her to open up about the war. I watch as she leafs through the pages, and then she gives a little gasp.

"What is it?" I ask.

"Nothing... I just saw something—something I'd completely forgotten."

I follow her gaze to the page. There's some writing in blue ink next to the recipe she's looking at, similar to the amendments to the Gateau Chocolat recipe I'd noticed. "You look as if you've seen a ghost."

"In a way I have," she replies enigmatically. "The ghost of my former self." She sighs. "This book is starting to feel like Pandora's box. I had no idea there were so many memories trapped inside."

"Would it help if you talked about them?" I ask cautiously, not wanting to make her clam up yet again. "Mom's therapist says that if we don't speak about the things we bottle up inside, they can become toxic."

My grandma raises her eyebrows.

"That's what I heard her yelling at Dad, anyways."

"Oh dear!" She laughs and shakes her head. "I'm afraid I'm going to have to disagree with your mom's therapist. There are some things it's really best we don't talk about."

I can tell she's going to close the conversation down again and I'm flooded with disappointment.

"Suit yourself," I say sulkily. "I'm going to go to my room."

She stares at me, shocked. "Raven, what's wrong?"

Deciding to put Suzette's therapist to the test, I choose to be honest. "I'm tired of being treated like my feelings don't count. You said you wanted to get to know me better."

"I do!" she exclaims.

"Well, it's a two-way street. I want to get to know you too. But every time I ask you about your life, you end the conversation."

"But I—"

"It's fine, don't worry," I interrupt. "I'm used to it. I only know what's going on with Mom and Dad because they yell it at each other. They never think to tell me anything to my face." I stand up to go, but she grabs my wrist to stop me.

"Don't go. Please." She looks back at the recipe book. "The truth is, I haven't told anyone about the secrets from my past, the secrets inside this book. I didn't even tell your grandpa."

"For real?" I stare at her.

"Yes. After the war ended, I just wanted to forget all about it. And when we moved here, I saw it as a chance to pretend that none of it had happened and start over, afresh. But maybe your mom's therapist is right. Maybe bottled-up memories do become toxic."

I sit back down. "Perhaps you could start by telling me just a little bit," I say softly and, to my relief, she nods and looks back at the book.

"I'll tell you the story behind the dinner I'm going to make you." She points to the recipe. "It was something I made for my friend Madame Monteux's seventieth birthday."

"That would be great." I give her a grin of encouragement.

She gets up and takes a joint of meat from the refrigerator and some onions and potatoes from the vegetable rack.

"But I suppose that if I'm to tell you that story, I need to go back to the beginning of the occupation, so that you have the background you need."

"That does sound sensible," I reply gravely, trying to contain my growing excitement.

I watch as she turns on the oven, then goes to a drawer and takes out a potato peeler. "Madame Monteux used to say that if you only wait long enough, you will see that there is a rhyme and reason to everything," she says with a sad smile. "Heartbreak, illness, loss, they all have their purpose according to my eternally optimistic benefactor and friend..."

I smile back at her and settle into my chair.

30

SEPTEMBER 1941, PARIS

I stood in front of the mirror on my closet door and peered cautiously at my reflection. It had been so long since I'd worn my special occasion dress—having had precisely zero special occasions to attend since the start of the German occupation—I wasn't sure how it would look, or how it would make me feel. My eyes scanned the teal satin and I felt a wistful pang as I noticed how the dress now hung in a shapeless rectangle from my shoulders rather than hugging my breasts and hips. Like most other Parisians, my curves had melted away a long time ago thanks to the rations. But still, it felt nice to be wearing something special again. Although many Parisian women were using their appearance as a form of resistance, refusing to dress dowdily despite the lack of material or even stockings, I'd been so busy with work I hadn't given it much thought. I turned to the side and pouted over my shoulder like a model in *Paris Vogue*. To hell with it. Today was a special occasion and I was going to make my best effort.

The occasion was Madame Monteux's seventieth birthday. Baptiste and I had thought long and hard about how we could celebrate, despite the growing tension in Paris. A couple of weeks previously, a member of the French Resistance known by his enigmatic nom de guerre, Colonel Fabien, had shot and killed a German soldier at the Barbès-Rochechouart Metro station as he was getting onto the first-class carriage of a train. But while Colonel Fabien had escaped, the German response had been swift and brutal. From that moment on, the German Commandant in Paris declared that any French citizen who was arrested for any reason would be considered a hostage. And any time a German was killed, a much higher number of these hostages would be killed in response. Posters went up all over the city informing us of the new rule. It felt like a turning point in the relationship between occupier and occupied, and one we'd never recover from.

Although Madame Monteux hadn't set foot in her beloved opera house since we'd seen Hitler there, I'd decided to take the risk and asked Baptiste if he could get the three of us tickets from one of his black-market contacts. I so badly wanted Madame Monteux to be happy on her special day and I was convinced that as soon as we got her inside the theater and the music started playing, she'd be swept away. Baptiste had got tickets for the matinee to avoid the issue of the curfew and we'd told Madame Monteux that we were taking her out for lunch so it would be a surprise.

I heard a knock on the store door and looked out of the window to see Baptiste, also dressed up to the nines, standing in the street below. I raced downstairs to join him, collecting Madame Monteux's birthday cake from the patisserie counter on the way.

"She's going to be so excited," I said as we hurried along the street. It was the first time I'd worn shoes with heels for months too, and I was wobbling like a drunk. I prayed that I didn't drop the cake box en route.

"It's about time she had something to smile about," Baptiste replied.

But as we reached the river, I saw something that made me freeze.

"Look," I whispered, grabbing Baptiste's arm and pulling him to a halt. I pointed to the entrance of Madame Monteux's apartment building, where two German soldiers were coming out, holding a large Art Deco radio. "Isn't that Madame Monteux's radio?"

"It looks like it," Baptiste replied, looking equally stunned. "But what are they doing with it?"

We watched as the soldiers put the radio on the back of a truck and drove off.

"I've got a really bad feeling about this," I said as we hurried toward the building.

"Me too," he replied, grim-faced.

For once, there was no sign of tittle-tattler Brigit, the concierge, and we hurried upstairs and I gave my customary three knocks on the door. After what felt like an eternity, it slowly opened an inch.

"Madame Monteux?" I peered in through the crack and saw her cowering in the hallway. "Thank goodness. We saw some soldiers leaving the building and thought that maybe they'd been harassing you."

Saying nothing, she opened the door wider. As soon as I stepped inside, I knew that something was terribly wrong. Madame Monteux was hugging herself and trembling violently.

"What is it? What happened?" I asked, gripping her arm.

"Duchess, what have they done to you?" Baptiste exclaimed.

"They—they took my radio," she stammered, her teeth chattering.

So it was hers. I shot Baptiste an anxious glance. "Why?"

"Apparently the Jewish people of France are no longer allowed to own them," she said flatly.

"But that's ridiculous!"

"No, it isn't!" she exclaimed with a wild look in her eye.

"What do you mean?" I frowned. "Of course it is."

"It's not! As far as they're concerned, we're just vermin."

"But you're not vermin!" I gripped her arm tighter.

"They even have an exhibition in Paris now about how disgusting we are."

I suppressed a shudder. I'd heard about *Le Juif et la France* exhibition from one of my customers a few days previously and it had caused another saucepan boiling over moment for me. I'd been hoping she wouldn't have known about it.

"They're the vermin, not you. They're monsters!"

"That's right," Baptiste agreed.

We went into the living room and I put the cake down on the table. The space beside the fireplace where the radio-set used to sit looked like a gaping hole. Madame Monteux sank down onto her chaise longue looking utterly defeated.

"We can't let them win," I said firmly, "especially today, on your birthday. You need to get dressed, we're taking you out, remember?"

She looked us up and down as if noticing our glad rags for the first time. "Oh goodness, I totally forgot. Where are we going?"

I glanced at Baptiste. "I think we should tell her." He nodded. "Baptiste has got us tickets for the opera."

I looked at her and held my breath, hoping against hope that this news would cheer her. But, to my horror, she dissolved into floods of tears.

"We aren't allowed in theaters anymore either. Or cafes or parks or restaurants."

"No!" I exclaimed. "This can't be right."

She nodded sadly. "They've brought out many more decrees. They're stealing our lives from under us."

I looked at Baptiste in despair, but for once he appeared to have been rendered speechless and he just stood there shaking his head. My anger bubbled and frothed inside of me. How dare the Germans do this? And how dare a French government agree to implement such cruel measures?

Madame Monteux hunched over with her head in her hands. I thought of how many times she'd pepped me up since we'd met—how she'd encouraged me to go for the job at the Lutetia and made me believe that a kid from Malakoff nicknamed Petit Four had every right to work as a chef in such a grand hotel. I put a lid on my anger and crouched in front of her.

"I have an idea," I said. "But I'm going to have to go somewhere and I'll be gone for about an hour. Baptiste will keep you company. And I need you to promise me that you'll do what you once advised me when I was nervous about starting my job at the Lutetia and I was worried the other staff would look down on me."

She looked at me blankly through teary eyes.

"Other people can only make you feel small if you let them," I echoed her words back to her.

She smiled weakly and nodded.

"So don't let them!" I exclaimed. "I'll be back soon."

I raced from the building and along rue des Saints-Pères, a mixture of anger and desperation powering my every step. I couldn't let Madame Monteux's spirit break, especially today of all days. I had to salvage things somehow.

It was only when I reached the Lutetia that my determination became diluted with fear. It wasn't my day to be working there; what if the guards didn't let me in?

Thankfully, one of them recognized me. He was about to wave me inside when he frowned. "Wait, it isn't Sunday."

"I know... I, uh—"

"She's here to see me," a woman said from behind me, and I felt a hand on my shoulder.

I turned to see Inga beaming her radiant smile at me.

"Oh, I see, I'm sorry," the guard stammered, standing back to let us in.

As I made my way through the revolving door, my mind raced. Why had Inga said that? After the way she'd snapped at me in the elevator the last time I'd seen her, her warm smile came as a huge surprise.

"Is everything all right?" she asked once we were both in the lobby.

"Yes. No. I..." I broke off. I could hardly tell her my real reason for being there.

"Come with me," she said, taking my arm and steering me over to the ladies' bathroom.

As soon as we got inside, she checked the cubicles were all empty, then joined me standing by the sinks.

"You look beautiful," she said, looking me up and down. In all the drama, I'd completely forgotten how dressed up I was.

"Thank you," I murmured.

"Are you sure you're all right?" she asked. "You seem very troubled."

Her voice was so gentle and she looked so concerned that for a fleeting moment I considered spilling everything out to her. But how could I? I wouldn't be confiding in another woman, I'd be confiding in Canaris's personal secretary, someone who'd rubbed shoulders with Hitler, and no matter what she'd said about his lack of charm or poor skin, he was responsible for the cruel measures being meted out to the Jewish and they were on the same side.

"I'm fine," I replied, forcing myself to smile. "It's just been a very busy day."

"I see." She nodded. "Well, I'm glad I ran into you because I've been wanting to apologize for how I spoke to you the last time I saw you." She said it so earnestly I couldn't help believing her. "I was, uh, very stressed about something and I took it out on you, and I shouldn't have."

"It's OK," I replied. "I could tell you were worried about something..." I paused and looked down at the sink. "Especially when the soldier joined us in the elevator." I risked glancing up into the mirror to try to gauge her response.

She sighed and nodded. "Yes, I didn't want him to..." She broke off.

"What?" I asked gently.

"Never mind. The important thing is that I make amends to you. You've been so kind and generous with your talents since we got here, and I've so appreciated your delicious baking."

I wasn't sure if she was just pretending to be nice, but in that moment I really didn't care. All I could think about was Madame Monteux crying and shaking in her apartment and how I had to do something to make her feel better. "There's really no need," I replied.

"No, I insist." She glanced back at the cubicles as if to make double sure that there was no one there. "I was wondering if you'd like the opportunity to make some extra money?" she asked quietly.

"How?" I met her gaze in the gilt-framed mirror above the sinks.

"Well, I..." She broke off as the door burst open and a German woman in a gray uniform walked in, instantly causing me to flinch. But I'd forgotten that I was standing with Canaris's secretary, and the woman gave Inga a respectful nod before disappearing into one of the stalls. "Perhaps you could come and see me with your recipe book before you start your shift tomorrow," Inga said loudly, and clearly for the benefit of the woman. "And we could go through some options for the menu." She gave me a pointed nod in the mirror.

"Oh, OK, of course. I'd be happy to," I replied.

"Excellent, thank you."

We went back into the lobby and Inga touched me on the

arm. "I'll see you tomorrow," she said quietly, before heading over to the elevator.

I hurried to the kitchen, my head spinning. What on earth had that been about? I pushed the question from my mind, remembering why I'd come to the Lutetia in the first place. I really hoped Reinhardt was here, otherwise my plan would be thwarted. Thankfully, I found him sitting at the counter, jotting in the notebook he used for menu ideas. Aside from a couple of junior kitchen staff prepping vegetables the kitchen was deserted.

"Coralie!" he exclaimed when he saw me, gazing at my dress. "You look... you look beautiful."

"Oh, this old thing," I quipped feebly.

"Are you going somewhere nice?"

"I was supposed to be going to the opera with my friend, but... our plans got changed, which is why I've come to see you."

"Yes?"

"I need your help," I blurted out.

He instantly looked concerned. "Of course, what's wrong?"

"My friend—the one you saw that time in the store?"

"Yes."

"It's her seventieth birthday, but she's had some very bad news." As I uttered the words, I felt my anger bubbling up again, but I forced it down. "Which is why we can't go to the opera as planned."

"I'm so sorry to hear that," he replied with a frown. "How can I help?"

"She hasn't had anything nice to eat for so long. Would it be possible..." I broke off, feeling angry and ashamed that I should have to go begging to a German. But Reinhardt wasn't like the others, I was becoming increasingly sure of that.

"You'd like to make her a special birthday dinner?" he said softly.

"Yes! And with your delicious onion gravy, now I know the recipe."

He smiled. "Of course. Wait here."

I stood and watched as he took some containers from the shelves, then set about filling them with vegetables and seasonings. Then he went to the fridge and, to my delight, he took out a joint of beef and wrapped it in greaseproof paper.

"Beef! Are you sure?"

"It's her seventieth birthday," he replied with a smile.

As he came back over, I couldn't stop myself from throwing my arms round him and hugging him tight. "Thank you!" I whispered, my eyes filling with tears. "You have no idea how much this means."

"I think maybe I do," he replied with a sad smile.

It was only as I was walking back to Madame Monteux's apartment that I pondered the meaning behind his words. Did he understand because he knew what it was like to have hardly any food, or had he guessed that I was talking about the latest rules to punish the Jews? Whatever it was, I was so grateful to him.

I stopped by the patisserie on my way back to pick up some extra cakes and found Raphael peering in through a crack in the shutters.

"Why have you closed early?" he said indignantly as soon as he saw me. I hated the way he spoke to me as if he was my boss, but I swallowed my feelings of annoyance. I had neither the time nor the energy to get in an argument with him today.

"It's Madame Monteux's seventieth birthday," I replied as I unlocked the door. "We were meant to be going to the opera, but Jewish people have now been banned from theaters and the Germans confiscated her radio today too. Can you believe it?"

"Sadly, yes," he replied as he followed me inside. "There are no depths to which the Germans won't sink. But thanks to Colonel Fabien they know the French aren't going to just take it anymore. The fightback has begun—which is why I'm here. I have something I'd like you to hide here for a while."

"More Resistance papers?" I asked, hurrying into the kitchen and taking some hazelnut éclairs from the fridge.

"No. It's something far more important and it needs to be handled very carefully." He took a package from his bag and gingerly placed it on the side.

"What have you got in there? A Ming vase?" I joked.

"No," he replied, his expression deadly serious. "It's a bomb."

31

SEPTEMBER 1941, PARIS

"A bomb?" My voice rose about an octave as I stared at the package Raphael had placed on the counter. It was the size of a large book and wrapped in brown paper.

"Keep your voice down!" he hissed, as if I had no right to be indignant, which only increased my indignance.

"You've brought a bomb to my patisserie," I whispered through gritted teeth.

"I need to keep it here for a couple of days," he said, as casually as if he were dropping off his pet budgerigar for me to look after.

"But what if it goes off?"

"It won't—unless of course you light the fuse... or there's a fire in the store."

"My God!" I began pacing the kitchen. "What the hell is it for?"

"I can't tell you that, I can't take the risk," he said in that irritatingly patronizing tone of his, at which point my saucepan of a temper didn't just bubble over, it blew its lid.

"*You* can't take the risk?" I exclaimed. "What about the risk I'll be taking keeping it here? If you don't tell me what it's for, then you can take your bomb and you can hide it up your backside!"

He looked at me, stunned. "Coralie!"

"I mean it." I went to pick up the package to thrust it back in his hands, then thought better of it and put my hands on my hips instead.

"All right, if you must know, it's to blow up the German bookstore here on the Left Bank, the Librairie Rive Gauche."

I nodded. I knew the store he meant. "And when exactly are you planning to do this?"

"I'm not the one planting it, that's someone else. They'll come and collect it from you in a couple of days."

A horrible thought occurred to me. "Are they going to set it off when there are people in the store?"

"I don't know. But why should that matter?" He frowned. "The Germans are now openly executing the French on the streets of Paris. Why should you care if any of them die?"

"I don't, but anyone could be in the bookstore." I thought of Reinhardt or Hans browsing for a read. "An innocent person could get killed."

"Hmm, I don't see how anyone who wants to read books in German could be innocent." His frown deepened. "Please don't tell me you're going weak on me. Maybe you're spending too much time in that hotel kitchen with them. Next thing I know, you'll be one of those loose French women I have to serve champagne to at the *Abwehr* parties."

Hearing his sneering words reminded me of Luc Laporte and only made my anger grow. "Of course I'm not! You know exactly why I'm working there. And I've been giving you information, haven't I? I told you about Luc Laporte and what he's doing up on the fourth floor."

"That's beside the point," he said dismissively. "Letting us use this place to hide things is of far more use. And if you care so much about your Jewish friend, you wouldn't hesitate to do this."

I thought of Madame Monteux and how broken she'd been by the outrageous new laws and I swallowed my desire to punch him on the nose. "All right, I'll hide it. But only for a couple of days."

"That's what I said."

"And I want it hidden in the cellar, as far away as possible from my customers."

"OK." He picked up the package and I followed him down the stone steps.

"How about in there?" I said, pointing to the old metal drum I used for storing flour.

I watched, numbly as he buried the bomb in the flour. From innocent people having their radios confiscated and Inga's strange request, to a bomb being hidden in my patisserie cellar, the world was increasingly feeling like a feverish dream.

I got back to Madame Monteux's apartment to hear music blaring from the gramophone inside. She opened the door, champagne flute in hand, looking considerably revived. Her long hair was now hanging loose and the color had returned to her cheeks—although that could have been down to the alcohol.

"Well, you look a lot better," I said as she led me into the front room. Baptiste was sitting at the end of the chaise, his face flushed and his bow tie hanging undone around his collar.

"Oh, uh, hello, Coralie," he muttered, looking distinctly shifty.

"What's been going on here?" I asked, glancing from one to the other. They looked like a couple of naughty children who'd been caught stealing sweets.

"Baptiste has been cheering me up," Madame Monteux said, and I looked at him just in time to see him give her a wink.

"Is that so?" I stifled a grin. There would have been a time when I'd have thought any union between the pair more unlikely than Hitler suddenly discovering a sense of compassion. But in this new upside-down world, it seemed that anything was possible and my heart lifted at the thought of them bringing each other joy. "Well, I have something that will hopefully cheer you up some more." I held out my box of food. "Everything we need for a roast lunch, including a joint of beef!"

"You've got beef?" Madame Monteux's eyes grew as wide as saucers.

"R-real beef—from a cow?" Baptiste stammered.

"Yes, from a cow." I chuckled.

"Where did you get it?" Madame Monteux asked, her eyes narrowing. "I hope it wasn't from the Germans at the hotel."

"Of course not." I felt terrible lying to her, but I so badly wanted her to have a nice birthday. "I got it from a black-market contact."

Madame Monteux gave a sigh of relief.

"Well, I say we get cooking." Baptiste sprang to his feet, rubbing his hands together excitedly.

The three of us hurried into the kitchen, where Madame Monteux supplied us all with fresh champagne. "It's my last bottle," she said, "but I can't think of a better occasion for it."

We raised our flute glasses in a toast and then I set to work seasoning the meat with salt and pepper and sprigs of rosemary, and Baptiste began chopping the vegetables. Madame Monteux floated around us, champagne glass in hand, directing us like she was choreographing a dance.

"It's the funniest thing," she said once I'd put the meat in the oven and started making Reinhardt's secret recipe gravy. "This is the happiest I've felt in ages and it's all from peeling vegetables."

"Er, who's the one peeling them, Duchess?" Baptiste asked, looking up from his potatoes with a grin.

"Well, technically you are, but I'm overseeing the operation."

I laughed. "I think you just created a brand-new kitchen role—Chief Overseer of Vegetable Peeling."

The other two burst out laughing, and it was a sound so welcome and warming, my eyes filled with grateful tears.

Madame Monteux raised her glass to us. "Thank you. Both of you. I don't know how you've done it, but you've somehow managed to turn my birthday from a disaster into a triumph."

"I know how," Baptiste said gruffly. "It's called love."

32

SEPTEMBER 1941, PARIS

The following day, I got to the Lutetia half an hour early and made my way up to Inga's room, recipe book in hand. While I waited for a response to my knock, I quickly flicked through the book, smiling at the memories of nights with Reinhardt that each recipe conjured.

Inga opened the door in a primrose-yellow dress and stockinged feet. As soon as she saw me, her face broke into a smile and she beckoned me inside. I quickly glanced around for anything that might be of use to the Resistance but the room was immaculately tidy and, apart from an ink bottle, there was nothing out on the desk.

"You wanted to go through some recipe ideas," I said, really hoping that this wasn't the case.

"Oh... uh, well, not exactly, no," she replied. She went over to the drinks cabinet in the corner and picked up one of the decanters. "Brandy?"

My spirits lifted. This was promising indeed. "Yes please. But better make it a small one. I have a whole shift ahead of me and I don't want to ruin my pastry."

"Of course," she said, returning my grin. She poured two

drinks into crystal tumblers and handed one to me. "I asked you to come here because, as I said yesterday, I have a proposition for you," she began, gesturing at me to join her in the chairs by the fireplace. "A way for you to earn some more money."

"OK," I said, perching down and placing the recipe book on my lap.

"I was wondering if you would deliver something for me."

"Deliver?" I blurted out. I really had not been expecting this.

"Yes, just some paperwork, to addresses in Paris. I've been doing it myself, but I'm so busy with my work for the Admiral, I thought I could pay you to do it. I know times are hard, so I thought you might appreciate the extra money."

Times are hard because of you Germans! I wanted to snap, but, thankfully, I was able to stay focused on the opportunity in front of me. Not to earn more money but to get closer to Admiral Canaris's personal secretary and find out more. Hopefully the addresses she was sending me to would be helpful in some way, and then I could get the arrogant Raphael to shut up once and for all.

"Some extra money certainly would come in useful," I replied.

"Oh, that's wonderful, thank you!" She looked so relieved, I instantly felt suspicious. Was this really about helping me, or was it more about helping her? But helping her with what, exactly? I thought of how nervous she'd been in the elevator, and how she'd bitten my head off when I'd tried to pick up whatever she'd dropped.

"So, what exactly would I be delivering?" I asked as nonchalantly as possible before taking a sip of my drink.

"Oh, just some paperwork," she repeated enigmatically.

"OK." The more I thought about it, the more it didn't make sense. As Canaris's secretary, she surely had numerous minions on hand to do deliveries for her. Maybe this was about helping me after all... Or she didn't want any other Germans knowing about whatever it was she wanted to deliver. Perhaps it was something so top secret, she felt safer giving it to me. I desperately wanted to ask what kind of paperwork it was, but I knew this would look suspicious, so I bit my lip.

"So you'll do it?" She looked at me hopefully.

"Yes, of course." I took another sip of my drink and watched as she went over to her desk.

"Thank you so much." She opened the top drawer and took out a couple of envelopes. "This is the first of the paperwork I need you to deliver." She came back to the sofa and sat down beside me. "I'm going to give you an address to take it to."

I took a pen from my bag and flipped my recipe book open. "Go ahead."

"Oh, I'd rather you didn't write it down, if that's all right."

"Oh, OK." I put the pen down.

"It's just that it's safer that way."

Safer for who? I wanted to ask, but again, I didn't want to arouse suspicion. In order to win her confidence, I had to look as if I'd fallen for her story that this was all about helping me earn some extra money.

"And if you get stopped and searched en route, you're to say that you're from the Lutetia and tell them to get in touch with me. Not that you should get stopped and searched obviously," she added with a nervous laugh.

"Obviously," I echoed, my unease growing. What on earth was this all about?

"This is the paperwork." She handed me one of the envelopes. It was sealed, with nothing written on it. "And this is for you." She handed me the other, smaller envelope. "Your payment."

"Oh, thank you." I put it in my pocket, feeling slightly sick. But then it occurred to me that I could spend the money on extra ingredients for the patisserie. I could try and source some sugar and cream on the black market and bake my customers a special treat.

"And if you could deliver it tomorrow that would be wonderful."

"Of course."

"When you get to the address, you're to say that you are Rose from the theater and you have the playscript."

"Rose, theater, playscript," I repeated.

"I know it seems strange, but such is life in the counterintelligence world!"

I shivered. If only she knew that I was already accustomed to such cloak-and-dagger activities. "I'll say anything you want me to, for some extra money," I joked, wanting to make it clear that I had no other, clandestine, reason for being there. "Times have been hard. I really appreciate this."

"You're very welcome." She looked so relieved, I felt a rush of excitement. I was really winning her trust.

We finished our drinks and she gave me the address. As soon as I got into the elevator, I jotted the arrondissement and apartment numbers next to the recipe for my Gateau Chocolat to help me remember. If anyone ever asked me what the numbers meant, I could just say that I'd been experimenting with different measurements.

I was hardly able to concentrate during my shift that night, too aware of the envelope in my bag and what it might contain. As soon as I got home to the patisserie, I took the envelope out and felt it carefully. It felt like a slightly bulky letter, but who was it for and why so hush-hush? Perhaps I'd have a better idea once I delivered it.

The next day, I set off for the 18th arrondissement, repeating my instructions over and over in my head on the Metro. I got off at Blanche and made my way down boulevard de Clichy, past the bright red windmill of the Moulin Rouge. German soldiers were everywhere, strolling along the sidewalks and sitting outside the cafes in the sunshine. I bristled at their carefree laughter and smug expressions. I only hoped that delivering Inga's mysterious paperwork would somehow end up helping the Resistance. I'd decided against telling Raphael yet, just in case it was all completely innocuous, and I'd ended up becoming a hapless carrier pigeon for the *Abwehr*. The last thing I needed was another of his patronizing putdowns.

I got to the apartment building and climbed the stairs to the fourth floor. When I finally reached number twelve, I took a moment to compose myself, then knocked on the door. After a minute or so, the door slowly opened and a woman peered out.

"Yes," she said, her voice wavering slightly.

"I'm Rose from the theater. I have the playscript," I said.

An expression of relief lit up the woman's face. "Thank you!" she exclaimed.

I took the envelope from my bag and she grabbed it with all the fervor of a child being offered a bag of candy.

"Thank you so much," she said again, before shutting the door.

I hurried back down the stairs feeling more confused than ever. Had I just given paperwork from the *Abwehr* to an innocent French woman, or was she a Nazi collaborator? Then I had an idea. Perhaps she would deliver the paperwork to someone else. I would wait and see if she left the building.

Thankfully, there was a little cafe across the street. I went inside, ordered a tea and took a seat on the terrace. Someone had left a copy of the paper *Le Petit Parisien* on the table. It had begun collaborating with the Nazis at the start of the occupation so I wouldn't go near it ordinarily, but now it provided the perfect cover. I sat there pretending to read while peering over the top at the apartment building.

About half an hour passed with no sign of activity, but then the large wooden door opened and the woman came out, now wearing a jacket and headscarf. I quickly drank the last of my tea, put down the paper and hurried along the street parallel to her. She turned left past the Moulin Rouge and up the hill toward Montmartre. For all I knew she could be going out on a simple errand and any minute now she might join a queue to collect her rations. She disappeared down a narrow side street and I increased my pace. When I drew level, I saw her deep in conversation with a man wearing a hat pulled down low. Nor wanting to be caught watching them, I turned my back to face a clothes shop. I could just make out their reflections in the window. Then I saw her take something from her bag and I risked turning to get a better view. It was the envelope, I was sure of it. She was giving it to the man. But why? And who was he?

They said goodbye and went their separate ways, with the woman heading back down the hill to Pigalle and the man going up toward Montmartre. I followed him at a safe distance on the other side of the street. At the top of the hill, he turned a corner and disappeared from view. I began walking faster, becoming out of breath. Where was he going? I wondered. The mystery of the envelope was becoming more and more intriguing.

I was just approaching the brow of the hill when I heard pounding footsteps coming toward me. I gasped as the man reappeared, running back down the hill. As he passed me, I saw an expression of terror on his face. Who was he running from? What had made him so scared?

I heard the hum of an engine and a black Mercedes cabriolet appeared—the car so beloved of the German soldiers. Sure enough, little swastika flags fluttered either side of the bonnet. The car sped past and I turned and watched the man flee up a narrow alleyway. The car screeched to a halt and soldiers in black uniform leapt out. SS men. They yelled, "Halt" in German and I began to shiver.

Not wanting to get caught watching, I quickly turned and carried on walking toward Montmartre, my mind racing. Why would someone with paperwork from Inga run at the sight of the SS? I thought of how she'd panicked that day in the elevator when the SS man got in. Weren't they all supposed to be on the same side? None of it made any sense.

33

JULY 1984, SAN FRANCISCO

My grandma gets up to check on the meat in the oven, and I sit watching her, my mouth gaping open in shock. If Suzette could see me, she'd probably say something snarky like, "Close your mouth, you'll catch flies," but I can't help it. I'm so in awe at what my grandma just told me. I'm so in awe of my grandma!

"Looks like dinner's nearly ready," she says, inspecting the meat. "I must have been talking for hours! Why didn't you stop me?"

"Are you kidding?" I stare down at the numbers scrawled in blue in the recipe book. "This is the most interesting thing I've ever heard. I can't believe you worked for the Resistance as a spy. You're like a female James Bond... who bakes cakes."

She bursts out laughing. "Now there's an image."

"But it's true. I think it's rad. I think *you're* rad."

"I'm what?"

"Rad. It means radical."

"Ah." She gives a little laugh. "I take it that's a good thing."

"Oh, trust me, it's a very good thing," I reply, unable to contain my relief. I still don't know the story behind the German love note, but she's told me enough to now know that she couldn't possibly have sympathized or collaborated with the Nazis. I look back at the numbers written in blue. "So, these numbers were a secret code?"

"Uh-huh, I guess so."

"This is the coolest recipe book ever!" I cannot wait to tell Melissa about this. She's going to die when I tell her I'm related to a spy for the French Resistance.

But my grandma's smile fades. "I wouldn't say that."

"Why not? It's a historical artefact!"

"Way to make someone feel really old," she laughs.

"Sorry, I didn't mean it like that, but it's an example of someone working against the Nazis—my very own grandma working against the Nazis!" Again, I'm filled with relief. This latest plot twist feels even better than something Judy Blume would come up with—and I don't say that lightly!

"I'm afraid I'm not quite the hero you think I am," she murmurs and I instantly frown. What's that supposed to mean?

"Why not?" I ask as she puts the joint of roast beef onto a plate.

"That's a whole other story," she says, her tone now somber.

Aware that she's told me loads more than I'd been hoping for, and not wanting to push things, I nod. "Maybe you could tell it to me tomorrow."

"Maybe," she says, and my heart sinks. She doesn't sound enthusiastic at all.

We spent the rest of the evening talking about music and movies and our favorite pizza toppings, but now I'm in bed, my thoughts keep returning to everything she told me about the war. It's like watching a cliff-hanger episode of your favorite soap. I still don't know what happened to the wonderful-sounding Madame Monteux, I still don't know what the myste-rious paperwork was. And I still don't know if my grandma was in love with a German! At least I've been able to figure out that the writer of the love note must have been the chef, Reinhardt. From what she's told me so far, he sounds pretty cool, and every time she talked about him she got a kind of coy and faraway look in her eye. So why did she say that she wasn't the hero I thought she was? Did she end up doing something bad? Something in support of the Germans?

The luminous hands on the alarm clock slowly tick their way around to two in the morning and I'm still no closer to sleep, so I decide to go get a glass of milk. I wish I was able to call Melissa and give her the scoop, but it's still only 5 a.m. in New York and I don't think her family would appreciate the early wake-up call. If only we all had our own personal phones! Maybe in the year 2000, when we're all whizzing around by jet pack and have pet robots, we'll have some kind of cordless phones to communicate with. That's if we have a future... I think back to a leaflet I saw at the peace protest in Mission listing the horrible ways in which people die from nuclear fall-out. I sit up in bed and turn on the lamp. It's actually been a pretty good day today. I am not going to ruin it by terrorizing myself with morbid thoughts.

I get out of bed and tiptoe down the hallway into the living room. I'd been hoping I might catch my grandma during an attack of insomnia, but all is quiet and dark. When I get to the kitchen and put on the light, I see that she must have been up recently as there's the remains of a herbal tea on the side and the cup still feels warm.

I pour myself a glass of milk and let myself onto the back porch. The balmy air smells of pine trees and it's instantly soothing. I sit down on the swing seat and notice a notebook on top of a stack of magazines in the wicker basket beside it. It's clearly a lot newer than the recipe book and photo album. *Could it be a journal?* I reach down and take it from the basket. *It might not be a journal*, I tell myself. It might just be for jotting down to-do lists or other mundane things. Perhaps I could open it quickly. Too quickly to read anything, but just enough to figure out what it is?

I glance up at the kitchen window to make sure no one's there, then quickly flick the book open. It's immediately obvious that it's a diary of some kind. The pages are full of writing and dates are written at the top of some of the pages. I snap it shut and put it back in the basket. I'm feeling so much closer to my grandma after today, it would feel really wrong to intrude on her privacy now. But what if she refuses to tell me anything more about her life during the war? What if I never find out the truth behind the love note, or the ominous admission she made this evening about not being a hero?

An annoying little voice in my head starts wheedling away. *You could just look at the very last entry. See if she's written anything about you coming to stay...*

Feeling slightly sick at my own behavior, I pick up the book again, turn to the last page of writing and hold it up to the light spilling out from the kitchen window.

... she's a lovely girl, really spirited and full of spark. I'd been so apprehensive about her visit, unsure what Suzette might have said about my failings as a mother, and after our initial altercation over the seat belt, I was certain she'd filled her head with reasons to hate me. But now I feel her anger is more toward her parents—and again I feel guilt. Are her grievances with Suzette in some way down to me? Did my inability to love my daughter the way she should have been loved mean that Suzette in turn has found it difficult to love her own daughter? Bob was such a good and dedicated father, so uncomplicated and so untainted by the war—to him it was all a thrilling adventure, arriving in Paris when he did, when the occupation was over. I've tried so hard not to think about those times. But Raven's arrival and looking at that recipe book have taken the lid off my Pandora's

box, and now I can't seem to get it back on. She seems so genuinely interested in my life back then, and I know she'll have more questions for me tomorrow. But how can I answer them? How can I talk about what happened to Madame Monteux? How can I tell her the terrible truth about Reinhardt? How can I confess that her grandmother was—is—a killer?

34

SEPTEMBER 1941, PARIS

I'd only been back at the patisserie an hour when Reinhardt
arrived for our evening cooking class. To my surprise, he was
dressed in a pair of slacks, flat cap and plaid shirt.

"I almost didn't recognize you in clothes," I said as I let him
inside.

"I wasn't aware that you'd seen me out of them," he replied
drily.

"No, I didn't mean... I meant out of your uniform," I stammered, and much to my annoyance, I began to blush.

He took off his cap and gave me a bashful smile. "I wanted
to see what it would feel like."

"Haven't you ever worn normal clothes before?" I asked,
raising my eyebrows, eager to turn the joke back onto him.

He laughed. "Yes, of course, but not in Paris. I thought it
might be..." he paused as if searching for the right word,
"easier."

"Do you mean more comfortable?"

"In a way, yes. It's definitely more comfortable not being
hated on sight by the French."

"Oh." I pondered this for a moment. I was so used to seeing

the Germans as our gloating oppressors, it never occurred to me that some of them might be bothered by the fact that most Parisians hated them being here. It gave me a small glow of satisfaction to think of them wincing at our cold glances and blank stares. But then again, how many of them were like Reinhardt? He was kind and considerate. He clearly had feelings. And I had to admit, he looked a whole lot better out of that hideous uniform.

"Come on, let's go upstairs," I said, ushering him behind the counter and trying not to think of the bomb ticking away, metaphorically at least, in the cellar.

"Did your friend enjoy her birthday lunch?" he asked once we were in the kitchen and sitting at the table.

"She did, very much. Thank you." I smiled at him. "It really cheered her up."

"Do you mind me asking what had upset her?" He picked up the recipe book and my pulse quickened as I thought of the numbers I'd added. *He's not going to notice them*, I reassured myself. *And even if he does, I can just say they're just an amendment to the measurements.*

I pondered making something up about Madame Monteux, but part of me wanted to tell him. I wanted him to know the consequences of his leader's cruelty.

"She's Jewish," I said simply.

"Oh." He looked away, clearly uncomfortable, and a horrible thought occurred to me. What if he was just like the others, and believed that he was somehow superior to the Jews? What if he hadn't seen Madame Monteux's Star of David that day after all, and he had no idea she was Jewish? "I'm sorry," he said softly.

"Hmm," I replied, unconvinced.

"No, I am." He looked at me earnestly. "You must believe me. Not all of us..." He broke off and looked around the room as if an *Abwehr* agent might be hiding under the bed.

"Not all of you what?" My skin prickled with goosebumps.

"Not all of us agree with what Hitler is doing," he whispered.

"Forgive me for saying, but I don't see any of you disagreeing," I said gently, encouraged by his show of defiance and deciding to nudge him a little.

"I understand, but you have to understand what would happen to us if we did."

I shivered. The punishment for a German openly disobeying Hitler didn't bear thinking about. Reinhardt had already taken a huge risk by admitting that he didn't agree with the German leadership and this made me ridiculously happy.

He reached into his bag and pulled out a bottle of wine. "Shall we have a drink before we start to cook?"

"Of course." I fetched two glasses from the cabinet.

"I'm very sorry your friend is suffering," he said as he removed the cork.

I studied his face. He certainly looked sorry.

"Why do people do this to each other?" I said with a sigh.

"Do what?" He poured the wine into the glasses.

"Hurt each other. Kill each other? It could be so different. Surely we'd all be so much happier if we agreed to live in peace." I thought back to Madame Monteux's birthday and how much love and fun we'd created in her kitchen simply peeling and chopping vegetables together and I wanted to cry. I didn't want a bomb in my cellar. I didn't want to be a part of the endless cycle of aggression and retribution. "Why can't we just learn to love one another. Or at least tolerate each other."

Reinhardt took a sip of his drink and cleared his throat. "Coralie, I want to tell you something, but I don't want it to change how things are between us."

I instantly felt worried. "What is it?"

He leaned forward and his hands brushed mine on the table. I didn't move mine away. "Over the past few months, as we've got to know each other I've—" He was interrupted by a loud rap on the shop door downstairs and we both jumped. "Who is that?" he said.

"I have no idea," I replied, but my heart was racing. The only people I could imagine calling at this time were Raphael or the person who was coming to collect the bomb. Or, of course, the police or Germans, who had learned about the bomb. Either way, it was very bad.

"What do you want me to do?" Reinhardt asked.

"Wait here," I replied. "Don't come down unless I tell you."

He nodded.

I made my way downstairs, my heart pounding, and opened the door to see Raphael standing in the dark.

"I have to take the bomb, it's—"

"Shh!" I interrupted as he barged in.

"Why?" He looked around suspiciously.

"I have someone upstairs."

"Who?" he whispered back.

"A friend." I led him into the kitchen. "You have to be quick."

Again, he looked at me suspiciously. "Is it the German chef?"

"No, of course not!"

"It had better not be," he hissed, instantly making my hackles rise.

"Just hurry up, please."

He went down to the cellar and I paced up and down in the kitchen, thinking of Reinhardt upstairs. Had he heard anything Raphael had said?

Raphael finally reappeared.

"Did you get it?" I whispered, looking at his bag.

He nodded curtly, then, before I could stop him, he barged past me and up to my room.

"What are you doing?" I hissed after him, but it was too late, he'd already disappeared from view.

Taking the stairs two at a time, I raced in behind him to find both men standing about two feet apart, glowering at each other.

"This is very cozy," Raphael said, looking at the glasses of wine on the table.

"We're planning the menu for next weekend," I said quickly.

"Isn't that something you can do at the hotel?" Raphael replied.

"I'd better get back," Reinhardt said, not meeting my gaze.

"Oh, I hope you're not leaving on my account," Raphael responded, his voice dripping with sarcasm.

"I'll see you on Sunday, Coralie," Reinhardt muttered, still not looking at me.

I so badly wanted to tell him not to go, and to tell Raphael to go to hell, but there was the small matter of the bomb in Raphael's bag, not to mention Raphael's big mouth, which had already done enough damage.

"OK, see you on Sunday," I replied. I looked at Raphael, hoping that he would go too, but his feet remained rooted to the kitchen floor.

As soon as we heard the door downstairs close and Reinhardt's footsteps disappearing off along the street, Raphael scowled at me. "Why did you lie to me? Why didn't you tell me he was here?"

"Because it's none of your business who I have here."

"That's where you're wrong—very wrong." He stepped closer, his frown deepening. "Who you're fraternizing with has everything to do with me if it means you're jeopardizing the Resistance." He looked over at my bed, which as usual was unmade. I grimaced as I realized what he would be thinking.

"It's not how it looks," I muttered. "He and I are just friends."

"*Friends?*" he spat. "You're friends with a German?"

He's been far kinder to me than you've ever been, I wanted to say, but bit my lip. I picked up the glasses and tipped the wine down the sink.

"I'm sorry for interrupting your cozy little soiree," he sniped.

"Oh, grow up!" I hissed. "You got what you came for, now I want you to leave. I have to get up in a few hours to start baking."

"Very well, but I'll be watching you, and if I get any inkling that you're working for those bastards, there'll be all hell to pay."

"Working for them?" The red mist descended and I flung a wet dishrag at him, landing on his head. "I hate them as much as you do. I hate them for what they've done to our country, and to my friend. How dare you accuse me of being a traitor! I happen to be working on something right now that could be of real use to the Resistance."

"What is it?" he asked, taking the dishcloth from his head.

"I'll tell you once I've gathered the intelligence," I said, mimicking his smug tone. "The less people who know about it at this stage, the safer."

"OK," he said grudgingly.

"So goodbye," I said firmly, praying he'd leave, and much to my relief he turned and stomped off down the stairs.

As soon as I arrived at the Lutetia kitchen the following Sunday, I could tell things were different with Reinhardt. Instead of his usual warm smile of greeting, I received a curt nod, and I trudged over to my station with a sinking heart. I'd been so concerned with how things had looked to Raphael, I hadn't stopped to consider what Reinhardt would have made of his sudden appearance.

When he came over later to fetch some butter from the refrigerator, I took the opportunity to test the water. "Is everything OK?"

"Of course, why shouldn't it be?" he said defensively.

"I'm sorry about Monday night."

"I hope my being there didn't cause any problems for you." His voice was so polite and formal, it was like talking to a stranger.

"Of course not, why would it?" I replied nonchalantly.

"The sommelier didn't look too pleased to see me there."

"The sommelier is never pleased with anything I do," I muttered.

Reinhardt stared at me for a moment as if trying to work something out.

"I'm afraid I'm going to have to cancel our Monday evenings," he said curtly. "We've been ordered not to go out on our own at night as it's no longer safe since the shooting." There was something about the way he said this that made me feel as if he had redefined things in his mind—and that I was no longer a friend, I was the enemy. It was a realization that stung like vinegar to a wound.

"I'm so sorry you no longer feel safe in the country you occupied," I muttered, turning back to the cakes I'd been icing and trying to ignore my hurt and disappointment. I picked up my piping bag and squeezed it too hard, sending cream shooting all over the counter.

Thankfully, Hans wanted to practice his French on me while he peeled a mountain of carrots and a few minutes in his cheery presence lifted me out of my gloom. I was just putting the finishing touches to a raspberry fraisier when I heard the clip of heels on the kitchen floor and turned to see Inga behind me, a vision of beauty in a fur stole and dusky pink dress.

"Good evening, Coralie," she said with a smile.

The noise levels in the kitchen instantly dropped as all the men turned to gawp at her.

"I was wondering if we could have a quick chat? I'd really like you to make a cake for a special reception the Admiral will be having here next week. Perhaps we could go and talk about it in the garden. It's such a lovely evening."

"Of course," I replied, picking up my recipe book and pen. I walked out of the kitchen with her and past Reinhardt without giving him a second glance.

The courtyard garden at the center of the Lutetia had been my favorite place to go and eat my lunch back when I worked in the hotel patisserie, but I hadn't set foot in it since the occupation. It was a lovely, balmy evening and the scent from the last of the summer roses hung heavy in the air. A couple of the gray-clad German women sat chatting on one of the benches. Inga led me to a bench in the opposite corner.

"How did it go?" she whispered as soon as we'd sat down.

"It all went according to plan," I whispered back. Obviously I couldn't tell her what had happened when I'd followed the woman I'd delivered the paperwork to.

"Excellent!" She gave a sigh of relief. "Thank you so much."

I so badly wanted to ask her what I'd been delivering, but I knew that would look suspicious, so I just smiled. "Always happy to help. And thank you so much for the money," I replied.

"You're very welcome. I was wondering if…" She broke off and looked around.

"Yes?" I asked, not wanting to appear too eager, but at the same time desperate to be admitted into her confidence.

"Would you like to help me again? I have some more paperwork that needs delivering but to a different address."

"Of course."

She opened her bag, then looked pointedly at my recipe

book. "Perhaps you could put the envelope in there, so no one else sees it."

"Absolutely." I opened the book and she slipped an envelope inside.

"I know this probably seems very strange to you," she said quietly.

I laughed. "Everything seems strange to me these days."

"Yes, quite, but I just want you to know that what you're doing—or, rather, what you're helping me to do—is a matter of great importance."

A breeze drifted across the garden, rustling the leaves.

"That's very good to hear," I replied, trying to hide my growing unease. Surely anything that was of great importance to the Nazi *Abwehr* could not be a good thing, and certainly not something I wanted to be helping with. Had the woman I'd delivered the paperwork to betrayed the Germans by giving it to the man? Is that why the SS had chased him? Was he a member of the French Resistance? My head began to hurt from trying to make it make sense.

"OK, now let's talk cake," she said in her normal voice.

"Of course," I replied cheerily, but my unease continued to grow. What was it that I was helping her and the *Abwehr* with? And, more importantly, who could it be hurting? In my eagerness to help the Resistance, had I inadvertently ended up helping the enemy?

35

NOVEMBER 1941, PARIS

As fall faded into winter, Paris life became more colorless and bland than ever. The city streets, which had once hummed with cars and people and music and chatter, now stretched out stark and lifeless as the branches on the skeletal trees. And into the resulting silence came the clickety-clack of our new, wooden-soled shoes, rubber soles having become another victim of rationing. I missed my Monday evenings with Reinhardt more than I cared to admit. The pages of our recipe book became filled with recipes in my writing only, containing the coded addresses for the deliveries I made for Inga. Despite my reservations, I continued working for her, hoping that one day it would pay off and I'd uncover some major intelligence for the Resistance. Reinhardt was perfectly polite when I worked my Sunday shifts in the Lutetia, but in a kitchen where light-hearted banter was the recognized language, his politeness seemed almost akin to rudeness. Raphael was also giving me the cold shoulder—not that I minded all that much. He hadn't called at the shop since our altercation that night, and the only time I saw him was when our paths crossed at the hotel.

One afternoon Baptiste turned up at the patisserie, breathless and excited at the news that a bomb had gone off in the German bookstore, completely oblivious to the fact that I'd provided said bomb with a hiding place. Apparently, it had been disguised inside a copy of Karl Marx's *Das Kapital*, and although it had gone off while the shop was open, to my relief, no one had been killed.

One day in November, I arrived in the hotel kitchen to find Reinhardt pacing up and down.

"Oh good, you're early," he said by way of greeting.

"Why what's wrong?"

"The senior officers are having a meeting and they've requested some of your cakes." Once again, his businesslike manner caused me to wince, but once again, I didn't let him see, simply nodding brusquely and heading over to my station.

I got to work making some choux buns with coffee-flavored crème pâtissière, reveling in the luxury of having access to real coffee instead of the insipid ersatz version we all had to make do with on our rations. When the cakes were ready, I took a tray of them into the lobby and walked straight into a commotion. A group of suited *Abwehr* agents with pistols drawn were frog-marching a handful of people through the revolving door. I stopped and stood as close to the wall as possible, trying to make myself invisible, my heart pounding nineteen to the dozen.

As they approached, I noticed a woman with jet-black hair and a short, blunt fringe amongst the prisoners and my heart went out to her. The thought of what she might be about to endure at the hands of Luc Laporte filled me with horror.

A couple of soldiers brought up the rear of the procession, laden down with wireless transmitters. As they all headed for the stairs, one of the male prisoners started singing "*La Marseillaise*" and I couldn't decide if he was really brave or really stupid. Did he not know where he'd been brought and what happened here? I thought of the golden pliers I'd seen on

Laporte's desk and the poor soul crying out from the room along the corridor and I was hit by a wave of nausea.

"You won't be singing soon," one of the agents said in French with a sneer. "By the time we've finished with you, you'll be screaming."

Again, I thought of Luc Laporte and I shuddered.

"And now we have your radios, many more of your comrades will be coming to join you," the agent continued before disappearing off into the stairwell.

I watched, horrified as the implication of his words sank in. I had to let Raphael know so that he could warn our network.

I took a breath to try to compose myself and noticed a German woman in her dreary gray uniform behind the reception desk staring at me. Obviously noting my horror, her mouth curled into a sneer.

Somehow, I managed to walk across the lobby to the elevators, where, to my relief, I spotted Raphael holding a tray of drinks.

"Have you seen what's happened?" I hissed.

He nodded. "Wait until we're inside," he whispered, pressing the call button.

The elevator doors opened and we stepped in, standing grim-faced and motionless until the doors closed.

"Thanks to an informant, the *Abwehr* infiltrated the Interallie Resistance network and they've arrested most of them, including their wireless operator," he whispered as the elevator began its ascent. "They're one of our largest networks. The Germans now have all their radios and they'll no doubt torture them to try to get their codes too."

"So they'll be able to lure other Resistance operatives into a trap?" I said, my nausea growing, and he nodded.

The elevator arrived at the floor and the door opened. Braying laughter drifted from the open doors of the conference room and as we walked toward the cheering officers, I felt sick to my stomach. They'd just delivered a crushing blow to the Resistance and I'd been asked to provide their celebratory cakes.

"I don't trust myself with these pastries," I whispered to Raphael, coming to a halt. "I'm afraid I'll stuff them right in their gloating faces."

Raphael stopped and leaned close. "You can't blow it now," he whispered in my ear. "The Resistance needs us more than ever. Take the anger you're feeling and channel it into revenge. And I don't mean throwing cream cakes at them." He raised his bristly eyebrows.

"You're right." I nodded. "But how?"

He glanced over his shoulder before continuing. "We need to find out what the *Abwehr* have learned about Interallie. We need to be the Resistance's ears and eyes here. The interrogations will be taking place on the fourth floor. We have to find out what happens up there."

"OK," I agreed, although privately I wasn't sure how this would be possible. How on earth would I get away with roaming around the fourth floor undetected? But then I thought of the black-haired woman who'd just been taken prisoner and the fear she must have been experiencing in that moment. I had to do whatever I could to help.

I followed Raphael along the corridor toward the conference room. As we drew closer and the gloating laughter grew louder, my determination intensified. Those brave members of the Interallie network had risked so much to try and free France. I mustn't let them down.

Thankfully, an opportunity soon arrived. Inga had asked me to collect my latest delivery from her a couple of evenings after the Interallie arrests, so I decided to have a snoop en route by pretending that I'd accidentally exited the elevator on the wrong floor. It wasn't the strongest of cover stories, but it would have to do.

As I was now a regular visitor to Inga, the guards waved me straight into the hotel and I headed for the elevators. Fortunately, no one else was present so I was able to press the wrong button without being seen. As the elevator made its way up to the fourth floor, I felt sick with nerves and I had to give myself a quick pep talk. Whatever I was experiencing was nothing compared to what those poor members of the Interallie network must have had to endure.

The elevator doors slid open and I emerged to the clickety-clack-ding of typewriters coming from the nearest room. Trying to ignore Hitler frowning down at me from his portrait on the wall, I mentally rehearsed my cover story in case I got caught. *"Oh goodness, silly me, I thought this was the third floor. I have an appointment with Inga, Admiral Canaris's secretary."*

I was about to start making my way along the corridor when a door at the other end opened and a man in a suit stepped out. Thankfully it wasn't Laporte. I quickly turned back to face the elevator, so it would look as if I was waiting for it to arrive, then glanced over my shoulder.

"This way," the man said and a woman stepped out of the room behind him. My heart skipped a beat as I recognized the jet-black hair and blunt fringe. It was the woman from the Interallie network. I watched over my shoulder as the man led her into another room and shut the door. This was it—my opportunity to find out what was happening in the interrogations—but how would I be able to hear?

Pushing my fear aside, I hurried along the corridor until I reached the room next door to the one they'd gone into. The door was slightly ajar so, after checking the coast was clear, I nudged it open a little more. It had clearly been turned into some kind of supply cupboard. The walls were lined with shelves full of paper and files and other stationery. I took a breath and stepped inside. I had no idea what I'd say if I was caught, but I couldn't think about that now, I had to stay focused on the poor woman in the room next door.

I looked at the adjoining wall and spotted a gap between the shelves. I quickly dashed over and pressed my ear against the ornate flock wallpaper. I heard the low mumble of the man's voice but couldn't make out what he was saying. The tone of his voice was surprisingly soft, though, for someone conducting an interrogation. Perhaps he was trying to soften her up, I pondered, before sending her to Laporte. I suppressed a shudder. I couldn't think of that monster now or I'd lose my nerve.

Then I heard the woman's voice and again I couldn't make out what was being said, but, to my relief, her tone was level and calm-sounding. On and on, she spoke, without a word from the man, and I started to wonder what on earth she could be saying. When I'd started working for the Resistance, Raphael had told me in no uncertain terms that if I ever ended up being arrested, I was to say absolutely nothing. Surely this woman would have had similar training. All I could think was that she was feeding the *Abwehr* agent some kind of cock-and-bull story in order to mislead him.

Finally, she stopped talking and I heard the soft, low voice of the man, followed by a loud peal of laughter—a woman's laughter. *What the hell?* She was supposed to be being interrogated by the enemy, so why did it sound like a conversation between old friends? A terrible thought occurred to me. What if the woman had switched sides?

I heard a door opening and the man's voice from the corridor.

"This calls for a celebratory drink," he said. "I'll have some champagne brought to the room."

36

JULY 1984, SAN FRANCISCO

The moment I wake the next morning, the last sentence from my grandma's journal flashes into my mind with all the drama of a newsflash. *How can I confess that her grandmother was—is —a killer?* I rub my eyes, hoping that I dreamed it and hadn't got up at all in the night. But then I notice the glass on my night-stand, cloudy with a film of milk. I stare up at the ceiling fan, my head filling with questions. *What had she meant? Who had she killed?* Oh how I wish I could talk to Melissa about it and try to figure out a way to discover the truth. *What would a Judy Blume heroine do in this situation?* I ask myself and the answer is immediate. She would try to get to the bottom of it.

I take a shower and get dressed, then head straight to the kitchen. Grandma is standing at the stove with her back to me. I can hear the sizzle of hot oil over the radio playing and the room smells of salty bacon. The table has been laid with a basket of freshly baked croissants and jugs of coffee and juice.

"Good morning," I say cautiously. Even though I was super careful to put the journal back exactly where I found it, I can't help feeling nervous that she might have somehow realized what I did.

"*Bonjour!*" she cries, turning to face me. Then she laughs. "With all our talk of Paris last night, I've started thinking and speaking in French again."

I sit down at the table, overwhelmed with relief. She doesn't know I've seen it. But how can I find out who she killed without her knowing? "It's so cool that you can speak two languages," I say, my mind buzzing. Perhaps if I can get her to talk some more about the war, she'll end up confessing.

"I used to be able to speak three," she replies, turning back to the bacon. "Well, two and a half would be more accurate."

"What was the half?" I ask, already guessing the answer.

"German. I wasn't fluent or anything, but I knew enough to..." She breaks off.

"To what?"

"Get by," she replies.

Hmm. What does she mean by that? Enough to have a relationship with the chef? Then I remember what she wrote about him in her journal and another question pops into my head. What was the "terrible truth" about him?

"The young boy in the kitchen I told you about—Hans—he taught me a lot." She sighs and takes the pan from the stove.

The song playing on the radio comes to an end and the show's presenter reads the news. The main story is about Russia, and I realize that for once nuclear war hadn't been my first thought upon waking. I'm not sure that discovering your grandma is a killer is much of a comfort, though. Now it's my turn to sigh.

"Are you all right?" my grandma asks, putting the bacon on a plate, which she places in front of me on the table. The rashers are perfectly crisp and golden at the edges and it's a measure of how distracted I am that I don't start to drool.

"It just seems as if nothing has changed," I say, pouring myself a glass of juice. "Since World War Two, I mean. Countries still want to kill each other. It's so depressing."

"Mmm." She sits down, looking thoughtful for a moment. "But if we allow ourselves to get fearful and depressed then they've won without even dropping a bomb."

"What do you mean?"

She pours herself a steaming mug of coffee. "Do you remember me telling you about the day I went to see Madame Monteux at the beginning of the occupation, and she told me that in a world governed by hatred and fear, happiness is an act of rebellion?"

I nod. "But how are we supposed to be happy when we could be killed at any minute?" My old anxiety begins clawing at me. "Isn't that just living in denial?"

She takes a sip of her coffee. "Ah, that's better!" she exclaims. "It's funny, even after all these years, I never take proper coffee for granted. It's not about denial," she continues. "It's about resisting." She takes another sip. "I'd been planning on taking a break from my war stories today, but maybe I should continue. There's one in particular that is the perfect example of what I'm trying to say, and it might make you feel a little better."

"Oh, yes, tell it to me, please!" I urge. If I can get her back onto the subject of the war, then maybe, just maybe, she'll end up explaining what she wrote in her journal and I'll discover if my grandma really is a killer.

"OK," she says, looking suddenly nervous. "So where was I...?"

37

JUNE 1942, PARIS

Over the next six months, the uneasy dance between the occupiers and occupied came to an end. There was no more mister nice guy on the part of the Germans, no more posters about how they were there to save us, but plenty detailing how and when they were going to execute French citizens, leaving us all on tenterhooks.

America had finally entered the war and despite the blow of losing the Interallie network, it only seemed to galvanize the spirit of the French Resistance. I told Raphael how I'd heard the woman from the Interallie network appearing to fraternize with a German agent and within a couple of months my suspicions had been confirmed. The woman, who was named Mathilde Carré, had indeed been turned and become a double agent for the *Abwehr*. Thankfully, once the Allies realized, they managed to lure her to Britain, where she was promptly arrested. Grateful for—and dare I say, even a tad impressed at—the role I'd played in helping first arouse suspicions, Raphael started bringing Resistance papers to the patisserie to be distributed again. Then, in June 1942, a new law was passed forcing all Jewish people to wear a yellow star with *JUIF* printed in black.

As soon as the law was announced, I hotfooted it to Madame Monteux's.

"It's like having a target pinned to my chest," she cried, as soon as I entered her apartment. The order had stated that the star had to be "level with the heart" and must not under any circumstances be hidden. "I'm never leaving my apartment again!"

The thought of Madame Monteux becoming a prisoner in her own home was too much to bear and I knew I had to do something. But what? I racked my brains, desperately trying to think of a way to cheer her up. Then I remembered the day she'd lifted my spirits after the *Abwehr* had arrived at the Lutetia.

"Do you remember saying to me that in a world where hate and fear rule, happiness itself is an act of rebellion?" I asked as we sat down in the living room.

She gave me a sad smile and it struck me how much smaller she seemed. Her thin shoulders were now permanently stooped, as if the cruel statutes against the Jewish were literally pressing down on her. "That does sound like one of the hopelessly optimistic things I used to say," she remarked with a sigh.

"It's not hopeless, it really helped me." A plan began forming in my mind that was either crazy or inspired, or both, but I felt as if we had very little left to lose. "I have an idea," I said, standing up.

"Does it involve cake?" she asked hopefully.

"No, for once it does not, although..." I paused, "cake could definitely be incorporated."

"Tell me more," she said, and it was wonderful to see the faintest spark of interest in her gaze.

"Stage one of the plan—we dress up in our most elegant gowns." I cleared my throat. "As I don't really have an elegant gown, would it be all right if I borrowed one of yours?"

Now she really looked interested. "Are you asking me to style you, Coralie?"

I nodded and she clapped her hands gleefully.

"I have waited for this day for years!"

I frowned at her, confused. "Really?"

"Yes! You have no idea how frustrating it is to see someone with your beauty hiding away beneath a flour-stained apron." She sprang to her feet and looked me up and down, as if inspecting a piece of meat in the butcher's. "Finally, I shall be able to transform the country mouse into a chic Parisian. Finally, I shall turn the dowdy—"

"All right, all right," I exclaimed. "No need to over-egg the pudding!"

"I'm sorry." She gave me a sheepish grin. "So, what else does this plan of yours involve?"

"Let's complete stage one first," I replied. "Then I'll explain stage two. Now I need to go and get some essentials."

"Cake?" she asked, her eyes now sparkling.

"Yes. I'll be back in an hour or so."

I raced to the patisserie, baked a batch of sables au chocolat with some chocolate I'd smuggled out of the Lutetia kitchen, and put them in a basket, along with some croissants, a piece of cheese and a baguette. Then I prepared a vital accessory for my outfit, before returning to Madame Monteux's, where I found her changed into a beautiful ruby-colored gown, her silver hair twisted into a topknot, with a couple of strands pulled out and coiled into ringlets framing her perfectly made-up face.

"You look incredible!" I gasped.

"Why, thank you," she replied with a little curtsey. "And now I must do the same for you. I've selected some outfits for you to choose from," she added, leading me into her bedroom. It looked as if a tornado had whipped through, scattering clothes everywhere. A scarf had somehow landed on top of the lampshade and a hat was perched on the dresser mirror. "It was so hard for me to choose," she said with a sheepish grin.

For the next hour or so, she buzzed around me, putting me into dress after dress until she decided upon the winner—a full-length goddess gown in emerald silk with a fitted bodice.

"Now you really are like my fairy godmother, getting me ready for the ball," I laughed.

"And you are as beautiful as a princess," she replied as she put the finishing touches to my hair and makeup. "*Et voilà!*" she ushered me over to the full-length mirror on the wall.

"Whoa!" I exclaimed as I gazed at my reflection. I looked like a totally different person. Like a Hollywood film star about to attend a premiere.

"Do you like it?" she asked anxiously.

"I love it. And I love you!" I replied, flinging my arms around her. "And now it's time for stage two of my plan."

"Cake?" she said hopefully.

"Yes. But not yet. We have to go somewhere first."

Her face clouded over. "But—"

"Shhh," I cut in. "Do you trust me?"

"Yes, of course."

"Then this is what we're going to do." I silently prayed that she'd agree before continuing. "We are going to go out on the town—well, on the Metro at least. And we are going to hold our heads up high, and we are going to be so defiantly happy that not even the Nazis can stop us. I just have to make one final addition to my outfit. Do you have a pin?"

She stared at me confused. "Oh—yes—I do." She fetched a pin from a box on her dresser and handed it to me and I took a yellow fabric star from my bag and pinned it to my dress. I'd made it from some leftover fabric from the patisserie tablecloths, so it was a paler yellow than the one she had to wear, but hopefully it would have the desired effect. Hopefully anyone who saw it would know that I was wearing mine in solidarity.

"Oh my goodness!" Madame Monteux exclaimed when she realized what I was doing.

"I'm choosing not to see it as a target," I said softly. "I'm choosing to see it as a sign of how much I love you."

She gave me a teary smile. "What did I do to deserve a friendship like this?"

"Everything!" I affirmed. "You're the best friend I've ever had. Now come on, we have a picnic to go to."

"A picnic, but where? I'm no longer allowed in parks, remember." She instantly looked crestfallen.

"Don't worry, I know just the place."

To my huge relief, she agreed and off we set for the nearest Metro. As soon as people saw us sashaying down the sidewalk in our ballgowns at two o'clock in the afternoon, they started to smile and cheer. To my delight, Madame Monteux began playing to the crowd, beaming from ear to ear and treating them all to a regal wave. But then the Metro station came into view and my heart sank as I saw German soldiers manning a checkpoint by the entrance.

"Happiness rebels, remember," I said, linking my arm through hers and trying to ignore my growing feeling of vulnerability. Madame Monteux was right. In the presence of German soldiers, the yellow star felt just like a target.

"I remember," she said, but her smile had gone.

The humorless soldier who greeted us didn't seem to notice our gowns, or my star, focusing instead on our identity papers. He thrust Madame Monteux's back at her and barked, "Jews in the last carriage!"

"Of course," she replied gaily and I noticed a flicker of confusion on his face, which made me smile. Like all bullies, the Germans got a kick out of seeing people's fear. Madame Monteux's joyful demeanor wasn't a part of the script and he wasn't sure how to respond to it. I was so proud of her, and so inspired by her courage.

As we made our way down the steps to the platform, my smile grew. It was possible to resist in the unlikeliest of ways if you were prepared to use your imagination.

We reached the platform just as a train was pulling in. As some passengers got off, a cry came up from the other end of the train and a man yelled, "Free France! Victory to Charles de Gaulle!" prompting a ripple of applause.

"See," I whispered to Madame Monteux. "There are so many of us rebels out there."

Her joyful smile warmed my heart.

We boarded the last carriage and I was struck by how subdued and nervous the occupants appeared, with their yellow stars pinned to their chests. For a horrible moment, I thought my plan might backfire and seem thoughtless and stupid. But Madame Monteux clearly had other ideas. As the rest of us sat down, she remained standing in the center of the carriage holding one of the leather straps hanging from the ceiling to keep her balance, then she took a deep breath and, to my surprise, she began to sing. As her powerful operatic voice filled the train, I instantly recognized what she was singing—the aria *"Un bel di, vedremo"* from Puccini's *Madame Butterfly*. She'd moved me to tears with this aria several times over the years, but to see her sing it on that Metro carriage was something else and I was so choked with emotion, I could barely swallow.

I realized that it was the first time I'd heard her sing since the law had been passed forbidding her to teach and I felt a stab of anger. *Damn the Germans and the Vichy government for keeping such a talent from the world.* As her voice soared louder and higher, rising above the clatter of the train on the track, tears began spilling onto my face. She looked and sounded like an angel.

I glanced around the carriage and saw that everyone else was watching, mesmerized, too, their troubled expressions replaced with looks of wonder.

Madame Monteux continued singing, eyes closed, and I wondered if she was dreaming of being back on stage at the opera house, singing to hundreds. Little did she realize the effect she was having on her audience in that shabby Metro carriage and the unexpected gift she was giving to everyone.

The train pulled in at the next station, but she continued singing and it was wonderful to see the looks of delight and amazement on the boarding passengers' faces. But then my heart sank as I spied a French policeman getting on.

"Papers please!" he barked as the train started moving again.

But, seemingly oblivious, Madame Monteux carried on singing and as the aria reached its stunning climax, even the policeman fell silent, watching open-mouthed.

Madame Monteux finished, her eyes still closed. There was a moment of stunned silence and then the carriage erupted with applause.

I glanced at the policeman, fearful that he'd try to put an end to this atmosphere of celebration, but his head was bowed and he brought his finger to his eye as if wiping away a tear.

"Goodness me!" Madame Monteux exclaimed, looking around the carriage at the passengers all cheering and clapping. Now it was her turn to look stunned and I was so happy for her, I felt my heart might burst. "Thank you—thank you so much," she stammered as the applause continued.

The train pulled into the next station and the policeman cleared his throat.

Determined to end the experience on a high, I stood up and took hold of Madame Monteux's hand. "Come on, diva," I said with a grin. "It's our stop."

Smiling at the other passengers, Madame Monteux gave a deep curtsey, causing another eruption of applause, and we skipped off the train and along the platform, giggling like kids.

"That was incredible!" I gasped as we made our way up the steps. "I had no idea you were going to do that."

"Neither did I!" she replied. "I don't know if it was the gown or all the talk of rebelling, but it was as if I'd become possessed by the spirit of Madame Butterfly."

"Well, I'm so grateful you did. And so was everyone on that carriage. Did you see their faces? You made them so happy."

She stopped walking and looked at me earnestly. "Do you think so?"

"Of course! Didn't you hear their applause?"

She laughed and shook her head. "And there was me thinking my days of performing were over."

We emerged into the sunlight and, mercifully, there was no checkpoint to dampen our spirits. We walked for a while laughing and talking until we found a little courtyard tucked away at the end of a narrow side street.

"And now it's time for stage three of my plan—a picnic," I said, taking the blanket from the top of my basket of food and laying it on the grass.

"Oh, Coralie!" Madame Monteux said as we sat down. "Do you know what makes me the happiest of all?"

I shook my head.

"Seeing the woman you've become. When I think of that shy little country mouse who arrived on my doorstep all those years ago..."

"I came from Malakoff, it's a suburb of Paris," I said indignantly.

"Exactly! And now look at you. You're brave and strong and funny and fearless. And the thing that makes me happiest is knowing that if anything happens to me, you'll be all right because you've become the woman you were always supposed to be."

"Nothing's going to happen to you," I said firmly, feeling suddenly teary.

"Well, just in case it does..." She fiddled with the moon-stone ring on her finger and held it out to me. "I want you to have this."

"What? No!"

"I insist. And every time you touch it, you'll be connected to me—no matter where I am."

"But—"

"No buts, Coralie. It will make me so happy knowing that you're wearing this. Think of it like a family inheritance."

"But we're not—"

"Of course we are! I love you like a daughter."

The tears that had been threatening overflowed.

She leaned closer and placed the ring on my finger and as it glinted, opalescent in the sunshine, I was filled with the most poignant and bittersweet cocktail of love and gratitude I've ever experienced.

38

JULY 1984, SAN FRANCISCO

My grandma stops talking and wipes her eyes. I look at the ring on her index finger, glowing pearly white in the sunlight streaming through the window, and it's as if I'm there with them all those years ago, sitting on the grass. And now my eyes are filling with tears too. I try to imagine what I'd do if Melissa was Jewish and we were living in France during the war. I'd like to think that I'd be as brave as my grandma and wear a yellow star in solidarity.

"That was such a beautiful story," I say, my voice breaking with emotion. "Is that the ring she gave you?"

"It is," she replies. "I wear it every day to remind me..."

"Of her?"

"Yes, and of what can happen if..." She stands up suddenly, wiping her eyes on a napkin. "Wowie, I'm an emotional wreck!" She picks up our breakfast dishes and takes them over to the sink.

"I'm so sorry," I say quietly.

"What for?" She looks at me, surprised.

"That you went through that. That your friend went through that." I think of all I've learned about my grandma so far and how brave she was standing up for her friend and working for the Resistance. But then I think of the love note and the Nazi photo album and the confession in her journal that she killed someone. It seems so hard to imagine that she could have done something so terrible. I'm not entirely certain, but I feel like the "terrible truth" about the German chef that she wrote about might hold some, if not all, of the answers. If only I can get her to open up some more about him.

"Thank you, Raven." She gives me a teary smile. "Right, I think you and I need to do some baking to lighten the mood, and I know just the thing." She goes through to the living room and returns with the recipe book. As soon as I see it, I feel a shiver of excitement. It could provide the perfect excuse to mention the chef. "It's funny," she says with a laugh. "There was a time when I could do this recipe in my sleep, when I didn't even need to measure the ingredients, but it's been so long, I think I ought to follow the instructions."

I stand up and join her at the counter. "What are we making?"

"Sables au chocolat," she replies. "The cookies I made for Madame Monteux that day. They're so rich and delicious if they don't cheer us up, nothing will." She takes some butter and eggs from the refrigerator and places them beside her mixing bowl.

I pick up the recipe book and look at the inscription on the inside cover. "What does this say?" I ask tentatively.

She glances down at the page and instantly her cheeks flush. "Oh—uh—it says 'the recipes of the best French pastry chef in the world and a lowly German cook.'"

"The best French pastry chef in the world?"

Her cheeks flush even redder. "Yes, he was joking, making fun of something I once said."

"It seems like you got on very well..." I hold my breath, hoping I haven't pushed it too far.

"We did." She cracks an egg on the side of the bowl so hard that the shell shatters and half of it falls inside. "Damn!" she exclaims before scraping it into the trash. "Clearly I'm no longer the best chef in the world," she says with a feeble laugh.

"Did you and he ever become friends again—after the night the wine guy turned up at your store?"

She frowns. "Oh yes, we became friends again, but..."

"But?" I echo softly. *Please, please, please keep talking,* I silently beg.

"But nothing was as it seemed." She sighs, and for a horrible moment I think she's going to change the subject. "OK, fetch me the sugar and I'll tell you the next instalment."

If there was an Olympic sport in fetching things from a kitchen cupboard, I think I just won gold, because I'm back at her side with the sugar in an instant, grinning in anticipation.

39

JUNE 1942, PARIS

My day out with Madame Monteux seemed to shift something in her, reminding her of who she used to be and who she truly was, and we saw the welcome return of her spirited self. Baptiste was delighted, and although they still refused to admit that anything of an amorous nature was going on between them, they were certainly openly playful and flirty with each other.

One night I headed back from an early supper with them feeling slightly wistful. I'd left early to give them some privacy and I felt a sudden loneliness descend upon me. Thankfully, the store and my work at the Lutetia kept me so busy—and tired —I didn't usually have the time or energy to feel lonely, but there was something about that balmy June evening that made me pine for how life used to be, and how every day in Paris before the occupation had seemed so ripe with possibility. As I turned into my narrow street, I noticed a man lurking in the shadows by the patisserie. My first thought was that it was Raphael and my heart sank. I wasn't in the mood to deal with his brusqueness or patronizing tone. But as I drew closer, the man removed his cap and I realized that it was Reinhardt. I was so surprised that I forgot all about our falling out and felt genuinely happy to see him.

"Reinhardt. What are you doing here?" As I reached him, I saw that his eyes were tinged red and ringed with shadows and I felt a stab of concern. "Are you OK?"

"Yes. No. I don't know," he replied quietly. "Can we talk?"

"Of course." I unlocked the door and led him upstairs. "Would you like a cup of tea?"

"Please." He hovered by the table nervously.

"Sit down." I gestured at one of the chairs.

"Thank you."

I put the kettle on and joined him at the table.

He looked as if he had the weight of the world upon his shoulders. "Was there something you wanted to tell me?" I asked gently.

He nodded. "I had some bad news yesterday."

"What was it?"

"My best friend from school was killed fighting in the east."

"In Russia?"

"Yes. We grew up together. He was the closest thing I had to a brother."

"I'm sorry." Ordinarily, I wouldn't have given much thought to a German soldier being killed, they had started the war after all, but Reinhardt looked so broken, it was impossible not to be moved by his pain.

"He didn't want to fight," he said softly, as if guessing what I might be thinking. "He was a really gentle soul."

My sympathy grew and I stood up and took the kettle off the stove. "I think perhaps we need wine more than we need tea."

He nodded and gave me a grateful smile and it felt so nice to feel the old warmth between us rekindle.

"I've missed you!" I blurted out. "I mean, I know I still see you every week, but I've missed this. I miss our friendship."

"I've missed you too," he replied. "And I'm so sorry for how I behaved before, when the sommelier came here. To be honest with you, I was..." He paused and cleared his throat, looking down at the table. "I was jealous."

I stared at him, stunned.

"I thought you and he were... He seemed so angry to see me here—I thought that you were..."

"In a relationship?"

He nodded, his face flushed. "I'm sorry. I hadn't realized. But I had no right to get angry about it."

"But we're not in a relationship. I would never be in a relationship with him!" I exclaimed.

His face lit up. "You're not?"

"No! Most of the time, I find him intensely annoying. Even his eyebrows make me want to scream!"

Reinhardt's face broke into a beaming smile and it was like seeing that first moment of sunshine after a storm. "I feel so stupid," he murmured.

"As well you should!" I retorted and, my God, it felt good to banter with him again.

He laughed. "I've missed this—you—us—so much."

"Me too."

He took a folded piece of paper from his jacket pocket. "I actually wrote something for you—a test of your German."

"Is this your idea of how to be friends again—by giving me a test?" I exclaimed.

"Yes, actually," he replied, a defiant glint in his eyes.

I unfolded the paper and saw three short sentences under the heading, *Deutschunterricht für Coralie*. "German lessons for Coralie," I translated in French.

Reinhardt nodded and I moved on to the first line.

"*Danke für dich*. Thank you for... for you?" I asked and he nodded again before looking down into his lap, clearly embarrassed. I read the next line. *"Ich liebe dich.* I love you?" I looked back at him, and he nodded without meeting my gaze. It suddenly felt as if all the air had been sucked from the room and I could hardly breathe.

"And the last one?" he said softly, still not looking at me.

I looked back at the page. *"Darf ich dich bitte küssen?* Please, I—you... What does *küssen* mean?"

"Kiss," he replied, his voice barely more than a whisper.

"Please can I kiss you?"

He looked at me and nodded. "Yes, you may."

I burst out laughing. "But I didn't write this, you did."

"I know." He continued to hold my gaze and suddenly we were both on our feet and there was a clatter of a chair being pushed back and landing on the floor. I'm not sure if it was his or mine; all I could think about, all I could focus on, was the fact that we were coming closer and closer together and then he was cupping my face in his hands and kissing me tenderly.

I'm not sure how long we were kissing for; I seemed to lose all sense of time. Then, finally, we came up for air.

"Wow!" he exclaimed softly. "That was even better than I dreamed it would be."

"You've been dreaming of kissing me?" My skin erupted in goosebumps.

His cheeks flushed. "Maybe."

"You mean to say that while we've been working together you haven't been focusing on the food you've been cooking?"

He grinned. "I have to admit that there have been several over-done lamb cutlets and poorly seasoned stews on Sunday evenings." He stroked my hair and his smile faded. "I've tried so hard to ignore my feelings, but then when I got the news about my friend, it didn't make sense to not tell you. Everything is so precarious now. Life is so fragile. I had to know if you felt the same way." He looked at me hopefully.

"I do," I said, feeling suddenly shy. I leaned forward and rested my head on his chest. "I'm so tired of this stupid war."

"Me too," he whispered.

"I've missed you so much."

"Me too."

"Is that all you can say, Chef? I hope your menu isn't as limited as your vocabulary," I teased, with a lightness I hadn't felt in oh so long.

He laughed. "How about I love you?" We looked at each other and in that moment everything else melted away, the war and the violence and the suspicion and fear, and all that was left was the word "love," hovering like a hummingbird in the air between us.

"I love you too," I whispered. And as I finally expressed what I'd tried so hard to deny it all felt so wonderfully simple.

We kissed again and he held me tight.

"So, what do we do?" he asked.

"I don't know," I said with a sigh as the complications of our situation came rushing back to burst our bubble.

"Should we wait until this stupid war is over and then find a way to be together?"

I frowned. "But we don't know how things are going to turn out. What if we don't live to see the end of the war? What if we never get that opportunity?" It had been so nice to momentarily escape the stress and lose myself in my feelings for him. I didn't want to give that up. I wasn't sure I'd be able to. "Perhaps we could start our Monday evening cooking classes again and..." I broke off, feeling embarrassed. "We keep our... *this* a secret."

He nodded and smiled and kissed me again.

For the next few days, I was barely able to concentrate, all I could think about was Reinhardt. I kept the note he'd written me in my apron pocket, sneaking peeks at it while I baked the day's bread and served the endless queue of customers. Then, at night, when I went to bed, I'd hold it to my chest and think of him in the Lutetia and wonder if he was thinking of me too. It felt so good to have something other than the horrors of the war to think about. And I was so grateful to be able to feel something other than dread or fear, I banned myself from worrying about the many potential problems our budding romance could cause.

That Sunday, when I walked into the restaurant kitchen and met his gaze, I felt certain the others would be able to detect the sparks flying between us.

"*Bonjour*, Mademoiselle Donnadieu," he said with a grin.

"Good evening, Chef," I replied in German.

"I had a special delivery for you," he said, following me over to my station. "It's in the refrigerator, look."

As I opened the refrigerator and looked inside, he stood right behind me, so close I could feel his breath on my neck, and my legs felt as if they'd turned to liquid. I leaned back slightly and felt his chin brush the back of my head.

"*Ich liebe dich*," he whispered in my ear, and a shiver ran up my spine.

"I don't know how I'm going to concentrate," I whispered. "All I want to do is kiss you."

"Trust me, that's all I've been thinking about all week," he whispered back.

Then Gunter yelled out something about vegetable peelings and the spell was broken.

I took some cream from the refrigerator and went over to my station. *Concentrate, Coralie*, I told myself. *Don't give the game away*. What we had was so precious—and so precarious—I had to do all I could to protect it.

· · ·

I was midway through making a batch of macarons when Inga appeared, delicate and beautiful as ever in a powder blue jacket and skirt and cream-colored satin blouse.

"Good evening," she said, approaching me with a warm smile. "I have some news."

I stared at her, confused. Surely it couldn't be to do with my mysterious deliveries. She never spoke about them in front of other people, least of all the kitchen staff. "What is it?" I asked apprehensively.

"I'm going to be leaving Paris... leaving France."

"Why?"

"I'm getting married." She held up her left hand and a diamond ring sparkled in the light.

"Congratulations!" I cried, and I meant it. The love I shared with Reinhardt seemed to have invaded every cell in my body, leaving me feeling dangerously like one of the heroines in the Victorian romance novels Olive had loved to read. I'd be clutching a satin handkerchief and reaching for some smelling salts if I wasn't careful. "How long will you be gone for?" I asked in what I hoped was a more business-like tone.

"For good. My husband-to-be is being posted to Hungary."

"Oh." I felt strange mixture of sadness that my one female friend in the Lutetia was leaving and guilt that I should view her as a friend in the first place.

"I'm really going to miss you," she said, "and not just for your cakes."

"I'll miss you too," I replied, feeling conflicted once again. While it had been nice spending time in her company, Inga worked for the Nazis, and judging by the size of the diamond on her ring, her fiancé could very well be a high-ranking officer.

"But I will have one last baking request," she said with a knowing look, and I nodded.

"Of course."

"Perhaps you could come and see me on Thursday?" she said. "I should know what I want by then."

"Absolutely."

"Thank you."

As I watched her walk back up the kitchen, her high heels clipping on the floor, I felt a real sense of urgency. I had one more chance to find out what she'd been getting me to deliver for the *Abwehr*, and I mustn't blow it.

40

JUNE 1942, PARIS

The following evening, when Reinhardt came for our cooking lesson, I'd barely closed the patisserie door behind him when we began kissing.

"Finally!" he exclaimed, hugging me tight. "It was torture being in the kitchen with you yesterday and not being able to hold you."

"I know!" I replied.

"I hope this doesn't make you angry," he said, breaking our embrace to open his bag.

"Oh dear, this doesn't bode well." I raised my eyebrows.

"I brought my camera," he said sheepishly, taking it out.

"Oh. I thought you were going to say that you'd brought me a turnip, or you'd asked Gunter to mentor me," I joked.

"Well, you didn't react very positively the last time I brought my camera here."

"True, but that was before..." I broke off, feeling suddenly embarrassed.

"Before?" he asked.

"Before I fell in love with you," I muttered, staring at the floor.

"I'm sorry, I didn't quite hear that."

"Before I fell in love with you," I said louder. I looked up and saw he was grinning from ear to ear. "You heard me the first time!"

"Yes, but it sounded so sweet, I had to hear it again." He pulled me back into his arms. "I love you too, which is why I brought the camera." Now it was his turn to look embarrassed. "I'd love to have a picture of you. Something to keep me from pining away when we aren't together."

"Oh." I felt a thrill of delight at this request. "Of course, as long as I can have one of you too."

"Play your cards right and I might let you have two," he quipped, taking the lens cap off.

"That would really be spoiling me!"

"I know exactly the picture I want of you," he said.

"Which is?"

"I want one of you baking, when you're lost in whatever you're creating and you have that dreamy look on your face."

"I'm not sure I know how to do that to order. I wasn't even aware I pulled a face."

"That's all right, I'll take it when you're least expecting, during our class this evening. And speaking of our class, what will you be teaching me to make?"

"The baguette," I announced. "Also known as the bread of equality."

He frowned. "What do you mean, equality?"

"Before the French Revolution, the rich people of France would have bread made from the finest wheat and the poor were left with the much harsher bran. After the revolution, a law was passed saying that bakers could only make one type of bread—the Bread of Equality—or face imprisonment. And so the baguette was born. They're made from a lean dough, with only flour, water, salt and yeast, so they're affordable for all."

Reinhardt looked fascinated at this. "I love that idea—that

everyone should be treated as equals, even when it comes to bread."

"Yes, it would be nice," I said wryly and there was an awkward moment of silence.

Reinhardt broke it by picking up the recipe book from the table and flicking through the pages. My pulse quickened as I thought of the coded numbers I'd added over the past few months, but, thankfully, he didn't notice them. He turned to a blank page and wrote *Bread of Equality* at the top.

"And what will you be teaching me to make?" I asked, eager to break the sudden tension.

"I shall be teaching you how to make the delicious Kartoffelpuffer," he replied.

I instantly giggled.

"The Kartoffelpuffer is no laughing matter," he said, pretending to look hurt.

"It just sounds so funny. What is it?"

"It is a potato pancake and it was my favorite thing to eat as a child. I've brought some apple sauce and sausage to go with it."

"Mmm." I immediately began to drool.

Our class began with me demonstrating how to make a baguette dough with my secret ingredient, a dash of honey for sweetness. Then, while I was busy kneading, I heard the click of the camera.

"Oh no!" I exclaimed. "I have flour on my nose and dough in my hair!"

"Exactly." He grinned. "That's how I wanted to capture you, completely at one with your ingredients."

"Very funny!"

Because the dough needed twelve hours for the yeast to ferment, I popped it into the fridge and took out a ball I'd made that morning in preparation.

"I can tell this one is ready now because it's doubled in

size," I explained. I cut the dough into three rectangles, then rolled and folded each one until they were baguette-shaped. I scored the tops, dusted them with flour and put them on the side. "They need to proof for thirty minutes before baking," I said, putting the oven on to heat and placing a pan of water inside. "The steam from the water helps the baguettes to rise."

While we waited, Reinhardt took the ingredients for the Kartoffelpuffer from his bag.

"Can I borrow your apron, Chef?" he asked.

I took it off and passed it to him. "Daisies really suit you," I joked.

"Yes, I'm always being told that. Roses, on the other hand, do nothing for my complexion." He picked up a wooden mixing spoon and twirled it like a baton.

"Ooh, that's the picture I want of you!" I exclaimed, grabbing the camera.

He twirled the spoon again and I got the shot.

Once Reinhardt had made the Kartoffelpuffer mixture and shaped them into flat circles, the baguettes were ready to go in the oven. While the bread was baking, he began frying the potato cakes in hot oil. Soon, the kitchen was toasty warm and the air full of the most delicious smells.

"This is so nice!" I exclaimed.

"Isn't it?" He smiled. "I love working with you. I love being with you!" Then his face lit up. "Let's get a picture together so we can capture this moment." He picked up the camera and held it at arm's length with the lens facing toward us. I looked up at him and he pressed the shutter. And oh how I wished we could have stayed in that picture-perfect moment forever.

Once the food was ready, we feasted on warm bread and butter and crispy golden potato pancakes with sausage and apple sauce. Then Reinhardt set off for the Lutetia. I was cleaning the dishes and wishing he'd been able to stay when there was a gentle knock on the back door. My first thought was that he'd returned and I felt a shiver of excitement. But I opened the door to see Raphael standing there, grim-faced.

"What's wrong?" I asked, hoping he hadn't got wind of me and Reinhardt meeting.

"There are rumors of another round-up," he said as he came inside.

My heart sank. "Of the Jewish?"

"Yes, and a lot bigger than before. Not just foreign Jews but French Jews too."

"No!" I thought of Madame Monteux and felt a jolt of panic. "When is it happening?"

"I don't know exactly. Our informant in the police only knows that it's being planned for some point in the future. Next month perhaps."

"Oh no." I leaned on the counter to steady myself.

"If you're worried about your friend, I might be able to help her."

"How?" I cried.

"I could try to get her false papers from a contact of mine in the Resistance."

"That would be incredible! Thank you so much."

He smiled. "You're welcome. I'm sure you will be able to repay me somehow."

"Of course. I'd do anything."

"Excellent." His smile grew and in that moment I felt the closest I'd ever felt to affection for him. If he was able to help save Madame Monteux from deportation, he would be a friend forever, and I would just have to learn to live with his annoying eyebrows and arrogant ways. "I'll have a word with my contact. How old is she? I need to know for the date of birth."

"Seventy."

"OK, leave it with me."

"Thank you!"

I locked the door behind him and went upstairs, my heart

pounding. If Raphael's contact came through, Madame Monteux could assume her new identity and come and live with me. I'd move down to the cellar and let her have my bed. There wouldn't be much room, but it would be so much better than the alternative. And she could take off that wretched yellow star once and for all.

41

JUNE 1942, PARIS

The following day, unable to contain my emotions, I went to see Madame Monteux as soon as I'd closed the store.

"I have some bad news and some excellent news," I said as soon as she let me in.

"Give me the bad news first," she replied grimly. "Then, hopefully the excellent news will compensate for it."

"I'm pretty sure it will," I said. "Well, the bad news is that there are rumors of another round-up taking place."

Her face fell. "When?"

"I don't know exactly, possibly next month. So you need to lay low for a while."

"Lower than I'm already laying?" she said drily. "What do you want me to do? Slither under the carpet?"

"No! I just mean don't go out anywhere. Baptiste and I will bring you food every day. Hopefully, it won't be for long—which brings me to the excellent news."

"It had better be excellent to make up for this!" she retorted.

"I'm getting you false papers! You're going to have a whole new identity—a non-Jewish identity—which means they won't be able to hound you anymore. You'll be free from all their stupid laws." To my surprise, she didn't exactly look elated. "What's wrong? You don't look happy."

"At the thought of having to deny my identity?" she said flatly and I instantly felt terrible. I'd been so concerned with keeping her safe, it hadn't occurred to me how upsetting this might be.

"I'm so sorry. I didn't think."

She patted me on the arm. "My dear, you have nothing to apologize for, and I really appreciate you going to these lengths, it's just so sad to think that it's come to this."

I sat beside her on the chaise longue. "We have to keep reminding ourselves that this is just a temporary thing. America have joined the Allies; the tide is turning against the Germans." As I said this, I felt a pang of concern for Reinhardt, immediately followed by guilt that I'd fallen in love with him. *He's not like the others*, I reminded myself yet again. *He's a chef who just happens to be German.*

"That's very true," Madame Monteux said and, to my relief, I saw the beginnings of a smile on her face. "And, I have to admit, the thought of having an alias is rather appealing. A bit like being a secret agent."

And that would make two of us, I thought to myself wryly. "Exactly. And you can come and live with me. There won't be much space, but you can have my bed and I'll sleep down in the cellar."

To my surprise, her eyes filled with tears. "You'd do that for me?"

"After everything you've done for me? Of course I would. And we'll make it fun because we're happiness rebels, remember?"

She laughed and squeezed my hand tight. "Of course. How could I forget?"

. . .

On Thursday, I went to see Inga to collect my final delivery. I arrived in her room to find it full of packing boxes.

"I can't believe you're leaving," I said, looking around the room.

"Me too." She sighed. "Obviously I'm excited to be getting married, but I'm going to miss France. I'm going to miss you. I only wish..."

"What?"

"We'd met in other circumstances."

I looked at her and smiled. "I do too." Hoping to capitalize on this moment of closeness, I decided to bite the bullet. "Can I ask you something?"

"Of course."

"What is it that I've been delivering for you?"

Instantly, her smile faded. "I can't tell you. I'm sorry. The Admiral would have my guts for garters if I let you know."

My heart sank. So I'd been making deliveries for the head of the *Abwehr* himself. What if the mystery envelopes contained information leading to the arrests of Resistance members? I felt like such a traitor.

Inga went over to her desk and took the two envelopes from the drawer. She handed me the smaller one first. "Your payment," she said. "There's double this time, to say thank you for your help over the past few months."

I took it from her feeling sick. It felt like blood money.

As if sensing my dismay, she touched me gently on the arm. "You really have been an incredible help. You've made such a positive difference."

Her words of consolation only deepened my dismay. The last thing I wanted to do was make a positive difference for the German Intelligence Service. I breathed a sigh of relief that I'd never told Raphael about my work for Inga. He'd have a field day lecturing me if he knew.

"And here's the paperwork," she said, handing me the larger

envelope. It felt thicker this time and I longed more than ever to know what was inside.

As usual, I had a completely different delivery address, and as soon as I'd left her room I jotted the apartment and arrondissement numbers in my recipe book by the measurements for the baguettes.

All the way back to the patisserie, my frustration at myself grew. Why had I continued delivering the paperwork for so long when I didn't gain any useful intelligence from it? How could I have been so stupid? And, worst of all, who had I hurt by doing so?

By the time I got back home, I was beside myself and the need to know what I'd been helping with was overwhelming. I put the envelope on the kitchen counter and started doing some baking to distract myself. But as I kneaded the dough for the following day's bread, all I could think about was the envelope. If only there was some way I could open it to look inside and then reseal it. I put the kettle on the stove to make a cup of tea and as it heated I had an idea. *What if I steamed it open?*

But what if you're not able to reseal it, my inner voice cautioned. *The* Abwehr *would know you'd looked inside and then they'd be having* your *guts for garters.* I pictured myself being frogmarched up to the fourth floor of the Lutetia and Luc Laporte pulling my guts from my body with his golden pliers.

"Stop it!" I muttered out loud to myself and I looked back at the envelope. This was my last chance to try to get some intelligence from my work for Inga. My last chance to turn the whole sorry affair into something positive. I picked up the envelope and marched it over to the kettle, where the steam was now hissing from the spout. Before fear could stop me, I held the seal over the steam and watched as the edge started to curl up. Then I fetched a knife from the drawer and very carefully slipped it into the gap, slowly sliding it down to open the seal.

My heart sank as I looked inside. It was full of other, smaller envelopes, all sealed. Surely I couldn't risk opening any more. I took one of them out and felt it for clues as to what might be inside, but it felt just like paper. The envelope was blank, apart from a number written in pencil in the top right-hand corner: 23.05.72.

I put the envelope down and fetched my recipe book, jotting the number in the back, but back to front. There were four other smaller envelopes inside, all with six-digit numbers in the top right-hand corners. I recorded them in my recipe book, then put them back inside the main envelope and tried to reseal it, but it wouldn't stick back down. *Damn!* Panic surged through me. I needed to reseal it, but how? Then I remembered how Arnaud had taught me how to make glue from flour and water as a kid.

My hands trembling, I quickly whipped some up in a cup and carefully spread a thin film along the seal of the envelope with a pastry brush. Thankfully, this time the envelope remained sealed.

I sat down at the table and tried to calm my racing heart. I had no idea what the numbers meant. They had to be some kind of code. Perhaps each one represented a letter of the alphabet. I spent the next couple of hours trying to crack the code, but nothing I came up with made any sense.

The next day, I delivered the envelope as instructed. The woman who opened the door practically snatched it out of my hand and shut the door again before I had a chance to say anything.

I returned to the patisserie feeling dejected. Later that evening I was about to go to bed when I heard a knock on the back door. It was Raphael.

"I've got it," he whispered, stepping into the kitchen.

"What?" I asked, hardly daring to believe he could be the bearer of such good news.

"The identity card for your friend." He took an envelope from the inside pocket of his jacket and handed it to me.

"Thank you so much!" All the day's frustration and disappointment disappeared in an instant and my body hummed with excitement.

He smiled. "Glad to help. I'd better get going as it's almost curfew."

"Of course. Thank you again."

I hurried upstairs and turned on the lamp. I couldn't wait to see Madame Monteux's face when I gave it to her. I held the envelope up to the light and my heart skipped a beat. There, in the right-hand corner was a six-digit number written in pencil, just like the envelopes Inga had given me. But surely it couldn't be one of Inga's; that wouldn't make any sense.

I grabbed my recipe book from the table and flicked back to the page where I'd written the numbers back to front. There, in the middle, were the exact same digits: 23.05.72. I held the envelope up to the light again and saw a greasy fingerprint shine in the light. Was that from me, when I'd held it earlier after kneading the dough?

I opened the envelope terrified it was some kind of trap, but there inside was an identity card. I studied the name on the card and the date of birth—23 May 1872, the same year of birth as Madame Monteux's. I felt a jolt of recognition as I looked at the number—it was the same as the one on the front of the envelope. The numbers weren't a secret code, they were the date of birth on the card inside.

I looked at the official stamp at the bottom of the card and had a flashback to the first time I'd gone to Inga's room and the wooden box I'd seen on her desk with the different compartments. One of them had housed a rubber stamp, I was sure of it. But how and why was Inga supplying false papers to the Resistance? Could Admiral Canaris's personal secretary be a double agent? It would certainly explain why she'd been so nervous when the SS soldier had got into the elevator with us that day. And why the SS had chased the man I'd seen being passed some of Inga's paperwork. I shivered as I thought of what Reinhardt had said about nothing being what it seemed at the Lutetia. But if Inga had been helping the Resistance, then I had too by delivering the cards for her. I felt a surge of relief. Could it be that I hadn't been betraying the cause after all, that I'd actually been helping people escape the Germans?

I looked down at the card and smiled. Whatever the truth, I was now able to help the most important person of all. Madame Monteux.

42

JULY 1942, PARIS

That night, I barely got a wink of sleep, I was so excited. It felt incredible to have some good news for once and I kept imagining Madame Monteux's face when I told her. It was going to be wonderful to see her smile.

This time, I didn't have to drag myself out of bed at four to start baking the day's bread; I positively sprang up and into my clothes and down the stairs. When I opened the shop door, I greeted the queue with a cheery *"Bonjour!"* and made time to ask each and every customer how they were. Every other minute, I'd glance at the clock on the wall, willing the hands to move faster until I could lock the door and hotfoot it to Madame Monteux. But then, midway through the morning, Baptiste appeared, pushing his way to the front of the queue.

"Hey, get to the back!" someone yelled. "I've been waiting for hours."

"I'm not here to get bread," he replied before turning to me, his expression deadly serious. "Have you heard the news?"

"No, what is it?" I asked, fear rising inside of me.

"The round-up has begun."

"No!" I tore off my apron. "I'm really sorry," I called to the customers, "but I'm going to have to close."

Cries of dismay filled the shop.

I grabbed the baskets of bread and brought them over to the door. Thankfully, the queue didn't stretch much further now. "Please help yourselves," I called, placing the baskets outside. "I have an emergency to attend to."

I locked the store door and Baptiste and I began running down the street toward the river.

"I have false papers for her," I gasped as we ran, feeling for the envelope in my pocket. "I got them last night."

"Oh thank God!" Baptiste replied. "I'm sure she'll be OK. She knows not to answer the door to anyone but us."

"Yes, and I'd warned her a round-up might be imminent." But, despite all of this, I couldn't help feeling nervous.

As we passed a side street, I heard a loud pounding sound and saw a group of policemen hammering on a door.

"Bernstein family, open up!" one of them called.

I gasped in horror. "Are the French police doing the round-up?"

"It looks like it," Baptiste replied grimly.

My panic grew. Madame Monteux knew not to answer the door to the Germans, but what if the French police tricked her into answering to them?

When we got to her building, I saw Brigit in her office.

"Have the police been here?" I asked frantically.

"Not that I know of," she replied, and I breathed a sigh of relief.

Thankfully, she clearly wasn't in the mood for gossip and disappeared off into her office. Not wanting to wait for the elevator, Baptiste and I raced up the stairs.

As soon as we reached the door, I gave my customary three knocks. There was no response.

"She might be hiding," Baptiste said.

"Good point." I took a deep breath, trying to calm myself, and fetched the spare key she'd given me from my bag. My hand was trembling so violently, it took a couple of attempts to get it in the lock.

"It's OK. She's going to be OK," Baptiste said, placing a reassuring hand on my shoulder.

I opened the door, and we hurried inside. Everything looked to be in place and my relief grew. A half-drunk cup of tea and an open book sat on the table next to her chaise longue. There was no sign of any kind of struggle.

"Madame Monteux?" I called. "It's all right, it's only us."

All remained silent.

"Maybe she's hiding in her closet and she can't hear us," I said to Baptiste and we hurried down the hall and into her bedroom.

I took the envelope from my pocket, ready to present her with her new identity.

"Madame Monteux?" I called again.

Baptiste went over to the closet. "Duchess? Are you in there?"

I watched, my heart in my mouth, as he opened the door.

"She's not there," he whispered.

"Then where is she?" My voice rose in panic. I looked around the bedroom for some kind of clue as to what might have happened. "Do you think she went out? Maybe she didn't realize that the round-up is happening. She could be back any minute."

He nodded, but I couldn't help noticing that the color had drained from his face.

We both jumped at a knock on the door.

"Shit! What if that's the police come to get her?" I hissed.

"We need to stay here, stay quiet, and hopefully they'll go away."

We stood motionless as there was another knock on the door, and another.

Finally, all went quiet. I crept into the living room and peeped out of the window. There was no sign of any police or soldiers.

"It looks like the coast is clear," I whispered, and then a horrible thought occurred to me. "What if Madame Monteux knows about the round-up and she's gone to the patisserie to hide there? She won't be able to get in."

"Oh yes." Baptiste nodded, looking alarmed.

"I'll go back there and check. You stay here in case she comes home. Hopefully between us we'll find her."

"Good plan."

Baptiste accompanied me to the apartment door, but as I opened it, I nearly jumped out of my skin. One of the neighbors was standing there, looking ashen-faced.

"I thought I heard you go in there," he whispered. "I wanted to let you know that they took her away."

"What? Who?"

"The police," the neighbor replied. "They came early this morning. Brigit showed them up here to the apartment."

"She did what?" I looked at Baptiste and my legs seemed to turn to water. It felt as if the bottom was falling out of my world.

43

JULY 1984, SAN FRANCISCO

My grandma leans back in her chair and closes her eyes and I notice the shiny trail of a tear making its way down her cheek.

"I'm so sorry," I say, my voice wavering.

"It was horrific," she whispers. "To have been so close to saving her, only to discover that they'd got her after all."

I get up and walk around the kitchen table and hug her from behind. Her hair is soft against my cheek and smells of coconut. "I'm so sorry," I whisper again. "I don't know what I'd do if that happened to my best friend. I can't believe Brigit showed the police where she lived."

"Oh, don't get me started on that woman," she mutters and it crosses my mind that maybe Brigit was the person she killed. I feel like I might have been driven to murder if anyone had done that to Melissa.

My grandma clasps my arm and her moonstone ring glows up at me and I think of Madame Monteux. Part of me is desperate to know what happened to her, but another part is scared to find out, certain that it must have been bad. "Thank you, Raven," she murmurs. "Thank you for being so supportive."

"You're my grandma," I exclaim. "Of course I'm going to support you."

She looks up at me, her eyes swimming with tears. "I bet you weren't expecting your visit to the Bay Area to be quite so dramatic," she says with a half-smile.

"No, I wasn't. I was actually expecting it to be hella boring," I reply and she bursts out laughing.

"Is that so?"

It's so good to see her laugh, I continue the joke. "Yep. To be honest, I'd been plotting all kinds of ways to be sent back home. Being rude and obnoxious. Refusing to wear a seat belt. Ignoring you. Going on a hunger strike."

Her laughter grows, then she gasps and leaps to her feet. "The cookies!"

"Just my luck to plan a hunger strike when I'm being fed by the best chef in the world," I joke as she takes the cookies from the oven. The smell of chocolate is so rich, it makes me feel giddy. "Please tell me they haven't burned."

"No, they're a little on the crisp side, but I think they're OK." She puts them on a plate and brings them over to the table. "I had no idea you'd been dreading coming here so much. Was it... was it something your mother said?"

I shake my head. "No, not at all. It was only because I didn't want to leave Melissa. But now I'm really glad to be here."

"You're not just saying that to make me feel better?" She looks at me so hopefully, it causes a weird kind of ache in my heart.

"Of course—and I'm not just glad to be here for your awesome food either." I glance at the cookies longingly. "I'm really loving hanging out with you and getting to know you better." And I really, truly mean it, despite her ominous diary entry.

"Well, ditto!" she replies and we smile at each other. "OK,

help yourself to the cookies while they're still warm," she says, "and I'll try to summon up the courage to tell you what happened next."

44

JULY 1942, PARIS

"I'm going to kill Brigit!" I cried as my shock began to subside, and I pushed past Baptiste toward the stairs.

"No!" He grabbed my arm and pulled me back inside Madame Monteux's apartment. "If she is in cahoots with the police and the Germans, you could end up in trouble too," he hissed. "And you'll be no help to anyone if you get yourself arrested. We need to try to find out where they're sending the people they're rounding up and see if we can save her."

I knew he was right, but I felt utterly defeated. The thought of Madame Monteux facing this new horror on her own was too painful to bear, and the notion that the busybody Brigit had helped them was making me incandescent with rage. "I should have got her to come to my place before," I cried. "I have false papers for her. She would have been OK."

"You mustn't blame yourself." Baptiste gave my arm a comforting squeeze. "Do you really think the Duchess would have left this place unless it was absolutely necessary? She—" He broke off at the sound of German voices outside and we exchanged frightened glances before hurrying over to the window.

"Oh no!" I exclaimed as I saw a group of soldiers standing on the sidewalk by a truck. I ducked out of sight as they looked up at the building.

"Do you think..." I tailed off, too afraid to voice my worst fears.

"They've come to loot the apartment?" he finished my question, looking equally horrified. "We need to get out of here."

I stuffed the false identity card inside my bra and we raced from the apartment. German men's voices echoed up from the stairwell.

"Shit!" I hammered on the elevator button and it began grinding into life painfully slowly. The sound of the voices and their boots on the stairs grew louder and louder. There was nowhere else to hide. If the elevator didn't come in time, we'd be sitting ducks.

There was a loud ping and we opened the door and stepped inside, pressing ourselves to the wall to try to make ourselves as inconspicuous as possible. Baptiste pulled the door closed and hit the button to go down over and over, but nothing happened. The German voices were so loud now, I knew it was only a matter of seconds before they appeared and then, mercifully, the elevator began its descent. I saw a flash of green-gray uniform in the shrinking gap just before we disappeared from view.

"What if there are more of them downstairs in the lobby?" I hissed.

"We have to look as if nothing's bothering us," he replied. "As if we've just been to call on a friend, but she wasn't there."

I nodded, grateful for his calmness under fire.

The elevator reached the ground floor and I took a deep breath, smoothed down my dress and fixed what was hopefully a serene expression to my face. The door slid open and to my horror I saw two soldiers standing there.

"They say it might rain later," Baptiste said loudly.

It took me a second to realize what he was doing. "Really? It's certainly hot enough for a storm," I replied.

As we crossed the lobby, I saw a flash of movement out of the corner of my eye—Brigit was in her office, and I saw a soldier standing beside her.

"Thank you very much," I heard him say. "You have been most helpful."

Rage coursed through my veins. So she had betrayed Madame Monteux after all.

As if reading my mind, Baptiste linked his arm through mine and practically frogmarched me toward the door.

"Good day," he muttered to the soldiers and they let us pass them and head out onto the sidewalk. I guess they had more important things on their mind, like stealing from my beloved friend.

We walked back to the patisserie in stunned silence. The only thing I could think to do was go and see Inga. If she'd provided the false papers, maybe there was something she could do to help. It was a high-risk strategy, but with Madame Monteux in such a perilous position, I had very little left to lose.

I said goodbye to Baptiste, collected my recipe book, and hurried on to the hotel. Thankfully, the guard on duty recognized me and waved me straight inside. I took the elevator up to the third floor and raced along the corridor to her room. When I got there, I found her door slightly ajar. I nudged it open and my heart sank. The room had been stripped bare. Inga had gone.

Feeling overwhelmed with despair, I decided to go down to the restaurant kitchen to see if I could find Reinhardt for some moral support.

The lunchtime shift was just coming to an end and the men were singing a song in German while cleaning up. Hearing their happiness was as grating as the sound of knives being sharpened and it hurt my ears. How could they sing while their compatriots were causing so much pain? I stood in the doorway feeling faint from shock and sorrow.

Suddenly, Hans appeared in front of me.

"Coralie, are you all right?" he asked in French. He looked so genuinely concerned, I couldn't stop my eyes from filling with tears and I shook my head. "Do you want to see Reinhardt?" I nodded. "Come, I'll take you to him." He took my arm and steered me out of the kitchen and up the back stairs. "He's in his room, resting before the evening shift, but I'm sure he'll be very pleased to see you."

"Thank you," I whispered.

He took me to a room on the first floor and knocked on the door. When Reinhardt opened it and saw me, his mouth fell open in shock.

"Coralie? What's wrong?" He glanced up and down the corridor, then pulled me inside, thanking Hans before shutting and locking the door. "What's happened? Please tell me you're OK."

The tears I'd been holding back began to flow. "They've taken my friend," I sobbed.

"Who have?"

"The police. They're rounding up the Jewish people and taking them away and I wasn't able to stop them. I wasn't able to save her."

He wrapped his arms around me and held me tight, but it was of no comfort and felt instead like being put in a straitjacket. I shook him off and turned away.

"I'm so sorry," he said softly.

"Why?" I snapped.

"Because she's your friend. Because I hate seeing you in pain."

"If you cared about my pain, you wouldn't even be here in France." As soon as the words left my mouth, I regretted them, but I was so grief-stricken and angry, I felt as if I was spiraling out of control.

"Do you really feel that way?" Reinhardt sounded so hurt, and I felt a pang of guilt, but that only angered me more. Why should I worry about his feelings? He was fine, living here in safety and splendor at the Lutetia, not having to live in fear.

"I shouldn't have come here," I said, going back to the door.

"No, please." I felt his hand on my shoulder. "Please stay."

"This occupation has ruined our lives," I said, quieter now and more in control. Although I knew that he wasn't personally responsible for the round-ups, I wanted him to know the pain his leaders were causing. I wanted him to know the true personal cost of the occupation. "And today the person who means the most in the world to me was taken from her apartment, taken God knows where, on her own. She's seventy years old and she's on her own." I turned back to face him. "And then your soldiers arrived like vultures to take her possessions. I was there. I saw them."

"You were there?" he said, looking shocked.

"Yes, I'd heard about the round-ups so I'd gone to check she was OK. But I was too late."

He stepped toward me, opening his arms as if to hug me, but I pushed him away.

"I was too late!" I cried and I began pummeling his chest with my fists, but he didn't move and he didn't try to stop me.

"Oh, Coralie, I'm so sorry," he said softly as I cried and cried. "I'm so, so sorry."

There was something so soothing and solid about the way he just stood there, allowing me to cry myself out, and it reminded me of how Arnaud used to be when I'd fly into a temper as a kid. How he'd hold me tight until I'd got all the anger and pain out of me.

But Reinhardt wasn't Arnaud, I reminded myself, he was a German, and because of the Germans, Madame Monteux had been snatched from her apartment and taken prisoner in her own country.

"How can you be sorry," I sobbed, and I felt his arms go around me. I tried to break free but he was too strong so I sank into his embrace, all of the fight gone from me. Reinhardt held me tighter, then began stroking my hair.

"I really am sorry," he whispered. "And believe me, I'm not the only German to be ashamed of what is happening."

I stared up at him, tears spilling from my eyes. "Do you mean that? Do you really feel ashamed?"

He nodded and gently wiped the tears from my face. "I love you, Coralie." And then he kissed me, but it was different to the times we'd kissed before. This time, it was full of pain rather than passion.

45

JULY 1942, PARIS

I returned to the patisserie that evening feeling sick to my stomach. Everywhere I looked, there were reminders of Madame Monteux and the huge role she'd played in my life. My gaze fell upon the cheery posters she'd created, proclaiming the store a boulangerie as well as patisserie, and it was like a knife to the heart. Since the first day I'd met her, she'd always looked out for me, showering me with her eternal optimism and generosity. What if she never came back? What if I never saw her again?

I sank to the floor in despair and looked at her moonstone ring, remembering what she'd said as she'd given it to me. Had she had some kind of premonition that this would happen, that one day we'd be parted? Whatever the reason, I was so grateful to have something of her with me and I clutched the ring tightly.

"Are you going to sit there on the floor moping forever or are you going to get up and do something?" I imagined her saying if she could see me, and I heaved myself up with a teary smile.

"All right, all right, I'll do something," I muttered, and I headed into the kitchen to make a start on the next day's baking.

But as I kneaded the dough, fresh tears began to flow. "Why? Why? Why?" I sobbed as I punched and pulled at it. I knew I shouldn't be kneading my sadness into the bread, but I couldn't help it. What difference would it make anyway? Everyone in Paris was grieving for someone or something, and the life they used to live.

When my first customers arrived the following morning, I served them like a silent machine, incapable of even the most basic greeting. All I could think about was Madame Monteux and where she was and what would become of her.

It was only when Baptiste arrived, pale-faced and unshaven at lunchtime, that I sprang into life.

"Have you heard anything?" I cried, grabbing his arm. "Do you know where they've been taken?"

He nodded grimly. "The velodrome."

"The cycling arena?" I stared at him, shocked. Why on earth would the police take people there?

"It's the only place big enough to house them all," he said, causing bile to burn at the back of my throat. The sports arena had been turned into a prison. A prison for innocent French citizens.

"How many have been taken?"

"Thousands." He shook his head in disgust. "Apparently even the velodrome isn't big enough."

"How is this happening?" I cried. "There must be some way we can rescue her."

I looked at him hopefully, but all of the spark had gone from his eyes and he seemed utterly defeated.

"There's no way. I've been down there. They have guards on every entrance."

The thought of Baptiste going to the velodrome to try to rescue Madame Monteux broke my heart all over again. It had been so wonderful to witness them growing closer, but it made the thought of them now losing each other even crueler.

"How do you think she's coping?" I asked.

"I don't know. She's a formidable woman, but there's only so much one person can take."

I hated seeing him so downhearted. "Are you going to be OK?"

He nodded. "Don't you worry about me. I'm tough as old boots. We have to keep the faith that she's going to be OK."

I nodded and forced myself to smile, but inside I was a churning mess.

By the time I'd served all the bread and closed the store for the day, I was exhausted, but way too anxious to sleep. I paced round and round the patisserie kitchen, my anxiety hardening into anger. Slowly, slowly, bit by bit, the Germans had stolen everything from us and now they'd taken the most precious person in the world. And to make matters even worse, our own government and police had been complicit in it. Was it really that easy for people to succumb to evil? Were we really so weak as a species? The fury inside of me built and built until I felt as if I couldn't breathe. Just when I thought I might explode, there was a knock on the back door. I opened it to see Raphael.

"Is your friend OK?" he asked straight away.

I shook my head. "I didn't get the identity card to her in time. They've taken her away."

"Shit! I'm sorry."

"I think the concierge in her building snitched."

He gave a heavy sigh. "There's been a lot of that happening, unfortunately. Sometimes they do it so they can move into the vacant apartment."

"No!" The thought of Brigit moving into Madame Monteux's apartment was horrific. How could people be so heartless and grasping? I forced the image from my mind to stop myself from screaming in despair. "Can I ask you a question?"

Raphael nodded.

"Where did you get the false papers from?"

"A contact in the Resistance," he replied vaguely.

"And can they definitely be trusted?"

"Of course. I've been getting false papers from them for months." He gave another sigh. "I'm so sorry you didn't get yours in time."

"Do you know where your Resistance contact gets them from?"

"No. But it must be another Resistance member who's an expert in forging papers." He frowned at me. "Why all the questions?"

I briefly contemplated telling him about Inga, then decided against it for fear that he would lecture me for working for her without telling him and I couldn't bear the thought of another of his arrogant putdowns. Not today. I couldn't trust myself to exercise restraint.

"No reason," I replied. "I was just curious."

Over the next couple of weeks, I felt as if I was fighting an undertow of despair and no matter how hard I tried to swim free, it kept sucking me under. Through Baptiste, I learned that the thousands of people rounded up and sent to the velodrome had been transferred to an internment camp in a suburb of Paris called Drancy, where they were being held in a half-finished construction site of apartment buildings. The thought of Madame Monteux and all those other innocent people living in such conditions was devastating. Baptiste had also discovered that the prisoners there were able to receive mail, so we sent her letters, and every day I prayed I'd receive a reply, but nothing came. Realizing that Madame Monteux might not have access to writing materials, I sent another letter including a pencil, sheet of paper and an envelope stamped and addressed to myself. But still nothing came.

The only comfort I felt during those terrible weeks was when I was with Reinhardt. He started coming to the patisserie two nights a week and staying until I had to start baking at four in the morning. Sometimes during the day I'd feel plagued by feelings of guilt that I should have become so close to a German, especially after what had happened to Madame Monteux. But then he'd arrive at the store and he'd wrap his arms around me and smile that smile of his and, momentarily at least, all of my tension and fear would melt away.

One evening, we lay in my tiny bed in the dark, dreaming out loud about how our lives might be after the war.

"I don't care where I live as long as I'm with you," he said, stroking my arm.

"Really? You wouldn't want to go back to Germany?" I asked, feeling a surge of relief. I'd been trying not to think about what might happen to us if and when the war ever ended, so certain was I that he'd want to return to his homeland.

"There's nothing there for me now," he said flatly.

I snuggled closer to him, resting my head on his chest. "That's kind of how I feel about France, especially now Madame Monteux has gone." I held him tighter as he kissed the top of my head. "Maybe we could go somewhere new. Start afresh?" I suggested and I held my breath as I waited for his response, praying he'd agree.

"That would be incredible," he exclaimed. "We could go to Holland or Austria—or Ireland. We could start our own cafe. I could make the savory dishes and you could make the desserts."

I wriggled into an upright position and stared at him in the dark. "Do you mean it?"

"Of course! It would be like our Monday evening classes but every day of the week." He lifted his hand to my face and gently stroked my cheek. "What do you say, Chef? Do we have a deal?"

"Yes, yes we do! But what would we call our cafe?" I asked, wanting to breathe more life into this wonderful spark of hope.

"Hmm, I think it should be something with meaning," he said. "Like your Patisserie Resilience."

My face flushed. No matter how close we'd become, I still wasn't able to tell him the truth about my role in the Resistance. "Maybe it should have peace in the title," I suggested. "To celebrate the war being over."

"Yes! How about the Café de la Paix?" he said.

"That would be perfect." I lay back down in his arms, gazing into the dark and praying that somehow, some day, we'd bring our dream to life and create something beautiful from bridging the divide between enemy sides.

One day in early August, Raphael paid me a visit.

"I need to hide something here again," he said, marching straight behind the counter and into the kitchen.

"Please tell me it isn't another bomb," I replied.

"It's not. Although I really don't see why that should upset you, especially given the latest developments."

He took a package from his bag. It had been wrapped in brown parcel paper and was tied up with string.

"What is it then?"

"Just some pamphlets and posters," he said nonchalantly and I breathed a sigh of relief.

The sweltering summer continued, the oppressive heat perfectly reflecting the rising tensions between occupiers and occupied. Then, one day late in August, the mail arrived and I saw an envelope addressed to me in my own writing. For a split second, I stared at it, baffled that I had seemingly written a letter to myself, and then I remembered and tore it open with trembling fingers.

I pulled out a piece of paper and my spirits soared. The page was covered in Madame Monteux's elegant, looping script.

46

JULY 1984, SAN FRANCISCO

My grandma stops speaking and stands up. "Wait here," she says, "I'm going to get something."

I sit motionless, stunned yet again by all she's told me.

She returns holding an envelope, yellow with age, and as soon as I see it, I feel a rush of excitement.

"Is it... is that the letter?" I whisper.

Uh-huh," she says softly. "But I haven't looked at it since I came to America. It was just too painful."

I watch as she takes a page from the envelope and carefully unfolds it and I see that her hands are trembling.

"Would you like me to read it to you?" she asks, looking down at the page.

"Yes, please." I wait and watch, utterly gripped.

She takes a breath and begins to read.

My dear Coralie,

Words cannot express the joy I felt when I received your letter. I was so sure you'd have no idea where I'd been spirited away to. Every day I have to pinch myself, I'm so convinced that this is all a bad dream, but if it is, there's no waking from it. I'll spare you the details of the living conditions here. And when I say "living," you wouldn't expect an animal to live like this, but I'm happy to report that I'm somehow managing to keep my spirits up. I say somehow, but really I know exactly how— through my thoughts and memories of you and Baptiste. Take it from someone in the know—don't worry about accumulating wealth or possessions, dedicate your life to accumulating wonderful memories, it's at times like these that you realize they are way more valuable than gold.

Some nights I lie here unable to sleep and the fear begins to creep in. They've started transporting some of the prisoners out of here and out of France, but no one is entirely sure where to. The rumor is that Hitler has created some kind of Jewish home-land in the east—but I can't see how this could really be true. Since when has Hitler ever done anything for the Jews? But then I entertain myself with memories of you, like the day we waged a happiness rebellion on the Metro and I sang the aria from Madame Butterfly *and all of a sudden I'm smiling again. And, of course, I think of dear Baptiste too. I wonder if he's told you what happened between us. I'm guessing he probably hasn't, being a true gentleman, but I know you had your suspi-cions! Well, you were right—all of his flirting and calling me the Duchess finally wore me down! In all seriousness though, the love that man showed me at a time when I felt so hopeless and worthless was one of the greatest gifts I've ever been given. I hope you get to experience a similar love one day.*

I'm very conscious that I'm running out of paper, so I want to make every word count and although it breaks my heart to write this, I know this could be my last chance to say something to you. You are a wonderful person, Coralie. I know you've always struggled to believe in yourself, due to your start in life. I know that you've been tortured by the question, how could your parents abandon you like they did? But I have an alter-

nate perspective. I love you like a mother, and I know Baptiste loves you like a father. And so did Arnaud and Olive. Four adults who had no obligation to do so have chosen to love you as their own. Never forget this, Coralie. I hope that one day you have the chance to have a son or daughter, so you'll experience that love too. And remember the ring I gave you. Any time you want to feel close to me, hold it tight and know that wherever I am, I'll be thinking of you too.

With all my love,

Suzette

My grandma puts the letter down on the table and I look at the faded writing, trying to picture Madame Monteux writing it in the camp at Drancy. I'm so choked up, I can't say a word, so I reach out my hand and place it over my grandma's. We sit in silence for a moment until I feel I'm able to speak without crying.

"Thank you for reading it to me, it was really beautiful."

To my surprise, my grandma frowns and shakes her head. "I feel like I let her down," she says, her voice breaking.

"How? You tried everything you could to save her. It wasn't your fault you didn't get the identity card in time."

"I don't mean that, I mean about being a mother."

"But you did become a mom."

"Yes, but I'm afraid I wasn't able to give Suzette—your mom —the kind of love she deserved."

I think of what she wrote in her diary about this and shiver. "What do you mean?"

"I was so shell-shocked by everything that happened during the war. I experienced so much loss and betrayal, it was as if part of me shut down. I couldn't bear the thought of being hurt like that again, so I never let people get too close to me—not even my own daughter, or your grandpa." She looks at me and sighs. "I'm not sure if that makes any sense."

I think of how I gave up trying to get my parents to understand me, how I couldn't bear to face yet another conversation where it felt as if we were from completely different planets speaking totally different languages, and I nod. "I think I get it," I murmur. "It's like you want to build a wall around your heart so they can't hurt it anymore."

"Yes!" she exclaims, then her face falls. "I'm so sorry you've experienced this too."

"Only with some people," I say. "When I'm with Melissa, I feel like I can take the wall down again."

"But not with your parents?" she asks softly, and I shake my head. "Oh." She looks really dejected at this. "I hope this isn't because of how I was as a mom."

"Why would it be?"

She starts fiddling with the edge of her placemat. "I was kind of distant as a parent. Don't get me wrong, I wasn't cruel and I didn't mistreat your mom, but I wasn't nearly as warm and affectionate as your grandpa. I wanted to be, but something inside kept stopping me. It was ridiculous—imagine being afraid of loving your own daughter."

"What were you afraid might happen?" I ask gently.

"That I would lose her," she whispers. "I remember the night after I gave birth to her, lying in the hospital bed looking down at her asleep in the bassinet beside me and she looked so tiny and vulnerable, it was terrifying."

"Why?"

"I didn't really understand it at the time. I thought maybe it was something to do with my birth parents. That maybe I'd inherited the same gene that caused them to abandon me. It's only been in more recent years, since your grandpa died, that the real reason has dawned on me. But now it's too late to do anything about it and your mom wants nothing to do with me."

She gives a sad laugh. "It's so ironic. I was so scared of losing her, I pushed her away."

"It's not too late," I say firmly, hating seeing her look so distressed. "I don't know how you were as a mom, but I do know how you are as a grandma, and I think you're awesome."

She stares across the table at me, her eyes wide with shock, as if this is the very last thing she expected me to say.

"You're the first adult who has shown a genuine interest in me and who hasn't tried to change me one bit," I continue. "Seriously, I think you're amazing and I know Madame Monteux would be proud of how you've been to me."

She lets out a little gasp of relief and reaches across the table and clasps my hands tightly. "Oh Raven, thank you so much. You have no idea how much it means to hear you say those things."

"Of course." I give her hands a squeeze and look back at the letter. "Did Madame Monteux ever write to you again?"

My grandma's smile fades, and she shakes her head. "No. This was the only letter I received, and after this, everything began to fall apart. It really was the beginning of the end."

I look back at the letter and my body tenses. As much as I want to know the next instalment, I'm afraid too.

47

SEPTEMBER 1942, PARIS

I wrote back to Madame Monteux with another stamped and self-addressed envelope but never received a reply, and then I heard from Baptiste that many more of the prisoners in Drancy had been put on trains going east. The only hope I could cling to was that the rumors of the Jewish homeland were true, although I too found it so hard to believe.

By the time Madame Monteux had been gone for two months, I felt like a horse pulling a heavy load through snow, dragging myself through each day, all the time feverishly praying that soon the snow would melt and the war would miraculously end.

One evening in September, Raphael turned up at the store, unannounced as always, just as I was about to bake a comfort batch of chouquettes—little pieces of choux dough sprinkled with sugar. My baking had been suffering due to my mood and I could no longer rely on my intuition when it came to measuring ingredients, so I was placing some butter on the weighing scales when he barged in through the door.

"I've come to get the package," he said, in that bossy way of his, marching through to the kitchen and down into the cellar.

"*I've come to get the package*," I mimicked, sticking my tongue out at his back.

He returned with the package and a smug smile on his face. "I'll be in touch soon," he said, going back to the door. He paused and looked at me over his shoulder. "I was thinking maybe you and I could have a drink one evening."

I suppressed a shudder at the thought but forced myself to nod. The last thing I needed was to upset him again. Life was stressful enough as it was.

"Excellent." He tipped his cap to me and disappeared into the night.

The following Sunday at the Lutetia, the men were in high spirits about an upcoming trip to the cinema and teasing Hans about his crush on the Hollywood actress Vivien Leigh.

"They don't understand that I'm a fan of her acting, that's all," a blushing Hans said to me in French.

"Just ignore the schoolboys," I replied, slipping him a chocolate éclair. "Your compensation for having to put up with them," I explained, and he grinned from ear to ear before biting into the cake.

It was only later that it struck me how unfair it was that the Germans should have taken over so many of our cinemas, replacing the signs with *DEUTSCHES SOLDATENKINO*, meaning German soldiers' cinema. Going to the cinema had been one of Madame Monteux's favorite pastimes. What if she never got to see a film again? I was hit by a wave of sorrow so strong, I dropped a tray of Paris-Brests all over the floor.

Quick as a flash, Reinhardt was at my side.

"Are you all right?" he asked as he crouched beside me to help clean up the mess.

I nodded, but inside I felt anything but. How could

anything be all right while Madame Monteux was being held captive?

A few days later I'd just served the last of my bread when Baptiste arrived at the patisserie, red-faced and out of breath.

"There's been a bomb," he gasped.

"The Allies?" I asked hopefully. I'd reached the point where I really didn't care if the British and Americans bombed Paris if it meant hastening the end of the war.

"No." He glanced around to make sure the shop was empty before continuing. "The Resistance," he whispered. "They killed several German soldiers."

I didn't feel any excitement at this news. Now the Germans had adopted their policy of killing French hostages, as they called them, it would mean many more innocent people being killed in revenge.

"Where was it?" I asked, picking up some empty trays to take back into the kitchen.

"By the Grand Rex cinema," Baptiste called after me. "They killed the soldiers just as they were coming out from a film."

I let out a gasp of shock.

"Are you all right?" he asked.

But I couldn't reply. I couldn't move. All I could think about was Reinhardt and the others talking about their cinema trip.

"Coralie, is everything OK?" Baptiste appeared in the kitchen doorway, looking at me, concerned.

I took a breath. I couldn't let him see I was upset. How would I ever explain?

"You look as if you've seen a ghost," he said with a cheery grin.

What if Reinhardt had been killed? What if I'd lost him too? I started to tremble.

Baptiste's smile faded. "Coralie, what's wrong?"

I tried so hard to maintain my composure, but there had been so much pain, so much fear, so much loss. I felt completely overwhelmed.

"Why should some haricots verts being killed upset you?" He frowned as he studied my face.

"It doesn't upset me," I said, turning away to fill the sink with water. I was so tired of all the deception.

"Is there something you aren't telling me?" he asked softly.

I so badly wanted to confide in him about Reinhardt, but how could I? He detested the Germans.

"I know you're working with them every week in the Lutetia, but they can't be trusted. You do understand that, don't you? We're at war and they're the enemy." His words were like a pail of cold water being thrown over me and I quickly came to my senses.

"Of course I know that. And you know that I'm only working there to help the Resistance," I whispered.

A relieved smile broke over his face. "Yes, of course. I'm sorry."

"I'd better get on with clearing up," I said.

"OK, I'll get out of your way." He shot me another concerned glance before heading out the door.

As soon as he was gone, I put on my coat and raced to the Lutetia. As I approached the main entrance, I saw that there were a lot more guards than usual on the door, all of them holding their rifles as if ready to shoot at a second's notice. I stopped and pretended to look in my bag to give myself a moment to compose myself, then I hurried over to one of the guards who knew me.

"I'm here to see Reinhardt about the menu for this weekend," I said, praying he'd let me in.

"Papers," he barked and he searched my bag before ushering me inside.

The lobby was abuzz with *Abwehr* officers, all talking in agitated tones. I hurried down the corridor to the kitchen and cautiously opened the door. It was so quiet that at first I thought there was no one there. Then I saw some of the men sitting at the counter at the back, but there was no sign of Reinhardt. They all looked shell-shocked.

As I began walking toward them, Gunter noticed me and his face flushed redder than ever. He barked something at me in German and although I couldn't understand what he was saying, I knew from his tone that it was hostile. The other men all stared at me coldly.

"Is... is Reinhardt here?" I said, my voice quavering.

Gunter jumped to his feet and started pointing his fat finger at me. "*Mörderin! Mörderin!*" he yelled, until one of the other men grabbed his arm to restrain him.

"Go," the man called to me. "Please go."

I stumbled from the room. What had happened? What did *Mörderin* mean? And where was Reinhardt? Why wasn't he there with his men?

I raced back to the patisserie to retrieve the book of German words and phrases Raphael had given me. I leafed through the pages until I reached the words beginning with M. *Mörderin*: murderer.

I dropped the book onto the table. Why would Gunter call me a murderer? There was only one explanation I could think of and it was terrible: Reinhardt had been killed by the Resistance bomb, and as a French woman, Gunter was holding me personally responsible.

48

SEPTEMBER 1942, PARIS

That night, I found it impossible to sleep as I kept playing and replaying the scene in the kitchen over and over in my mind. Even though it was a mild night, I was filled with an icy dread and I couldn't stop shivering. It had been hard enough coming to terms with the fact that Madame Monteux was no longer in Paris, but the thought of Reinhardt being blown to pieces by a bomb was so horrifying, it felt as if my mind was spiraling out of control.

Unable to bear it any longer, I got up and went down to the kitchen. The only thing I could think to do, the only thing that might stop me from going insane with worry, was to bake. I took some butter from the fridge and some flour and sugar from the pantry. I needed to make something stodgy and comforting. Something that would fill the icy hole inside of me. I mixed the ingredients together and began feverishly kneading the dough. Then I heard a sharp rap on the shop door and almost jumped out of my skin.

I glanced at the clock on the wall. It was one in the morning. A terrible thought occurred to me. Had Gunter called me a murderer because they'd somehow found out that I worked for the Resistance? Had the *Abwehr* now come to arrest me?

There was another knock on the door, louder this time. An image of Luc Laporte sprang into my head, smiling his evil smile at me and cracking his knuckles. Resigning myself to the worst, I went through to the store and slowly opened the door. My first thought was one of relief as I could only see one man standing there in the dark. But then my heart sank—what if it was Raphael, there to gloat about the bombing?

The man stepped closer and took off his hat and I held onto the wall to steady myself.

"Is it really you?" I cried, fearful my eyes were playing tricks on me.

"Of course it is," Reinhardt replied, and he stepped inside and shut the door behind him. "What's happened? What's wrong?" He took my hands in his and I felt some of his strength soaking into me.

"I thought you were dead," I gasped. "I heard about the bomb at the cinema and I went to the Lutetia to check you were OK, but there was no sign of you and the men all looked so sad and Gunter—he called me a murderer." I touched his chest, checking again that he wasn't some kind of apparition. "But you're alive."

"I am, but..." He broke off.

"What?" I asked, my dread returning.

"Hans isn't." His voice cracked. "Hans died."

"No!" I gasped.

"That's why the men were upset. He was killed in the explosion."

"Not Hans!" A flurry of memories came rushing back to me. Hans's sweet smile and the way he'd made me feel so welcome that first day. The praise he'd lavish on my cakes, the fun we had during our French and German lessons and how he tried so hard to learn.

Reinhardt looked away, clearly close to tears. "I was there. I saw it happen. I saw him die."

"Oh no." I reached out to touch his arm and felt it trembling.

"He was only eighteen, just a kid."

"I'm so sorry." My words felt so impotent and I was flooded with sorrow.

"He had so much potential. He could have been a great chef. I was teaching him everything I know. I wanted him to..." He fell silent.

"He really loved you," I said softly. "I could tell, from the way he looked at you and the way he spoke about you."

"Why did this have to happen?" Reinhardt cried, his eyes filled with despair, a despair I knew only too well. "Why him? He didn't do anything to hurt anyone."

I stepped closer and wrapped my arms around him and he rested his head on my shoulder. "I hate this war," he muttered. "I hate it."

My skin prickled with goosebumps. To hear him say this made me love him even more. "I hate it too, but I love you," I whispered and he looked at me.

"Things are going to get a lot worse now," he said. "I probably won't be able to come here for a while. The German command have said that we mustn't fraternize with the enemy and we've been forbidden from having relationships with French women."

My sorrow grew. "What about my job at the Lutetia?"

"That should be OK. French staff are still allowed to work in the hotel. And I'll have a word with Gunter, get him to calm down. But for now I think you and I should just be work colleagues." There was a dullness in his eyes, a sense that he had somehow given up.

"I understand," I said, although inside I felt crushed. "But promise me you'll keep dreaming of the day we can be together. Café de la Paix, remember? Please don't give up on us."

He gripped my arms tightly. "I won't. I promise. And you must promise that you'll stay safe until then."

"Of course."

He hugged me tight, then turned to go and I felt a horrible wrench inside.

At least he didn't die, I reminded myself. *At least you still have the chance to be together one day.* But I could feel my hope slipping away.

"I'll be thinking of you always," he said, as he opened the door.

"And I, you," I replied.

After he left, I slid to the floor and sat holding Madame Monteux's ring in the dark, too numb from loss—so much loss—to do anything else.

I was finally about to go up to bed when there was a knock on the door. I hoped for a moment that Reinhardt had changed his mind and come back, but I opened it to find Raphael standing there, holding a bottle of wine, and grinning from ear to ear.

"I was just about to go to bed," I muttered as he barged past me.

"You can't go to bed yet, we're celebrating," he said, marching through to the kitchen and returning with a couple of glasses, which he placed on the counter.

"Celebrating what?" I stared at him, baffled.

"Killing the Boche." He pulled the cork from the bottle and filled the glasses. "We killed four of them coming out of the cinema and injured quite a few more."

He carried on speaking, but his words all blurred into one long drone. I couldn't concentrate on what he was saying. All I could think of was Hans. How could I celebrate the killing of such a sweet young man?

"Cheers!" he said, passing me a glass and chinking his against it.

"I'm not really in the mood," I mumbled and he instantly frowned.

"What do you mean?"

"I'm not in the mood for celebrating." I placed my glass down on the counter.

"Why not? Those bastards have killed so many of our people, of course we should celebrate this victory."

I searched for an excuse. "I—uh—I'm missing my friend—the one who was taken to Drancy."

"All the more reason to celebrate," he exclaimed. He picked up my drink and tried to hand it back to me, but I refused to take it. I was sick of him telling me what to do. "I want to have a drink with you," he said, with a darker tone to his voice, implying that he wasn't going to take no for an answer, which, of course, only made me more determined to refuse.

"Well, I don't want to have a drink with you. I want to go to bed."

"Is that an invitation?" he said with a smirk.

"No!" I exclaimed. "It most certainly is not!"

His smile vanished. "I see. So you'll invite the German chef up there, but not a fellow Frenchman, a fellow resistant."

"Are you seriously saying that I should sleep with you because we're both French?" I snapped.

He took a step closer. "Don't you feel any kind of bond with me, after everything we've been through together?"

I stared at him, scarcely able to believe the words coming from his mouth. "You need to leave."

He put his drink down. "And you need to think about where your loyalties lie."

My heart began to pound. "I know exactly where they lie."

"Well, I hope that's true because it would be a very sad state of affairs if your sympathies were to now lie with the

Germans..." He paused for a moment as if for effect. "Especially given your role in what happened at the cinema." He gave another of his smug smiles, like a poker player about to reveal his winning hand.

"What do you mean, *my* role?"

"You hid the bomb for us."

"No I didn't, I—" I broke off, horrified, as the awful truth began to dawn. "Was the parcel you stored here...?"

He nodded, his smug smile growing.

"But you told me it was pamphlets and posters."

"Yes, because you'd caused such a fuss about the bomb before," he replied nonchalantly.

"So, the bomb at the cinema was kept in my cellar?" My voice became shrill as I thought of Hans and how I'd inadvertently helped to kill him. I felt sick to my stomach.

"It was indeed."

Oh, how I wanted to punch the smirk from his face, but if I showed the extent of my rage, he would start questioning my loyalties again.

"Go!" I gasped, marching to the back door and yanking it open. "Get out."

He came over to me and leaned so close, his face was just an inch or two away. I could smell stale liquor on his breath, and it made me want to retch. "Why are you so upset?" he hissed. "Is it because of that chef?"

"No! If you must know, one of the men who was killed worked in the kitchen. He was only eighteen."

"He was a German," Raphael replied, seemingly devoid of all feeling.

"He was a kid."

Raphael took a sharp intake of breath. "Do you know how many children those bastards have rounded up and sent off to their deaths? My brother was only eighteen when they killed him in the Battle of France."

"They killed your brother?" I murmured and he nodded.

"The Germans who were killed today never should have been here," he continued, his voice breaking with emotion. "This isn't their country, so I don't care how old he was. He didn't have to come here. So yes, I am going to celebrate when we kill some of them, and if you had any sense, or any loyalty, you would too." And with that he marched out of the door.

I stood there, motionless, still reeling from his revelation. I had hidden the bomb that could have killed Reinhardt. I had hidden the bomb that had killed sweet, kind Hans, and no matter what Raphael said, I was overwhelmed with guilt.

49

JULY 1984, SAN FRANCISCO

So, it's ten after two in the morning and yet again I cannot sleep. After my grandma broke the news about Hans dying, she said she needed to have a break from her World War Two story for a while, and I couldn't blame her. Even I was affected by learning of Hans's death and I never even knew him. I wonder if there are young Russians who are just as sweet and kind as Hans, and who don't want a nuclear war any more than Melissa and I do. There have to be. I feel kind of dumb for not thinking of this before. I guess I'd gotten hung up on seeing all Russians as the enemy, just liked I'd assumed that during World War Two all of the Germans were. Now I find it reassuring that my grandma got on so well with a couple of them. It gives me hope that ordinary people are the same all over the world, it's just our leaders that get us into these messes with their crazy power games. But then why did she write about the "terrible truth" about Reinhardt in her diary? And why did she call herself a killer? It must be because she'd hidden the bomb that killed Hans, but if it is, I think she's being really hard on herself—she didn't even know that that's what she was hiding, thanks to that hellacious sneak, Raphael.

I think of the journal tucked inside the basket by the porch swing. *Is it still there?* I wonder. *And has she updated it since I looked?* The urge to find out becomes overwhelming and once again I find myself doing a deal with the annoyingly persuasive voice in my head. I could just flick to the last page again and see if there's been an update. It wouldn't be snooping as such. Well, only in a very minor way.

So up I get and off I creep to the kitchen. There's no trace of my grandma having been up, the kettle's stone cold and the table is just as we left it, so I head straight for the porch. At first, it looks as if the journal has been removed, but then I find it hidden at the bottom of the pile of magazines. I sit down and quickly flick it open to the last page of writing and my pulse quickens as I see she's made a new entry. I hold it up to the light coming from the kitchen window and almost jump out of my skin. My grandma is standing there, staring out at me. I drop the journal like it's a hot coal, sending it clattering to the floor.

When I look back at the window, my grandma has disappeared, and I wonder if maybe I'd imagined it. But then the porch door creaks open and I see her in her over-sized T-shirt and bed socks, silhouetted against the light from inside.

"What are you doing?" she asks, her tone flat and emotionless.

"I couldn't sleep, so I thought I'd come out here and—uh—and read one of your magazines."

"But you weren't reading a magazine," she says, her voice still eerily calm. "You were reading my journal."

"I wasn't—not really. I just wanted to see if..." I fall silent, unable to come up with any plausible excuse.

"If what?"

"If you'd written anything in there about the war," I mutter, staring down at my lap, my face burning with shame.

"But I've been telling you about the war every day." She

comes over and snatches up the journal and holds it tight to her chest.

"I know, but I couldn't sleep, and—and—I had to know what you did."

She frowns down at me. "What do you mean?"

"I read what you wrote—about being a killer."

"Oh no!" she cries.

"I'm sorry. I literally only read that page."

"Oh, Raven."

"I'm sorry. Please don't send me home. Please let me stay." The irony that I'm begging to stay after trying so hard to get sent home at first isn't lost on me.

"Of course I won't send you home." She sighs. "But I am hurt, and disappointed. I thought you of all people would appreciate the importance of respecting a person's privacy."

"I do!" I exclaim, stung by her words because I know that she's right. "I was just so desperate to find out more."

She's silent for a moment and somewhere in the distance an owl hoots.

"OK. Well, let's go back to bed and try to get some sleep and I'll tell you the rest in the morning." She still sounds really disappointed.

"Thank you, and I'm so sorry." I stand up and throw my arms around her. For a moment, she stands there, stiff as metal, still clutching the diary to her, but then, thankfully, her body softens and she wraps her spare arm around me. "Did you write that you were a killer because of the bomb?" I murmur into her shoulder. "Because if you did, you shouldn't have. It wasn't your fault at all. You didn't even know you were hiding it. It's not like you wanted to kill anyone."

"Oh, but I did!" she says softly.

I pull back a little so I can see her face, but she looks down at the floor like she can't meet my gaze.

My stomach tightens. "What do you mean?"

"What I wrote ... it wasn't about the bomb. It was about something else entirely."

50

DECEMBER 1942, PARIS

That night in the store, the night of Raphael's revelation, felt like the fatal axe blow that fells a tree. All of the blows that had come before—the Germans arriving in Paris, the *Abwehr* taking over the hotel, the curfew and the rationing and the punitive statutes, and losing Madame Monteux—had weakened me, but the revelation that I had helped kill an eighteen-year-old boy who'd shown me nothing but kindness caused something inside of me to completely shut down. I guess my brain couldn't cope with the enormity of it. And so I became a kind of automaton, seeking solace in my routine—baking, serving, cleaning, sleeping—day after day after day. Every Sunday I would go to the Lutetia to prepare pastries for the Germans, standing next to the station left empty by Hans, pretty much ignored by the rest of the staff, and all through my shift, I would think of his smile and his kindness and I'd relive my role in his death. I never, ever got a wink of sleep on Sunday nights.

Three months passed and, other than fleetingly at the hotel, I didn't see Raphael at all. I'm not sure if it was down to his doubting my commitment to the Resistance or his bruised pride from my rejecting his advances—or both—but I was glad he no longer came to the store. My guilt about Hans also made no more visits from Reinhardt easier to bear. How could I have faced him alone, knowing what I'd done? How could I have let him tell me he loved me, knowing that I'd helped kill someone he was so fond of? He appeared to be numb from loss too, simply going through the motions of running the eerily somber kitchen. Then, in the run-up to Christmas, he came to see me at the end of my shift.

"I was wondering if you could stay a little later this evening," he said as the other men all cleaned down their stations and prepared to leave. "I'd like to talk to you about the menu for Christmas and New Year. Is there something special you could bake, a traditional French Christmas cake, perhaps?"

"Well, there is the galette des rois," I replied. "We bake it in France every year on the twelfth day of Christmas."

"The cake of kings," he translated into German.

"Yes, it's to celebrate the day the three wise men visited the baby Jesus. It's one of my favorite cakes, and not only for the delicious frangipane filling," I added, "but because a charm is baked into the cake and whoever gets the slice containing the charm is given a paper crown and declared king or queen for the day."

He smiled, a sight I hadn't seen since Hans had died, and it warmed me to the core. "That sounds like fun."

"It is. I loved it as a kid. I'm not sure how he did it, but whenever my adoptive father made a galette des rois, I always ended up with the slice containing the charm." I laughed. "He probably realized there'd be hell to pay if I didn't get it."

He smile grew. "Yes, I can imagine!"

"I'd been hoping to make some individual galettes de rois for any children who come to my patisserie on the day—if I can find the ingredients."

"Oh, I'm sure I can help you with that," Reinhardt said. "I

don't suppose..." He broke off for a moment as if unsure whether to continue.

The other men all began filing out of the kitchen, calling goodnight over their shoulders.

"What?"

"Could you show me how to make it?" He looked around the deserted kitchen. "We should be free from any interruption."

"You want me to show you now?" I asked, surprised.

He nodded. "I've missed our cooking classes so much," he said softly, causing me to shiver.

I felt so conflicted. I wanted nothing more than to fling my arms around him and hug him tight, but I knew that if I did, I'd be overwhelmed with guilt. So I hurried over to the refrigerator and took out some pre-made pastry instead.

"Are you all right?" he asked.

"Yes, yes, I just need to get some pastry ready."

"OK, I'll write down the ingredients," he said, spying my recipe book on the counter. He flicked it open to a blank page. "So what do we need for the cake of kings, Chef?"

I called out the ingredients for the frangipane and began beating together some softened butter and sugar and eggs, then I folded in some ground almonds. As soon as I was mixing and stirring, I felt better, on firmer ground. Once the filling was made, I asked Reinhardt to cut out two circles of pastry and line a pie dish with one, onto which I spooned the frangipane.

"And now for the lucky charm!" I said, looking round the kitchen for inspiration. "I think I'll have to use a hazelnut. When the cake was first created, they used a bean, so I suppose it's kind of the same."

Reinhardt pulled a face. "I think I'd prefer a hazelnut to a bean in my cake."

"Yes, me too!"

Once we'd placed the pastry lid on top and put the cake in

the oven, we sat at the counter at the back of the kitchen, waiting for it to bake.

"When we have our Café de la Paix, we'll have to make this cake every January," Reinhardt said and I felt a sharp twinge of pain. Would he still dream of having a cafe with me if he knew what I'd done? He took my hand in his and my guilt grew. "The thought of one day being with you is the only thing keeping me going."

"Really?" It had been so long since we'd been alone together, part of me had been wondering if his feelings might have faded.

"Of course," he replied. "Everything else is so bleak."

"It is." The urge to hug him was so strong now, it began to override my guilt. I didn't know that Raphael had hidden a bomb in my store. If I had known, I never would have let him. Maybe I was wrong to be so harsh on myself. Maybe Reinhardt wouldn't judge me if he knew the full story. I obviously couldn't tell him now, but maybe one day, when this was all over and if we were lucky enough to make it out alive, I could come clean and hopefully he would understand. But in the meantime... "I've missed you so much," I said quietly.

"Oh, thank God!" he exclaimed. "You've seemed so distant lately. I was worried you might have gone off me. Or found someone else."

I grinned. "Well, it is true that I've developed feelings for another man."

His face fell. "Who?"

"Gunter, obviously. Haven't you noticed the chemistry between us and the way he always scowls at me in order to disguise his true feelings of deep attraction? It's electric."

"Ow!" Reinhardt cried, clapping a hand to his heart. "Cast aside for a man whose head looks like a giant beetroot!"

I giggled. "I've always found the beetroot to be a very attractive vegetable."

"Ha!" He laughed. "And you say I'm obsessed with vegetables!"

"You're obsessed with turnips. The beetroot is so much more colorful."

"That is true." He leaned toward me and kissed the tip of my nose. "But are you sure you can't be tempted by a humble turnip lover?" he whispered.

"I suppose I'd be willing to let you try to tempt me," I whispered back.

He stood up and offered me his hand. "Come."

I took it, my heart pounding as he led me over to the storeroom. As soon as we were inside, he closed the door behind me.

"I can't stand it anymore!" he exclaimed. "I have to be with you." He cupped the back of my head with his hand and began kissing me. All the way up my neck at first, then my ear, causing me to moan with pleasure. He pushed me back against the door as our mouths met, and as we kissed, it was as if all the guilt and pain and fear of the last three months was finally draining from my body. "This has been the hardest three months of my life," he said when we finally pulled apart. "Not being able to be alone with you."

"Mine too."

"I've missed you so much."

"I've missed you too."

"Are you just going to copy everything I say, Chef?" He grinned. "I hope your menu has more imagination than your conversation!"

"Hmm, says the man whose menu revolves entirely around root vegetables," I shot back, and, my God, it felt good to be joking again.

He shook his head. "How dare you! My menu now revolves around onion gravy, as well you know. And I've even been known to include a sausage or two."

I threw up my hands in mock defeat. "I'm so sorry for

doubting you. Your onion gravy is indeed an act of artistic genius. I've heard that Picasso himself is jealous of your creative prowess."

He laughed. "Now I know things are OK. You're being rude to me again."

"Likewise."

He shook his head and gave a labored sigh. "And once again, she has nothing of her own to say."

"Actually, I do." I took a step closer to him and looked him right in the eyes. "I love you."

We stood like that for a moment, and then he kissed me again. It was so passionate, it was as if we were trying to make up for lost time.

"I love you too," he said finally.

"So unoriginal," I joked, rolling my eyes.

"You want something original?" he said, with a glint in his eye, and he took a key from his pocket and locked the storeroom door.

"What are you doing?"

"Being original," he replied, before taking my hand and leading me past the rows of shelves to the back of the room, where he began kissing me again. "Is this OK?" he whispered, as he undid the top button on my blouse.

"Yes!" I whispered. "This is so much better than OK."

Afterwards, we sat on the floor, leaning against the wall.

"I will never, ever think of this storeroom in the same way again," I said, looking up at the jars of spices in front of us.

"Me too," he laughed. "It's going to be a lot more exciting coming to get the seasonings now."

"I've missed you so much," I sighed, leaning into him. Feeling his strong arms around me felt so good. I felt so safe.

"I tried so hard to do the right thing and not see you," he

said softly. "But it only ended up feeling like the wrong thing. I've been so miserable."

"Me too." I nodded. "This—being here, with you—is the only thing that's felt right in so long."

"So, should we risk seeing each other again?" he asked. "Should we restart our cooking classes?"

"Yes," I replied. After what had just happened, there was no way I could say no.

"Excellent." He kissed the top of my head, then got to his feet and held out his hands to help me up. "We'd better get out of here. I'll walk you home." But just as we got to the door, Reinhardt put his finger to his lips. "Shh!"

My skin prickled with goosebumps as I heard the low drone of men's voices in the kitchen.

"Who is it?" I whispered.

He shrugged.

Then one of the men laughed and it sent a chill right through me. I'd know that gloating laugh anywhere; it was Luc Laporte.

"I was up at Drancy today," another man said, immediately catching my attention. I heard drawers being opened and the clink of cutlery. They were obviously helping themselves to a snack.

"Oh yes?" Laporte replied.

"They sent three more trainloads of the vermin off."

"To the labor camps?" Laporte replied.

I thought of Madame Monteux and shuddered.

"If that's what you want to call them," the other man said, and I could tell from his tone that he had to be smirking. "Most of them won't be doing a day's work ever again."

Laporte laughed, but this time it sounded menacing rather than gloating.

Reinhardt's fingers laced through mine and he clasped my hand tightly, but I was too shocked to respond. What did the man mean? Were they transporting the Jews out of France to kill them?

They can't be, there's far too many of them, I tried reassuring myself. But all I could think of was Madame Monteux facing yet another untold horror on her own and it made me sick to my stomach.

I heard a refrigerator being opened and closed and then finally their voices and footsteps faded into the distance.

"Are you all right?" Reinhardt whispered.

I nodded, but I couldn't trust myself to speak for fear that if I opened my mouth, I'd start sobbing. I just wanted to get out of there, as far away as possible from monsters like Laporte.

"The... the cake, we need to take it out of the oven," I stammered.

He opened the door cautiously and we emerged into the kitchen. The air was full of the almondy aroma of the galette, but it only made my feelings of nausea grow.

"I'm so sorry," he said again, as I took the cake from the oven.

"I need to go," I said, plonking the tin on the side. "I need to get home."

"I'll walk you."

"No, it's OK, I—"

"I insist!" he said firmly.

We walked back to the patisserie in total silence. It was a moonless night and pitch black. But for once I liked how the suffocating darkness wrapped itself around me. I didn't want Reinhardt to see my heartbreak and despair.

51

Just as my grandma stops speaking, the phone in the kitchen starts to ring, causing us both to jump.

"Saved by the bell," she says wryly, getting up from the breakfast table to answer it.

I'm too shocked to say anything. I'd been so enjoying her story about Reinhardt and the storeroom—although it is a little gross thinking of your grandma doing the deed—but then, when she said what she did about Madame Monteux and Drancy, I felt really sick. I'll never forget my history classes on the Holocaust, and the horrors that happened in the concentration camps. But now I know all about someone who probably ended in one, someone who meant so much to my grandma, it suddenly feels personal, and even more horrific. I look at the half-eaten croissant in front of me and push my plate away.

My grandma takes the receiver from the phone on the wall and clears her throat. "Hello?" She looks at me, surprised. "Oh, hello, Suzette. How are you?"

Instantly, my heart sinks. The last person I want to speak to right now is my mother. All I want is to hear more of my grandma's story. The unanswered questions are piling on top of each other inside my head. *What happened to Madame Monteux? What was the terrible truth about Reinhardt? And who did my grandma kill?* I'm getting so close to the answers now, I can feel it.

"Yes, of course," my grandma says, smiling at me. "She's right here."

She leans across the table and hands me the receiver.

"Hey, Mom," I say flatly.

"Hi, Cindy," she replies, sounding equally fed up. "I was just wondering how you were getting on?"

"Excellent, thank you."

"Oh!" She sounds genuinely shocked at this, making me even more convinced that her sending me here was supposed to be some kind of punishment.

"Yes, I'm having a great time," I add for good measure. "How are you?"

"Oh, not bad, I suppose."

I feel a pang of concern at how down she sounds. *But why should I care how she feels?* I remind myself. *Since when has she ever considered my feelings?*

I contemplate asking how she and Dad are getting on but decide against it. She'll only brush me off with some vague and slightly patronizing answer.

"So, you're having a good time with your grandma?" Once again, she isn't able to hide her surprise and it really annoys me.

"Yes. I'm loving it here. We're having a ton of fun." I glance across the table and my grandma gives me a grateful smile. "Was there anything in particular you wanted?" I ask. "We were kind of in the middle of something."

"In the middle of what?" Suzette says and I feel a prickle of annoyance at her sudden interest in my life.

"Oh, just something." For once, I'm the one being vague and evasive, but to my surprise it doesn't feel satisfying, it feels kind of icky.

"OK, well, I won't keep you then," she says in a tight little voice. "I'm glad you're both having such a great time."

You're the one who sent me here, I want to yell, but instead I say, "Thanks, Mom," and hand the receiver back to my grandma.

"So, how are things going, Suzette?" she says, then gives the receiver a puzzled look. "Oh, she's gone."

"Good! I want to get back to your story."

I watch on tenterhooks as she puts the receiver back in its cradle on the wall, but instead of coming back to the table, she stands there for a moment. "Can I just say something before I continue?" she says, looking slightly awkward.

"Sure."

"That time when your mom snooped in your diary?"

"Ye-es," I say apprehensively, unsure where this is going.

"Maybe she was doing it for the same reason you were when you looked in mine."

"What do you mean?" I ask, instantly feeling defensive.

"Maybe she just wanted to get to know you better."

"Hmm—or maybe she was just looking for a reason to punish me."

She looks unconvinced. "Promise me something, don't be too hard on her. If she offers you an olive branch and tries to make things better between the two of you, please take it." There's something about the plaintive way in which she says this that makes me wonder if she's talking from her own personal experience. Did she try to make things better with Suzette only to have her attempts rejected? I think back to the last time I'd seen her, when she came to visit us in New York. Was the cake she brought her attempt at an olive branch? I wince again as I think of how Suzette had told her she wished she'd died instead of my grandpa.

"OK," I say with a nod.

"Thank you." She gives me a relieved smile and sits back down at the table.

"So, what happened next?" I ask, eager to move the conversation away from my mom. "After what you heard in the hotel kitchen?"

Her smile fades and she visibly pales. "Everything began to unravel."

52

JANUARY 1943, PARIS

Reinhardt was good to his word and on the eleventh day of Christmas, I woke to find a delivery of all the ingredients I'd need to make my galettes des rois for the children. I didn't mind the extra baking at all. I stirred hope and joy into the frangipane filling and I felt like a fairy godmother as I put a charm into each of the tiny cakes, picturing the children's faces when they discovered them. As the cakes baked, I thought of Madame Monteux and how she would have loved what I was doing, and I was hit by a fresh wave of sorrow. I touched the moonstone ring she'd given me and prayed for her protection and my strength. I couldn't give up hope on her. I couldn't let what I'd overheard in the kitchen make me lose faith.

"I hope that wherever you are, you're OK," I whispered. "I miss you so much, and so does Baptiste. Stay strong. And stay happy." My voice wavered and I felt a lump growing in my throat.

Don't be sad, I imagined her scolding me. *Remember that happiness is an act of rebellion.* I gave a weak smile and returned to my cakes.

. . .

The twelfth day of Christmas was a huge success. Every time I served a parent, I'd hand their child a mini galette and their eyes would grow as wide as saucers. I'd spent half the night making paper crowns to go with the cakes and seeing the children leave the patisserie with smiles on their faces and crowns on their heads made my soul sing. It was a much-needed reminder that happiness was possible in even the grimmest of circumstances, and that we could create our own warmth in the harshest of winters.

I was still glowing that evening as I cleaned the pans and prepared the ingredients for the next day's baking, but then I was startled by a rap on the back door. I opened it to find Reinhardt standing there dressed in his civilian clothes and holding a cake box.

"What are you doing here?" I asked, surprised.

"Well, that's a fine way to greet a man who has just spent five hours making you a cake."

"You've made me a cake?" I stared at him as he stepped inside. The last person to have made me a cake was Arnaud.

"Yes. And let me tell you, making a cake for the best cake maker in Paris—sorry, the world—is an intimidating experience. That's why it took me five hours; I kept messing up, I was so nervous."

"What kind of cake is it?" I asked as he carefully placed the box on the table, touched by the sweetness of his gesture.

"A galette des rois, of course." He grinned at me. "How did it go today, with the children?"

"It was wonderful!" I exclaimed. "They were so happy. Thank you so much for the ingredients."

"You're welcome." He looked as delighted as I was. "OK. Here goes." He glanced at me nervously, then opened the box. Inside was a perfectly baked galette; the puff pastry on top was the perfect shade of gold and in a leaf design.

"It's beautiful," I said.

"Thank you. I only hope it tastes OK." He went over and fetched a knife. "Shall we?"

"Yes please."

"I brought some wine too." He took a bottle from his bag.

"This is champagne!" I exclaimed as he placed it in front of me on the table.

"Is it?" He gave me a mischievous grin.

"Are we celebrating something?"

"Possibly." He put a slice of the cake on a plate and handed it to me. Then he cut himself a slice and opened the champagne. "To dreams coming true," he said once he'd filled our glasses.

"To dreams coming true," I echoed. "Especially our Café de la Paix!"

"Yes!" He chinked his glass to mine, then watched intently as I took a bite of the cake.

"It's delicious!" I cried.

"Are you sure?"

"Yes, but then I did teach you everything I know."

"Very true, Chef, very true." He watched as I took another bite.

"Aren't you going to have any?" I said, feeling suddenly self-conscious.

"Yes, I just wanted to check that you really like it."

"I love it!" I exclaimed. "I—oh!" I stopped talking as my teeth bit into something hard.

"What is it?" He looked at me eagerly.

"I think I have the charm." I took it from my mouth and began removing the frangipane. "But it isn't a charm," I cried. "It's a ring."

"How on earth did that get there?" he said, before sliding off his chair and onto the floor.

"What are you doing?" I removed the last of the cake from the ring. It was beautiful. Silver with a solitaire diamond that shone up at me like a star. "Why are you...?" I looked down at Reinhardt to see that he was on one knee. "Oh!" I gasped.

He gently took the ring from my fingers. "Coralie, will you do me the honor of being my queen?" he said softly.

"You mean...?"

He nodded and smiled. "Will you marry me?"

"Marry you, but—"

"I know we can't get married yet," he cut in, "but after the war... If we're going to have a cafe together—and live above it together—it would only be right to—"

"Yes!" I interrupted, kneeling down in front of him. "Yes! Yes! Yes!"

"You mean it?" His eyes lit up, greener and brighter than ever.

"Of course!" I had never, ever experienced a joy like I felt in that moment, and part of me was certain that I had to be dreaming.

He put the ring on my finger.

"It's all sticky from the cake," I giggled. "I can't believe you put my engagement ring in a cake!"

"Well, how else does one propose to the best pastry chef in Paris if not the world?" he said, raising his eyebrows.

"Very good point, Chef. I appreciate your thoughtfulness. Although I'm also glad that I didn't choke to death on it."

"Don't worry, I was ready to slap you on the back just in case."

"Is that why you were staring at me so hard?" I exclaimed.

"Yes! I was terrified I might accidentally kill you!"

We both laughed and then he kissed my ring finger.

"Oh, it tastes good!" he said. "Come on, let's have a toast." He stood up and helped me to my feet.

"Just a moment," I said, "there's something missing." I

hurried into the store and returned with two of the leftover paper crowns I'd made for the children. I placed one on his head and one on mine.

"To us," he said, raising his glass.

"To us," I echoed, and in that moment I truly believed that the love we shared was strong enough to save us, strong enough to survive the war. I had no idea of the devastation to come, and how the ones we trust the most are capable of the cruelest deception.

53

SEPTEMBER 1943, PARIS

Months passed without incident—now Raphael was out of the picture, I was able to focus solely on providing the bread rations in the patisserie and my Sunday shift at the Lutetia. No one seemed to know where Raphael had disappeared to, but Baptiste heard on the grapevine that he'd gone to join the armed resistants hiding in forests outside of Paris.

"I'd go and join them too," Baptiste said to me, "if it wasn't for my weak knee." He'd taken to walking with a stick now and it pained me to see him looking so frail. The war was ageing us all prematurely, it seemed and I couldn't help wondering if his decline was also due to his heartbreak over Madame Monteux. "I'll be joining them on the streets of Paris though," he continued. "When it's time to fight for our liberation, and that time is coming, Coralie. The tide turned the minute the Germans were defeated in Stalingrad."

I smiled, but inside my stomach churned. As much as I wanted liberation from the Germans, what would become of Reinhardt if and when that day came? I knew that he wasn't a Nazi but would the Allies be as discerning, or would they tar all of the Germans with the same brush?

Reinhardt and I continued with our secret cookery classes and our secret engagement. I only wore my ring on Monday nights while we were together, and week by week the pages of our recipe book filled with my desserts and his savory dishes. On those nights, it was easy to imagine that our dream of the Café de la Paix would come true—cooking together in my tiny kitchen made me feel as if we were already living it.

But then, one fateful evening, my house of dreams came tumbling down. It was a Monday and I'd been preparing for my cooking class with Reinhardt, dressed in my best dress, complete with engagement ring, when there was a knock on the back door. Thinking it was Reinhardt, I went racing downstairs, only to open the door and see another man standing there. His cap was pulled down low, with only a bushy black beard visible, and his clothes were shabby and smelled musty.

"What are you doing?" I cried as he tried to barge past me into the shop kitchen.

"I need your help," he said gruffly and I froze. It was Raphael!

"What... what are you doing here?" I stammered, quickly shutting and locking the door.

He took off his cap and I saw that his face was streaked with dirt. He looked as if he'd been living wild for months. "I told you; I need your help."

He looked me up and down and my face flushed as I realized how overdressed I must have appeared.

"Going anywhere special?"

"No—uh—yes—I..." I broke off as his gaze fell upon my engagement ring.

"Are you getting married?" he asked, raising his eyebrows, which were even more unkempt than ever.

"No—I—It's..." No matter how hard I tried, I couldn't find the words and I could feel my face growing redder and redder.

"Who is it?" he asked, taking a step toward me. "Who's the lucky man?"

"It's not—I'm not..." I jumped at the sound of four jaunty knocks on the shop door. Reinhardt had arrived. "You have to leave," I hissed at Raphael. "It isn't safe for you to be here."

"Why not?" He stepped so close I could smell his stale breath.

"Because you could get caught," I hissed.

"By who?"

There was another knock on the door, more insistent this time.

"Aren't you going to answer that?" he asked, almost mockingly.

"I can't with you here. I told you, it isn't safe."

"Answer it!" he said sharply, and he reached inside his jacket and pulled out a gun.

I stared at him, horrified. "Have you lost your mind?"

"No, but I have a horrible feeling you might have lost yours. Now answer the door!"

"Keep your voice down!" I hissed.

He aimed the pistol at me. "Answer the door!"

Realizing I had no choice, not only because of the gun pointing at me but also because Reinhardt would panic if I didn't, I went through to the shop feeling utterly sick. I couldn't let him in with Raphael brandishing a gun in the kitchen. I'd have to make up an excuse to get him to leave. I unlocked the door and opened it about an inch.

"Good evening, Chef," Reinhardt exclaimed cheerily, and I winced as his voice boomed around the store.

"Good evening." I quickly pulled a pained expression and clutched my stomach. "I'm so sorry, but I'm not feeling very well."

"Oh no, what's wrong?" He looked so concerned, I felt even worse lying to him, but what else could I do?

"I've been really sick. I think I ate some cheese that had gone off."

He gently stroked the side of my face. "You poor thing. Let me come in and take care of you."

"I don't know if—"

His face lit up as if he'd just had an idea. "I know. I'll make you some of the ginger tea my mother used to make me when I got sick. I have some ginger back at the hotel; shall I go and fetch it?"

Recognizing that this was probably my best chance of saving a potentially disastrous situation, I nodded. "That would be great, thank you."

He kissed me on the tip of my nose. "OK, I'll be back soon. You go and sit down."

I nodded and shut and locked the door, then took a breath before heading back into the kitchen. I felt as if I was about to meet my executioner.

Raphael was standing there with his gun trained on the door. I wondered hopefully if he hadn't heard.

"You traitorous bitch," he hissed, now pointing the gun at me. "You're engaged to the chef."

"My God, you are so stupid!" I yelled, for once fully in control of my temper but wanting to take him by surprise. Thankfully, it appeared to work and Raphael instantly lowered the gun and took a step back, looking shocked. "Why did I go to work in that kitchen in the first place?" I asked angrily.

"Clearly to get a German husband," he muttered.

"No, you idiot, to work for the Resistance, which is what I have been doing for nearly three years. And I've been able to get closer and closer to the enemy."

His scowl faded and he looked at me, clearly interested. "Go on."

I took a breath and said a silent prayer for forgiveness to

Reinhardt before continuing. "And now I'm in a position where I've completely won the trust of the chef, which means he'll tell me anything."

Raphael sighed and shook his head, like a deeply disappointed parent.

"What?"

"He's probably doing exactly the same thing to you."

I frowned at him. "What do you mean?"

"I mean, he's an agent for the *Abwehr* and I'm certain they're using him to find out about the Resistance."

I felt a rush of panic, and the palms of my hands became hot and clammy. "That can't be true. I'd know if that was the case."

"Clearly not." He gave another patronizing sigh. "He's completely deceived you."

My panic grew. Surely this couldn't be true. "How do you know?" I looked at him suspiciously. I wouldn't have put it past Raphael to make it up just to get one over on me.

He took something from his pocket and held it out to me. It was a photograph of two men standing in front of the Eiffel Tower—one of them was wearing the dreaded uniform of the SS and the other was in civilian clothes. I could tell instantly from the curly hair and smile that it was Reinhardt.

"This is him meeting with a member of the SS," Raphael said smugly. "Passing information to them about the Resistance."

"What?" I leaned against the side, feeling dizzy.

"Apparently he works directly for Canaris."

"But—"

"And judging from your hurt expression, you've been lying to me, and you do have feelings for him."

"I don't," I said quickly. "I'm just furious that he's been working against the Resistance." I looked away, feeling sick. "Has he always been working as an agent for them?"

"I'm not sure. This photograph was taken a year ago."

A year ago. I cast my mind back to the previous September and I felt sick. It was when the Resistance planted the bomb outside the cinema. The bomb that killed Hans. Had that been the motivation he needed to work against the French? Another thought occurred to me, filling me with dread. Had he heard on the grapevine that the Resistance had stored the bomb in my patisserie?

"Don't worry," Raphael said. "At least you now have the upper hand because you know the truth about him."

"But does he know the truth about me?" I murmured, my dread growing.

"I don't know," Raphael replied, and my heart sank. Surely if he was making this whole thing up to hurt me, he'd have said yes, absolutely. "He's probably been asked to keep tabs on you," he continued. I thought of how Reinhardt had started coming to see me again three months after the bomb and how he'd managed to get around the rule banning Germans from getting involved with French women. If he was doing this on Canaris's orders, it made complete sense that he hadn't got into any trouble for doing so. "But it's all right," Raphael said, "because now you can turn the tables and keep tabs on him. And we're about to hit the Germans where it hurts."

"How?" I asked, my mind racing as it tried to catch up with his revelations. Could it really be true? Could Reinhardt really have been spying on me?

"We have something big planned, here in Paris," Raphael said with a smile.

My stomach clenched. "Another bomb?" Even after everything he'd told me, I really didn't want to be a part of more killing.

"No. I can't tell you what it is, but I need a place to stay."

"You mean here?"

He nodded. "I can sleep down in the cellar. It's just for tonight. I'll be gone first thing tomorrow."

I nodded numbly, then remembered what Reinhardt had said about the ginger tea. "The chef's coming back. I told him I was feeling sick to try to get rid of him and he said he'd bring me a remedy."

Raphael gave a sarcastic laugh. "He really is working hard to win your trust."

I grimaced and glanced down at my engagement ring. Had it all been a sham? Could Reinhardt's warmth and kindness really be an act? It was so hard to believe. But there was no denying the photograph. It was definitely Reinhardt deep in conversation with an SS officer, and even worse, smiling at him like they were old friends.

"OK," I said. "You can stay. I'll tell him I'm too sick to see him when he comes back."

Raphael nodded. "Thank you."

I fetched him a pillow and some blankets and left him to set up a makeshift bed in the cellar. Then I paced around the store, my heart pounding as I waited for Reinhardt to return. Could it really be true that he'd been deceiving me all this time? Had nothing about our relationship been real?

I was torn from my thoughts by a knock on the door and I opened it to see Reinhardt, a worried expression on his face. "How are you? I've made you some tea." He held out a flask to me. If it was all an act, he deserved to win an award.

"I was just sick again," I said weakly. "I think I need to go straight to bed."

"Would you like me to stay with you for a while? I could try to take your mind off it."

"No," I said more sharply than I'd planned and he instantly looked hurt. "Sorry, I just feel so awful, I need to be by myself."

He nodded. "I understand. I hope the tea helps."

"I'm sure it will, thank you."

He looked at me intently, as if trying to work out if everything was all right. Or had he realized I was on to him?

I forced a smile onto my face. "I'm really sorry," I said softly.

"No need to apologize!" he exclaimed and he kissed me gently on the cheek. "I'll see you on Sunday at the hotel."

"Yes, see you then." I shut the door, my eyes filling with tears.

54

Thankfully, Raphael wanted to go straight to sleep in preparation for whatever he had planned the following day, so I left him down in the cellar and went up to bed. For the next few hours, I tossed and turned, my mind like a pendulum swinging between evidence of Reinhardt's innocence or guilt. The thing that most convinced me that Raphael was right was the timing. If anything was going to get Reinhardt to work against the French Resistance, it was Hans being killed. It had affected him so badly. But did that mean that he was spying on me? *What does it matter?* I thought to myself bitterly. Even if he didn't suspect me and his feelings for me were genuine, if he was working against the French that changed everything.

I got up at four to begin the day's baking and found Raphael pacing nervously in the kitchen.

"I couldn't sleep," he muttered.

"Me neither." I filled the kettle and set it on the stove. "Tea?"

"Please." He sat down on a chair in the corner. "There's— uh—something I want to say to you, just in case..." He broke off.

"In case?" I looked over my shoulder at him.

"In case things go wrong today."

I shivered. Even though I didn't know what he was doing, it was clear what he meant. "Well, hopefully it won't come to that," I said breezily.

"But just in case it does." He cleared his throat and looked down at the floor. "I'm really sorry."

"What for?" As the most irritating person in my life, he could be referring to a multitude of things.

"For what I did the time I came here with the wine. The way I tried to..." He tailed off, looking embarrassed.

"It's OK," I said softly, stunned that he'd found the humility to apologize, even if he wasn't able to verbalize his wrongdoing.

"What crazy times we are living in." He gave a sad laugh.

"Yes, indeed." I sighed. "I can't imagine France ever going back to normal again after this."

"We have to keep hoping." And for once when he smiled it wasn't smug or annoying, but warm and genuine.

"Is there a real risk you might not come back from today?" I asked, my voice wavering. As much as he annoyed me, I couldn't bear the thought of him being captured or killed. And at least I knew for sure that he was on the side of the French. A sobering thought occurred to me. He and Baptiste were the only people I could now trust entirely.

Raphael nodded. "But I don't care." He sighed. "I used to. I used to pray that I'd make it through all this alive, but things have got so bad. So many innocent people have been killed. If it takes me losing my life to help defeat the Boche, then so be it. They're evil, Coralie. Never forget it."

His words sent a shudder right through me and I went over and placed my hands on his broad shoulders. "Whatever it is you're doing today, I pray you stay safe."

He looked down at me, his eyes glassy. "Thank you. If anything does happen to me, someone will come here to let you know. They'll tell you that it's been a bad year for the Beaujo-

lais. Beaujolais is my code name, due to my being a sommelier."
He gave a wry smile.

"Ah, I see."

"And you must reply to them that the better wine is with
the Priest."

"The better wine is with the Priest," I repeated.

"Yes, the Priest is the code name for another member of my
network. I've left some of my belongings with them in case
anything happens. Things that will need to be collected," he
added stoically.

"OK."

As I watched him leave, I felt an icy chill pass right
through me.

It didn't take long for me to find out what Raphael had come to
Paris for. Word reached the grapevine of the patisserie bread
queue by early afternoon.

"Julius Ritter has been assassinated," I heard one woman
say to another as I took her ration coupon. "He was shot in his
car this morning, outside his home."

"Ritter?" the other woman said questioningly.

"Yes, the bastard in charge of the *Service du Travail*. It's
because of him my son is now working in Germany."

I had to fight to stop myself gasping. The compulsory order
forcing young French men to go and work for the Germans had
been introduced in February and was universally unpopular,
with many seeing it as akin to a death sentence. Assassinating
the man in charge would strike a blow right to the very heart of
the German command.

"Did they catch whoever did it?" I asked casually as I
handed the woman her bread.

"No." She leaned across the counter and lowered her voice.
"Thankfully, the heroes managed to escape."

I breathed a sigh of relief.

Baptiste showed up later just as I was about to close the store.

"Have you heard?" he whispered, his eyes sparkling with excitement.

"I have indeed," I replied. If only he knew that one of his former Lutetia colleagues had played a part in it.

"The tide is turning, Coralie. It won't be long before we send them all packing."

I nodded but found it hard to feel excited. How could I, now that I knew what I did about Reinhardt? I'd pinned all my hope for the future on us being together—on him being a decent human being. It was like waking up and realizing that my hope had been nothing but a meaningless dream.

The German reprisals were swift and brutal. The front page of the *Paris-soir*, a paper that had been taken over by the Germans at the start of the occupation, denounced the shooting as an abominable act and fifty French prisoners were killed in retaliation.

While I was relieved that Raphael and his fellow resistants had managed to escape, the German retaliation left me feeling utterly disheartened. It seemed that no matter how hard the French fought back, we were always trampled all over in response. It was like we were ants trying to defeat an elephant. I found myself increasingly relating to what Raphael had said— things had got so bad, I no longer cared what happened to me. I no longer cared about baking cakes or bread. All I wanted to do was devote myself to making this nightmare end. And I had to find out for certain if Reinhardt—my fiancé—was working against the French.

55

OCTOBER 1943, PARIS

That Sunday at the hotel, I couldn't tear my gaze from Reinhardt, but unlike before, when watching him had sent shivers of desire coursing through me, I only felt dread. It was a relatively quiet night in the kitchen and the shift passed without incident. As I cleaned down my station, I dared to think that maybe Raphael had been mistaken, maybe there was an innocent explanation for the photograph. Maybe Reinhardt had met with the SS because they'd asked him to cook for them.

I was cleaning cream from my whisk when Reinhardt came up behind me, causing me to jump.

"It's only me," he laughed. "No need to be afraid."

"I thought it was Gunter, so there was every reason to be afraid," I joked lamely, but now everything Reinhardt said seemed loaded with a sinister subtext and all I could think was, *Should I be afraid of the man I'm supposed to be marrying one day?*

But I couldn't allow my fear to win. I had to do what Raphael had said and use my new knowledge to my advantage.

"I was thinking," I whispered, tugging on his chef's jacket

and pulling him close. "What are the chances I could stay here tonight?"

"Here? In my room?"

Was it my imagination or did a look of alarm flicker across his face?

"Yes." I stood on tiptoes and whispered in his ear. "I miss you so much. I just want to be close to you."

I felt his breath quicken and he put his arm around my waist and pulled me toward him. "I want that too," he whispered. "But we have to be careful not to get caught."

"Of course, but that makes it all the more exciting."

He nodded, his eyes wide with longing, but all I felt was sick. If I found anything incriminating in his room, that would be it. We would be over forever. The one positive thing I'd had in my life since I'd lost Madame Monteux would have all been a pretense and I wasn't sure how I would cope with that.

After we'd cleaned up and the other men had gone to their dormitory in the old hotel mail room, we snuck up the back stairs to the top floor. As soon as we got inside his room, Reinhardt locked the door behind me, something that would have made me feel safe before, but now it made me panic.

He took my hands and held them tight. "I've missed you so much." He kissed me passionately, then broke away. "That reminds me, I've got something for you." He went over to the desk and opened the top drawer. I watched carefully as he lifted an official-looking folder and took a leather-bound album out from under it. "I finally got my film developed. Do you remember these?"

He opened the album and showed it to me. My heart twinged as I saw the photos of me lost in my cooking and him in my apron, one waving a mixing spoon and another with a baguette balanced on his head. And then, beneath them, there was the photo of me in his arms, gazing up at him longingly. That evening had felt so special. So magical. I remembered wanting that moment to last forever. Surely he couldn't have been pretending.

"They're lovely," I said, but I was unable to hide the flatness in my tone.

"Are you all right?" he asked, looking concerned.

"Yes. I'm just tired. And I've been missing you so much."

He closed the album and handed it to me. I noticed a swastika on the front and my stomach churned. It was a stark reminder that he was here with the enemy. But was he working for them? "I want you to keep this," he said. "Then, whenever you miss me, you can look at our photos and dream of the day we'll always be cooking together like that in our Café de la Paix."

How was he able to lie so convincingly? For a fleeting moment, as I put the album in my bag, I wondered if Raphael could have been wrong? But I couldn't allow myself to think like that. I couldn't afford to lower my guard. Not unless I could find proof that it was all an innocent misunderstanding. The dread in the pit of my stomach grew as I realized what I would have to do.

Later, we lay in bed with our arms wrapped around each other and I prayed for Reinhardt to fall asleep. Finally, his breathing slowed and his arm slackened on my stomach. Could I risk getting up and snooping around? What if he woke? What if he saw me? But I felt as if I had no choice. I couldn't live with the doubt and suspicion hanging over me. I had to try and find out the truth. I decided to go to the bathroom first, so I had an excuse if he did wake and find me up. I slowly wriggled out from under his arm and slid out of the bed, and although he murmured, he remained asleep.

I tiptoed into the bathroom and took a moment to formulate a plan. I would start with the desk drawer, and the official-looking folder. Then, if he was still asleep, I'd check his pockets and his wallet. It was a high-risk strategy and I didn't know what I'd say if he caught me, but I had to know if he was working for the *Abwehr*.

I ran the tap for a few seconds just in case he'd woken, then crept back into the room. I breathed a sigh of relief at the sound of soft snoring coming from the bed and I crept over to the desk and slowly inched open the drawer. Now came the really risky part; I would have to take the file into the bathroom to read whatever was inside. If he woke and saw me doing that, the game would be up for sure.

I tiptoed back into the bathroom and shut and locked the door. Then, heart thudding, I opened the file and peered inside. After all the build-up, I didn't know whether to be relieved or disappointed when I saw a menu in German on the top sheet of the pile of papers. I lifted it to look at the page underneath. It contained two recipes in Reinhardt's distinctive square-shaped handwriting. One of them was for Strasbourg sausages—I recognized the list of ingredients instantly from when he'd shared them with me in my own recipe book. I was about to move on to the next page when I noticed something strange. There was an extra word in the list, and one that didn't make any sense.

I held the page up to the dim lamplight to make sure I wasn't seeing things, but it was there, clear as day. *Beaujolais Zwiebeln*. *Zwiebel*, I knew, was the German for onion, but I'd never heard of Beaujolais onions before and I'd never heard mention of them in all the time I'd been working in the hotel kitchen. The only Beaujolais I knew of was the wine. I looked closer at the other ingredients and noticed another discrepancy —before *Schweinefleisch*, the German word for pork, he'd written *Priest*. I frowned. Why did those two words together sound weirdly familiar?

My stomach lurched as I remembered. Beaujolais was Raphael's code name; the Priest was code for another member of his network. Had Reinhardt incorporated them into his recipe as some kind of secret message? Did he know their identities?

I flicked to the next page and saw a recipe for bread—another one that he had shared with me. And, once again, there was something strange hidden in the list of ingredients—the word Montparnasse next to the word for yeast. My frown deepened. Montparnasse was a neighborhood in Paris that was most definitely not known for its yeast. I sat down on the edge of the bath, my head beginning to ache. Was Reinhardt, like me, using his role as a chef as a cover for his clandestine activities, but, unlike me, *against* the Resistance? I turned to the last page, feeling sick.

I heard a movement from the bedroom and almost dropped the file to the floor.

"Coralie? Are you OK?" Reinhardt called out sleepily.

"Yes, yes, just going to the bathroom," I called back, my heart racing. What was I going to do? I could hardly put the file back in the desk now; he'd see me.

I looked around the bathroom in desperation and spotted a small closet in the corner. I opened it and saw a pile of towels on one of the shelves. That would have to do. As I went to tuck the file inside, I felt something hard hidden beneath the towels. I lifted them up to see a wooden box. I took it out and turned on the tap, then opened the lid. I had to stop myself from gasping as I looked inside. It was a radio transmitter. But what on earth was Reinhardt doing with it? One thing was for certain—it wasn't anything to do with his work as a chef. Then I remembered what Raphael had told me when the Interallie network were arrested. The Germans were going to use their transmitters to lure other Resistance operatives into a trap. My skin erupted in a clammy sweat. Is that what Reinhardt had been doing, and using Raphael's code name?

I heard a movement from the bedroom and quickly shut the

box and put it back under the towels along with the file. Then I took a deep breath to try to compose myself before returning to the bedroom.

Reinhardt was propped up on his elbow looking at me. "I thought for a moment that I'd dreamed you'd stayed."

I forced myself to laugh, but it sounded false and shrill. "No, it wasn't a dream. I'm still here."

"Good." He reached out for me.

I slipped in beside him, feeling chilled to the core. He wrapped his arm around me, but instead of feeling comforted, I felt like an animal caught in a trap. I lay there, rigid, staring up into the dark. If Reinhardt was using his wireless transmitter and coded menus to lure Raphael and his network into a trap I had to warn him, and fast. But how?

56

OCTOBER 1943, PARIS

After what felt like forever, Reinhardt finally fell asleep and I managed to get the file from the bathroom and back inside the desk. I returned to the bed and lay there, plagued by increasingly panicked questions. What if Reinhardt knew that I'd been helping Raphael's network? What if he knew about the role I'd played in the cinema bomb? Did he want revenge for Hans's death? What if, instead of dreaming of a future together, the man lying asleep beside me had been dreaming of my downfall? How could I have been so gullible, believing that he'd fallen in love with me? Believing all his talk of one day owning a cafe together. He was a German. Of course his loyalty would be with his men, not the French.

I thought back to when we'd first met and how bitter he'd been about the lack of food the Germans had after the Treaty of Versailles and the enforced starvation of his people. The clues had been there all along, but I'd chosen to ignore them. Then an even more terrible thought occurred to me. What if he'd been working for the *Abwehr* from the start and not just since Hans's death? I recalled the time he had arrived at the patisserie and bumped into Madame Monteux holding the leaflet about the student protest. Had he seen what was in her hand that day? Had he warned the *Abwehr* about the protest? Is that why Oskar Reile had turned up there? And what about the time Reinhardt had dropped by when I was burning the Resistance papers? Had he seen them smoldering in the grate and realized that I was working for the Resistance? My stomach lurched. What if he'd been spying on me ever since? As much as I hated to admit it, Raphael was right, I'd been a naïve fool.

Finally, I heard a clock somewhere striking five and I got out of bed. The curfew was over. I could go back home.

"What are you doing?" Reinhardt asked sleepily.

"I need to get back to the patisserie to make the day's bread," I said, unable to look at him.

"Oh, OK. I'll walk you." He sprang out of bed with a grin. "Thank you for last night, it was wonderful."

As he took hold of my hands, I wanted to yell at him and demand to know what the file and transmitter meant, but somehow I managed to smile sweetly. "You don't need to walk me, but perhaps you could make sure I get out of the hotel OK."

"Of course. If you're sure?"

Oh, I was sure. The sooner I got away from him, the better.

We made our way down the back stairs and into the lobby. Thankfully, it was deserted.

"So will I see you tonight for our class?" he whispered.

"I don't know." I faked a yawn. "I'm feeling very tired. I hardly slept at all last night."

"Oh no." His face fell.

"Perhaps we could leave it this week, as I stayed here last night?"

He frowned. "Are you sure you're all right?"

"Yes, I..." I stopped at the sound of men's voices in the street outside. The revolving door slowly spun into life and two soldiers marched in, brandishing their rifles. Reinhardt and I stepped back and my heart sank as more guards entered, frogmarching a group of male prisoners inside. One of the prisoners looked barely out of his teens. The others were slightly older. Then I saw a sight that made me gasp.

"What is it?" Reinhardt asked, studying my face.

"Nothing—I... I..." I stammered as I glanced again at the stocky man with the bushy black beard. It was Raphael.

"You seem shocked?" Reinhardt said, still staring at me intently.

"I just wasn't expecting to see something like this so early in the morning," I whispered. Then, to my horror, the guards began marching the prisoners our way.

"We've captured an entire Resistance network!" one of the guards said triumphantly to Reinhardt as he walked past.

"Excellent," Reinhardt replied and I felt sick to my stomach at the realization that he and his coded menus and transmitter radio had probably played a key role.

Raphael drew level and our eyes met. I wanted so badly to do something, say something, to give him some kind of show of solidarity. But how could I? His gaze flicked to Reinhardt beside me and my spirits sank. It was still so early, it must have been obvious that I'd spent the night there. I hoped he didn't think I'd gone back on my word. I hoped he realized that I'd spent the night with Reinhardt to help the Resistance, although of course my attempt to help had been too little, too late.

"Wasn't that the sommelier?" Reinhardt asked as the prisoners were jostled and shoved up the stairs.

"The who?" I said, praying my cheeks didn't betray me and start to blush.

"The sommelier who works here at the hotel," he replied. "Wasn't he one of the men who was just taken past?"

"I don't know." I shrugged nonchalantly. "I don't think so."

Reinhardt continued studying my face. Was he searching for some sign of upset, a clue that my sympathies lay with the

Resistance? Well, if he was, he sure as hell wasn't going to get one.

"Look at the time!" I exclaimed, gesturing at the lobby clock. "I need to get going or my customers won't have any bread!" I stood on tiptoes and kissed him lightly on the cheek as if everything was tickety-boo and I hadn't just discovered that my fiancé was a treacherous snake. "I love you," I whispered in his ear for good measure.

He gave me a relieved smile. "I love you too."

I somehow managed to walk out of the hotel without my legs buckling, and I made it to the patisserie in one piece, although I couldn't remember a single detail from the walk, I was so distracted. As soon as I got inside the store, I locked the door behind me and kept the shutters closed. I hated letting my customers down, but there was no way I could open that morning. I had to take some time to regroup and work out what to do next.

I went upstairs and sat at the kitchen table, where I tried to process everything that had happened. I thought of how the guard had told Reinhardt that they'd arrested an entire Resistance network. Had he said it to Reinhardt randomly because he couldn't contain his excitement, or was it because he knew Reinhardt was an *Abwehr* agent? Was it because he knew Reinhardt had helped orchestrate their capture? Surely if Reinhardt knew about my own involvement with the Resistance I would have been arrested too. Or was he saving that for later, in an attempt to find out more from me first? I hated having such paranoid thoughts, but I couldn't afford to be taken for a fool again. I owed it to Raphael and all the other brave resistants who'd been captured to keep my cool and retaliate, but how?

All morning, I heard people knocking on the door of the patisserie looking for their bread, but I ignored them, too preoccupied with trying to work out what to do next. Then, in the middle of the afternoon, I heard what sounded like a stone hitting the window. I peered out to see Baptiste standing in the street below.

"Oh, thank God!" he exclaimed as I opened the window and leaned out. "Can I come in?"

"Of course," I replied and I ran downstairs.

"I thought they'd got you too," he said as soon as I opened the door. He took off his hat and hurried inside.

"Who?" I asked, shutting and locking the door behind him.

"The Germans. They arrested an entire Resistance network this morning. The Manouchian network." He stepped closer and lowered his voice. "They've got Raphael."

"How do you know?" I asked, my pulse quickening.

"An old army friend who works for the Resistance told me. I came by earlier and saw the shop was closed and when you didn't answer the door, I panicked. I thought Raphael might have roped you into joining their network, given that you work at the hotel."

"Oh, no, not at all." I hated lying to him and part of me longed to tell him everything, but I didn't want to put him at any risk.

Baptiste sighed and shook his head. "I don't know, Coralie. What with the Duchess and now Raphael, I'm starting to think there's no hope left."

"Don't say that!" I exclaimed. "We can't give up. Madame Monteux needs us to stay strong."

He sighed and shook his head.

"What is it?" I asked, his ominous expression filling me with dread.

"I've heard more rumors about the camps in Poland." He paused and looked down at the floor. "They say... they say they've been killing the Jewish prisoners with poisoned gas."

"What? No!" I shook my head. "No, that can't be true." But

then I thought back to that night in the storeroom with Reinhardt and the conversation I'd overheard. I shivered as I remembered how the man had joked with Luc Laporte that most of the Jewish prisoners wouldn't ever work again. I'd tried to ignore the sinister implication behind his words, but that was no longer possible. "She has to still be alive!" I cried in panic. "She can't be dead!"

Baptiste placed a comforting hand on my shoulder. "We have to prepare ourselves for the worst, Coralie." His voice cracked. "She might not be coming back."

"How can you give up on her?" I snapped, but, of course, my anger wasn't really at him, it was at the Nazis and their evil regime. It was at the French government and police for going along with it. And it was at Reinhardt for being on the side of such monsters. I was so, so angry at him.

"I haven't given up on her." Baptiste gave a weary sigh. "But I think I might have given up on humanity." His eyes filled with tears. "How has it come to this? How can this be happening?"

I shook my head. The thought of the Germans gassing people to death was beyond all comprehension.

"One thing I do know," Baptiste said quietly, "is that if it came down to it, I would die to save my country."

"Don't say that!" I implored.

"It's true." He gave a sad smile. "But that's what makes us French so dangerous to the Germans."

A shiver ran up my spine as I realized what he meant.

"They've pushed us to the point where we have precious little left to lose," Baptiste continued, "where we'd be willing to die if it made a positive difference. And that makes us a formidable enemy."

I nodded. I understood because I was almost certain I'd reached that point too, and the implications were strangely liberating. What if I no longer cared if I was captured or killed?

What would I be capable of doing to make a difference? Standing there, in the half-light in the Patisserie Resilience, the seed of an idea began taking root inside of me. An idea both terrible and thrilling.

57

OCTOBER 1943, PARIS

All week, my idea grew, twisting its tendrils throughout my mind, until I could think of nothing else. By Wednesday, my mind was made up, and by Thursday, I'd sourced everything I needed to put my plan into action. Any time I felt a pang of doubt or fear, I'd remember what Baptiste had told me about the Jews being murdered in the camps and I'd think of Madame Monteux facing such horror and I'd feel emboldened once more.

I arrived at the hotel on Sunday feeling sick with nerves. As I pushed my way through the revolving door, I wondered if I'd ever emerge onto the streets of Paris again, or was this it? Was this the beginning of my end? Reminding myself that I had nothing left to lose, I strode purposefully into the kitchen.

Reinhardt looked up from dicing an onion and greeted me with a smile of delight. But now I couldn't even trust his facial expressions.

"You're early!" he exclaimed, placing his knife down on the chopping block.

"Yes," I replied with a smile, just as phony as his. "I have something special planned for dessert and it's going to take some time to get it right."

"Sounds intriguing, what is it?"

"The croquembouche," I announced. "A tower of cream-filled pastry puffs, all bound together with spun sugar and caramel."

His eyes widened. "That sounds delicious."

"It is." As I nodded in agreement, I was struck by the irony that the croquembouche was one of the most popular French wedding cakes. I probably would have made one for our own wedding—if Reinhardt hadn't turned out to be such a deceitful rat.

"And it's perfect timing for something special," Reinhardt continued. "Admiral Canaris is here this evening for a meeting with his top staff."

My heart skipped a beat. The stakes had just been dramatically raised and if my plan worked, the repercussions would reverberate across the world. It would also mean my certain death, but Baptiste was right. My no longer caring if I lived or died made me a lot more dangerous to the Germans and useful to the Resistance. I would finally be able to make a powerful difference.

"That's great!" I exclaimed. "I'd better get to work then."

I made my way to my station and took off my coat and put on my apron. All around me, the kitchen hummed with the usual chatter and bellowed instructions, but I felt completely detached from it all, consumed by the enormity of the task ahead. This would probably be the last thing I ever baked, so I had to pull out all the stops, and I needed the dessert to be as enticing as possible.

I opened my recipe book and turned to the right page, frowning as I scanned the list of ingredients. Should I really have written *poudre de succession* beneath flour? Was it too much of a clue? But there was no way the Germans would know what it meant and writing it down had given me a rush of satisfaction, a written record of my final act of resistance.

I poured some flour into a mixing bowl and then, when no one was looking, I took a small velvet pouch from my purse. Back in the seventeenth century, the French elite had named arsenic "*poudre de succession*," meaning powder of inheritance, because so many of them had used it to kill relatives in order to claim their inheritance. I shook the powder onto the flour and began stirring it in. I should have really named it powder of revenge for my recipe. I thought of Madame Monteux and Raphael and it felt as if my heart had clenched as tight as a fist.

"May all who eat this pastry die a miserable death," I whispered as I stirred.

"There you are, talking to your food again!" Reinhardt suddenly appeared beside me, causing me to jump.

"I'm just praying that the pastry will be light and fluffy," I said gaily.

"I'm sure it will, I can't wait to taste it," he replied and I felt a jolt of panic. Even after everything he'd done, I hadn't been planning on Reinhardt eating my poisoned pastries. There was still a part of me stuck in the old story of us—or the old lie, as had it turned out to be.

"This dessert is far too extravagant to be wasted on kitchen staff," I joked.

"Ouch!" He clutched his chest as if fatally wounded, and again I felt a surge of panic. If he ate any of the pastry before it was served to the *Abwehr* officers, my whole plan would be ruined. "Don't worry," he said. "I'll wait and see if there are any leftovers for us lowly kitchen staff to scavenge."

I forced myself to grin. "Thank you, Chef, glad you know your place."

He laughed and returned to his station and I set about heating some water, butter and salt in a pan. As soon as it reached boiling point, I began adding the flour. My palms started to sweat as I realized that what I was making had the power to kill a person stone dead. I pictured Arnaud and Olive looking at me and shaking their heads. *"Whatever happened to my little sugar-snatcher?"* I heard Arnaud asking sorrowfully. *"I always knew that temper of yours would get you in trouble one day,"* I imagined Olive adding. But this didn't feel like one of my saucepan boiling over moments. Quite the opposite, in fact. I felt completely in control and almost devoid of emotion. Discovering Reinhardt's deception and the terrible truth about the camps had broken something in me.

Once my mixture had formed a ball, I removed the pan from the stove and began stirring in the eggs until the dough became velvety soft. Then I transferred it into a bag and piped mounds onto a baking tray. It was something I'd done a thousand times before, but my hands were trembling so much it took a couple of attempts before I got the mounds exactly the right size and shape.

Focus. Focus, I urged myself. So I focused on all of the horrors I'd witnessed since the Germans had arrived in France and there at the hotel. All of the prisoners I'd seen dragged through the lobby, from Greta the German artist on the first day, who disappeared never to be seen again, to the brave creators of the Resistance newspaper, and the members of the Interallie and Manouchian networks. And, of course, I thought of Madame Monteux and all the others deported from their own country to face who knew what horrors in the camps in Poland. I started piping the pastry with more confidence. The *Abwehr* officers deserved what I was making for them. They were literally going to get their just desserts.

Once the pastry puffs were baking, I washed the pan thoroughly and threw out the piping bag, then I began making the cream to go inside. I'd decided to make four different flavors—chocolate, coffee, praline and vanilla—to make the dessert all the more enticing. Now I'd made the poisoned pastry, I was able to relax slightly and I tried to appear as nonchalant as possible, humming a tune as I melted chocolate and ground hazelnuts for my flavorings.

Once the pastries had cooled, I filled them with crème pâtissière, then began heating some sugar and water in a heavy pan. While the sugar was heating, I quickly constructed a large pyramid of the pastry puffs on a silver platter. Then, when the sugar and water had formed a light golden caramel, I removed it from the heat and waited until it had cooled just enough for the caramel to form wispy strands when lifted with a fork. I began drizzling the caramel over a rolling pin and onto the pyramid of pastry puffs in web-like strands. I was so focused on what I was doing I didn't realize that a crowd had formed behind me.

"That looks incredible," I heard Reinhardt say, and I turned to see him and a few of the other men gazing in awe at the croquembouche. "Seriously," he said, placing a hand on my shoulder, "that is a masterpiece." He looked so genuinely proud and impressed, it caused a lump to form in my throat. *Why did you have to betray me?* I silently implored. *Why did you have to be as bad as all the rest?*

"Very good," Gunter grunted and, to my surprise, he even smiled. It was the first time in three years that he'd actually been nice to me and I found the irony of that fact darkly amusing.

"*Danke,*" I said, giving them a jokey curtsey.

The men all returned to their stations, apart from Reinhardt, who stayed smiling warmly at me.

"It's true," he said quietly. "You really are one of the most talented chefs in the world."

"Oh, I wouldn't say that," I muttered. Nothing he said felt genuine anymore and it made my skin crawl to think of how I'd fallen for his lines before.

"You are." He leaned closer and whispered in my ear, "And I'll be so proud to one day be married to you."

Over my dead body, I thought to myself, shuddering at the realization that it probably would be.

But what if he doesn't know about your involvement in the Resistance, a little voice whispered inside my mind. *What if he genuinely loves you?*

I shrugged the thought away. What difference did it make? The fact was, he was an agent for the *Abwehr*, he'd been seen meeting with the SS, he had a wireless transmitter and he'd made some kind of coded message about Raphael, who was now facing execution.

"Thank you," I replied stiffly. "I'd better get on with adding the final touches."

"Of course, I wouldn't want to keep a genius from their work." He grinned. "Perhaps we could have a drink together after our shift."

"Absolutely," I replied, although obviously there would be no drinks with him ever again after tonight. The thought sent another shiver through me.

The servers began taking the main courses through to the restaurant and as I placed some decorative flowers on the croquembouche, I heard an arrogant laugh.

"Oh no," Reinhardt muttered, and I looked up to see Luc Laporte swaggering into the kitchen, his shirtsleeves rolled up and his collar undone.

"So, what's on the menu this evening?" he called. "I've been torturing Resistance members all day and it's hungry work!"

My face burned with rage as I thought of Raphael and the others at the mercy of this monster.

Gunter sniggered, but I noticed that Reinhardt was glowering.

"Shit! He's helping himself to my sausages," he muttered before striding off through the kitchen.

I looked down at the completed croquembouche and fear began roiling in my stomach. Feeling the sudden urge to go to the toilet, I slipped out of the back door and made my way to the staff bathrooms. Once safely inside a cubicle, I sat down and took stock. My plan was to try to leave as soon as the dessert had been taken through to the restaurant. When I got back from the bathroom, I'd tell Reinhardt that I wasn't feeling well. Then, as soon as the dessert was served, I'd say that I was feeling even worse and ask if I could leave. I wasn't sure how long it would take for the arsenic to work, but at least this would buy me some kind of head start to get to Baptiste's place. As far as I knew, Reinhardt knew nothing of my friendship with Baptiste, so I should be relatively safe there. As long as I was allowed to leave, that was. If I wasn't, I dreaded to think of the fate that awaited me.

I washed my hands, splashed some cold water on my face and returned to the kitchen.

I got back to see Laporte and Gunter standing by my station and my unease grew. Having to contend with them when I was trying to stay calm was the last thing I needed. But then I remembered how Laporte had laughed about people being killed in the camps and my anxiety hardened into anger. I refused to be intimidated by such a traitor to his country.

I walked down the kitchen toward my station and as I drew level with Reinhardt, he shot me a smile.

"Not long now, Chef, and we can relax with a drink."

"Yes," I replied tersely. I looked back at my station and saw a sight that made my blood freeze. Laporte had plucked one of the pastries from the base of the croquembouche and was about to put it in his mouth.

"No!" I yelled at the top of my voice.

"Coralie, what is it?" Reinhardt asked.

"No!" I yelled again, breaking into a run. But it was too late. Laporte popped the entire pastry into his mouth with a smirk.

"Oh shit," I heard Reinhardt say, coming up behind me. "Why can't you leave our food alone?" he called to Laporte.

"She's been working for hours on that. You've got no right to come in here and help yourself."

"Says who?" Laporte sneered through a mouthful of cream. "I don't take my orders from a cook. Get back to making your sausages."

"And I don't take my orders from a petty thug!" Reinhardt yelled, as he reached him. The kitchen fell deathly quiet as everyone watched Reinhardt bring his fist back and send it smashing into Laporte's face.

Laporte teetered backwards, clutching his jaw. "You'll be sorry you did that," he spluttered before advancing on Reinhardt.

I stared, stunned, as Reinhardt stood his ground, squaring up to Laporte, and a second later the two men were grappling with each other and careering into the counter. I watched, feeling totally bewildered. Why had Reinhardt done what he did? However odious Laporte was as a person, they were on the same side. And judging by the file in his desk and his wireless transmitter, Reinhardt had been providing Laporte with prisoners to torture.

There was an almighty crash as a saucepan was sent flying to the ground.

"Stop!" one of the young dishwashers cried anxiously.

I looked at the croquembouche on the counter and the hole at the bottom left by Laporte. The servers had only recently taken the main course through to the restaurant, which meant that dessert wouldn't be requested for at least half an hour, maybe longer, by which time the effects of the arsenic would surely become apparent. Damn! What should I do?

The men staggered toward me and Laporte shoved Reinhardt, sending him flying into the counter housing the croquembouche. We all watched mouths agape as the pastry structure crashed to the floor, sending pastry puffs and splinters of spun sugar flying. All of my hard work, destroyed in an instant.

"Now look at what you've done!" Reinhardt yelled before charging at Laporte like a bull. Laporte pulled back his fist, preparing to throw a punch, then suddenly doubled over, clutching his stomach. Frowning in confusion, he let out a low moan.

"What's wrong with you?" Reinhardt said, looking at him with suspicion.

"My stomach!" he gasped.

Shit! I edged my way over to the shattered dessert on the floor.

"If this is some kind of trick, I'm not falling for it," Reinhardt said.

"It's not," Laporte gasped. "It's—"

"There's something wrong with him," Gunter said, hurrying over as Laporte collapsed to the floor.

As the men all gathered round, I fetched a broom and quickly began sweeping the remains of the dessert into a dustpan, my palms clammy.

"We need to get a doctor," someone called.

"But I don't understand, I didn't even hit him in the stomach," Reinhardt said.

"I think I've been..." Laporte gasped, and I froze.

"What?" Reinhardt asked and he crouched down beside him. Laporte whispered something in his ear, then let out a low moan, before going deadly still.

Heart racing, I scraped the remains of the dessert into the bin, trying to get rid of the incriminating evidence, as pandemonium broke out.

"He's dead!" Gunter yelled and my stomach lurched. "You've killed him!"

"I hardly touched him," Reinhardt replied.

I spotted a stray pastry puff in a corner under one of the counters and rushed over to pick it up. Reinhardt appeared at my side just as I was putting it into the bin. "What are you doing?" he hissed.

"Cleaning up the mess," I replied, barely able to breathe.

He frowned and stepped closer, and I saw that his face was glistening with sweat. "Did you put something in the dessert?"

I frowned back as if personally affronted. "What do you mean?"

"Laporte told me that he thought he'd been poisoned," he whispered.

"Of course I didn't!" I hissed.

He looked at me for a moment, then, to my horror, he reached into the bin and took out one of the pastry balls.

"What are you doing?" I yelped.

"I just want to try one."

"No!" I exclaimed, hitting it from his hand and back into the bin.

He stared at me with an expression of horror, and I realized that the game was up. He knew what I'd done. I swallowed hard, preparing for what would come next. Being marched through to the guards. Taken up to the fourth floor to be interrogated. And then... I was filled with an icy terror. Once the *Abwehr* officers found out that I'd planned to kill them, including Canaris, I'd surely be executed on the spot.

"You need to leave, now," Reinhardt whispered urgently in my ear.

"What? But..."

"Now!" he snapped. "And don't come back. You need to disappear."

I grabbed my coat and bag with trembling hands, but I wasn't quick enough. I watched in horror as four soldiers came rushing in, guns drawn. My heart sank as I saw Gunter walking in behind them. He must have gone to fetch them.

"What's wrong with him?" one of the soldiers barked as they formed a circle around Laporte.

"I think he's been poisoned," Gunter said, his chest puffed out, suddenly full of self-importance.

"By who?" another of the soldiers asked.

"The only thing I saw him eating was the cake," Gunter said, looking at me accusingly.

"What cake?" the soldier asked, and all eyes turned to me.

I opened my mouth to speak, but no words came out.

"Don't be ridiculous," Reinhardt said, moving to stand right beside me.

"Where is this cake?" one of the soldiers asked, marching down the kitchen toward us, his boots clipping loudly on the floor.

"It—it's in the bin," I stammered, my face flushing.

"And why is it in the bin?" he said, his cold eyes staring into mine.

"It got knocked to the floor in the..." I broke off. If I mentioned the fight, I'd get Reinhardt into trouble and despite everything, it still went against my instincts to do so, especially as, for some bizarre reason, he seemed to be trying to protect me.

"Laporte and I got involved in an altercation," Reinhardt said calmly. "Unfortunately, the cake got destroyed in the process."

I glanced sideways at him. Why was he doing this? Why was he trying to save me?

"You were fighting?" the soldier said, and you could have heard a pin drop, the kitchen was so deathly silent.

"Yes," Reinhardt replied, still miraculously keeping his cool.

"Over what?"

"Over Laporte eating some of her cake," Gunter chimed in and Reinhardt shot him an angry stare.

"I need to see what remains of this cake," the soldier said, taking a step toward the bin.

"It wasn't her cake," Reinhardt said, stepping to the side to block him. "It was the sausage."

The soldier frowned. "What are you talking about?"

"I poisoned the sausage," Reinhardt said calmly, "because I was sick of that French bastard coming into my kitchen like he owned the place and talking to me like I was a piece of shit."

There was a collective intake of breath as everyone stared at him, shocked, none more so than me. Why on earth was he saying this?

"But how did you know he'd eat it?" Gunter asked, shooting me another suspicious look.

"Because he's always coming in here, helping himself to the food," Reinhardt replied. "I thought it was time he was taught a lesson, so I left it out on display for him."

As I watched him speak, I felt as if I no longer knew him. There was a coolness, a hardness, about him that I'd never seen before. But, of course, if he was an *Abwehr* agent, he'd be used to putting on a performance like this and he'd be cold and hard to the core.

"So you deliberately poisoned him?" the soldier asked, looking as stunned as me.

"No, I deliberately set a test for him." Reinhardt stared back at him defiantly. "I didn't make him take the sausage. I didn't make him eat it. I didn't even offer it to him. He'd still be alive if he hadn't felt entitled to help himself to our food without asking."

His argument was so compelling that for a moment I almost forgot that I was the one who'd poisoned Laporte and I had to stop myself from nodding in agreement.

The solider beckoned one of his colleagues over and they each grabbed one of Reinhardt's arms.

"But..." I muttered and he shot me a pointed stare over his shoulder as if to tell me to keep quiet.

I stood, frozen to the spot, as the soldiers frogmarched Reinhardt over to the door and the other two picked up Laporte's body. I watched numbly as they carried it out of the kitchen, still reeling from what had just happened.

The men started talking quietly in huddled groups and I noticed some of them looking over at me. I needed to get out of there and quickly. I began walking through the kitchen, my heart thudding and my legs as wobbly as a newborn calf's.

"Where are you going?" I heard Gunter call from behind me, but I ignored him and quickened my pace.

Somehow I made it to the door of the kitchen and into the corridor. I heard yells coming from the lobby, but I had no choice; it was my only route out of there. As I reached the end of the corridor, I saw that the lobby was swarming with soldiers and *Abwehr* officers. Was Reinhardt somewhere amongst them? My eyes darted left and right and I saw a brief flash of white from his chef's jacket before he was bundled off toward the stairs. I froze for a moment, horrified at what might become of him. But then I remembered his last words to me. "You need to leave now... You need to disappear," and a survival instinct kicked in.

I marched across the lobby, the place that had once held so many fond memories for me, and over to the door. I was half expecting a guard to come running after me and grab me by the back of my collar. But they were all running in the opposite direction toward the kitchen. I pushed my way through the revolving door and out into the chill air, and disappeared into the cavernous dark.

58

"So now you know," my grandma says with a sigh and she leans on the table, head in hands. She looks as if she's just run a marathon, and I guess that, emotionally, she has. "I'm sorry," she mumbles through her fingers.

"What for?" I stare at her, shocked.

"For what I did, for being a killer." Her shoulders start to quiver and I realize that she's crying.

"Grandma!" I leap to my feet and go sit beside her. "You're not a killer."

"Of course I am. I killed someone, and I'd planned on killing a lot more." She looks at me and I see that her cheeks are shiny with tears.

"Yes, but it's not like you were some psychopath like... like the Boston Strangler or the horoscope one."

"The Zodiac Killer?"

"Yes. You didn't kill for kicks. It was totally different. You were at war. They were your enemy. It's like... it's like..." My mind buzzes as it tries to process her shock revelation. "It's like you were a soldier."

"But doesn't that make you hate me?"

"No! Why would it?"

"You're a pacifist."

"Yes, but..." I break off, feeling momentarily stumped. "Maybe there are some times when it's OK to kill another person—if it means you're going to save others' lives by killing them." I'm aware that this was the argument America used for dropping the atomic bombs on Japan, but I can't think about that now. All I can think about is my grandma, who is looking so unbearably sad. "Please don't cry. I don't hate you, I love you, and I'm so proud of you."

To my horror, this only makes her cry more.

"You are? You do?" she gasps between sobs.

"Of course. Like I told you before, you're like a female James Bond... who bakes cakes," I add and, to my relief, she lets out a laugh. "You are though," I say. "You were so brave." The phone on the wall starts to ring, causing us both to jump. "Shall I get it?" I ask and she nods.

"Yes please, I'm not in any fit state to talk to anyone right now. Could you tell whoever it is I'll call them back later?"

"Sure." I hurry over and pick up the receiver. "Hello?"

"Oh, Cindy, is that you?" I can't help sighing at the sound of my mom's voice. Talk about terrible timing.

"I'm sorry, Mom, Grandma can't talk right now, she's, uh—out running some errands."

"That's OK, it wasn't Grandma I called to speak to, it was you."

"But we only just spoke."

"I know, but..." She goes silent and for a moment I think we might have been cut off.

"Hello?"

"Yes, I'm still here."

"I'm really sorry, Mom, but I can't speak either. I—uh—I have some chores to do."

"Oh." Once again, she sounds really flat.

"Is everything all right?"

"Yes, I just..." There's another long pause. "I miss you," she says quietly.

"Really?" Now I'm the one unable to hide my shock.

"Of course. It's not the same without you here. It's so much quieter."

"I'd have thought that would have been a good thing," I joke.

"Yes, well, it's not."

There's another silence and my grandma gets up and goes out onto the porch. "I'd better go."

"OK. Well, hopefully we can have a proper chat soon?"

"Sure. Bye, Mom."

"Bye Cin—Raven." There's a click on the line as she hangs up and I stare at the receiver in shock. That's the first time she's ever called me Raven.

I head out onto the porch and find my grandma leaning on the railing, gazing out at the garden. It's a riot of color with flowers growing everywhere, even in the middle of the grass, which is flecked with daisies. "Is your mom OK?" she asks as I join her.

"Yes, she just wanted a chat."

"Oh, that's nice."

"Uh-huh," I reply, but I don't allow myself to get too carried away. I can't bear the thought of lowering my guard only to get hurt again. "Does Mom... does she know what happened to you during the war, what you just told me?"

Her eyes widen. "Oh God no—no one does."

"Nobody?"

She shakes her head. "I didn't even tell your grandpa. I was too ashamed."

I think about her carrying this dark secret deep inside of her for all these years and it makes my heart ache with sadness. I place my hand on top of hers on the railing and I feel Madame

Monteux's smooth round moonstone pressing into my palm. It feels strangely comforting, like she's there with us. "Thank you so much for telling me."

She looks at me and smiles. "Thank you so much for not hating me."

"Stop saying that! I love you!"

"Oh Raven!" She starts crying again. "I love you too." She takes a tissue from her pocket and blows her nose. "Shall we sit down?" She gestures at the swing seat.

We sit down and I link my arm through hers, the way I would do if I was sitting with Melissa.

"So, what happened after you escaped from the hotel? That's if you want to still talk about it?" I add, not wanting to make her cry again.

"It's fine," she says. "There's not much left to tell, really. I collected some belongings from the patisserie and hotfooted it to Baptiste's place and hid there for the next few months."

"Did you ever find out what happened to Reinhardt? Do you really think he was working for the *Abwehr*?"

She nods. "Absolutely. The evidence was too overwhelming. The photograph of him meeting with the SS. The file and the radio transmitter in his room. Raphael's code name hidden in his recipe. And the way he was that final day—the way he fought with Laporte and lied so effortlessly to the soldier—it was like seeing a totally different person—a trained *Abwehr* agent."

I can't help shivering despite the warmth of the morning sun. "But why would he have taken the blame and allowed you to escape if he was on their side all along?"

"I can only think that his feelings for me were genuine," she answers sadly. "So I guess that was something. I wasn't completely taken for a fool."

"You weren't taken for a fool at all!" I exclaim. "He was the fool for supporting Hitler."

She nods.

"So how long did you live in hiding?"

"Until the start of the following year, 1944. Baptiste heard on the grapevine that Canaris had been called back to Germany and then the *Abwehr* fell into disarray."

"Did you go back to the patisserie?"

"Only once the Germans had left in the summer, and by that point, it had fallen into such a state of disrepair, I didn't have the energy or motivation to fix it up again, so I ended up selling it." She gives a sad laugh. "Well, it might be more accurate to say that I gave it away, I took such a low price for it. Not that I cared. I was so disillusioned with everything. Even the liberation of Paris and the sight of the Germans being driven out didn't cheer me up." She sighs. "Looking back now, it's pretty obvious that I was suffering from depression, but we didn't talk about things like that back then, we just got on with it. Or tried to, as best we could."

I nod. "And then you met Grandpa?"

"Yes. He arrived in Paris just after the liberation, to cover the story for the *San Franscico Chronicle*." She gives a sad smile. "It was so refreshing to meet someone who hadn't been through what we had, who was untainted by the years of oppression. He was so bright and sunny. So *American*, with all his talk of dreams and fresh starts. When he asked me to come back here with him, I jumped at the chance. Like I said before, I saw it as an opportunity to put an ocean between me and all the heartache." She sighs. "I didn't realize that we wear our pain on the inside, and it can't just be cast off like a coat."

I squeeze her arm tighter. It must have been horrible to arrive in a brand-new country hoping for a fresh start, only to realize that you've brought your heartache with you.

"But at least I didn't have to speak about it anymore, and I could try to pretend it had never happened." She looks at me and laughs. "I thought I'd take the story of what happened to the grave. Little did I know that I'd be blessed with a grand-daughter as inquisitive and stubborn as me."

"I'm sorry," I say nervously.

"Don't apologize! It feels strangely good to have shared it with you—like a weight I didn't know I was carrying has been lifted."

I give a sigh of relief. "Did you ever go back to France?"

She shakes her head. "No. Just the thought of returning felt way too traumatic. I'd gotten so used to pushing my memories away, I was terrified of coming face to face with them again." She gives another little laugh.

"What?"

"Well, thanks to you, I've been forced to face them and the world didn't end after all; in fact, it's starting to feel like it could be a new beginning."

"That's excellent!" I exclaim, warm with relief that all my snooping and questioning might have actually helped.

"Maybe I should go back to Paris one day," she says thought-fully. "And really confront those memories once and for all."

"Well, if you want someone to come with you, just say the word," I offer hopefully.

"I will indeed." She smiles at me, but I'm not sure if it's because she thinks it's a good idea or she's just trying to humor me.

A blackbird swoops by, then circles back and perches on the railing in front of us, chirping loudly. I think to myself how nice it must be to be a bird. To just fly around all day singing at the top of your voice and not have to worry about things like death and war.

"Can I ask you one more question?" I say cautiously.

"Only one?" She raises her eyebrows.

"Yes—for now anyways," I giggle.

"Go on."

I take a breath. "Did you—did you ever find out what happened to Madame Monteux?"

Instantly, her face falls.

"It's OK, you don't have to talk about it if you don't want to."

"I know, but I guess I have to. It's the last chapter of my World War Two story. And the last chapter of my time in the Lutetia."

"The hotel?" I look at her surprised.

She nods. "If you thought the *Abwehr* taking it over was a shock, what happened after the occupation was a twist no one saw coming." She stands up and for a moment I think she might have changed her mind and decided not to tell me after all. "Wait there," she says. "I need to fetch something."

59

JULY 1984, SAN FRANCISCO

My grandma returns to the porch holding an old brown envelope and the German photo album. Of course, I can't let on that I've already seen the album, so I pull an expression of what I hope looks like genuine curiosity.

She instantly frowns at me. "Are you all right?"

"Yes, why?" I reply defensively.

"You look really startled."

Shoot, I guess I over-egged the curiosity pudding, as Madame Monteux might have said. "No, I was just curious about what you're holding." Really annoyingly, my cheeks start to flush. One thing's for certain, I have not inherited my grandma's talent for being a spy.

She sits back beside me on the swing seat. "I'm holding the final items in my Pandora's box," she says ominously.

"Oh," is all I trust myself to say without giving anything away and I watch as she reaches inside the envelope and takes out a black and white photograph and passes it to me. It's a headshot of a beautiful older woman with large dark eyes and long silver hair. "Is that...?"

"Madame Monteux," she finishes my question and nods.

"She's so beautiful."

"Yes." She gives a heavy sigh. "After your grandpa had written about the liberation of Paris, the *Chronicle* sent him off with some other journalists to join a company of Allied soldiers and write about the defeat of the Germans. He was with them when they arrived in Poland and liberated the concentration camps. I'd told Bob all about Madame Monteux and he wrote to me, telling me that I should prepare for the worst, but, of course, nothing could have prepared me for what happened next."

"What did happen?" I ask quietly, dreading the answer.

"The survivors of the camps started arriving back in Paris in April, and Charles de Gaulle, the man who'd led the French Resistance and became the leader of France, decided that they should be sent straight to the Lutetia."

"But why?" I stare at her, shocked.

"As soon as the first survivors got to Paris, it was clear that they needed urgent medical attention, and Gare d'Orsay station, where they were coming in, just wasn't equipped to deal with the task. They needed food and baths and beds, so de Gaulle thought it best that they were sent to a hotel and he nominated the Lutetia—he did honeymoon there after all, so I guess he had a soft spot for it." She leans back in the seat and gazes up at the pine trees. "As soon as the people of Paris got wind of what was happening, anyone who'd had a loved one deported descended upon the Lutetia. It was bedlam. The whole square outside became crammed full of people desperate for news, desperate for a glimmer of hope. And, of course, I was one of them—on the first day at least, then I heard that the Red Cross needed volunteers to help inside the hotel."

"Did you go back to work there?"

She nods. "And in the kitchen too."

"No way!"

She nods gravely. "As soon as the Red Cross heard I'd worked there before as a pastry chef, they asked me to come and

make bread for the returning deportees. How could I say no?"
She places her hand on my arm, and gazes at me, eyes wide.
"Oh, Raven, I'd thought it was bad seeing people suffer on
rations, but nothing was worse than the sight of those poor
people arriving at the hotel. They were like walking skeletons in
those horrible striped uniforms. And the smell..."

"What smell?"

"They hadn't been able to wash for weeks, or maybe even
months. And some of their clothes were caked with blood."

I shudder, thinking back to the pictures of the concentration
camp victims I'd seen in my history class.

My grandma gestures at the photo of Madame Monteux. "I
stuck this picture to the wall in the main corridor of the Lutetia.
Hundreds of relatives and friends stuck photographs of their
loved ones there, as a way of trying to find them. And every day
I prayed I'd see her coming through that revolving door with the
next group of arrivals. Although I'm not sure she would have
liked being sprayed with the pesticide." She gives a dry little
laugh.

I frown. "What do you mean?"

"Most of the returning deportees had lice and the Red
Cross didn't want the hotel to become infested, so as soon as
they walked through the revolving door, a soldier would spray
them with a white powder to delouse them."

"Wow."

She smiles. "Yes, it certainly wasn't the customary warm
Lutetia welcome. Madame Monteux would have probably
hollered the place down."

"Yes." I nod and smile in agreement, as if I knew her too.

"Did she ever return?" I ask hesitantly, as I'm pretty sure
what the answer will be.

My grandma shakes her head. "I worked there until
September, until the last of the survivors had returned and the
Lutetia became a working hotel again, but there was no sign of

her and no one I asked had ever come across her." Her voice cracks and I take hold of her hand.

"We don't have to talk about it anymore if you don't want to."

"It's OK, there's not much left to say. At the end of 1945, Baptiste heard from a friend of his who'd been sent to Auschwitz that Madame Monteux had been in the same transport as him from Drancy but she hadn't survived." She pauses and clears her throat. "They sent her to the gas chamber as soon as she arrived at the camp."

"Oh no. I'm so sorry," I murmur, looking back at the photo, and speaking as much to Madame Monteux as to my grandma.

"Thank you. As you can imagine, I was devastated. And then Bob returned from Poland and I could tell immediately that he'd been really affected by what he'd seen. It was as if someone had turned the dial on his cheeriness right down low and he wanted to get back to America as quickly as possible, so he proposed to me and we arrived in the Bay Area at the start of 1946." She looks at the photo album and my pulse quickens. "So, this was the album Reinhardt gave me."

"Ah, I see," I say as nonchalantly as possible.

"I haven't looked inside it for years. I hadn't looked at any of the things I brought with me from France. I'd hidden them all away in a box in the garage until I wanted to get the recipe book so I could make you the cake."

"Oh wow."

She opens the cover and turns the page past the pictures of the Eiffel Tower and other landmarks, then lets out a gasp when she sees the pictures of her and Reinhardt. I watch as she traces her fingertip along the edge of the photo of him waving the mixing spoon.

"What do you think happened to him?" I ask. "After he took the blame for poisoning Laporte?"

She sighs. "I dread to think. I can't imagine the *Abwehr*

would have looked too kindly on him killing their chief torturer."

I looked down at Reinhardt's grinning face and feel sad. Even if he was working for the *Abwehr*, he saved my grandma's life. "Holy cow, I just realized something."

"What?"

"If he hadn't done what he did and saved your life, I wouldn't be here either."

"That's right." She looks at me and smiles. "Thank you."

"What for?"

"Making it a whole lot easier to forgive him."

I smile back. "You're welcome."

She turns the page in the album and gasps. "Oh!"

I follow her gaze to a photo of her fast asleep, her dark hair fanned out around her like a halo on the pillow. "You look really beautiful, like an angel."

"Thank you. He must have taken this one night without me realizing. I'd completely forgotten it was in here."

She turns the page and there's another picture of her, this time piping cream onto a cake, smiling joyfully.

"You look so happy," I say.

"Baking always made me feel that way." She smiles shyly. "Reinhardt always used to comment on how happy I looked in the kitchen. I had no idea he'd taken this one either."

I picture Reinhardt focusing his camera lens on my grandma, perfectly capturing her radiance and beauty and something hits me. "Can I say something?"

She gives me a funny look. "When have you ever not said something?"

"Ha ha, very funny." I give her a playful nudge. "Seriously, though, I really think he did love you."

"You reckon?" She shoots me a sideways glance and I notice that the tips of her cheeks have flushed a rosy pink.

"Yes. I mean, for a start he was willing to risk losing his life to save yours. That's like a Romeo and Juliet level love—although obviously they both died and you didn't, and of course, the Montague family weren't Nazis."

"OK, you've made your point," she says with a chuckle.

"And look at these pictures he took of you." I point back to the photo of her piping cream on the cake. "Look at what he wanted to capture. Look at how he saw you."

We both gaze down at the album and a drop of water plops onto the picture.

"Grandma?" I look at her, concerned, and she wipes her eyes.

"Oh dear." She sniffs. "I don't know what's gotten into me."

"I'm sorry. I didn't mean to upset you, it's just that I don't think you should think of him as the enemy anymore."

To my relief, she nods. "You really are a wise soul, Raven, has anyone ever told you that?"

"No! Never!" I stare at her in shock, and she bursts out laughing.

"Don't look so surprised. You're making me see things very differently, and you're helping me enormously."

"I am?" I feel a warm glow inside.

"Yes."

She takes hold of my hand and squeezes it tightly. "How would you like to help me some more?"

"I'd love to!" I exclaim.

"Good, because I've had an idea, and I'm not sure if it's inspired or insane."

Now it's my turn to laugh. "I reckon all the best ideas are like that."

"Quite possibly." She stands up and reaches her hand out to me. "Come. We need to call your mom."

"What?" My heart plummets.

"Don't worry, I'm not sending you back to New York—

although I guess we will have to pop back to New York to collect your passport. I take it you have a passport?"

I nod, hardly daring to guess what she might be planning. "Is it—are you—are we..."

She grins. "Yes. We're going to Paris. It's time I laid some ghosts to rest once and for all."

60

AUGUST 1984, PARIS

My grandma and I emerge from the Paris Metro into a small square lined with benches and dotted with trees. It's mid-afternoon—in France at least—having just arrived, we're still on US time and I'm feeling a little drunk from the sudden dazzling sunshine and lack of sleep. Not that I'd be able to sleep, I'm way too excited.

I plonk my backpack on the ground and turn and look all around, drinking in my first proper sight of Paris. A huge department store sits behind us on the corner of the square and I recognize the name, Le Bon Marché, immediately from my grandma's story, which means the hotel must be close. I turn back and see an even bigger white stone building on the other side of the square at the corner of a wide crossroads. The word LUTETIA is displayed in huge, illuminated letters at the top. As soon as I see it, I shiver, despite the summer heat. I've become so immersed in my grandma's memories of the place, it's almost as if they've become my own.

I glance at my grandma and see that she's visibly paled, as she stands motionless, staring at the hotel.

"Are you OK?" I ask, touching her arm.

"I never thought I'd see it again," she whispers.

"We can always go someplace else. We don't have to stay there if you don't want to."

"No," she says firmly. "We did not fly all the way across the Atlantic and suffer that terrible airline food for me to chicken out at the last minute."

I laugh and hoist my backpack onto my back, then link my arm through hers. "That's the spirit!" We start walking slowly through the square, and as the hotel looms larger, I think of my grandma treading this exact same path all those years ago and it makes me shiver. So much of her life was tied up in that building. I can't imagine what it must feel like for her to be back here again.

"Well, here goes nothing," she mutters as we reach the crossroads and the pedestrian light turns green.

The hotel is so big it takes up an entire block and I notice a concierge standing in front of an entrance about halfway along. As we get closer, I think of my grandma when she was younger, approaching that same entrance on her way to work. It's almost impossible to imagine Nazi soldiers standing guard there and it makes me realize what a shock their arrival must have been to the people of Paris. I picture my grandma racing out onto the street after poisoning Laporte and I squeeze her arm tighter. She gives me a grateful smile.

As we approach the entrance, I notice a stone plaque on the wall a little further down. A bouquet of roses has been tucked inside a brass ring beneath the plaque, the petals withered and yellowing at the edges. My grandma notices it too and points up at it.

"I wonder if that's for..." she says and we walk past the door to take a closer look. "It is!" she exclaims. "It's a memorial for the deportees."

I stand there in silence as she begins translating the inscription into English.

"From April to August 1945, this hotel, which had become a reception center, received the greater part of the survivors of the Nazi concentration camps, glad to have regained their liberty and their loved ones from whom they had been snatched. Their joy cannot erase the anguish and pain of the families of the thousands who disappeared who waited here in vain for their own in this place."

I think of what my grandma told me about all the people who came here, desperate to find their loved ones, and as I look up and down the street, it's as if I can feel their ghostly presence and their pain and, to my surprise, my eyes fill with tears. I quickly blink them away. I need to be strong for my grandma.

"OK, let's do this," she says, as if hyping us up for a track event.

We walk back to the concierge, a twinkly-eyed man with graying hair, who smiles at us warmly, and I wonder if my grandma is thinking of her friend Baptiste. "Welcome to the Lutetia," he says. "Is this your first time here?"

My grandma smiles. "First time as a guest."

"Well, you are in for a treat." He ushers us into the revolving door.

"It's the exact same door!" my grandma gasps as we push our way inside. "Oh goodness!"

She puts her case down and clasps her hands, gazing around the lobby. Straight away, I see the mosaic of the ship on the floor above the motto for Paris. I guess it came true in the end—they were beaten by waves but they didn't sink. Someone is playing the piano softly in the corner and three incredibly beautiful women with immaculate hair and makeup are standing on duty behind the reception desk. It all looks so elegant and peaceful and once again I struggle to imagine what it must have been like filled with German soldiers and agents.

Once we've checked in and received the keys to our suite, my grandma shows me to a corridor leading off the lobby.

"That's where the patisserie used to be," she says, pointing to a hair salon.

"Oh wow."

"And this is where I first saw Reinhardt, gazing in the window at my cakes." She looks down at the thick burgundy carpet and I think of his feet once standing on that very same spot.

"Shall we go up to our rooms?" I suggest, worried that if we stay here any longer, she'll get upset.

"Yes, let's."

We go over to the elevator and press the button for the seventh floor. When my grandma had phoned the hotel to book a couple of weeks ago, she made it very clear that she didn't want to stay on the third or fourth floors. I wonder if the guests staying in those rooms know what once happened there. I'm guessing not. You'd have to be a pretty dark person to want to stay in a room where people were once tortured.

Once we get to our rooms, I head straight to the window. The view is spectacular, with the ornate white buildings of Paris all glimmering in the sun.

"I can't believe we're here!"

"Tell me about it," she laughs, sitting down on her bed.

"I still can't believe Mom let me come."

As soon as my grandma had suggested our trip to Paris, I'd been convinced Suzette would put her foot down and refuse, but after much begging and pleading on my part, and much gentle persuasion and reassurances from my grandma, she'd given in.

"Well, I'm very glad she did as I don't think I could have done this alone." My grandma reaches for the phone on her nightstand. "And speaking of your mom, I promised I'd call to let her know we arrived safely."

I sit down on the end of the bed and wait while the call is connected.

"Hi, Suzette, it's Mom. We've arrived safely and we're at the hotel." My grandma pauses and frowns. "Suzette? Are you OK?"

"What's up?" I mouth at her, feeling a pang of concern.

"Oh sweetheart, I'm so sorry to hear that," my grandma continues, and my concern grows. "Yes, of course you can, she's right here." She beckons at me to move closer and hands me the receiver.

"Hey, Mom, is everything OK?" At first, I think the line's crackling, but then I realize that she's sniffing. "Mom?"

"Oh, Cin—Raven, I'm afraid I have some bad news."

My first thought is that something's happened to Melissa and it feels as if my heart is being squeezed tight. "What is it?" I squeak. "What's happened?"

My grandma takes hold of my hand, which only makes me panic more.

"Your father and I—we're, we're getting a divorce."

"Oh," I exhale with relief. "Oh!" My grandma squeezes my hand tighter.

"I'm so sorry, I tried so hard to make it work." I'm not sure if it's the long-distance call, but Mom sounds smaller and more vulnerable than I've ever heard her before.

"It's OK, Mom, it's not the end of the world." I give a wry smile as I think of my favorite Judy Blume book. Reading *It's Not the End of the World* made me wish my parents *would* get a divorce, so they would stop fighting and hating on each other just like the parents in the book.

"You're not upset?" She sounds genuinely shocked.

"No. It's obvious you guys..." I was going to say *hate each other* but think better of it. "It's obvious your marriage isn't working. Hopefully, this way everyone can be happier." Then a horrible thought occurs to me. "Wait, we're not going to have to move, are we?"

"No, you and I will stay in the apartment and your dad's

moving to a place in the Village, so you'll be able to see him whenever you want."

"OK, cool."

"Are you sure you're OK?"

"Yes, I am," I say firmly. "You never know, we might all get along better now."

There's a pause and I wonder if I've said the wrong thing, then I hear her clear her throat.

"I'm so sorry for all the fighting." Her voice is weird and high and I realize she's crying.

"Oh, Mom, it's OK. Honestly. And now I can say my life is just like a Judy Blume novel."

There's another moment's silence and I feel certain I've blown it this time, but then she laughs.

"Oh, Raven, I really miss you!"

"I miss you too, Mom." And in a weird way, I kind of do. This new, softer Mom feels a lot easier to miss.

"Well, I'll let you get back to your grandma. You guys must be so tired from the flight."

"Yes a bit," I say, although the truth is, hearing her news has made me feel kind of wired. My parents are getting a divorce. My dad's moving out. Even though I'm not devastated by the news it's a lot to get my head around.

"Love you," she says and for the first time in ages she sounds like she really means it and this makes me feel wobbly all of a sudden.

"Love you too," I reply, a lump growing in the back of my throat.

I pass the receiver back to my grandma and look down into my lap. I mustn't cry. This trip is about my grandma. The last thing she needs is me being an emotional wreck.

My grandma puts the phone down and moves closer so that our legs are touching, which feels oddly comforting. "I'm sorry, honey."

"It's OK, it's hardly a surprise."

"I know, but still, it's a big deal."

I nod and swallow hard.

She looks at me for a moment, then stands up. "Would you like to come on a little adventure with me?"

"Does a bear shit in the woods!" I exclaim, momentarily forgetting that I'm with my grandmother and not Melissa. "I'm so sorry! I meant to say, yes, yes of course."

She bursts out laughing. "It's OK, that's exactly the kind of enthusiasm I was looking for or I might back out."

"Why, where are we going?" I stand up, grateful for the distraction.

She gives me a nervous smile. "We are going to find the Patisserie Resilience—or what's left of it at least."

61

AUGUST 1984, PARIS

After a quick freshen-up, we head out of the hotel and away from the square. The sidewalk is bustling with suited men who look as if they've just stepped out of commercials for aftershaves with names like *Le Debonair* or *Eau de Suave*. And as for the women, well... I can now safely say that I've seen the living definition of *très* chic, although in my jetlagged state, they're making me feel *très* grody. I look down at my saggy sweatpants and sigh.

"Are you all right?" my grandma asks, linking arms with me.

"Sure. How are you doing? It must look so different to how you remember it."

"It's the strangest thing." She gazes up at the buildings lining the boulevard. "The buildings are all the same, but everything else has changed." A car speeds by, its horn honking. "And there were hardly any cars during the occupation," she continues, "apart from those belonging to the Nazis, and their tanks and trucks of course. They were the only ones who could get gasoline."

I look at the pretty tree-lined street and again it seems impossible to imagine what happened here forty years ago. It seems impossible to believe that I'm here right now. Melissa practically passed out when I called to let her know I'd be coming to Paris to retrace my grandma's wartime footsteps. She's booked me in for a three-night sleepover the second I get back to New York so I can fill her in on all the details. She's also made me swear on both of our lives that I won't fall madly in love with a swoony French boy and want to emigrate.

"OK, I'm pretty sure we need to take a left down here," my grandma says, gesturing to a cobbled side street, "and then it should be the second street on the right. Oh boy!"

I grip her arm tighter. "It's OK. You need to do this, remember, to lay those ghosts to rest."

"Absolutely. I don't know why I'm feeling so scared. It's probably nothing like it was before. The building's probably been turned into apartments."

We take the second turning on the right, onto a street so narrow you'd barely be able to fit one car along it.

"This is it!" she exclaims, eyes wide. "This is the street." She unlinks my arm and takes hold of my hand, gripping it tightly.

"Was that it?" I say, spying a quaint little bookstore.

She shakes her head. "No—no, that's it." She points to a cafe a couple of doors down and I notice that her hand is trembling. It must be so emotional for her to be back here, given all that happened.

"Ah, it looks really cute," I say, taking in the pale green walls and sky blue shutters. "And it's great that it's a cafe because we'll be able to look inside. That's if you want to?"

I turn back and see that her mouth is gaping open in shock.

"Are you OK? We don't have to go in if you don't want to. I understand if it's too emotional. And we could always come back another day."

She shakes her head and points at the cafe again, her hand trembling even more. "Look."

"At what?" I stare at the cafe, then back at her, confused.

"The name," she whispers.

I look at the lettering painted in gold across the top of the building. "The Café de la Paix," I read out loud. Then I gasp. "Holy cow! Isn't that..."

"The name of the cafe I was going to have with Reinhardt," she whispers, her face deathly pale.

62

We stand frozen in shock for a moment, then I tug on her arm.

"Come on, we have to investigate."

"I'm sure it's just a coincidence," she says as we make our way closer. "It has to be. Maybe someone had the same idea as us after the war and wanted their cafe to be a celebration of peace."

I frown. "Maybe, but it's kind of strange that it would be on exactly the same site as your old patisserie. Did you tell anyone else about the idea?"

She shakes her head. "How could I? It was all top secret."

As soon as we reach the cafe, I see that it's dark inside and obviously closed for the night and I'm flooded with disappointment. "Oh dang!"

We press our faces up to the window.

"They've taken the counter at the back out," my grandma says. "I guess to make room for the tables. But the shelves on the back wall are the same. And look, they still have the same bar at the window for people to sit at."

I look at the wooden bar beneath the window in front of us.

A brightly colored menu has been propped against a pair of silver salt and pepper pots.

"It's so cool to think that you once owned this place," I whisper, peering inside. "To think that you once made and sold your cakes here."

"I think we should get back to the hotel," my grandma says sharply and I see that she's already retreated a few steps along the street. Then I remember that Madame Monteux had bought her the patisserie and I realize that it must be bringing back a whole load of painful memories.

"Of course," I say, running to catch up with her. She keeps marching faster, her gaze fixed firmly ahead. "Are you sure you're OK?"

"Yes. I just came over all tired all of a sudden. Must be the jetlag catching up with me."

"Yeah." I pause. "I'm sure the cafe name is just a weird coincidence." Although the truth is, I'm not sure at all. I mean, what are the chances? If Melissa was here she'd probably be having a cow at this latest shock twist.

"Yes. Yes it must be," my grandma says in that weird matter-of-fact tone again.

She barely says another word all the way back to the hotel and we go straight to bed. She can't have been that tired though because I hear her moving around a lot from my adjoining room before I fall into a bottomless sleep.

I wake the next day with a jolt and as I sit up in bed and take in the velvet curtains and dark wood paneling, it takes me a minute to remember where I am and realize that, no, I've not woken up inside an episode of *Falcon Crest*. Then I remember how shaken my grandma had been the day before and get out of bed and knock on our adjoining door. There's no answer, so I quietly open the door and tiptoe inside. The bed is made and the curtains are open with sunlight spilling in, making the dust in the air shimmer like glitter. I spy a piece of paper with my name on propped on top of the bank of pillows.

> *I woke up ridiculously early so I've gone for a walk. I'll meet*
> *you in the hotel restaurant for breakfast at 9! Grandma xx*

I look at her travel alarm clock on the nightstand and see that it's eight. Perfect. I have enough time to take a bath and try to make myself look *très* chic—or my version of *très* chic, anyways.

One hour later, I head to the elevator wearing a black fishnet vest over a bright pink crop top, my baggy stone-washed jeans, and all of my necklaces and bangles like that new singer Madonna. As I step inside the elevator, I wonder if it's the same one my grandma was in that time with the woman who was making the identity cards for the Resistance. It certainly looks old enough and I feel as if I've stepped back in time right into her memories.

When I get to the restaurant, there's no sign of my grandma, but I don't mind. As the maître d' shows me to a table, I imagine I'm a famous popstar just arrived in Paris for a gig. Practically as soon as I've sat down, a smiley waiter appears with a basket of croissants and a jug of water. While he pours me a glass, I look around and try to imagine this same room full of people returning from the concentration camps. It must have felt so bizarre to come from somewhere like Auschwitz to this. I gaze up at the huge chandelier sparkling in the center of the ceiling and I think of how my grandma had said that many of the returning deportees couldn't cope with the splendor after where they'd been and chose to sleep on the floor instead of the comfortable beds. I give a heavy sigh. Why oh why do human beings have to be so cruel to one another?

In keeping with my *très* chic popstar in Paris image, I order a coffee, which arrives in a tiny doll-sized cup. I'm not sure if I ordered it wrong, but I don't want to look like an idiot, so I don't say anything. As soon as I take a sip, I realize why it hasn't come in a mug. It's so strong, I almost spit it out. Then I spy my grandma in the restaurant doorway looking around, so I stand and wave and she comes hurrying over. I can tell straight away that there's something different about her. Her cheeks are flushed and she looks—excited.

"Hey, Grandma," I say as she reaches the table, "did you enjoy your walk?"

"Oh Raven." She stands there staring at me, her eyes sparkling.

"What is it? What's happened?"

"The most incredible thing," she gasps.

My pulse starts to quicken. "What?"

"I went back to the cafe and..." She pulls out her chair to sit down and the waiter reappears.

"*Bonjour, madame,*" he says, offering her a menu. "Will you be having breakfast?"

"Oh—oh, yes please," she stammers.

After what feels like forever, she orders some coffee and toast and he leaves.

"Well?" I exclaim, my eyes on stalks. "What happened?"

"I saw a ghost," she whispers.

63

AUGUST 1984, PARIS

After seeing the cafe yesterday, my mind wouldn't stop racing and I barely got a wink of sleep. I probably could have accepted that the name was a bizarre coincidence, but when I saw the menu in the window, I knew it was way more than that. Admittedly, there's nothing strange about seeing baguettes and éclairs on the menu of a French cafe—in fact it would be strange if it didn't include them—but it was when I saw the Strasbourg sausage with the special onion gravy that my heart almost stopped beating. And then I noticed Kartoffelpuffer in the list of side dishes. The chances of German potato cakes being on a French menu were slim to say the least and surely way beyond coincidence and it sent me spiraling into a panic. In all my imaginings of coming back to Paris, I never for one moment thought that I'd find a trace of Reinhardt here.

All night long, I tried figuring out possible explanations. The best I could come up with was that he'd told someone about our plan and they'd taken it for their own. But I knew I wouldn't be able to rest until I knew for certain, so as soon as morning rolled around, I decided to go back there and try to get to the bottom of it. I got to the cafe just as it opened at seven, so there were no customers yet, and no sign of any servers either when I looked inside. But as soon as I pushed the door open, a bell above it jangled so loudly I practically jumped out of my skin and a man appeared from the kitchen.

"*Bonjour!*" he cried cheerily and as soon as I saw that smile, I knew it was him. The curly hair might have been gray instead of caramel and his skin might have crinkled like fans around his eyes, but those eyes were still as bright green. "Come in, come in," he said to me in French, and I realized that of course he didn't have a clue who I was. Why would he? It had been over forty years. Knowing this made me feel slightly better, like I had the upper hand somehow, so I sat down at the table closest to the door, just in case I needed to make a quick exit.

"Looks like being another lovely day," he said, gesturing at the sunbeams dancing on the cobblestones outside.

"Yes," I said bluntly, terrified that if I said too much he might recognize my voice.

He handed me a menu and I thought of those same hands once touching me and my breath caught in my throat. "Can I get you anything to drink?"

"Water will be fine, thank you," I replied, and he went into the kitchen to fetch me some. "Quite an interesting menu you have here," I called after him.

"Thank you," he called back.

"It's unusual to see a mixture of German and French dishes like this."

He returned with a glass of water and placed it in front of me. "I'm afraid I've been a little self-indulgent with the menu. The dishes are all my favorites, specially selected because they bring back happy memories." He smiled wistfully. "That's one of the things I love the most about food—the way it can transport you to a different time or place."

"Yes." I cleared my throat, trying to maintain my composure. For so long I'd thought of him as someone who'd betrayed me in the worst possible way, every memory I had of him had been called into question and felt false. This smiley man in front of me, talking so fondly of happy memories didn't fit the picture I'd built of Reinhardt at all. I cleared my throat, trying to maintain my composure. "So, how long have you had this cafe?"

"Twenty years," he replied, and I quickly did the math. Twenty years meant that he bought it in 1965—twenty years after the war ended and enough time for a German to be able to return to France.

"It certainly has a lot of character."

He nodded. "Yes, for sure."

I looked back at the menu. "I think I'll have the Kartoffelpuffer please."

"Excellent choice!"

He disappeared into the kitchen, giving me time to mentally regroup. Not only was Reinhardt alive, but he'd set up the Café de la Paix in my old patisserie. I glanced around and noticed some framed black and white photos on the wall. One of them looked familiar, so I went over to take a closer look. It was the one he'd taken of my cakes in the window during the war. Then I saw the picture he'd taken of the patisserie. Both were the same as the pictures in the album he'd given me. He must have had prints developed from the negatives.

"Ah, you're looking at my photo collection," he said, appearing in the kitchen doorway. I heard oil sizzling behind him and the air began to fill with the delicious smell of potato frying. As I breathed it in, I was sent hurtling back in time to the night he taught me how to make Kartoffelpuffer, in the tiny kitchen upstairs, and I had to lean on a table to steady myself.

"Yes. I like the look of these cakes," I said, pointing to the picture. "Did you make them?"

"Oh no, those were made by the best pastry chef in Paris." He chuckled softly and my heart twinged.

"If not the world," I added quietly.

There was a beat of silence.

"What did you say?" he asked with a frown.

"The best pastry chef in Paris, if not the world," I said louder, looking straight at him.

His mouth opened, but no words came out, and as we stood there, staring at each other, it was as if the past four decades had melted away and there we were, back in the patisserie, back in the place where it all began.

"Is it—is it you?" he whispered.

"Speak up, Chef, I can hardly hear you," I tried to quip, but my voice wavered.

"It is you!" he gasped, and then, to my surprise, his eyes filled with tears. "It worked. It finally worked!"

"What worked?"

"This place." He gestured around the cafe. "I knew that if you were still in France and still alive, you'd come back here someday. But then you never showed up, so I thought you must be..." He wiped his eyes and shook his head. "What took you so long, Chef? I thought you were dead!"

"You thought *I* was dead!" I exclaimed. "I thought *you* were dead."

"What? But why?"

"After what you did at the Lutetia. When you took the blame for killing Laporte. I thought the *Abwehr* must have killed you."

"Oh!" He laughed and shook his head. "No, thankfully Canaris hated Laporte too, so I was let off with a punishment—I was sent east to cook for the troops."

Instantly, my mood soured. "You were let off because you were an *Abwehr* agent?"

"No!" He frowned. "What made you say that?"

I noticed wisps of smoke in the air behind him and smelled something burning. "I think your Kartoffelpuffer might be on fire, Chef, and I don't remember asking for them to be well done."

"Shit!" He raced into the kitchen and the sizzle of oil quietened. Then he marched back in and over to the door and locked it and closed the shutters in the windows. "We need to talk," he said, pointing to the table beside me. We both sat down and my heart started beating, fit to burst. Finally, I was being given a chance to confront him over what he'd done, and the enormity of that fact was overwhelming. "Why do you think I was an *Abwehr* agent?" he asked.

"Because I was told you were from a very reliable source. And they showed me a photo of you meeting with a member of the SS."

He looked stunned and shook his head. "Did you really think I'd help those monsters?"

"What was I supposed to think? I saw a photo of you meeting with them." I took a breath before revealing my trump card. "And then I found the file and the radio transmitter."

"What file? What radio transmitter?" he asked, and I felt a surge of panic, before reminding myself that forty years had passed and my snooping around his room really didn't matter anymore.

"The ones you had hidden in your hotel room. I saw them the night I stayed over. And I saw the coded messages in your recipes," I added.

He looked puzzled for a moment, then he gasped. "You saw the recipes, the ones in the file?"

"Yes. I found them when you were asleep."

He shook his head in disbelief. "But how did you know there were coded messages in them?"

"Because I'd been doing something similar, in my recipe book—the one you gave me."

He frowned. "What do you mean?"

"I'd been working for the Resistance," I said defiantly. "And delivering false identity papers for Canaris's secretary, Inga. I hid details about codes and addresses in the recipes."

But instead of looking surprised, he gave a knowing nod. "Ah yes, I heard how she'd been doing that after the war."

"You heard that she was helping Jewish people?"

"Yes, and with Canaris's blessing."

"Canaris knew?" I stared at him in shock.

"Of course."

"But..."

"Canaris hated Hitler and what he was doing to the Jews. He was even involved in a plot to kill him."

"Really?" I stared at him incredulously.

He nodded. "They planted a bomb at a meeting Hitler attended, but sadly he survived and he had Canaris executed for his part in it."

"I had no idea." It felt as if the room had tilted on its axis and I had to grab the edge of the table to steady myself. Everything I had thought to be true seemed to be unravelling right before my eyes and, like Alice disappearing down the rabbit-hole, I found myself in bizarre land where the head of the Nazi *Abwehr* had been helping the Jewish and had plotted to kill Hitler.

"Nothing was as it seemed at the Lutetia. But I wasn't working for them." He smiled across the table at me. "If you must know, by 1942, I was working for the British."

"What?" I stared at him, completely blindsided.

He nodded, his smile growing.

"But that doesn't make any sense."

"Why not?"

"Because—because you're German," I stammered, clutching at whatever I could to convince myself that I wasn't going crazy.

"Yes, but I hated what Hitler was doing too. Don't you remember me telling you that?"

"Yes, but once I'd been told you were working for the *Abwehr*, I assumed that was just a line you'd been feeding me."

"A line?" He sighed and shook his head. "All I wanted was for the war to be over so that..." He broke off and gazed down into his lap.

"So that?" I asked softly.

"We could be together!" He looked back at me and I saw that he looked really hurt. I felt a pang of concern before my voice of caution piped in again.

"But what about the code names you had in your recipes?"

"What about them?"

"Weren't they for French Resistance members?"

"Yes."

"But why would you have them if you were working for the British?"

"The British were the ones who gave me them, so that I could transmit messages to them on the radio they gave me."

My mind raced as I tried to compute what he was telling me. "Did you ever pass any messages to Raphael?"

He frowned. "Who was that?"

"The sommelier who worked at the hotel. His code name was Beaujolais."

"Ah, yes! Only a handful of times, but then their network was captured."

"So he knew that you were working for the British?"

"No, I only ever passed messages to him via the radio transmitter, using my own code name, Springerle."

"Springerle, but that was my..."

"Nickname, yes." He smiled.

"My God..." I broke off, thinking back to the night that Raphael told me Reinhardt was a German agent. "The sommelier was the one who told me you were working for the *Abwehr*."

Reinhardt looked stunned. "Why would he have done that?"

"He was the one who showed me a picture of you meeting with a member of the SS." I studied Reinhardt's face for any sign of discomfort, any sign that he was lying, but he just looked confused.

"Was the picture taken by the Eiffel Tower?" he asked.

"Yes."

His face lit up in recognition. "Canaris had sent me there."

"Canaris?"

"Yes. He told me the SS wanted some menu ideas, but it was obviously a cover for a message he was sending them."

"What do you mean?"

"Canaris gave me a letter to put inside the menu."

I frowned. "So, you did pass a message to the SS then?"

"Yes, because I knew Canaris was briefing against them."

I stared at him, stunned. "Canaris was briefing against the SS?"

"Yes, the *Abwehr* and the SS hated each other. Canaris regularly fed them false information to try to thwart Hitler." He gave a sad smile. "Honestly, Chef, your pastries might be the best in the world, but your knowledge of history is appalling. This all came out after the war."

"I had no idea. I've tried to avoid the subject of the war, to be honest, I just wanted to forget everything that happened."

"That makes sense." He looked down at the table. "And I suppose you wanted to forget all about me, given that you thought I was the enemy."

"Yes," I said quietly, still trying to make sense of the world of smoke and mirrors we'd been a part of. The world where the head of the intelligence service had been working against Hitler, Reinhardt had been working for the British, and my fellow resistant, Raphael, had unwittingly caused me a lifetime of heartache due to his own misunderstanding. I had a flashback to that awful morning in the hotel lobby when we'd seen Raphael and the others from his network being dragged inside. When Reinhardt had asked me if it was the sommelier, I'd assumed it was because he was trying to see if I knew he worked for the Resistance. But it must have been because he was genuinely concerned that one of his contacts had been captured. "What a crazy world we were a part of," I murmured.

"Indeed."

I glanced across the table. Reinhardt was looking so glum, it made my heart hurt.

"Did you think I was working for the *Abwehr* the whole time?" he asked, still staring down at the table.

"No, only at the end, when Raphael told me."

"So up until that point your feelings toward me were genuine?" He looked up at me hopefully.

"Of course. And were yours?" I hardly dared breathe.

"Of course!" he exclaimed. "Why wouldn't they be?"

As soon as he said those words, I felt a lifetime of pain begin leaving my body. Reinhardt hadn't been a traitor. He hadn't deceived me. He had loved me. And I had loved him. Oh how I'd loved him.

"I can't believe you're here," he said.

"I can't believe *you're* here."

"Seriously, Chef, can't you think of anything original to say." He grinned. "I hope your menus have more imagination than your conversation."

"Very funny!" I laughed, and it felt so good to relieve the tension, and so good, if totally surreal, to be back there with him.

"So where are you working now?" he asked. "Do you have another patisserie?"

"Oh no. I haven't worked as a chef for years. Not since the war."

His eyes widened in shock. "Why not?"

I told him all about Madame Monteux and how devastated I'd been to learn of her death in Auschwitz and how Bob had offered me an escape to America, and I'd jumped at it.

"So you're married?" he said, once I'd finished my tale.

"*Was*. He died a few years ago."

"Oh. I'm sorry."

"Thank you. How about you? Did you ever marry?" Once again I found myself holding my breath as I waited for his response.

He shook his head. "I guess you could say I became married to my job. No one I met ever..." He fell silent and looked away.

"What?"

"Measured up to you," he said softly, and my skin prickled with goosebumps. "I mean, you are the best pastry chef in France, if not the world."

"So you only ever wanted me for my pastries!"

"No!" He pulled a hurt face. "Of course not. I wanted you for your witty repartee, not to mention that hot temper!"

His mention of my temper brought the memory of what I'd done to Laporte rushing back and I felt a surge of shame and regret.

"But don't you think badly of me after what I did to—to Laporte?"

"He was a monster."

"But I could have killed a lot more people that night if he hadn't come in and eaten one of the pastries." I clasped my hands in my lap. "I think I'd been driven half mad with grief and I felt as if I had nothing left to live for. I'd just heard what was happening to the Jews in the concentration camps and I'd been told you were working against me. I wasn't thinking straight."

He leaned forward, placing his hands on the table in front of me. I wasn't sure if it was an invitation and I so badly wanted to take hold of them, but I didn't dare risk it in case I was mistaken.

"We were at war," he said, his voice calm and strong. "Normal rules didn't apply. Normal behavior couldn't be expected. Everything had been turned upside down and inside out. I mean, the leader of the *Abwehr* was secretly helping the Jews and plotting to kill Hitler!" He let out a laugh and then his smile faded. "Think of how many ordinary people ended up becoming killers on the battlefield," he said softly. "Even people like my best friend from school, who wouldn't have hurt a fly ordinarily."

Hearing him say this felt a bit like receiving a blessing from a priest. Reinhardt had been there. He knew what life had been like back then and he wasn't blaming me at all. His empathy felt like one of the greatest gifts I'd ever been given and I was flooded with relief. I looked at him and nodded. "Thank you."

He raised his hands from the table and held them out to me and this time I took them gladly. His grip was warm and firm and I felt his strength traveling up through my fingers and arms and filling my body.

"I'm just relieved I didn't help myself to one of those pastry balls." He grinned.

I smiled back at him. "If you remember correctly, I hit it out of your hand the second you tried to."

He laughed. "Yes, so you did care about me, even if you thought I was a German spy."

"Of course I did," I blurted out. "I loved you."

We fell silent and my cheeks grew warm. It felt so strange to say those words to him after so long. But then our eyes met and once again it was as if no time had passed and suddenly, magically, our dream had come true and we'd turned the patisserie into our cafe of peace.

"I loved you too," he said softly, gripping my hands tighter. "And, if I'm totally honest, I still do."

EPILOGUE
APRIL 1985, PARIS

I watch, hardly daring to breathe, as my grandma weaves delicate strands of golden spun sugar over the pyramid of pastry puffs, a look of pure concentration upon her face.

"Wow," Mom whispers beside me. "It looks more like a work of art than a cake."

"I know," I whisper back.

My grandma puts down her fork and steps back to examine her masterpiece. "There! Now we just have to add the sugar flowers." She turns to us, a radiant smile lighting up her face. "Perhaps you guys could help me."

"Of course!" I exclaim and hurry over to join her at the kitchen table.

"Suzette, would you like to help too?" my grandma says.

"Are you sure?" Mom asks nervously. "You know what they say about too many cooks spoiling the broth."

"Nonsense," Grandma replies firmly. "And, anyway, it isn't broth, it's my wedding cake—so decorating it absolutely should be a family affair."

"I can't believe you're getting married tomorrow," I say, taking a lilac sugar flower from the bowl.

"Neither can I," my grandma says, and I watch as she takes a pale pink flower and attaches it to a strand of the spun sugar on the side of the cake. "Thank you so much for coming. It means the world to me to have you here." She looks so much lighter, so much younger than she did before we first came to Paris last summer, and it makes me so happy.

"Are you kidding?" I exclaim. "There's no way we would have missed it, is there, Mom?"

Mom nods and smiles as she comes over to join us. "Of course not. So, what should I do?"

"Take one of the flowers and stick it to the spun sugar like this," I say, demonstrating with mine.

Mom does as instructed and the three of us work together in silence for a while, planting the pretty pastel colored flowers all over the cake.

When my grandma told me she was moving back to Paris to be with Reinhardt, it had felt so bittersweet. Selfishly, I was heartbroken—I'd only just gotten to know and love her and now she'd be moving to a whole other continent. But, on the other hand, having met Reinhardt last summer and seen how happy they were together, I knew without a shadow of a doubt that she was doing the right thing. I guess part of growing up is realizing that you can't always get what you want all the time, and that's OK. When you're a kid you see life as a story all about you. You don't realize that other people aren't there just to be your supporting cast, they have their own stories to live too. And having been trusted with my grandma's wartime story, I know better than anyone that she deserves a happy ending.

"*Et voilà!*" she cries as she places the last of the flowers on the top of the cake. The moonstone in her ring glimmers pearly-white as it catches the light and I think of Madame Monteux and wish that she could have been here to witness this too.

"It looks wonderful," Mom says and I can't help giving the cheesiest grin as I watch my grandma link her arm and pull her close. They've gotten so much closer since last summer and this makes me so happy too.

"Thank you, Suzette." Grandma kisses her lightly on the cheek.

It turns out that Judy Blume was right and that divorce isn't the end of the world at all. In fact, in my case, it was the start of a much happier new life. Mom and I get on so much better now it's just us in the apartment. And when I go see my dad for my weekly visit, it's like he's seeing me for the first time and he actually wants to get to know me.

"Shall we get back to the Lutetia?" my grandma says, checking her watch. "I told Reinhardt we'd be out of here by six." She laughs. "It feels a little silly, avoiding my groom-to-be on the night before our wedding when we're both in our sixties."

"It's not silly," I say, "it's romantic, and anyways it means the three of us get to have a sleepover tonight."

"Yes." Mom nods in agreement. "And I've brought us all matching pajamas and face packs specially."

We all laugh and start making our way out of the kitchen and into the cafe. As I watch my grandma close the shutters and turn out the lights, I picture her younger self, not that much older than I am now, going through so much here, and suddenly, my heart is filled with so much hope and joy, it feels like it might burst. The world might sometimes teeter on the brink of war and disaster, but there's so much good in the world, and so many good people, that's what I'm going to choose to focus on from now on.

We step outside into the warm spring evening and link arms, before making our way, giggling and chatting along the narrow, cobbled street. Just before we reach the turning I glance over my shoulder at the words Café de le Paix glimmering gold in the setting sun and my heart fills with gratitude that my grandma's story isn't over yet and that in fact, the happiest chapter is yet to come.

A LETTER FROM SIOBHAN

Dear reader,

Thank you so much for choosing to read *The Resistance Bakery*, I hope you found it an interesting and mouthwatering read! If you want to be kept up to date with all my latest releases, just sign up at the following link. Your email address will never be shared, and you can unsubscribe at any time.

www.bookouture.com/siobhan-curham

Anyone who knows me—or follows me on social media—will know that I'm a huge fan of baked goods, especially the French kind, so writing this book was a real labor of love. And I'd like to reassure you that I took the research side of things very seriously. Many a cream cake was consumed during the writing of this novel! On a more serious note, until I began my research I had no idea how important food was to Nazi Germany and the role it played in helping Hitler rise to power. I hope you found the food history woven into the story as fascinating as I did.

I love using my historical fiction to throw a spotlight on lesser known yet fascinating facts from World War Two, and when I discovered what went on at the Hotel Lutetia during the war I knew I had to set *The Resistance Bakery* there. I'm not sure if any other hotel has had such an interesting and colorful past. Although Reinhardt and his kitchen staff are all works of fiction, all the senior *Abwehr* officers featured in the novel were real people, as was Inga Abshagen, secretary to Admiral Wilhelm Canaris. Learning what Inga did in Paris during the war, and with Canaris's blessing, blew my mind, and I was thrilled to be able to bring attention to such an incredible woman.

Similarly, although the character of Raphael is a work of fiction, the Resistance network he belonged to did exist, as did the Interallie network and the woman who betrayed them, and all the major acts of resistance that Raphael and Coralie are involved in, such as the student protest, the Resistance newspaper, the bookstore and cinema bombs and the shooting of Julius Ritter actually happened.

As for the 1984 storyline, I have to say that the character of Raven was loosely inspired by myself at that age and time, when I too made some 'interesting' fashion choices, adored Judy Blume and was terrified of imminent nuclear war. Through Raven's relationship with Coralie I wanted to show how the trauma of war can ripple down through the generations of a family but also has the potential to be healed. I hope you found this storyline uplifting, and the eighties references entertaining!

Siobhan

siobhancurham.com

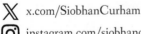 x.com/SiobhanCurham
instagram.com/siobhancurhamauthor

ACKNOWLEDGEMENTS

MASSIVE thanks as always to Kelsie Marsden, my wonderful editor, for your expert insights, brilliant brainstorms and thoughtful gifts. And thank you to Jade Craddock for bringing so much as always to your copy edit. Huge thanks to Richard King, aka the Father Christmas of the Foreign Rights world, for all the gifts of good news you bring, and to all the foreign publishers who have bought the rights to my World War Two novels. It's been so exciting to see your editions of my books on my travels around the world. And none of this would be possible without the incredible support of the whole team at Bookouture. I'm so thankful to be with such a supportive and dynamic publisher. Much gratitude to publicist extraordinaire Sarah Hardy, Kim Nash, Noelle Holten, Jenny Geras, Ruth Tross, Alex Crow, Melanie Price, Alba Proko, Ria Clare and Sinead O'Connor, to name but a few.

When this book was in its very earliest stages—i.e. I'd decided to write a World War Two novel about two chefs—I was blessed by two highly serendipitous events. The first happened at a family party in Arkansas, when I found myself sitting eating hotdogs around a fire with a lovely guy named Don Walsh. We'd only just met and when I told him I wrote World War Two fiction for a living he instantly asked how I researched the food from the time period. "Funny you should mention that," I replied, "because I'm about to start a novel revolving around food." He told me he knew just the person to help me, Dr. Sevin Gallo, an American historian who specializes in how food culture intersects with national identity and politics, and he wasn't wrong. Thanks so much, Don, for putting me in touch with Sevin and huge thanks, Sevin, for enlightening me about the role food played in German political history—your advice and reading recommendations were so helpful.

The second serendipitous moment happened about a month later when I found myself on the worst seat of a plane (jammed in the middle of the back row, right by the toilets). Having worked out the historical background for *The Resistance Bakery*, I was still trying to get inside the head of the character of Reinhardt, and wondering how he might have ended up becoming a chef. As I scribbled some notes on my phone the guy sitting next to me asked if I was a writer and told me that he used his phone to make work notes too. 'I'm a chef,' he added. I mean, what were the chances?! I told him I was about to start writing a novel about a chef and he very graciously offered to help me with some on the spot research. By the time we'd landed and cleared the long line at passport control (the only time I've been thankful for Brexit!) I was completely clear on Reinhardt's background and motivations. And it was only when I googled my helpful fellow passenger later that evening that I learned he wasn't any old chef but a Michelin star chef no less! Massive thanks, Lee Westcott, for being such a great sport and so helpful.

HUGE thanks also to all the lovely people who take the time to review my novels on their social media, blogs, Goodreads, NetGalley and Amazon. There are so many, it's impossible to mention you all here, but please know that I read and deeply appreciate every review. I also really appreciate all the messages I receive from readers; it's so encouraging to receive your feedback about my books.

Last but never least, much, much love and gratitude to my friends and family. Massive thanks to my family: Jack and Zirka

Curham, Michael Curham, Anne Cumming, Alice Curham, Bea Curham, Luke Curham, Katie Bird, Dan Arthur, John Arthur, Lacey Jennen, Gina Ervin, David Ervin, Sam Delaney, Carolyn Miller, Amy Fawcett, Rachel Kelley, Charles Delaney. And to my friends who feel like family: Tina McKenzie, Steve O'Toole, Sammie and Edi Venn, Sara Starbuck, Pearl Bates and Caz McDonagh.

And huge thanks to my friends who have been so supportive of my books and writing over the years: Sass Pankhurst, Sandra McDonagh, Stephanie Lam, Abe Gibson, Linda Newman, Lesley Strick, Lara Kingsman, Diane Sack Pulsone, Thea Bennett, Jan Silverman, Marie Hermet, Mara Bergman, Jan Silverman, Patricia Jacobs, Mavis Pachter, Suzanne Burgess, Liz Brooks, Fil Carson, Jackie Stanbridge, Gillian Holland, Doug Cushman, Glenn Bryant. And to the new writer (and artist) friends I've made on my travels: Linda Joy Myers, Ruth Mitchell, Wendy Taylor Carlisle, Andrea Silva, Dora Santos Marques, Alexandre Gaudencio, Rosária Casquinha da Silva, Natalie Normann, Gul Mir. It's been so much fun getting to know you!

Lastly, thank you to everyone who subscribes to my weekly Substack letter, Wonderstruck, to follow my writing and travel adventures. I'm so grateful for the lovely community we've created over there and I love writing to you every Sunday. (If you don't subscribe to Wonderstruck I'd love it if you joined us! You can subscribe for free at siobhancurham.substack.com).

PUBLISHING TEAM

Turning a manuscript into a book requires the efforts of many people. The publishing team at Bookouture would like to acknowledge everyone who contributed to this publication.

Audio
Alba Proko
Sinead O'Connor
Melissa Tran

Commercial
Lauren Morrissette
Hannah Richmond
Imogen Allport

Cover design
Eileen Carey

Data and analysis
Mark Alder
Mohamed Bussuri

Editorial
Kelsie Marsden
Nadia Michael

Made in the USA
Monee, IL
07 October 2024

67329843R00245